LAMMAS

LAMMAS

by
Michael Kelly

The White Water Press

This book is a work of fiction. Names, characters, events and places are the product of the author's imagination or are used fictitiously. Any similarity to real people, events, or places is coincidental.

Copyright ©2003 by Michael Kelly

All rights reserved. No part of this book may be reproduced, transmitted in any form or by any means, electronic, mechanical, photocopying, recording or otherwise, or stored in a retrieval system, without written permission from the publisher, except by reviewers, who may quote brief passages in reviews.

First Edition, 2003

ISBN: 0-9730428-0-X

Published by
The White Water Press
P.O. Box 26060
206 King Street East
Oshawa, Ontario L1H 8R4 Canada

National Library of Canada Cataloguing in Publication

Kelly, Michael (Michael John)
    Lammas / Michael Kelly.

ISBN 0-9730428-0-X

    I. Title.

PS8571.E58664L34 2002   C813'.6   C2002-902848-5
PR9199.4.K44L34 2002

Cover Design: Kimberley Young
Cover Painting: Roxana Kelly
Publishing Services: Melinda Tate

Printed and bound in Canada

To Roxana

Chapter 1

IN THE LAKE WAS A WOODED ISLAND. His mind's eye reverted to it constantly for he believed it held a mystery that he had to penetrate. This inward conviction abided even as he rushed from one deadline to the next in the feverish life of his outward self culminating in this day of ceremonies. Even here on the campus his obsession possessed him: nothing else beside it mattered but everything in his urgent rushing life excluded it. Glimpsed years before in a magic day's trip north, his mind had plucked the vision as it streamed away from him. The landscape's loveliness made him shiver, adding another jewel to his hoard of hidden treasure.

The day was turning strange! Ywain felt that his head, detached from its surroundings, rode above a nerveless body. Here in the open among the angular canyons formed by the glossy buildings of the enormous university only the blue sky went on being itself; a transparent cloud or two drifted on; the cold breeze expended itself in the valleys and passage ways of the small city the university had become.

He could feel his gorge rising. Four years of determined application had brought him to the realization of his own and his mother's dream, but instead of being elated at his success he felt sick at being corralled, emotionally and socially, in a spiritual slum. Somewhere, close at hand if he could only find it, his vision waited.

Yet again the cold sweat that visited him so often these days was breaking out accompanied by the usual nausea. Psychosomatic masochism Debra had called it in one of her unkinder moods. He didn't doubt she was right.

Miles away the speaker barked into his microphone under the brilliant flags whose barbaric colours opposed the mystic mauves of sleeve and cap. There were over eight hundred candidates for bachelor degrees. Each fresh squad of bodies discharged itself into the aisle with electric rustles of nylon like an elaborate salvo fired off to impress the audience with the solemnity of academic buffoonery.

He tried again to lose himself in the rapt beauty of his morning vision over the lake.

Two minutes later he started out of his transport. It was his turn to centipede to the platform.

Somewhere in the crowd his mother must be waving to him. She was far back and he had trouble finding her. When he did, she held up her scarf and blew him a kiss. A cloud settled on him again as he realized his debt to her, realized that this occasion arose out of her sacrifice, not his. This thought troubled him. As he waited to stumble along his row, another eye caught his. A man of indeterminate age smiled slightly at him. He was certain that he had never seen him before, but there was something familiar in his expression, a trace of his dead father, perhaps, whose features he knew only from photographs. If he had lived! He did not really have any idea what difference the death of the man he never knew had made to the little family, but there had been times when he yearned for him in spasms of impossible desire.

On this day of triumph for his mother, of surfing success for all the mothers, fathers and their progeny, he alone was waterlogged, an unwilling jetsam caught by and borne along with them in this flotilla of tossing success on the flood tide.

Afterwards he and his mother had a curiously formal lunch together. He loved his mother, sometimes almost to the point of awe, but they were not really close. She was an intensely private woman, cold at heart, but with the instinct of a somewhat abstracted love centred wholly on her divine twins. Money had always been tight: her job managing a small travel agency was ill-paid and this combined with variable interest on the insurance money, the sole asset her husband had left for the support of his family, amounted to no more than about $25,000 in a good year. Yet she had managed to save something and had put both of them through university at the same time, God knows how, refusing to allow either of them to take a government loan. Having kept her good looks, she was able to moonlight from time to time. She had spent herself for the two children she had secretly dedicated herself to, almost to the point of worship. Of the veiled intensity of her devotion Ywain knew nothing.

The children were bound to their mother by her sacrifice. In the absence of a father their loyalty was undivided; but the children's love, although less abstract than the mother's, was weighed down by this ballast of duty: they owed everything to her. They showed their consideration for their mother in every way they knew. But they had never been a touching family. The mother's bond with her children was a transcendental rather than a human one. Ywain could not remember ever being hugged or kissed by his mother, let alone Mira.

Mira, the first-born of the twins, still had a year to go, for she was reaching high, for a good M.B.A. Once she had that, she could go into a bank or financial house as an investment consultant. She had been unable to come to the graduation ceremony because she had a summer job downtown in the Ministry of Transport earning a great deal more than her mother.

As for Ywain, he was still working in a store along Bloor West repairing bicycles. He did not know what to do with his life, and, superficially, felt no particular concern about it. He had his vision to help him ride out the daily grind, the discouragement of driving competition and the stalking nightmare he tried to ignore, that at the end of his labour there would be nothing for him to do, and he would be no further ahead than when he began – still working in Total Cycle. Mira had her field of fire and her sights set. He hadn't.

There were several options open to the undecided, the armed forces, for example. He was fit, Canadian-born and well-qualified, although he did not know for what. But his spirit flew above regimentation. His mother had several tenuous connexions, and at this moment there might be careers other than the army he could jump into, but underlying all his meandering attempts to focus on some definite way of keeping himself in milk and honey *and* forging ahead (a favourite expression of his mother's) was a prevalent sense that all this was formless in a formless setting: there was no real plan or destiny in it. The chasms of the great city delved by the technology of men concealed a dark chaos beneath. He could express it no further. Some essential breath of life was absent.

It had come upon him suddenly on a dark day that at the centre of the wood on the island was a hidden divinity.

So there it was: he had a secret dream and a secret fear.

He had never been out in a restaurant with his mother before, and was almost shocked at her extravagance. She saw his thought and smiled.

'First time for both of us, I think, but not the last for you. There'll come a day when you'll find it difficult to remember the days when you had no money. You can do anything you want, you know. You have the brain.'

Ywain had no appetite. His mouth was dry, his hands clammy as he leafed through the menu. He couldn't swallow and wished only for a sip of water. The forced conviviality of meetings, congratulations, overdone modesty and over-warmed wishes for success had drained him, but he dreaded much more the question he knew was coming sometime. The *con-*

sommé à la julienne was luke-warm and tasteless and the *gigot à la sept heures* was papier mâché soaked in warm dripping. He drank without thirst, but no amount of water could prevent his mouth from drying up. He forced enjoyment but his mother must have noticed his reluctance to eat.

'And what are you going to do?'

'Marry a rich wife,' he said jocularly.

She nodded to herself, but said nothing for a while.

'You didn't reconsider teaching?'

Two further years of grind at phony subjects in a college of education followed by a nervous breakdown somewhere down the line. Besides, it was no longer advisable for men enter fields where they would have dealings with children. No thanks.

'Only at the university level. I could enter a Master's programme, but it's a gamble that I'd make it through to a doctorate. That's another four years at least – probably a college in the States at some point – on spec. We haven't got the resources, Mom. I mean, you have to have a vocation to go into school teaching. I haven't got it. The army's always there, but that's a last resort.'

He needed a pre-emptive diversion. It came unsummoned.

The mother wished she hadn't asked the question on this occasion. The same old tape began running.

'I did have one idea, if you didn't object.'

'Ah?'

'I thought that if I could travel somewhere, just for a short time, I'd have time and the detachment to think.'

'Ywain! You've got to make up your mind!'

Oh dear! On this day of days! With a frustrating effort she restrained herself.

'You have to have some fairly definite idea of where you want to go and make a plan to get there. Oh, travel if you must. You deserve a break, but you have to stop this procrastinating. I'll agree to anything that helps you decide what part you want to play in society. If you don't make up your mind, the world will make it up for you, and you won't like what you get. How long have you been waiting to spring this on me? Very well. Travel, then – but with the sole condition you *know* what *stable* career you want when you get back. Where do you want to go?'

'Well . . .'

'Never mind!' She stopped and caught herself again. Not today. She must not display impatience on this day of all days. After all, he had one very solid achievement on the table. 'Let's see what kind of desserts we get here.'

'None for me, thanks. And the coffee's probably too old for you. I can smell it from here. Let's finish off at home.'

'Sure?'

'Quite sure.'

Debra was the only girl he really knew. He was inward- rather than outward-directed, reticent in his relations with others. He had no real friends apart from her, possibly because others sensed his unwillingness to give of himself. He liked her because, light and easy in her outward ways, she was as stable as a rock and gifted with unusual strength and determination, the qualities his mother thought her son lacked. She had asked him to accompany her to a party that evening, but he felt so sick that he was tempted to call it off. Knowing Debra, he realized he would spoil her evening if he did. He would be exploiting her sympathy on her special occasion. Sick? He did not know what else to call it. His energy had gone. In its place he felt an impotency that now became physical as if he had a severe pain suppressed by a drug. He had no appetite, or thirst either if it came to that and his inner self wanted to vomit. He wondered if he had caught something which he hadn't had time to notice in the rush and stress.

Debra, like himself, preferred to be in the background of things. Nevertheless, it was she who had arranged to encounter him rather than the other way round. In the library he could not miss her longing glances, but he was shy of others, even of an intelligent girl he found striking but not particularly attractive at first. After a week or so of the eye-beam stuff, he came back after his usual stroll in the fresh air at eight in the evening to find a note wrapped round his pen. *Greetings, O Studious One*, it ran, *She whom you choose to ignore marvels at your truly superhuman power of scholarly detachment, and would it be a good idea if we went down for a coffee right now as both the sight of you slaving so damned industriously and this cretinously boring academic crap utterly drain me, from She Who Must Be Obeyed.*

As he finished, he realized that she had moved into the chair opposite. They both started to laugh and had to leave anyway.

He admired her adroitness, alien to his own inflexible mentality.

The academic crap in question led to the party, for it was thrown with the aid of one of the girls in the small section undertaking a special history topic, The Changing Status of Women in the Mediæval Household, led by a fanatical tutor doing a Ph.D. on the subject. The twenty students were larded with handouts and referred to brick-like books written in the dull technical obtuse styles of second-rate scholars publishing for their lives. This gruel being thinner and nastier than usual, they had vowed to celebrate the last supper in various spectacular ways, but the tame outcome was the party to mark the ritual burning of the hated handouts. A Joanne had persuaded her parents to allow the use of the lower floor of the house for a party limited in numbers.

Debra was on the point of dancing in her delight. She had landed a pretty good job that afternoon.

'Graphics, advertising, printing, that kind of thing. It's not everything I hoped for but it's much more than I expected. Could be a growing outfit – anyway, they seem to like me, for now at least, so my worries are over. I'll be into some real money, even if I do have to live at home and use most of it to pay back the bank. You know, my parents have been absolutely wonderful. They're not well-off but they've given me everything they could. I feel that I have to get myself off their hands. They haven't told me, but I *know* I've cost them any savings they might have had. And I think they've borrowed money, for my sister Angela is in her second year, and I couldn't have taken on any more debt this year.'

'Wonderful!' exclaimed Ywain, kissing her. But she felt the feebleness and halted.

'You'll do much better. You have a pass with distinction.'

'Yes,' he said brightly.

'Come on, Jeremiah. You must be getting some idea of where you want to go by now. You didn't go to all that trouble for nothing.'

It was the mention of her parents that made him groan inwardly. She drew him to her in sudden appreciation of his pain. 'You loved the Elizabethans, especially Nashe, didn't you? You told me that that was where Blake had started. You worked for love, not to get somewhere as the rest of us did. I knew that very soon after we ran into each other. I know you better than you yourself do, but your obsession to justify yourself to your mother keeps you from admitting that it's love of your subject, not of your mother, or duty, that keeps you going. I know you, Ywain, and I think it's about time you talked to her about it. The conflict is causing you a lot of stress.'

For a time they were insulated from the rushing party in their own bubble of loving warmth.

'You're happy for me, aren't you?'

Happy? He loved her. What had Eliot called this? Pneumatic bliss. What a monastical old chump! He knew the touch of her breasts was divine, but what he was thinking of was that his mother had never asked anything, never complained. He tried to give himself up to Debra's warmth and inviting, but kept thinking that his mother had always found ways to meet all his demands. What was he doing for her? He didn't even know what he could do.

She embraced him.

'Oh God,' he exclaimed in a tidal rush of fervency, 'you're all the happiness I have and want. It's enough for me to know that you are happy – I can love that alone.'

For all her frank friendship, Debra always drew back at any mention of love. Love for her had to be implicit in every single expression of heart and soul. Declarations frightened her.

'Let's laugh a little. This is not a night for big dramatics. We've all won. Isn't that a trick? What's your next move?'

'Oh, I think I'll travel,' he said, trying to grasp a thread of gaiety.

'Great! What do you plan to use for money?'

'Well –'

'Well?'

'I have to think.'

'Think? You know, I believe you're exhausted, mentally, emotionally and physically. Hasn't your mother noticed?'

'I don't feel –'

'You certainly don't look or feel like yourself.'

'It's just that I'm still having trouble . . .'

'Finding a full-time job. So have hundreds of others. But you, you have a brain. It won't be difficult for you. I'll help you. I've got a few leads. Seriously, I believe you can do anything you set your mind to. Very few people have your gift for mental organization.'

The moment in her embrace he had blasted passed away. Was it possible that his imbecile behaviour with Debra could bring on the sick feeling of emptiness that gripped him again. He remembered E. M. Forster writing of 'the inadequate heart'; over all his directions impotency loomed. Had Debra rejected him? Had she really a heart? Had he?

From that moment he felt cold all over.

He could not sleep. He piled on rugs, but they made no difference. He was chilled from within. Some desperation in his mind was shaking him up, saying, 'Get away from here before you're well and truly trapped.' If he could only slip through the entanglements that lay between him and those he loved he could search for his dream. His father would have known what to do, would have seen him through, somehow. He lay semi-conscious and dreamless, as he thought, passively hearing a dialogue that ran on all night. When he started out of a drift of sleep he was aware of a rush of words that vanished from his memory as if some external menace rased out parts of his mind at will.

With a start he shot out of bed as the radio shouted the weather into his right ear. He still had a job to do. He did not have to think about it. Automatically he found himself in the bathroom bathed and shaved. There was a headache spread out behind his eyes. In the mirror he saw another self, the face already deeply-lined, the face of one whose fate is revealed, a face without any future in literal time. A life run-out, a discard, the sudden overwhelming heaviness of a body whose life drains away. Only death, he suddenly realized, is the comfort of despair. A tumbling chaos of unsummoned thoughts swept away conscious control. He swooned, his head cornered between the basin cabinet and the bath, dull and obstructive. His head was numb.

He heard and saw nothing directly. Some third party remotely connected with him brought vague awareness of a voice. What it said was not comprehensible. He was excused from responding to it and this was how it was going to be. He was thankful for that.

Mira found him in the same position when she came in at five. Ywain was hardly aware, even at third-hand of being run to his bed. He knew no feelings and was conscious only of not being part of anything external to his skull.

Mira telephoned the family doctor just in time to catch him in, in spite of the defensive barriers put up by his secretary.

'Do you want him to go to hospital?'

'Yes. I can't get through to him at all and I'm afraid of what he might do to himself. We can't handle him here.'

'You or your mother will have to sign the papers. Are you prepared to do that?'

'Yes.'

At seven that evening Ywain was in a psychiatric ward, still cut off from what he would twenty hours before have called reality. The silent servant within him watched for him. Through a glass window cloudy green and white figures, aseptic ghosts, moved slowly and mysteriously. Troubled by the light, he was moved to sit down at the desk sometimes used by the duty doctor during the day. He rested his head on his arms, finding the hard neutral Formica gentler than the soft mattress which invited dreams but not sleep.

No one disturbed him that night.

Chapter 2

GROUP THERAPY: the first day's session badly frightened Ywain. He watched old men and young girls alike break down and weep miserably as they told their pitiful little tales, and he was terrified, for he too was always at the point of collapse. The clever manipulations of the psychiatrist continually drew him to a treacherous brink where he was in imminent danger of helplessly blubbing out his own wet little story. He would be mortified out of his manhood. And always at the back of his mind was the secret. It was sacred and not to be divulged. He sat with the others in a circle during the thunderous silences. He volunteered nothing, said nothing, but for the first three or four days was always on the verge of giving way to tears with all that that entailed. After that, he got a better grip on himself.

He was labelled 'obstructive' by the psychiatrist unsuccessful in unloading him.

When he returned to his semi-private ward he lay on the bed, sleeping or in a conscious dreamless stupor. His roommates changed almost daily. Sometimes one of them would fulminate to Ywain that it was ridiculous for him, the newly-arrived inmate, to be there. These were always alcoholics. He replied, if at all, in monosyllables. Sometimes he walked the circuit of the corridors, but avoided conversation. He had to take meals with the others, but again, he avoided talk, ate little and took his drink back to his ward. This went on for ten days until he got a weekend pass.

At home, he drew the curtains, did not answer door or telephone and kept to his own little room.

He responded politely, too politely, to his mother and sister, but did not talk to them.

They did not know what to do with him and were worried. The clever psychiatrist had told them that Ywain was in a state of psychotic depression, but this did not tell them anything. They simply did not know where the familiar Ywain they had known was. He had become a stranger to them.

He experienced involuntary vivid memories of early childhood, scenes recalled in the sharpest detail. In these compulsive impressions he was always standing outside a white house. The light was subdued but beautiful, from within himself. He saw glistening pale lawns in the early dawn, over which strange netted funguses, feather-light, rolled gently in the soft breeze not strong enough to stir odd squat trees with long flat dark green leaves, or bushes with huge complex globular flowers in pale blue. The sun never shone there. Sometimes the lawns were dark, the atmosphere threatening. He sensed the faint redolence of ionization as if thunder were in the offing.

The oddest thing was that none of this was any part of his actual remembered childhood. These reveries were completely foreign to him. They should have been intensely familiar to him, he knew, but this new and dense reality had never been part of his life.

In later recurrences of the visions he could hear voices whispering, usually two or more conversing, but occasionally one alone insistently demanded his attention. Yet however urgent it was he could understand nothing of the language.

Sometimes he heard far off the sucking rumble of what must be waves pounding a beach, some sea flowing in and out upon a remote pebbly shore. He knew he had never heard this sound before.

After the second week these illusions or accessions became less frequent but they did not leave him. He went home every weekend of the three remaining weeks he spent in hospital. Gradually he began to distinguish more clearly between inward vision and external reality, but he remained passive.

Arriving back in his ward on Sunday night, the fourth of his stay, Ywain found Victor in the bed nearest the window.

Victor was the most striking figure Ywain had ever seen. He was tall, gaunt and white-bearded with a clear untroubled eye and a soft voice. He looked exactly like a pre-Raphaelite apostle. He had one other peculiarity: he had lost one of his eyes, doing without patch or prosthetic. This grotesque lapse in appearance merely underlined the wave of presence exuding from him, and reinforced the impression Ywain had of having walked into the unreal dimension of a mediæval painting. He lay upon his back perfectly still but watched Ywain carefully as they exchanged names.

That courtesy done, Ywain returned to his own bed and nothing further was said between them that night.

Victor did not attend group therapy next morning, or in fact leave the ward at all. He would not take drugs, and when the orderly administered a suppository he waited until the man had left and promptly got rid of it. In all his refusals he was gentle but firm.

Ywain went to group therapy because he thought he ought to go, but once there did not participate. He had discovered that the hospital therapy pursued by its self-important practitioners was doctrinaire, irrelevant and did further damage to the ego it was supposed to restore.

Victor had no possessions. Of all the patients, he was the only one dressed exclusively in the unisex hospital gown to which had been added a white terry cloth hospital bathrobe. He refused to eat because it was against his principles to accept anything that was the property of another. Nor would he say an unnecessary word to anyone, except, oddly, Ywain, whom he seemed to recognize from the beginning. He presented the nurses with a dilemma that was apparently insoluble, and it was only a day or so before he was moved to a mental hospital.

Before that, however, Ywain had several interesting though short conversations with Victor, who told him that he, Victor, was a 'child of God'. A bible that he had been reading had gone missing. Ywain offered him one out of a whole carton that he had found abandoned. He explained to Victor that, as the property had been abandoned by its unknown owner, it became salvage, that is, ownerless. Anyone could help himself to it. It was therefore no longer anyone's property. In keeping it, he, Ywain, had possession but not ownership. In passing it on to Victor he could transfer the former but not the latter. Victor seemed to accept this argument, but instead of reading it he allowed Ywain to put the book into his bedside drawer, and went on making little diagrams or pictures by impressing the bed linen with his thumb nail. He would not accept pen or paper from Ywain.

Finally Ywain asked him what he was making. For the first time since admission his curiosity was piqued.

When Victor at length answered, he said softly but with great deliberation, 'Trees, a forest, dark under looming storm clouds. From a single tree hangs the figure of a man. Approach it when the moon rides the clouds in an angry sky, Ywain, and you will see. I must begin again, for I now see what I never understood before: I shall have to approach death quite soon, my friend.'

His clear gaze clouded for a moment or two and he smoothed the creases out.

Ywain tried to make his own sense of this lucid though hallucinatory description. He remained on his bed looking at Victor, who, for his part, having ceased to mark the linen, lay stretched out on his bed like a corpse prepared for burial. When he was like this neither light nor noise penetrated his ascetic tranquility. After a minute or so Ywain put out the light and lay down in his turn to sleep.

His dream was totally unexpected and intensely vivid. He found himself in a moderately large room whose three visible walls were vague, for most of the scene on his left was occupied by a beach of dazzling white sand. A sea wall, now nearly submerged divided the ocean from a perfectly rectangular pool not much bigger than a full-sized bath. Its water was as blue, as calm and as deep as the sea's. He picked up a flat stone from the beach with the intention of sending it skimming over the water, but as he did so a sense of mystic awe at the beauty and clarity of the scene overcame him. Instead, he took off his clothes and bathed in the pool, which was cool but not uncomfortable. When he did this, the sea's calm was replaced by waves running over the sea wall and buffeting him in the pool.

As he got out, he realized that the room was not his, so he went into a dressing room adjoining. That was when he woke up.

He looked at his companion. Victor lay in exactly the same attitude as before. His eyes were lightly closed. Getting up, he went over to the window and looked out over a cheerless barren winter city beyond the flat of the hospital's roof. There was a faint suggestion of dawn in the thick clouds obliterating moon and stars.

This time his dream was even more insistent than its predecessor. He was walking up a broad snow-covered path ascending ever more steeply to a mountaintop. He had an idea that Debra was slightly behind him, to the left, but he did not see her. Before him an enormous brilliant sun filled the fabulous horizon with blue-white rays radiating like incandescent swords. He was intensely aware that the scene was hallowed and mystic. As he struggled to reach the overwhelming light from the sun of suns, his heart opening out to divine wonder, he abruptly found himself in a very different setting: he was inside a garishly-lit department store or supermarket wandering among innumerable advertisements. There was an evil stale and rotten smell and the heavenly sun had become a tasteless yellow advertising balloon shrinking and wrinkling before his gaze. 'Rotten vulgarity,' he said aloud.

In a tent there was a small table covered with deep crimson cloth. Two men were sitting at it. They offered to reveal a secret to him if he would attend midnight mass. He demurred, offering instead to show them a house he had built on the summit of Mount Everest. The two did not think highly of his property and with gestures refused. He had the impression that he had met the younger of the two once long before, but could not place him.

What followed did not seem to be part of the sequence. He thought the dream had ended, and something else now interposed itself. The vision was startling in its soft realism, like islands seen through mist. He was in a field descending a slope and saw before him a perfectly symmetrical hill with neatly-flattened top. It was spring. Water moved gently in its course as it emerged as a spring from a fissure in the rocks. The turbulence stirred a chalky silt in its bed and it ran like milk. The green of the surrounding country was a marvel.

He awoke and dressed. Few patients used the bath regularly. The nurses on station nodded to him.

He spent about five minutes having his breakfast, bringing his coffee, a spare supply of sugar and juice back to his ward. He offered Victor the juice but the latter refused gently.

'Do you ever dream, Victor?'

'Sometimes. I do not remember dreams.'

'I had some vivid dreams last night, which is strange, for I haven't dreamt for ages, and certainly not since the beginning of my illness.'

'Ywain, you are a very generous man. You always offer me what you have,' said Victor inconsequentially. 'I would offer you something if I had it, but God has forbidden me to have any property of my own or to accept the property of others. Perhaps I am giving dreams to you, perhaps not; perhaps they are your own. Who can say? But something at least I can offer to you in exchange for the possession you have allowed me. If I had pencil and paper, I could write, but that would be to deface the property of others, so that is not permitted to me. I love letters. Do you?'

'I'll write to you when I get out.'

Victor smiled. 'Yes, you have true generosity, Ywain. You seek something to love, and you wish to be a prince in spirit. However, I did not mean pieces of paper with writing on them, but the alphabet. It is strange, isn't it, that the letter which stands for love also stands for nothing.'

'Whoever invented the alphabet was pretty smart, that's for sure,' said Ywain carelessly.

'Who could invent such a thing? The alphabet is a gift from heaven. First there is *B*, taller than a tree. A beautiful letter, *B*, don't you think?'

Ywain was fascinated by the lucidity of complete madness. 'I thought *A* came first.'

'You have to be careful of *H*. It can be unlucky, but *G* has the strength of the female and *M* is the sunniest. I shall give you *O*. It is the perfect letter:

it means nothing and is as symmetrical as divinity. I do not own the letters. No one does. Then it is like the bible. It belongs to no one. You merely show me where it is so that I can pick it up. I will show you O.' With his left forefinger he touched the base of his right forefinger. 'But when you do this, do it quickly and keep your hand closed so that no one can see what you are doing except the one you want. Do you understand?'

'Yes,' said Ywain, wondering at Victor's unwonted intensity.

'On your travels you will sometimes need to know if people are your friends or not. That is very important, for you will be travelling, Ywain, I know that.'

'I had thought of going somewhere for a bit, but now I don't feel like it and in any case I've got no money.'

'God will decide what you are going to do, Ywain, and I see you as a traveller, moreover, as a traveller who sets out on his way quite soon. So remember. *O* is the letter of love, the first step. Let one or two, not everyone you meet, know that you love them, perhaps only one, and you will find that love will serve you better than all the money you could wish. And if you are cold, this gesture of the *O* can look like no more than the clasping of chilled hands.'

Ywain stared at him for a moment. No one speaks so convincingly as the deluded man, he thought, and yet, even given that, his words had conviction.

'What were my dreams, then?'

'I do not know, but I believe that in dreams we can meet angels. Did you meet angels or demons.'

'I don't know whether they were demons or angels, but I met two men who wanted to show me something, but only if I went to midnight mass.'

'Do you go to mass?'

'No, never.'

'Do what you are told in your dreams. Perhaps a messenger from God is speaking to you. Was it God's command you heard?'

'I don't know. It was more like a – something like a temptation. I cannot talk of God. Who knows where God is to be found?'

'Ywain, you speak as the rest of them do. Do you wish to cut yourself off from God when he has sent word to you? Or was there something more to your dream that you are keeping to yourself. That may be just as important.'

Ywain did not know what to say for a minute or two.

'I had other dreams too. I dreamt of a hill.'

But Victor had stretched himself out and closed his eyelids lightly in preparation for sleep. He looked as though he had been in a state of suspended animation for hours.

Ywain went out and got himself a two-hour pass to walk in the park. When he came back, Victor had gone and his bed was stripped.

He went to the nurses' station.

'Where's Victor?'

'Oh, he's been moved back to the psychiatric hospital.'

'But I was getting along so well with him. I could have persuaded him to eat. And I had something for him.'

'Yes, Victor's a dear, isn't he?'

He went back into the ward and opened the drawer of Victor's night table. The bible was still there, together with a scrap of toilet paper that Victor had been using as a bookmark. He put them into his grip.

On Tuesday of the following week Ywain was discharged and went home, still on heavy doses of anti-depressant drug.

For four months he remained passive and listless except for occasional periods of wild elation in which he dreamed vividly of finding some earthly paradise where happiness was freed from the restrictions of having to earn a living and dealing with other people. On T.V. he saw a film about the idyllic life of an old man on some island off the east coast of Australia, and for a while he wove fantasies of getting just enough money together to enable him to go there and sit on the beach or under a tree in beautiful weather, feeding himself from the sea. What more could he need there? Why should he slave in the darkness of winter afternoons merely in order to eat more than was good for him or to own multiple sets of clothing? In this cloud-cuckoo-land he regarded himself (together with the old man) as being the sole representative of sanity in a world of self-incarcerated slaves.

More often he spent days sleeping.

His mother worried and his sister was alternately sympathetic and contemptuous. From the first she had led and he had followed.

It was clear to Ywain that money or no money he would have to live somewhere else.

Late one afternoon in the Fall he went down to his old boss, got his job back and was promised a full-time position in a matter of months. Ywain had learned a great deal about all kinds of bicycles in his time with Total Cycle and was a better man than his replacement, who was still struggling with the basics. He began to look for lodgings.

His intense longing for privacy made him choosy, but at length he managed to find some space not licensed for accommodation in a big industrial building in the south-east of the city, sharing a common area with an artist called Pendar Whitlan. Pendar had recently split with his artist girlfriend and did not want another artist sharing his studio and living space. Though the quarters were crude they were enormous, allowing ample room for subdivision into private areas.

He gave his mother Pendar's telephone number, telling her he would be getting his own phone soon, but not his address. He didn't even know the postal code. He did not know why he refused to give her his address and nor did she. Having so recently learned that her son was mentally unstable, she worried and tended to exaggerate his condition, but Mira laughed. She said it was the best thing for all of them.

Meanwhile Ywain did not neglect Victor even though it was difficult to reach him without the use of a private car. Considering that Ywain had been the only person actually to persuade Victor to accept something, he had a lot of trouble getting in to see him. He was told that visitors caused Victor 'distress' and that as a rule only close relatives were allowed. Bluffing, Ywain told the reception nurse that not a single family member had been to see Victor, and in any case he had come to return something.

Finally, he got in 'just for a few minutes'.

In his inexpressive way Victor was delighted to see him and pleased when Ywain proffered him the bible that no one owned. He did not take it but, as before, indicated the drawer of the night table. Ywain for his part was pleased to see that Victor had been successful in preserving himself from the flood of drugs used to control patients in a mental hospital. He also had the presence of mind to write out several requests that Victor wished Ywain be allowed to visit him. These were dated at suitable intervals.

'What can I do for you now?' asked Ywain as he sat down.

Victor gave him a warning look and pointed to his ear. Ywain bent over him.

'Nothing,' Victor whispered. 'God gives me comfort.'

'Where will you go when you get out?'

'They will not let me go. But if they did, to Ireland first, then to England where I am called. Perhaps I shall join the dance.'

'You come from Ireland?'

'From the north, further north than Ireland or Britain, once, long ago. From the old lands, Ywain. Our roots are there. You may start in Ireland.'

At that moment a male orderly came in, ostensibly to check that Victor was not being over-excited, and signed to Ywain to leave.

'I'll try to visit you again soon.'

'You are a generous man, Ywain. Wherever you go, may God go with you.'

Chapter 3

Ywain's second and final visit was even briefer than the first. After a short five minutes he was asked to leave by the same male nurse who had ushered him out on the previous visit. The man stood there until he left, so there was no way he could exchange any final private remarks with Victor. The latter insisted that Ywain take back the bible and became so distressed when he showed unwillingness to do this that he felt obliged to put it into his pocket. As he did so the orderly winked at him as if he, Ywain, was a fellow-scoffer at his friend's delusions. Victor's final words were: 'I shall be discharged soon, Ywain. You have helped me to recover.'

Outside the ward, the orderly, a complacent little know-it-all, told him, 'Not a chance. That guy would just lay down and die on his own without no twenty-four hour supervision. And visitors just make him worse. He sits up, takes notice and starts raving off again. Sorry, but there it is, chum. Nothing against you personally, understood? That's the way it is and I can't help him any and you can't. Religious nuts! Worst kind – I'm not saying anything against him personally, understood?' he added hastily.

Why the unnecessary deliberate lie? Ywain asked himself as he left. To justify the constant stream of obliterating drugs? Or was this slander of the gentlest quietest creature he had ever known a cover for some other more sinister purpose?

Whitlan was out. Ywain threw the bible on to a salvaged sofa laden with junk mail, flyers, newspapers and his small budget of current reading and hung up his jacket. He went over to the large window door that served as exit to a fire escape and stepped out on to the tiny steel balcony to get some fresh air four storeys above the traffic fumes. In the low light of late afternoon he could look out over the commercial buildings, gaunt variations on industrial brick. It was the perfect setting for a film on life in the Great Depression. On an impulse he could not explain he took another identical Gideon bible from a carton of twenty or so that lay in this cargo hold of impedimenta, part of the accumulated flotsam and jetsam of utilitarian objects that dwellers in commercial space inherit – discarded office chairs, sofas and easy chairs, typewriters, bits of plumbing – Whitlan was very skilful at using this kind of thing – old filing cabinets, unused carpet and rugs, a desk or two, a small refrigerator which Whitlan would get running some day, shelving and odd pieces of lumber, some hundreds of navy-blue aprons, even a moth-eaten polar bear skin, bulky paraphernalia not worth taking away at the end of the lease or picked up elsewhere by Whitlan, some of it dating back forty years, most of it never used – and placed it on the sofa. He jammed Victor's bible into the bottom of his overnight grip between the stiffener and the leather.

Depression had not left him. It had been alleviated by the tiny yellow pills he gulped down three times daily, but the sense of life's darkness still oppressed him. As the result of years of combined grind and classroom politics culminating in academic honours he was now privileged to be working full-time at the only trade he knew, repairing and sometimes selling bicycles. Well, but so did the Wrights. For his arts as for his dreams there was no echo in the waking world. A silent undiscovered forest called futilely to him.

On a thought he retrieved the bible from its hiding place. Had Victor left him a message? He flipped the pages, wondering why they were called leaves. He held it up by the covers, but nothing fell out. He looked for pencilled messages in the text. He could see none.

The strength of Victor's delusions amazed him, but he reflected that there was at least some happiness in being so obsessed. No such distraction alleviated his own chilling reality once the diverting pressure of the university had been taken off him, for, he thought, depression is not necessarily a mental disorder. It is more often the terribly clear perception of the intelligent who have found that there is far more dark than light matter in their circumscribed universe.

'Funny,' he thought, 'approaching the twenty-first century, we make books much the same as they've been for hundreds of years. And *still* we can't make one that piles the leaves perfectly evenly when you lay it down or stand it up, even though Caxton would have been ashamed to let a book so badly bound as to show the faintest hint of a crack in the pages go out of his shop. Yet take any book here. Every one shows cracks between sections of pages.'

This particular bible had indeed been well-used. The red edging on the pages had almost worn away. He picked it up and opened it where the spine gave, at page 561. A careless reader had left a stain there. 'Nevertheless, my loving kindness will I not utterly take from him, nor suffer thy faithfulness to fall,' he read as he turned the page. What was this, for God's sake, a divine domestic quarrel? 'My covenant will I not break, *How long* shall they utter *and* . . .'

He turned back to the previous page. Something didn't make sense. It was then that he noticed the verses ran 32, 33, 34, 4; that page 561 was followed by page 564, because two pages were stuck together. Dirty feeder had used a tiny patch of moistened sugar, probably, to seal them. When he separated them a scrap of thin hospital toilet paper fell out. On it a message had been impressed in thumb-nail marks. It took him a while to make out the grotesque script: 4 THE BOOK OF CAIN.

Reading through Genesis 4 did not take him anywhere, scrutinize the text as he might, searching for some clue to Victor's mind. Did he regard himself as bearing the mark of Cain, convinced that he was an irredeemable outcast with a curse upon him, the curse of lacking everything? The magnifying glass he borrowed from Pendar's desk was no help either, but the artist's dioptre lamp produced some result. With the greatest difficulty he was able to make out a pin prick beside Verse 10. Further examination with the 8" lens enabled him to descry an even smaller pin prick under the fourth word, *what*. He must have spent an hour methodically traversing the page, but he found no more pin pricks. The uneven tissue of the cheap thin paper made them hard to spot, for the varying density scattered minute holes or near-holes in profusion. He was almost sick with frustration.

At this point he decided to give his eyes a rest. It was going to be a long night.

When he resumed, he caught his second wind, his patience held and he made better time. There was a definite pin hole on page 7 indicating Chapter 9. Verse 12 yielded *said* and *is*, and Chapter 10 Verse 12 gave up *between*. At the end of Chapter 10 a faint pencilled note which he had completely missed seeing on his first examination was added to the last sentence: *These are the families of the sons of Noah, after their generations, in their nations: and by these were the nations divided up in the earth after the flood* (explained in Judges).

Even Ywain knew that there was no connexion between Genesis and Judges.

Again, the problem with Judges was distinguishing the actual pin pricks amid the constellations of tiny holes in the imperfect paper, and it was symmetry rather than size which made them visible. The first one occurred in Chapter 3, Verse 16, the ninth word, *two*. So far, then, *what is said between two*. It didn't look very promising, and Ywain had the momentary fear that this was indeed mere madness. There were no more pin holes in The Book of Judges, and no indication of where to go next in order to complete whatever sense there might be. He didn't know what made him persist, but he wanted to. The trouble was that he had run out of clues.

It was long before he thought to look closely at the alphabetical index. The characteristic pin-hole was in the *R* of 'Revelation', and he could take up the thread again. Someone in obscure jest had crossed out the last word in Chapter 1, Verse 1, *John*, and substituted *Matthew*. 4, 2, 5-6, 4, 3, 30 and 16, 20, 3 yielded another four words, *in the emerald island*. It didn't take Ywain long to extract the one remaining word from Matthew 10, 16, 18, *serpents*.

He now had: *what said is between two in the emerald island serpents*.

The obvious arrangement was: *what is said between two serpents in the emerald island*. But where did that take him?

At least he could go to bed knowing that he had solved part of a puzzle. What did it mean, and where was the rest?

He climbed to his aerial perch and unfolded the bed the artist had cunningly built to fold up against the pillar and lie out along the beam. As soon as his head touched the pillow he heard Pender trying to unlock the door. His landlord came in too drunk to do anything except relieve himself noisily and collapse on to a sofa.

Back in the factory quarters after work next evening, he watched the artist at work in complete silence. Ywain was at a dead end. When he retrieved the bible from his grip to scrutinize it for the umpteenth time he saw for the first time a little scrap of toilet paper that Victor had apparently used as a marker when he was in the same ward as Ywain. On it something was written so faintly as to escape notice altogether: *For Ywain to keep*.

His instincts now stronger than ever, he made sure that Victor's bible was well hidden and that the decoy was lying carelessly on the gather-all sofa. He carried all the other bibles downstairs and disposed of them in the dumpster.

Hadn't Victor told him pretty clearly that he came from Ireland and England and lands further north, but Ireland most recently?

Chapter 4

He awoke early in the morning. A departing dream rushed back into its subterranean bed leaving a shellburst in his vision. All his effeminate melancholia and indecision were swept away in a tide of absolute conviction. Destiny in a white bed sheet pointed out a path that would surely lead to some fantastic wonderful end. All that stood in his way was his bank balance. He had his fare, no more.

He did not want to hang around the studio too much, especially as Pender in his golden period was frequently drunk and invariably morose, so he spent much of his spare time in the libraries trying to get a feeling for his destination. Sometimes he called Debra, but she worked some evenings. However, they agreed to meet on Friday and go to experimental theatre. Admission was free as the performance was subsidized. A friend of Debra's was involved in the thing. There was a double billing: *Nescience*, in which the entire cast was covered with black pigment, and *Poisonous Parallels* (spelt incorrectly), in which each scene was entirely static. Debra had many friends in theatre and believed in every one of them. Ywain was not keen on going, since 'experimental' meant student-written, student-directed and student-acted. Both plays were guaranteed disasters mitigated only by the fact that the entire audience consisted of sympathetic drama students and their friends and relatives who had been morally coerced into attending. But this was the ordeal exacted for Debra's lovely company.

On Friday evening Debra was excited, almost dancing in her joy. She had found the job far more congenial than she expected. Her drawing had impressed; her section head made no secret of the firm's desire to keep her and a recent change of government made it certain that some juicy contracts were in the offing for its friends. Corporations become fixated upon persons, at least temporarily, just as lovers do. She was sorry Ywain still had nothing. For some reason he could not explain even to himself, he said nothing about his own abrupt change of plans, even though he was bursting with the sheer marvel of his quest. He knew she would not understand, and instinctively he wanted to make a complete break with the whole of his past life.

Although the theatre was small well over half the seats were empty. He set himself to enjoy it as much as he could, suspecting that the real entertainment would come from the audience. The first play started twenty minutes late. There was only one constantly visible and mobile character, blacked from head to foot and supported by a chorus of wailing furies of equal nigritude lost in the shadows at the back. The protagonist responded to voices coming from various directions. His projection was not good, but it was far better than his enunciation, so that a good deal of the dialogue (if that is the right word) was lost on Ywain. Debra was rapt. It appeared that the protagonist was acting as an oracle on Life, particularly as it concerned the coexistence of the two sexes, but every answer depended on some other answer, so that he really got nowhere. There was no plot, no character, no progression and absolutely no humour.

'Isn't he marvellous!' exclaimed Debra. 'He's directing *Poisonous Parallels*! What ability! What talent! Oh, don't you think he's a genius!'

Ywain nodded as non-commitally as he dared short of bruising Debra's enthusiasm. Even more bored than he had anticipated, he looked around, stifling a yawn. A few souls must have arrived late, for several more seats were taken, not exclusively by young *afficionados*. One of the newcomers at least was no student. He was a tall lean man of indeterminate age with scrub-cut brown hair, thin glasses and a narrow straight mouth. As Ywain gazed in his direction he caught his eye, but the other man simply blinked and looked elsewhere. It was obvious that he had little interest in the play. Ywain wondered why he had come. He was alone. Not scouting for talent, surely? Evidently his patience was short, for he had disappeared from the audience when the lights went up.

After a beer with Debra and a few of her drama pals, he walked her to the subway before striding off through the concrete valleys in the soft light.

Now that his mind had something to work on, Ywain was less prone to disabling fits of depression. He had scraped up enough money for the lowest fare, but had so little left over that he could not possibly exist for more than three or four weeks without finding work. In times of high unemployment most countries protected their own citizens by enacting immigration laws designed to prevent visitors from taking jobs. But never mind. For the first three weeks it ought to be sweet. He didn't allow himself to become concerned about this obstacle to his progress.

It was after 1 a.m. when he got back. 'Ten days to go,' he said to himself. At the end of each day he crossed it off his mind's calendar.

Whitlan was still out.

Chapter 5

WHEN THERE WERE NO FURTHER ARRANGEMENTS for him to make he became more desultory in his daily activities. Even his boss, with whom he normally got on very well, found something to complain of in him.

Going out to eat his lunch in the Philosophers' Walk where he hoped to meet Debra, he began to take notice of a white car that he remembered seeing often for the past week. It was too far off for him to see who sat behind its tinted glass. He stopped at an intersection to let the car catch up with him, but the driver changed lanes abruptly, signalled for an illegal left-hand turn and swung away, bringing a clamour of angry horns upon him. Ywain caught a glimpse of a face behind the glinting sunlight that he remembered seeing fairly recently, but it took him a while to place it. He was still puzzling over this when he got to the Philosophers' Walk.

He was troubled. Hunger had left him.

Debra was there, earlier than usual, still delighted with life. Again he listened to all her news but did not confide his own plans to her. While they were talking, he suddenly remembered where he had seen the driver before – of course – at the play. He described him to Debra and asked her if she knew him. She shook her head.

'No. Not on my list at all. Why do you ask?'

Ywain told her.

'Probably a coincidence. After all, who'd be interested in you? You're not working for the F.B.I. or Interpol, are you? Or are you one of Toronto's drug barons on the quiet? Hey, I bet you're an old married man and your wife's having you tailed – and possibly docked, eh? Wait a moment, though. Could have something to do with someone you've known, perhaps? No? Well, unlikely, isn't it? Tell you what, I'll leave a minute or two early and walk towards Queen's Park as usual You stay here, go when you usually do while I stand somewhere inconspicuously and see if you're really being tracked or if you've just got a bad case of boiled-head paranoia.'

It was so pleasant here with Debra. He wondered why his instincts rebelled against the sunny prospect of life with such a fine woman. She knew he was troubled and gave him a single gentle kiss as she got up. Throwing the remains of his lunch into the garbage basket, Ywain watched her leave. She was wearing a skirt, and the fall and undulation made him exclaim aloud: 'She's a classic.' He tried to look as though he was not watching out. He didn't see any sign of a car on the way back. He should have noted down the licence number when he had the chance. But where would that have got him?

At work during the day he was uncharacteristically morose in contrast to his evening fits of elation. Strangely, the prospect of new adventure did little to lighten his spirit among the bicycles.

His walk home was a long one, mostly along Bloor West until he dipped into a warren of small streets on the other side of a huge railway overpass. Bloor was packed solid with cars and people, although the latter thinned out once he got well beyond Dufferin. A tiny park, a patch of lichen on a rock, dragging sparse life from the shaded and infertile ways, breathed desperately in the hydrocarbon-charged air.

To approach his own dwelling he had to unlock a gate, walk for about a hundred-and-fifty feet between the high buildings to a double door, usually left unlocked and take the stairs on the left in the five-storeyed converted factory warehouse where tiny importers and little manufacturers of jewellery plied their trades amid the artists, the photographic processors and the dog-training school. He went down the path towards the double door where another path intersected it. Seldom did he see another soul here at this time of night, but on this occasion a tall man came out of the building. At this moment Ywain's instinctive fears still slept, but in spite of the darkness he recognized the stranger in the theatre. As yet his daylit fantasies suppressed the dream of menace.

'Hold it!'

Ywain stopped. No mistake about the man now.

'Just want a word with you. You don't have too many friends, do you?'

'What's this all about?' Ywain tried to sound nonchalant, but he sensed the aggressive vitality of the man. He made as if to walk on, but his interceptor seized his arm and there was no mistaking his grip.

'Don't make it tough on yourself. Feel here.'

Ywain felt the outline of a revolver under the man's jacket.

'What are you up to?'

'I'm not up to anything. I'm just coming home from work as usual.'

'Now isn't that nice! And what's a man like you working in a place like that for, a man with a university education?'

'Jobs are hard to get.'

'I've got plenty of work to do, do you mind me? I've got lots of work. Know what my work is?'

'No.'

'It's dealing with stubborn people like you.' The stranger tightened his grip on Ywain's elbow. 'How many people in Toronto dissolve into the wind every day?'

Ywain, thoroughly frightened now, tried to sound stupid. 'Dissolve –'

'How many are put on ice, upholstered in lead, dunked in the lake, fed lead – you know. Take your pick. What would you call it? Something fancy I bet – set at peace, brought home to harvest, passed on. Me, I'm not fussy. The deed, not the word, is all I'm concerned with. So how many?'

'Why do you ask me?'

'Matter of general interest. An aimless young nerd like you, why, who would have a motive? I'm talking about the ones the cops don't find out about. Most of these jerks like you wind up in cement, and why? Because they're stubborn stupid. Now, all you have to do is cooperate and I'll leave you alone – unless you tell anyone. If you do, and especial if you tell the cops, you'll – how shall I put it in poetry? – vanish, dissolve, totally deteriorate – cheap for your family. No casket to buy, no funeral, nothing. There'll be nothing left over. Very convenient for all.'

He spoke in a deliberate, casual, almost toneless voice.

'What do you want?' Ywain forced himself to say.

'What did you get from that maniac – you know who I mean, the loony dork in the hospital?'

'Nothing.'

'Ah,' responded the intruder, putting a lock on Ywain's neck, 'that is disappointing. A little birdie tells me he gave you a book.'

'He gave me *back* a book. He wanted a bible but wouldn't accept anything that belonged to anyone else. He refused to keep it and gave it to me back.'

'What a touching tale. And what did you do with it?'

'It's in my apartment. If you want it I'll go up and bring it down to you. I don't need it.'

'Was that the one laying on the couch?'

'Yes.'

'O.K. I believe you.' He spoke something unintelligible into a small two-way radio.

'Can't you just leave me alone? I don't know what's going on. I'm not involved in whatever it is. God knows why you think a book in the hands of a mentally-disturbed patient is important. What's all this about?'

'Come on. We've got a call to make.'

Ywain began to protest but the stranger put his hand into an inner pocket.

Outside a large white car was parked.

'Get in.'

There were two men in front as Ywain was pushed into the empty rear seat followed by his captor. The two did not turn their heads.

'I got the bible and the slips of paper.'

'Good,' said the man on the right. 'Now get out and watch him from the entrance. If he gives any trouble, kill him and we'll throw him into the lake.'

He had a plummy English accent, somewhat overdone and cultivated an air of exaggerated coolness.

When Ywain's tormentor had removed himself to stare fixedly at the victim through the glass from the sidewalk, the man with the over-rich voice spoke again.

'Sorry about the inconvenience, old chap, but if you knew our reasons you would understand. Our friend outside is a little crude, but he gets results and that is what counts. Now listen carefully. If you have anything to tell us about your friend Victor, or if there is anything having some connexion with him, however trivial or remote, tell us now. It will save you enormous trouble. Come on. You were with him in St Michael's for a day or two, weren't you? What did he talk about? You see that I am dealing with you as a gentleman; our friend outside certainly won't if I have to turn you over to him.'

'He hardly spoke. He told me that he was a child of God and that God had forbidden him to accept the property of others. He wouldn't eat, drink or take his medication, so he was moved to the mental hospital in short order.'

'What about these slips of paper?'

'I noticed that he was pretty much alone and thought someone should visit him. I went to him because I thought I could help him.'

'How?'

'By talking his obsession out of him. I didn't think he was getting much help or understanding from the staff.'

'Why did you insist on getting these slips from him?'

'They made trouble about my visits, so I got him to give me written requests –'

'What does this mean?'

He held up a slip of toilet paper.

'I haven't the faintest idea – I wouldn't assume it means anything, except perhaps to him.'

'You must have studied it pretty closely. After all, you're the one who was taking such an interest in him.'

'I tried. Everything he said was completely incoherent as far as I can see. I mean, he never made any sense to me in St Michael's. He was obsessed. Everything he said, and he didn't say much, was governed by his obsession. He was trapped in it. I can't be expected to follow his ravings.'

'Did he have any other visitors?'

'None while I was with him.'

'Anything else?'

'No. I have no idea what this is all about. Why is he so important?'

'Who said he was?'

'Well –'

'Never you mind what it's all about. Tell me anything you can now.'

'There's nothing to tell.'

'Very well. If we think you've played fair with us, we're prepared to make up this little unpleasantness up to you. If we think otherwise, we'll kill you after we've got what we want out of you. It's better, far better, for you to be absolutely frank with us now than to suffer what we'll put you through to get the truth out of you. Do be perfectly clear about that, won't you? Any misunderstanding on your part, however minor, could be fatal to you. Are you hearing me?'

'I hear you.'

'Good. We mean business and we're going to keep an eye on you. By the way, who is this?'

He turned on the dome light and showed Ywain a photo of Debra. Ywain said nothing.

'It's your girl, isn't it? Name, address and phone number, please.'

There was no point in lying. This was so obviously a test.

'Fine. Now if anything should happen to you, if, for example, you tried to disappear, she could get into trouble. You've met our simian friend out there. It's very easy for someone like Debra to run into the wrong people. It happens all the time these days. He likes dealing with women, he says, because there are so many things you can do to them. Now run along and take care. Life is full of hazards.'

As Ywain turned to open the car door, the plummy voice added a footnote: 'I'm sure you know your *Hamlet*. Hamlet's mistake was in underestimating Claudius. Don't make the same blunder. Claudius' error lay in not being ruthless enough. We are quite ruthless. Do keep that in mind.'

Ywain got out, the bully got in and the big car glided off.

Hardly pausing, Ywain bounded up the steps to his quarters.

At first he didn't notice much amiss. The place was a mess any time. But gazing up, he noticed that the two beds Whitlan had ingeniously constructed to fold into the loft beam during the day had been discovered by someone. They were up-ended and thoroughly rifled. The artist had not escaped: everything had been moved around, his desk drawers had been emptied out on to the floor, the furniture upholstery was slit and slashed, and his paintings thrown around and left face-down on the floor. However, it was Ywain's own little domain to which the invader had devoted the major part of his energy. In addition to the destruction of the furniture and the desolation of his desk, his modest rack of garments had been cut or torn to pieces. The searcher had slashed out the linings of the jackets and the seams of everything, dashing the mess on to the floor as he methodically ruined each one. The small tallboy one place removed from the junkyard which Ywain had salvaged was destroyed and empty, its contents discarded with the rest. Oddly, although the grip had been turned out, the man who got results had missed the concealed bible. As far as he could tell, the decoy was missing.

Ywain paused, but absorbed the shock well and then moved. He stuffed into his grip and a surviving rucksack all the usable small clothing on the floor. All the outer clothing except what he was wearing was beyond repair and his shoes had been cut up. There wasn't much to pack.

Then his mind took over with racing thoughts. They've got Victor. If he's still alive they may force him to incriminate me in whatever's going on. The sense of deep menace was overpowering, but he salvaged some paper and envelopes and wrote two short notes.

> *Dear Mom,*
>
>   *You won't understand why I have to leave so abruptly, but it's not only on account of wanderlust. I'm pursued by forces I don't understand. I flee them in order to find out what lies beyond the life I've been leading.*

> *If I come back I'll know more than I can tell you now.*
>
> *Thanks, dear Mom, for all that you have done for me. At least my failure is not one of love for you. I hope to be back, so last out for my sake.*
>
> *Your loving son,*
> *Ywain*

To his sister he wrote an even briefer message which, however, cost him more thought.

> *Dear Mira,*
>
> *Sorry to have been a disappointment to you recently. I've disappointed myself as well. I have to leave now, but I'll drop you a line if anything significant happens. What's the use of degrees if you don't want to carry on in Ulro?*
>
> *Born together, we're poles apart, but perhaps we'll meet again before the end.*
>
> *Your brother,*
> *Ywain*

He then wrote a terse note to Debra warning her to hide and protect herself.

He addressed and stamped the envelopes to post on the way.

Now cold and collected and in the grip of fear, he was cautious and deliberate.

Before he left, a lucky thought struck him. He went over to see that he had locked the door behind him. An envelope addressed to him was pinned to the wall beside it. The contents were four $500 bills and a laconic note: *No need to make a fuss, old boy.* It was unsigned.

This time he used the utmost care to make sure that there were no watchers before he fled into the warren of criss-crossing streets the narrow lane at the foot of the fire escape debouched into.

Chapter 6

SUNDAY WAS A BEAUTIFUL EVENING sparkling with brilliants. The severe cold air from Toronto to the coast of Labrador revealed the lights of cities and settlements and, briefly, the moonlit sea. It was succeeded by ever-thicker cloud cover all the way over the Atlantic. Ireland Ywain glimpsed only patchily in the dull morning as the captain began his long descent, an obscure passing of a dark green below.

Rain slashed razor cuts across the ports.

At 6.30 a.m. Dublin's airport was depressing. He felt his soul gripped by the familiar undertow of despair, but he possessed himself. Here there was neither friend nor hostile stranger.

Tourist Information booked him into a B&B costing £8.50 a night, plus single supplement, another £1.75. He might as well splurge the first night. Getting a bus to take him to the centre of Dublin was no problem, but once there he thought he might as well walk all the way to Clontarf where his B&B was. The sky had lightened a little. So had his heart. Shouldering his pack, he started off. After an hour the sky closed in again and rain resumed. He paused for rest with increasing frequency throughout his soggy journey.

The generality of the Irish people might be practising their elfin humour behind their doors that day, but his hostess was reserved, polite and strict after the manner of those who like to remind strangers of their place. She offered him the obligatory tea and scone, collected his voucher from Tourist Information and the balance of his lodging and disappeared. The 60p charge attached to the bank transaction in addition to the ruinous rate spread on exchange had shaken him. How would he manage to live at this rate? It was obvious that he must gravitate downwards, beginning on the morrow. A recollection of Victor flashed through his mind.

A walk along the bleak shore revealed only the industrial development of the whole area, sending him back to the room he thought he could not afford, sick and disgusted. Where was the magic realm?

He had trapped himself again.

He slept. He awoke. He sorted out his meagre stock of possessions for the third or fourth time. He went out, sniffed the air, went back into the lounge, examined the out-dated advertisements of events no longer current in a rack of stale papers, and knew again despair.

He slept again, fitfully disturbed by the swashing of jets arrowing down into Dublin as if the aircraft he had travelled on had pierced his heart. He knew the second stage of desperation, a cold insulation from life that invited him to dwell on what was no longer the worst.

Morning welled up under dense black clouds bringing rain in coarse drops.

In the dining-room he ate his greasy breakfast of fried egg, sausages and fat bacon more out of a sense of duty to his lost £10.25 than with any relish of the culinary archæology that was supposed to fascinate tourists. It added a fetching extravagance to his desperate melancholia.

His hostess, still businesslike but less discouraging than the day before, asked him where he was going. She saw that he was uncomfortable in his reply and his perception that she did tied his tongue. He mumbled something about youth-hostelling around Ireland.

She nodded and left, returning immediately with a leaflet. He could get a youth hostel card for a modest fee and with it stay at any youth hostel for two or three pounds, a trifle more if one was over 26. He took the address and thanked her.

Not knowing what else to do, he went back to the centre again, found the Tourist Information Office, purchased his youth hostel membership and took a bus south, planning to stop in Cork and look for a job.

On the way some of the clouds lifted and things looked brighter. He still had something over $2,000, but once he started seriously to spend it he would be staring either poverty or the return half of his air ticket in the face, both equally unpalatable. He was determined never to ask his mother for help (she had surely done her part) and almost equally resolved never to ask Mira for anything. She just might refuse.

After a promisingly bright spell, the clouds gathered again and a louring sky threatened the cut hay as the underpowered bus laboured up Ireland's gentle slopes and complained around bends. Every now and then a small car scuttled around them cutting it fine on blind curves like a worker ant with an obsession about business.

How did one get to own a car? By going out and getting a job. But the wasteland of work was more futile than the rotting hay cultivated only to spoil. He could not face entering the blind alley of years of repetitive work striving to make the time when life would be a burden to him as comfortable as possible.

Almost as depressing as Clontarf under rain were the mud flats of Wexford. What could this small country hold? What *idée fixe* had driven him here? He recoiled from this question and comforted himself with the thought that all travel is a valuable experience and one must not expect it to be uniformly pleasant. 'Senile cliché!' he exclaimed aloud to himself.

Although it was high summer (if 50°F can be called summer), there were few passengers in the bus whose number varied, as there were frequent stops and diversions. All the people were pleasant, natural and kindly. He tried to throw off his own inner tension by taking an interest in his fellows. Black hair and pale skin were predominant, but red hair was also common – and everyone had hair, lots of it. He couldn't remember seeing a baldy. He fitted in. He looked just like one of them.

Until he walked down the long main street in Youghall he wasn't fully aware that his journey to escape the future was in fact a step into the past: apart from a liberal sprinkling of tiny box-like coloured cars parked over gutter and footpath and the headlines of newspapers, the whole scene might have been set in 1920, or even 1880. Behind the nineteenth century street façade the grocer presided over a dangerous-looking hand slicing machine on which he cut lovely fleshy bacon that bore no relation to the pale rashers of fluid-cured fat that passed under the name in Toronto supermarkets; there was a sweet shop that displayed nothing but masses of colourful hand-made sweets in a nursery variety of shapes, a painted illustration in a child's book: all the shops were small and specialized except for the shoebox of a 'supermarket' that was nearly empty and seemed out of place. The butcher wore a white-and-blue striped apron; the grocer and greengrocer, white. Children played the street games long abandoned by the street-wise youngsters of his own city, chanting over the ritual rhymes and looking up in silence, making way for him to pass. For them, the adults were still Olympian. Girls stared in momentary frank interest and in the same moment glanced away. Very young women in their teens held on to their infants or pushed strollers. They ignored him. On the quay old men sat in the sun, drawing on contented pipes or talking in slow voices. It was like a photograph from the eighteen seventies. Fishing boats lay on the mud, for the tide was out. The life of the town quickened along its streets and in its public houses. Stopping at a familiar-looking pub for a beer, he was surprised when men – they were all men – greeted him as he entered. They were bearded, leathery and gently human. There was a long-lost quality of community here which was quite new to him. Once again on the bus bound for Cork he wondered at this. It was so uncannily different from the automatic smile and polite hostility of Toronto.

Encouraged by the gentle conviviality of Youghall, the sun showed its face in a space between clouds bestowing warmer hues of soft green upon the rounded contours of breast-like hills. Now and then the pines took a hill or two in force while hedgerows or stone walls defended irregular squares of pasture or cash crops in sombre green or morning yellow.

In Cork he was back in Dublin. The place was citified, a chaos of endless narrow streets in the last stage of sclerosis brought on by the internal combustion engine. The buildings were layered over hills where each successive generation of building was founded on the obliteration of an essential and more beautiful past. There was work, there was industry. Busy men in nice suits – they all wore three-piece suits, for this was still a man's country – industriously walked forth doing the things they had done yesterday and would do again tomorrow.

This life at Cork, strange and eventful though it was to him, crushed his spirit again. At Youghall there had been a simple monument to patriots tortured hanged or piked by the British in 1798. He had stood for a minute or two, feeling a momentary fierce elation as though the stone had some concentrated psychic force within it: there was some spirit in that place. Compared with Youghall, Cork, with all its splendid buildings, did not seem to amount to anything in particular that could not be expressed, for example, in statistics. He felt again the sickness of despair as he went in search of the nearest YH without having definite desire or will to do so.

He must go on as long as he could. An intense desire to be directed by a power outside of himself came over him.

It was no great effort for him to chat naturally with his fellow hostellers, deceptively frank. Seeking troubled sleep in the long night, he wondered if he was a mental case who ought never to have been released by the hospital.

No dreams complemented whatever it was that had stirred his inner life during the day.

His money was the time fuze of a huge disaster ticking away more ominously with each day's levy of expense. He had solved part of the puzzle and would have bled to understand the whole enigma. He feared that if he could not do this he would be rudderless, unable to act.

It was Merrick who suggested that Ywain get rid of his surplus stuff and buy a second-hand bicycle. Merrick was one of his Youth Hostel acquaintances of the previous evening. The two had struck a common chord, the one a native, the other a visitor, both cyclists, both intending a tour of exploration, not only of Ireland, but of themselves.

'You've got a lot of stuff you don't really need. You need two shirts, not more. One pair of spare pants, waterproof – just a single change. Sometime later on you get a blow-up nylon tent. That's a luxury, though. Keep the double-knit nylons, flog your other socks and get a lighter-weight nylon jacket.'

'What about winter?'

That's months off. It's not too cold – and you'll be inside most of the tine. You'll see. It's a whole new culture, man. Throw out the idea that you've got a rôle to play in society. You haven't, unless you want to be a mental and physical slave for the rest of your life.'

'What about money?'

'Money? That's the least of your worries. Who's got a bank account these days? That's just giving yourself up as a hostage to the government. You pick up the odd job – and don't be too fussy what it is – you put your hand out – that can be very profitable if your act is good and you rap with people – you look helpless, you tell a good yarn, show them a photograph of your sick kid, or your wife has cancer – something like that, you find out where the soup kitchens and food banks are and latch on to everything that's going. That's why you need to hang out in a big city over winter. You get yourself some new identification – lots of suggestions in the graveyards – and an address and go on the dole. All of us who travel light know what's going. Just get there first. In the swim you survive. You owe nothing to anyone because you've nothing to give.

'Another good way is to pick up a bird or two. There are always birds who are too scared to be out on their own. They're so scared that they'll do anything you tell them, especially if you persuade them that there's a lot of danger around. And birds collect cash in bucketsful. You have more than you can spend. That's something I've never done. It's too much like the world of work and bank accounts. You leave traces. You've got to run to rules – set them up and maintain them strictly. You have to live with them. They're always bellyaching. I don't give a shit for straights. They don't give a shit for me. Why should I ape them by going into business? Waste of energy. But it might suit you. Don't be too scrupulous.'

It sounded too good to be true. Was there a way for him (Ywain) to sock his cash away safely in a bank and live the life of an errant fish out of school? What scruple should he have? He had divorced himself from his country and any intended career. He could always escape if he had ready cash in a bank somewhere.

When he got up in the morning Merrick had gone. Was he a good or a bad demon, or neither? A new reality? What he had said sounded tempting. If one had the means of saving oneself . . .

The day was drizzly and misty.

Chapter 7

He knew the bicycle was stolen: the price was definitely 'hot'. A few days in the youth hostel and on the streets of Cork had taught him that. He had run into several boys and a girl younger than he who made a living by stealing and transforming bicycles so radically that their former owners would never recognize them. So what? He could not restore it to its rightful owner, or owners, since it now combined the parts of several bikes. He had expended more precious pounds in laying in some legitimately-gotten goods to enable him to be more self-sustaining, such as a nylon tent, sleeping bag, bedroll and mess gear. Ireland is a lovely country for cyclists as long as the rain stops and there are no headwinds.

In acquiring the cheapest and most reliable transport, though, he had again reduced his reserves, his margin of safety. In spite of Merrick's youthful wisdom, he could not see how one could possibly move around without using any money.

On Friday he left, glad to be out of Cork, despite the south-west headwind, the intermittent rain and occasional rough going on the shoulder – the verge – as cars raced each other on the straight stretches. At least there were lyrical instants of brief sunshine. He wanted to get to the coast, to follow it around for a bit. The gentle misty contours of Ireland gave promise of a mystical beauty at present hidden from him, echoed, miles back, by the tuneful notes of a penny whistle in some old reeling melody. He stopped at nearly every narrow bridge taking the old way over the stream and gazed down at the waters of Ireland, seeking for some reflection of his soul or an answer to his riddle. On his way he saw many, many ruins, of cottages, towers and churches, some looking recent, and marvelled at the all-too-obvious flood tides of ill-fortune. Yet these wayside digressions did nothing to prepare him for the next development on this day of wonder.

Scattered all over Ireland are thousands of shrines to the Virgin Mary.

He had passed many, but this one arrested him. She stood just inside a grotto high on the slope of a low hill. At her feet a single worshipper in a blue veil and a white robe was depicted in prayer. Less common was the extensive crowd, hundreds strong, completely blocking the narrow country roadway. They were singing. A tiny altar was crammed with burning candles. At the sudden realization awe seized him, perhaps in sympathy with devotion that filled the air. He had never experienced anything like this before.

Locking his bicycle to the wire fence, he joined in. He asked a woman what the occasion was. She told him that the figure of the Virgin Mary had moved on its pedestal the previous evening without any sign of the change showing in the brittle plaster of the base. As she spoke she could see that he was a foreigner and feel his lack of belief. Part of him, the part driven by his Toronto upbringing, rose in spontaneous derision. Part of him, the larger and deeper part, commanded him to understand. He tried to enter into communion with those around him, but did not know how. In spite of the mediæval simplicity of the image with its tinge of the vulgarity that is an essential of common faith, he did not in this company doubt that the Blessed Virgin was, in a sense he could not grasp, the spirit of the place.

Clambering up the steeper slope on the opposite side of the road, he got a better view, and saw that there were many more people than he had noticed at first. A great many were, like himself, watching from this higher ground, all eyes fixed on the effigy in the grotto, waiting for a visible sign of grace. He stood gazing as men and women went through rituals he could not follow. Finally he went down again and stood in the midst of the ever-growing crowd. Few left and many more arrived, often women bringing their children.

At last he turned to go, his gaze still drawn to the grotto. He bumped into a red-haired girl, accidentally brushing against her breast.

'Sorry –,' he began.

'Sure, and there's no need,' replied the girl. He noted her pale skin, blue-green eyes, freckles and the straight full lips of the Celt. 'You're a stranger. What do you think of it all?'

Others were listening and smiling. The Irish spontaneously take part in any conversation within earshot.

'Lovely,' he replied. 'Of course I don't understand it.'

'There's nothing to understand. The Blessed Virgin Mary has made a miracle to remind us of our faith. What's hard about that?'

'It's hard for me.'

'Where do you come from?'

'Canada.'

'Ah, Canada!' She pronounced the word languishingly, as if all that was far-off and alluring might be found in that place. 'That's grand. And are you staying with relatives here?'

'No, I just came over on my own. I wanted to see what Ireland was like.'

'Ah, your family's Irish, then?'

'My father was born in Ireland, I think. I don't know where. My mother could never remember.'

'Then you're one of us – you're Irish. What's your name?' she asked as innocently as an infant.

'Ywain.'

'Sounds Welsh. I'm Ilona – MacBride.'

She offered him her hand, rather narrow and sensuously cool. As he took it he could feel a tingling in all his nerves. He could sense that she felt it too.

'And where are you moving on to?'

'I don't have a plan. I'm interested in shrines, though.'

'Are you a Catholic, then?'

'I suppose – well, I don't know.'

'You don't know! That is strange.'

'Well, I don't know what my father was. My mother didn't bring us up in any religion. She always felt that the churches were no real good to anyone. But of course she knew nothing about places such as this.'

'And where have you just come from?'

'Cork.'

'And where did you say you were going to?'

'As I said, I don't have any unalterable plans. I'm just following the coast, roughly.'

'All by yourself?'

'All by myself.' He laughed in sudden lightness of spirit. 'Why not?'

'You'll be needing company some time. Why not now? Come home with me and I'll cook you up something. You look as though you need it.'

'All right,' replied Ywain, somewhat lost in the girl's presence of mind and unashamed good nature. 'I've got my bike. How do I get there?'

'We'll go together. It's amazing. The Virgin Mary has wrought many miracles.'

'You mean, others besides moving statues?'

'Oh, there are things much harder to move than statues. That was only a tiny miracle for the Blessed Virgin. I knew it was a sign for me. And so it is.'

She crossed herself and gave silent thanks to the image. Then they went over to the bicycle.

'Where do we go?'

'Ah, we could walk it, but it's a little far for me in my high heels. I hitched a ride here to Ballinspittle. Let's walk a little till the road gets smoother and then we can ride double. I'll spell you for a bit and you can have a rest.'

This is what they did, except that Ywain would not let her 'spell' him, but instead insisted on doing all the pedalling.

There was quite a lot of it.

They took a road in the direction of Clonakilty, sometimes brushing the purple heather that bled from the hills. As is the case with many Irish villages the one they entered consisted of a tiny main street flanked by painted rough-cast houses. Two small shops and the standing gables of two ruined cottages at the nearer end completed the picture. Next to the second of these stood another abandoned house, also well on its way to extinction. She led him around and behind this one. The back door she opened by prising open a reluctant window and reaching for a key lying on a bench or shelf beneath.

The furnishings were starkly simple: an old peat stove, a bench with a tub and a single tap. A wooden ladder loosely nailed to the floor gave access to a makeshift loft. Apart from a decrepit green sofa, there was practically nothing else in the place. He sat down while Ilona brought his bike around and propped it against the outside wall.

'Everyone's honest here,' she said, 'but it's best not to leave temptation in their way.'

Ywain now had an idea that this was not perhaps the best place he could have chosen to come to, but it was too late for second thoughts. The girl threw open a cupboard and brought out some scraps of vegetables and the jagged end of a flat loaf.

'I know what we need,' she said, 'a little beef for the stew. Ywain, you wouldn't happen to have a pound or two we could use to buy a little bit of beef with, have you?'

Ywain gave her one of the two five pound notes remaining in his wallet, glad that he had no more visible. The rest of his money was in his belt. Nevertheless, he watched it disappear into her hand with a sinking feeling in his heart.

'Oh, that's lovely. Don't worry – you look worried. Are you a worrier?

– I'll make it up to you. I know that these days a fiver is not so easily come by or thrown away. I'll not be long. Best keep inside. Some of my neighbours are not very understanding, but I'm a daughter of the Church just as much as those venomous old bitches are.'

Ilona left, taking a plastic bag with her. Ywain wondered whether he ought to leave too, but on second thoughts he might as well get at least one meal out to credit against the loss of his cash.

After about fifteen minutes Ilona came back. She took out some meat, a loaf, several slightly fresher carrots, a single very large potato and half a dozen little pats of butter wrapped in grease-proof paper such as appear in some restaurants. Presently the aromatic temptation of a stew cooking seized irresistibly on his hunger. He suddenly realized that he had not eaten a proper meal for several days, and his appetite was unleashed.

Ilona turned round to watch him now and again as she worked. She smiled happily.

'I see you're hungry too.'

'My God, I didn't know.'

'That's how it seizes you if you've been off proper food for a while. You didn't know you were hungry, did you?'

'No, I didn't. How did you know?'

'Because I'm hungry too. I know the signs without feeling hungry myself. That's all we hungry people can do. Not eating lessens the desire to eat. Were you ever this hungry in Canada?'

'No, never.'

'I'd like to visit that place, but there's no hope. I'd never get the money together in my whole life. You must be rich.'

He laughed aloud, gladly, knowing that his hunger was about to be satisfied.

'No, I'm poor too. I only had a part-time job before I left. I got a bit of money unexpectedly, but I'd already paid the air fare.'

'Holy Virgin! What a rich country that must be if you're one of the poor ones, now.'

Soon the fragrant steaming mess was on the table in front of him. Ilona put the pot on a flat stone that wobbled, pouring out the contents with the aid of a spoon on to two enamelled plates much chipped. Each of them ate, hardly pausing to talk or even look, heedless of how hot the food was. Finishing it didn't take long. He didn't know what to do with the whole loaf, so she tore a piece off for him, another for herself. The pat of butter made it heavenly.

'We ought to keep the rest for this evening,' she said, 'but we've still got some bread and there's tea in the house.'

Between them they finished the whole loaf and wished for more.

Ilona rinsed the plates clean and scrubbed out the pot using a pinch or two of earth from the yard. Then she put the plates away in the cupboard and hung the pot up.

'Time to rest,' she said. 'The loo is outside.'

When he came back in, Ilona had gone up into the loft. She called to him, 'Come on up. Bring your roll because I'm a little short on pillows.'

He got it and climbed up. There was one mattress, not over-clean. On it lay Ilona who had the only pillow and a single large pallet stuffed with straw which she used as a quilt over her.

Ywain looked for another bed.

'This is it, the only one,' giggled Ilona. 'Take off your clothes. You won't need pyjamas. It's plenty warm under here. Hurry up. All right, I'm not looking. She laughed a little, not unkindly, and turned her face away.

Ywain undressed and got in at the farthest edge. She took his hand and pulled him over.

'I hope you didn't bring one of those awful things. I'm a good Catholic.'

She crouched like an animal to heap the cover on Ywain. He saw her naked breasts, not over-large and not small, but petite and perfectly firm with erect nipples over large areolas. As he hesitated, she grasped his hand and moved it to her bosom. 'This is the one you touched. Touch it again, touch it again, please!'

His heart was beating fit to burst, paralyzing him. She held his hand to her breast. Nervousness suppressed desire in him.

'Be yourself and rest, Ywain. I said I'd make it up to you, but you're as taut as a trap spring. How does this feel?'

She covered him with her naked body and moved over him gently. Then with the most sensuous caress she drew her hand languishingly around his scrotum which almost disappeared as the phallus stiffened into soft bone. She withdrew her hand up the shaft to the head, where she manipulated the pit of the heart. As she did, he felt his life spring through the lovely piercer in a wave of ecstatic pain from beneath his belly.

Ywain had ejaculated.

'Oh, most Holy Mother! You're a virgin I do believe.'

Never had Ywain felt so inadequate or miserable. A wave of blackness akin to that which had swept into hospital overcame him and he disgraced himself again: he wept.

She disposed of the mess in her hand and wiped him fairly clean with some straw.

She lay beside him propped on one elbow and stroked his hair. He resisted at first, but soon she had turned him round and caressed him again with her whole body, kissing his face gently. He felt that she was both cool and warm simultaneously, a paradox of synthesis he could feel but not understand. Her fingers were alive on his back and shoulders and neck.

When he awoke, it was twilight and she had gone. He realized that he did not know whether she really lived here or if she was coming back. He threw on his clothes and went out to the loo. The bike which she had so carefully propped against the wall was gone.

There was utter silence. There was not the cry of a single human voice to be heard, the crunch of stones underfoot the creak of a door or a busy motor, even in the far distance, not even the slightest sough of wind.

A sullen hybrid of mist and drizzle enshrouded the village.

There were no lights.

It was possible that she had gone to get something, perhaps for supper. After considering this thought for a while, he was prompted to look in his wallet.

The other £5 note was gone.

Fortunately she had not thought of examining his belt.

As the dusk and drizzle conspired to rob the western world of light, Ywain sat on a chair and waited. As the hours lengthened, he occasionally dropped off for brief periods, but he was unwilling to commit himself to unwatched sleep. He was waiting for the faintest hue of dawn. When that came, he disposed his equipment for carrying as well as he could and left the village the same way as the two had entered it on the previous day. In the back of his mind was Ilona's face, thoughtful and sympathetic. He did not feel that he was her victim.

Chapter 8

IT IS VERY EASY TO HITCH IN IRELAND. Nearly everyone does it at one time or another – children surprisingly young, pairs of young women hiking about in smart jeans and absurdly incongruous high-heels, even couples in advanced middle age getting a holiday on the cheap. Having lost his bike, Ywain looked at his map and plumped for Dingle for no particular reason except that it was on the coast and the name rang quaintly without suggesting (as did Ballinspittle) the plucking of a chicken.

He got himself to Dingle in three hitches with ease, considering his baggage, more easily than he could have done by bicycle, and much more enjoyably, considering that it rained most of the way. He kept a hopeless eye out for his bike, which Ilona had almost certainly turned into money by now. The lurching lorry which stopped for him was driven erratically by a kindly but uncommunicative old farmer. He was next given a lift by two very young newly-married American school teachers in a rented Fiesta which struggled along in convulsive jerks accompanied by the sound of shredding steel as they struggled with the unfamiliar manual transmission, making frequent stops to consult a completely inadequate road map supplied by the government tourist bureau. They had picked him up in order to get an authentic Irishman into conversation and were visibly disappointed to find that he was only a Canadian, a kind of insignificant lesser American. For the last stage two middle-aged ladies had picked him up and driven him in practically utter silence to Dingle. With hardly an acknowledgement of his thanks they left him as if they had just made an inconvenient though charitable delivery.

His youthful hostel acquaintances had told him that once a machine came into their hands it could be made unrecognizable in less than an hour. Like the demon in the bottle, it fetched less with every subsequent transaction.

He did not expect or desire to encounter Ilona. That young lady, he had to admit, was even more of an adept than Merrick in the trade of surviving on nothing. If she had any self-esteem she would do rather well. Had she? He tried to reconcile her devotion at the Grotto of the Blessed Virgin and her tenderness towards him with her treacherous behaviour, but could arrive at no solution of the paradox.

With each ride he was a comet temporarily captured by other people who had their own definite plans, while arriving at no clearer definition of his own. And with each new perturbation of his orbit he seemed to be cast a little nearer to some lurking planetary giant and destruction.

A grim gale from the north west tore into Dingle. He was surprised to find everything open on Sunday in staunchly Catholic Ireland, and annoyed to see that the rock fraternity had taken over the place. Anything was better than that, so he decided to hitch north on the morrow.

Again, it was easy to hitch on Bank Holiday Monday. Drivers accepted that thumbers had their rights. In this way he managed to get to the south bank of the Shannon where he again passed the point of being famished. He had enough money, but most of it consisted of travellers' cheques which could not be cashed out of banking hours except at the ruinous rates inflicted on the unwary traveller by the numerous so-called exchange bureaux found in many shops doing a very good thing out of Ireland's restricted banking hours.

He pitched a miserable tent for the night, intending to hitch the following day with a driver taking the ferry.

Getting across the Shannon proved unexpectedly difficult. Motorists out of Listowel making for Tarbet were less inclined to pick up hitch-hikers because they had to pay £5.50 for the ferry; passengers therefore were looked upon as an expense as well as a liability. Nonetheless, he managed to get as far as Limerick from where he could strike out for the coast again. But Limerick turned out to be a mistake. In Cork he had been impressed by the relative absence of street children, called tinkers. In Limerick there were hosts of them, not only the usual pre-teen girls and boys, but very young women carrying babies. Limerick was slicker, more empty than Cork, the size of Cork without the charm. It trespassed against his desire to travel in order to find more significance in life than the empty words of a university Vice-Chancellor. In Limerick he encountered depression again, so much so that it was only with an effort that he could think to leave. When he did, he made directly for the coast. Again three motorists in succession took him first to Ennis and then to the cliffs of Moher. The last one, a bulky Irishman, gave him a lift because he wanted the stranger to see the famous bluffs, but Ywain's confidence in his ability to control the events of his life had been shattered again, temporarily, in Limerick. He could respond to his host's terse questions about his background and his motives in coming to Ireland only with insincere smiles, acquiescence, artificial good nature and fake curiosity. He knew as he made each conversational remark or gave each fatuous smile that he was being silly and bogus, but he could not do anything to prevent his automatic persona from taking him over. As a result the Irishman was glad to set him down at the car park near the cliffs. He drove off without making much attempt to conceal his poor opinion of his passenger.

Ywain pulled his hood over his head, for it was still raining lightly, although out at sea the interplay of light and cloud gave promise of patches of sunshine.

He followed the crowd aimlessly, up the path to the O'Brien Tower, pausing to view the rain-beaten waves rolling in ceaselessly to explode on the bases of the cliffs to the south. A barrier of slaty slippery stone in slices piled three feet high discouraged weaker spirits from approaching the very edge. An unwary watcher would have no chance to reflect on his fate. A furious south-easterly in vicious gusts blew those going up the path along to the tower and those coming down back, so much so that one had to turn one's back to the gale in order to breathe.

He could almost touch the unformed veils of cloud chasing overhead. But the real storm was the hopelessness and blackness assailing his own soul. He knew that he was useless. He hadn't the nerve.

There were quite a few lined up, waiting their turn to use the panoramic binoculars at the top of the tower. As he loitered up, not really interested enough to join the queue, he noticed that the man in possession of the glass had ceased to scan the cliffs or seas. He was trying to depress the binoculars to their limit in order to focus on some object much closer.

Indecisive in the constant crises of his life, Ywain became aware, secondhand, as it were, that the watcher had evidently found what he wanted and fixed his observation on that point. In the same moment he knew that the object now in focus was himself.

There was no mistaking the man who now left the instrument and began to push his way through the crowd on the stairs. He had first seen him in a theatre in Toronto.

Chapter 9

SIOBHAN WAS LUCKY IN HER PARENTS. They were solid citizens who had worked hard to achieve their lot. Her father taught geography and mathematics at the local high school. He also gave photography classes in his spare time and did a little commercial work, chiefly in bringing out travel brochures for the local area, on which he was an expert, particularly in its geology and plant biology. The house into which he had put all his small capital and, for a time, all his effort outside of his job, had room for seven B&B guests, and he worked at this aspect of his useful life, as he worked at all the other aspects, to achieve the highest possible standard. It was conceivably the friendliest, cleanest and nicest B&B in the West. The enormous garden that took up three sides of the half acre property was a neighbour's wonder. Over the years he had removed tons of the unforgiving stony slope into which the house was built, had chipped out barrel- and tun-sized craters which he had then lined and filled with peat moss and top soil to grow a variety of small trees and bushes that included climbing roses, several cabbage trees and the great flax bushes native to New Zealand, together with a mixed hedge of holly, may and ninebark, the latter another introduced species, and flourishing rhododendrons. Apart from the hedge, he had not got round to finishing the front, which consisted of a little gravel raked to even out the worst troughs and holes in the rough stone. This provided parking for guests' cars. On the sheltered side he tried to cultivate some of the wild flowers from the Burren. In this, however, he had only very limited success. He probably knew more about the Burren than anyone else and never tired of exploring it.

His wife, Erin, had been born and brought up in Winnipeg, but had gone through university in Dublin where she had met her husband. He was a student existing upon scholarships and very little else. They had fallen in love.

When Siobhan was twelve they had been married for thirteen years.

She was their only child. Oddly, although she had her parents' undivided love and was used to playing up to and being petted by the numerous guests, she was not really spoiled in any important way, partly, perhaps, because her mother sometimes took in other children of working or absent mothers during the day and practised no favouritism. Yet as she passed the first birthday of her adolescence when the latest age of childhood blends into the greeny teens, she became aware that she was really not much like other girls of her own age who were at that magic age when sex and chocolate were equally alluring. As an infant she had always been possessed by powerful verisimilar fantasies. As she grew older her dreams occasionally turned into visions.

Although her visions were rare yet they had come upon her in her earliest memories, intermingled at first with the dreams and fantasies of paradisal infancy. If she were to consider, the first definite time when another reality came at her out of the blue in the midst of other occupation, when she saw something and *heard* something totally different from what she was doing or thinking about, something totally different from this world, well, it happened when she was walking down the steeply sloping path of packed stone that led to the road, hand on the latch of the gate, she began to open it – a sudden gust of wind and the clapping of huge white pinions, they must have been all of two metres high – and she saw an angel. Yes, an angel. There was no doubt about it, none. She couldn't remember whether or not she'd heard about angels, or perhaps learned about them at school, but what did that matter? She'd seen one. She could quite understand even at the age of eight that if she were to try to describe this vision to anyone else, the important thing to the audience, whether her father, her mother or a friend would be the question of whether she'd had the image of an angel in her head before she 'saw' one. She couldn't even be certain if he'd looked at her or not. He turned his head towards her; she remembered his profile with its straight strong lips, devoid of hair. He was on her left.

Later in the summer, on a transparent evening following one of those clear days on the west coast of Ireland that leaves a ghost of itself in the sky, a deep dark mystic blue like a Mediterranean dream, she had got up in the dark of the morning to gaze out over the sea. As she looked up she became aware of a barely discernible black patch against the blue. It was roughly square and losing height as it moved slowly across the sky, perhaps heading for the sea. It wavered once or twice as though it was thin like a sheet, but its motion was steady. When it was a good deal lower – the size was impossible to guess – some fragments or figures descended from the leading edge. At this point she could see it had depth, appeared in fact to be a cube with sharp edges, but did not behave quite like a solid since it wavered once in a while like fabric in a gentle breeze. She thought it might have been sent to rescue some people floating helpless on the sea. It would not have been much more than a mile offshore, but she could see nothing further.

She kept both these appearances to herself, but there was one strange sight she did tell her father about. Getting out of bed in the small hours of a scented summer's night, she saw a tall woman in a white dress cross the front yard and disappear into the thick foliage enclosing an empty house on the other side of the road. Her father got up to find her on the front steps. He had no idea of how she had got the double-locked front door open, but put the whole thing down to sleepwalking and dreaming, and didn't think much more about it. However, the following day, being curious, she cautiously went down the neglected driveway of the ruined house and was surprised to find it in better order than she remembered. Not only that, but someone was living there. The front door opened and there she stood, a woman not very different from her own mother, who told her to come and play as often as she liked.

Again, on an impulse she could not explain even to herself, she made no mention of the woman or her invitation, to her parents, or anyone else, but went there quite often. The name of her new friend was Nera. As the two grew fonder of each other, Nera began to teach Siobhan all kinds of things that no one else knew.

Neither her parents nor anyone else knew about this secret part of Siobhan's life.

After Nera came there were no more visions or visionary dreams for some years.

She was always a capable and self-assured young lady entirely unaffected by the rare visions which blurred the limitations of the empirical world, but perhaps because of them she was unusually self-possessed and private, at least to the point where her mother was concerned for her, for she became so much older than her years, from the first more an adult than a child. She did not willingly enter into the spirit of her contemporaries or their amusements, although she had her own special friends.

Apart from those, the girls at school left her alone because she was 'different'; they did not know what to make of her. She seemed larger of life than they, yet the presence she cast could not be put down to anything specific in her outward demeanour. The boys stood in awe of her. They did not know what to make of her. They regarded her as untouchable. Yet she had many friends outside of school who were anxious to do anything they could for her.

In everything she was the well brought-up Irish girl. Her teachers called her 'the little lady'. On the whole, she was neither very good nor very bad at her studies. She did very well indeed in English, Irish and art; she was fascinated by history, which she thought the greatest game in the world, but did not do well in it because (her history teacher thought) she arrived at strange relationships of facts and did not present coherent developments or logically-derived conclusions (meaning that her teacher did not understand what she was getting at). She did poorly at mathematics and all branches of science (but had a good grasp of shapes and measurements), had no interest in P.E. or sports, and not much more in the domestic arts of home economics in spite of her wide practical experience in helping her mother run the B&B. Religion was mediocre; geography was average.

She had several hobbies apart from walking and cycling. She collected books and would visit all the bookshops in any town she visited. She had an eye for the unusual. She read Yeats and Muir, though with love rather than with critical understanding, but kept this treasure from her friends. She had taken over part of her father's rock garden. He had helped her to sink the holes to put in two hollies, male and female, which she was trying to prune back into trees.

What else? She had always spent a good deal of her spare time alone, often going on long walks or cycling along the rocky shore or exploring the Burren. On many a rapturous morning she would wheel along the hill face road in the direction of the Burren to try a new angle of approach, or find a fresh turlough or another way of coming on to the dolmen. Her father had a good pupil.

Like most Irish youngsters she was confirmed in her fourteenth year, but took no more than the average interest in the church expected of her. She was much more taken by the figures of the Virgin Mary in their thousands found outside of the church and enjoyed sketching them.

At seventeen she was an intelligent young lady bound for university. She was petite, having the pale skin, luxuriant black hair (which she kept long) and grey-blue eyes of her Irish ancestry. At home she was sometimes mistaken for the lady of the house by arriving guests, except that her brow was unmarked by any line, and her whole face was almost flawless alabaster, a disconcerting combination of the unformed and the ideal. She had the high forehead and habitually noble and humane expression that one sees in late mediæval sculpture, nearest, perhaps, to the lovely Uta in Naumburg Cathedral, a vision of embryonic wisdom.

She was now nearly eighteen.

On this lovely morning she was sketching a shrine. While working on the supplicant, Bernadette, she was impelled to turn the face away from the Blessed Virgin and towards herself, the artist. As she drew automatically she noted all the details in colour. The young woman had long auburn tresses surmounted by a braided plait binding her head in a circlet at the hairline. She wore a simple dress or robe, beautiful but unadorned. Her shoulders were covered. She had pale blue eyes – grey, Siobhan might have called them. The expression was gentle – what else? – but behind the slight smile lay hard determination mingled with the love. She knew she ought to recognize his face. She resembled, but was not, Nena.

When she got back home she found the house packed with its maximum of seven guests, all of whom wanted the evening meal, high tea. Although silent on matters that were important to her, Siobhan could be a great chatterer, and it was this quality that helped endear her to the guests and smooth over things for her mother. Later on in the afternoon she helped her mother and was kept so busy that she thought no more of her sketch until late at night. While clearing away the dishes at about eight, she felt an irresistible impulse to go outside. On the porch she turned her gaze towards the northering coast, towards the Burren, hidden beyond bays and hills, quite out of sight from the Ward property, yet *she* saw it in vivid detail in a clear perspective that no earthly instrument could have yielded. She was looking at a spot near the cromlech not far from where she had been sketching that morning. It occurred to her that she had missed out on something there. She would go in the first light of morning. The scene vanished like a map rolled up and she went back into the kitchen.

When she had finished cleaning up, she prepared some bread, two hard-boiled eggs, wrapped some salt in a twist of grease-proof paper and filled a plastic bottle with water drawn through a carbon filter to which she added some sugar and the juice of a lime.

Chapter 10

THE BURREN is one of the most remarkable karst landscapes in Europe. It lies between Galway Bay on the north, the Atlantic coast on the west and a line drawn roughly through Doolin, Kilfenora, Gort and Kinvarra. Neither the great extent of the Burren nor its nature can be recognized by the casual driver or wayfarer because it changes its character according to the ground one views it from. For the traveller taking the coast road from Doolin to Ballyvaghan, the Burren emerges, at first gently, as a mass of terrace, the lower steps partly sheathed in green but with layers of grey stone showing through clearly enough. Further along the road the slaty brow of the summit dominates, oddly crossed by unbroken strung-out walls of raw stone dividing the greyness into long segments. An observer on the road below would swear that not even the bramble could take hold here for, from his viewpoint, the Burren can appear as barren as Mercury. But climb up from the ravine traced by the road running inland from Ballyvaghan: from above one sees the turloughs, or hollows in which a rich deposit of soil, sparse remnant of the forest that flourished here before the mediæval farmer cleared the trees, has allowed grasses and wild flowers to flourish in unexpected pockets that may become miniature lakes, appearing and later disappearing in their season. Indeed, under the ledges of the shelving rocks are thickets, even miniature forests, of stunted hawthorn, blackthorn and hazel. And except for those stretches of almost rectangular pavements, the clints and the grykes, there are tufts of small delicately-scented flowers in every crevice. The west coast of Ireland has a fairly high rainfall and there are often skyscapes of dark threatening clouds in a constantly transforming welkin; yet even under the blackest louring the Burren seems to exist in a light of its own, perhaps the effect of the frothing whiteness of the shattered waves a mile or so away, or possibly some peculiarity in the albedo of the place, or perhaps a spell quite as magical as the sight of three white horses far-off in the mist beyond silver rivers in a softly-dropping twilight under the mountains.

The Burren is within sight of the Cliffs of Moher, but Ywain had no time to note this or any other feature of the landscape as he tore himself away, jostled along the waiting line and hurried back to the car park. There he grabbed a bicycle left unchained by its unwary owner. At that moment he had no idea of what the time was, what day it was or even what the name of the place was. He had no idea of the landscape except in the vague foreshortened panic of the badly frightened man busy cycling for his life. The stalled lines of cars blurred as he passed them and flung out along the marvellous coastal road in the direction of Lisdoonvarna. He had no time to ascertain where he was going. He was praying that now the rain was clearing and the light sky promised fair weather, all the holiday traffic in the world would flock to this thin road snaking along he coast, walled in on the sea side by jagged rock teeth that appeared to stand by mere affinity for one another and the unyielding hills on the land side. On this merciless highway only one thing could save him: hordes of impatient cars. It must have been less than half-an-hour since he had taken his first long look at the Cliffs of Moher, clambering over the slate wall in defiance of the posted warning, thrilling slightly at the immensity of wash recoiling from the dark land. Before he had gone up towards the tower he had noticed a blood-red Rolls-Royce gliding in. The driver had parked without so much as a glance around him. Ywain had not bothered to see who the passenger was.

Yet now on a fifteen-speed derailleur at least he had a chance. It was a pity that he did not keep his wits about him or he might have seen the second Rolls-Royce which swerved slightly to avoid him as he shot out of the entrance.

In a few minutes he was on a down slope crossing a bridge at a respectable pace, glancing back at the road behind him. He knew the pursuit would not be more than a mile away, but, as cars slipped past him, he almost began to think he had escaped unnoticed and was beginning to ease back on his long pumping when he glimpsed in the flash of a curve behind the unmistakeable outline of a black Rolls-Royce tailgating the car in front. He laid into his stroke and sped, looking all the while for a way of escape. Traffic was fairly thick, as thick as it ever gets on the Lisdoonvarna road, but few cars can stand in the way of a well-driven Rolls-Royce whose horses have been given their head. He would lose this game in short order.

Cut and dash as he might where cars slowed down briefly at cracks or runnels in the road or hesitated at the sharper curves, he could not, in the long run, keep up with any of them. He would tire; they would not.

Desperation made him note every gate or track entrance running down on his left, but there were none of the latter and a paddock or yard was a trap. The road went on forever uninterrupted. He could see the nearer of the two Rolls-Royces not more than four or five cars back. He knew that the first would overtake and block him while the second would come in behind and scoop him.

And that was what happened. He saw it was all over when the black car swept by. Knowing that they would try to run him off the road, he abruptly swerved over to the right hand side of the road. He could see the approaching driver blanch, heard the sharp squeal of brakes call out a chorus of other panic stops behind it. Edging in to put the oncoming cars between himself and his enemies, he braked. The black car also slowed, but Ywain's manoeuvre succeeded as the red Rolls, having no room in the centre, slipped past the cyclist stalled on the opposite side of the road behind a string of cursing drivers getting underway again.

After regaining his breath, he slowly began crawling towards the curve in the same direction. He knew his time was short. No explanation or profession of ignorance would save him. They were ruthless and probably wanted his blood.

The narrow road – hardly more than an asphalted track – debouching on to the main road from below came as a benediction. Braking and wheeling, he darted down it, rushing towards the sea, curving and cornering, for it was by no means straight, with here and there the swift vision of a gate or barn or blind yard. Suddenly panicking, he rushed into one of these and rushed out suppressing an instinct to pick up the bike and hide in the fields or the thin brush. They would surely know where to look for him then.

At this point he could not see far up the track, but he knew that one of the Rolls-Royces would have turned around, come back and would be about to crawl down the tiny road.

He flung himself again on the machine and tore recklessly down. Reaching the bottom, he turned right, uphill along the coast, shifted gears and trod furiously. There were houses and a pub here. A car parked right at the intersection of the track with the lower road would hold them up while they manhandled it out of the way.

They must have stopped, for there was no sign of them as he pedalled on, straining into the slope. After an age of sweat and pulsing calves he passed a pale cream and blue church. Just beyond was an intersection where the right hand way took him back up to the main road into the path of his pursuers. Directly facing him were some trees overhanging a wall. A large tower or fortified house, partly in ruins, rose above it.

Taking no heed, he turned left and sped downhill again as the road curved and angled towards the sea. As soon as he saw a gap in the stone wall skirting the sea side of the road, he rushed through it with the wheels flexing under the terrible shocks if the rocky terrain. Even panic could not prevent him from pausing in a moment's wonder. The day was changing. The sun, now low in the west, threw its beams through the towering cloud temples of the sky and the drifting veils of vapour thrown high into the air by the huge Atlantic rollers dashing against the tall crags of the coast in a dark bronze age gold. Dismounting, he gripped the bike and carried it towards the sea roaring in to collide against the great fissured rocks. He was exposed. If they saw him now he had no chance. There was, however, a place to hide which might not occur to them. He made his way over towards the enormous fountains of spray and foam. Picking the highest perch at hand, he raised the bicycle above his head and hurled it with all his strength into the devastating surge. Then wet, soaked by the salt spray, he clambered down a few feet to find a precarious hold on the ruined ledges of the rock. Strangely the gold and steel sun glinted as it went down into the western ocean attended by brilliant vapours heavenly-hued in a heroic sky of battling clouds. He was invisible from the road. Anyone, even someone looking very carefully at the line of precipitous rocks lit by the fountaining white water, would be hard put to it to guess that even a frightened water rat might be able to hide there.

Clambering back up for a look was difficult and dangerous for a single mistake would hurl him on to the rocks below to be dashed by the gigantic Atlantic waves. Worse, if he were glimpsed, he would have no chance of escaping torture and death. Therefore he hung on shivering as much with cold as with the reaction of cold fright. When it was absolutely dark he would move cautiously, taking care to flatten his profile against the western skyline.

He imagined them arriving at the junction. One car would trace the Lisdoonvarna road and the other the lower coast road back to the village. Unless they were anxious to contemplate the last moments of sunset, he thought, they would not bother to look where there seemed to be no cover whatever.

He was right. They didn't.

Chapter 11

COLD, WET, BREATHLESS: he realized that he was shivering violently as the agony of his long wait forced itself upon his consciousness. Why had he such dread of the men who apparently had Victor in their grip, those who were now, his instinct assured him, determined to capture and take his life? It was a most immediate and touching fear that possessed him, knowing that some people with power wanted very badly to kill him, but a greater fear even than that one rose up behind it: what was the unknown that he was up against? What was the scheme of events in which he was now entangled? His complete ignorance oppressed him even more than the fear of death. And the proximity of death is imminent to one clinging to several rather precarious holds fifty feet above a destructive sea whose every roller punches the solid rock of the ancient land in the belly with the force of an earthquake.

After a spell he moved to a more comfortable position as quickly as he could and keeping low.

He was still terribly cold.

He knew they would watch both roads, but thought he might climb up over the hills to some building sites over the brow, and make his way in the fields and bush to the area he had glimpsed during the afternoon, where green was interspersed with large patches of grey rock. If he could reach the high ground he might at least find a perch from which he could see danger coming. But this might mean that he would have to retrace his steps to the village, and he was sure he would never get past the junction.

In the end, the only plan seemed to be to work along the rocky margin between the sea and the narrow road running along the shoreline. There ought to be some vegetation, odd thickets at least, to provide some cover.

When dark came he struggled up and moved away from his hostile hiding place. The chill wind cut him.

Early the next morning, having seen that the steep hillsides made it impossible for him to move to higher ground, walking between the road and the sea, he was doing pretty well, resting now and then when the ever more frequent clumps of bush and briar gave seclusion. Seeing a miniature stone building like a small chapel on the other side of the road, he could not resist crossing over and entering it.

Inside it was so dark that he could see nothing for a minute or two. But he could hear the trickle of water, and found that he could slake his thirst at a spring-fed drinking well. The traveller was provided with a bronze cup on a chain, the gift of a long-dead king, perhaps. As he paused and drank, an ancient blessing, weak but still protective of travellers, covered him. He could feel it. Perhaps the goddess Brigit still watched over wayfarers. Cold as he was, he felt more tranquility than discomfort.

And well it was that he paused: from back in the deep shade he saw the red Rolls-Royce with driver and three passengers scanning both sides of the road. He froze back into the darkest corner adjacent to the entrance, sweating cold. He heard the car door open and realized that no prayer could save him now. He flattened himself along the wall in the darkness cast by the shadow of the open door. There was the tread of feet on loose stones. The intruder, who had no feeling for the place, gave a cursory glance at the well, completely failed to see Ywain drawn up flat against the wall, and went off, evidently to look elsewhere, for it was a little while before he heard the door of the Rolls-Royce clunk softly. The man, whose eyes were probably a little tired by this time, was evidently unaware that the bright sunlight outside had blinded him to the shadow within. Ywain moved quietly and glanced obliquely up and down the road. After a while, he edged out. They were gone. He now had to think of being ambushed.

With great care he took cover and scanned the road in both directions. Then he crossed to the shore side and moved like a one-man commando unit, in rapid dashes with frequent pauses in cover.

When fear was momentarily absent hunger took its place.

He realized that he was not going to get far on his own, and decided to do what he had done before, namely, hitch. But not in a car, for then he could be seen. He would be better off in a van or a lorry where he would be high up, in a position to spot his enemies before they saw him. Unfortunately this was a scenic road; most of the vehicles were cars or RVs carrying holiday makers. He was too exposed on the open road, even among the vacationers, but he had no choice.

It took him until early afternoon to get to Ballyvaghan. There he went into a pub where he got stout, soup and bread, heaps of bread, followed by a large plate of fish-and-chips. It was heaven, but fear made him eat too fast and hunger made him gobble, and the drinkers made it clear that they were too polite to stare at him. As he went out, his eyes searching for pursuers, he had no idea where to go. While he was gazing at the multiplicity of names on a signpost, a man spoke to him.

'Need any help?'

The speaker was a young man of about thirty with a short slight figure. Ywain looked at him dumbly and nodded. He did not know what to say, could hardly trust himself to say anything.

'Are you going to Corofin – or Kilfenora? Ywain asked his benefactor, stumbling, glancing at the signpost.

The man smiled. 'You don't seem too sure of where you want to go. Both of them – or anywhere else within a reasonable distance. Got any gear?'

'No, I lost it.'

'Right then.'

He crossed the road and led the way to a small commercial van parked at the kerbside.

'I'm Brian. What's your name?'

Ywain told him.

'Ywain?' replied the other, surprised. 'That's an old name, sure. Is it in your family or did your mother and father pick it because they fancied it?'

'I'm not sure. I think my father's family is old and that's where the name comes from.'

The battered and underpowered van hadn't too many more miles to go. The doors didn't fit properly, the passenger's side window was jammed open and the upholstery had worn through. Bare metal was visible. The engine clattered like a threshing-machine as it choked and roared to drag off its burden.

The straight roads and clear directional signs of North America are a poor preparation for driving in Ireland whose roads often follow the mysterious ways and contours of the old tracks trodden out centuries before. Even the signs themselves were confusing. Brian knew where he was going, though. He never had to pause and read the road signs. For the first time in forty-eight hours Ywain began to relax. Now and then Brian said something to him, but his voice came to Ywain as if delayed by long distance. He was overcome with fatigue and the heady stout and began to drift off.

'Ah, you're weary. Get in the back and lie down,' said Brian.

The next thing he was aware of was a lurching. There were voices, a sudden jolt and a metallic thud as the van lurched again, and Brian's voice, raised. Then came confused sounds of voices and scuffling, then a yell and a sudden screaming of tyres and a rushing of wheels as a faintly audible engine of enormous power accelerated.

Ywain got out carefully, climbing out over the front seat. The van leaned over to the right so much that he could hardly open the door enough to get out.

When Brian saw him, he motioned him back. 'The bastards,' he said.

He had been changing a tyre and they had wanted to look inside. He had told them to go to hell. They had pushed the van off the jack before leaving.

'If I hadn't had this tyre-iron in my hand they'd have killed me. Ah well, someone will be along soon enough. We know each other around here. You're in trouble, lad. Why are they after you?'

'I don't know. I wish I did.'

'O.K. The best thing I can do for you is to tell you the best way out of here, if it is a way for you. They're watching for you. Fucking English! They really put my back up! And I'll swear those boyos are a real nasty bunch. Whatever you do, stay as far away from them as you can. If they're not a bad lot then my name's not Brian. If we meet again you can tell me all about it, but for now you'd best get out of sight as quick as lightning. They haven't gone away – don't think it for a moment – wanted to look inside – but I told them to go to hell. Who do they think they are? Come to that, who do you think they are? No idea? Holy Virgin, I hope you get no closer to them to find out. Up the ravine wall here, then, and move among the tree cover *quietly* farther up. Get yourself a pozzy where you can keep a good lookout, and hide until nightfall. After that, I hope your guardian angel takes charge. All the best, Ywain.'

'I don't know how to thank you.'

'Never mind that now. Be off. God send you good friends.'

They shook hands.

He was getting leaner and more agile now. The puppy fat and wanton lassitude induced by years in sedentary schools were dropping away. He pulled himself up. After about fifty feet he found himself on a broad shelf of curiously formed limestone sparsely covered with thorns and grasses. After walking some distance he found himself level again with a curved stretch of the road. There was no sign of any car. He struck away up, clambering over the merging shelves until he reached the next miniature cliff with a miniature forest of miniature trees at its base. Here he hid among the dwarf hazels and hawthorns awaiting the dark, but he did not neglect to look about him. They must know he was here, somewhere. There was nothing in sight and he did not think that anyone could possibly see him.

When he woke up, the sun of a new day was already tinting the sky. Now rested, he ran in and out of the trees, following the contour, ascending around the edge of the next rise. When he reached the top, as he thought, it was bare. He was completely exposed. He despaired for a moment, but ran up over a fold to find a crude ruin of a few huge stones heaped to form a shelter near the remains of a wall. Too obvious. The wind caught at his hair. Anything was better than standing out under a morning sun. The most casual passer-by could not fail to notice him. He pushed through a breach in the wall and hunkered down. His heart raced and there was a rushing in his ears. He was beginning to realize how hopeless his position was, for apart from this fingernail-sized wall, there wasn't so much as a leaf or tiny flower to offer concealment, only some defensive baulks of lichen manned by grubs.

Fear did not completely obliterate awareness: again the light was thrown up over the rocky terraces as though this landscape had a foot in another world.

Here he hadn't a chance.

He sat wearily with his face in his hands and remained where he was, motionless, for minutes on end.

He was roused by a voice speaking to him, the voice of a woman as clear and lovely as the speech of a mountain stream in the chill morning.

'What kind of trouble are you in?'

Chapter 12

IN A FLASH HE WAS ON HIS FEET. He looked around carefully. There was no one. He clambered back over the partial breach in the wall and went around. Again, no one.

'Well, what's the matter with you? You're filthy, wet and shivering a little. Can't you speak?'

Again he scanned the ground on all sides. There was no possible place to hide except the cromlech. It was as empty as the shivering wind, and in any case, the voice was much closer at hand.

'Never mind, I'll help you. We'll take a short rest and then we'll go on. Don't worry. I know this place. I know its ways.'

He was speechless and paralyzed. He could not come at the source of the voice.

'You'd better come over here. Anyone for miles around can see you out in the open like that. That old pile of rock is the first place anyone would look in.'

He went towards the stones.

'Not there! *This* way.'

He went in the direction from which the voice seemed to come, finding himself at the wall again. As he gazed back over the ground he had covered, an arm and then a head appeared over the lip of a hollow that was completely invisible from the sloping ground running up to the dilapidated wall unless one were within a yard of it. He slipped over to it and almost tumbled headlong down into the rocky depression whose floor was miniature garden. Under the lip it shelved back somewhat, towards the road. At any time during the night he could have broken his neck before he knew what was happening.

'Careful! If you break your leg, then what am I to do?'

She was sitting on a tiny grassy knoll. Her bicycle lay beside her. She was simply dressed in jeans and a flannel top. She had thick hair, midnight black, gathered into tresses. Her face was pale with a few freckles.

Incongruously, she wore high heels. She was possibly three or four years younger than he.

'Hullo, I'm Siobhan. Who are you?'

'Ywain.'

He took her proffered hand awkwardly.

'Well, you look a bit of a mess. I've been watching you tear around ever since I woke you up. You're scared of something. What's bothering you? You're not a bank robber or anything like that, are you?'

Her tone of voice was that of a mechanic asking what was the problem with the car.

'Some people are chasing me.'

'And they're going to find you if you're not a bit more careful. Do they know that you're up here somewhere?'

'Yes.'

'Well, that makes it a bit awkward, but we'll manage. I've been over almost every inch of this whole place with my father, and there's not much he doesn't know about it. That old wreck there is the first place they'd look in. You know, when I came up here this morning I thought that something might be going on.'

She gave him the bread and the hard-boiled eggs she had brought for her breakfast and watched him carefully as he ate, his eyes on her as he wondered at her words.

'You thought –'

'Yes, thought. But don't ask me to explain it.'

'I don't understand. Did someone tell you – Ilona, perhaps?'

Like all very young men, no matter how intelligent, confronted with a striking and dominant woman, Ywain was capable of the most gormless gaucherie.

'I've never heard of this Ilona. Your eyes tell me bad things about her, whoever she is. No, I can't explain. What's your family name?'

Again, her tone of voice suggested a matron of thirty-eight addressing an adolescent.

'O'Keefe.'

'Ywain O'Keefe, come to dance with me in Ireland.'

'What?'

'Just a line from an old song.'

She laughed a pure and joyful laugh. 'Evidently you're my first task. What am I to do with you? There's a fellow down in the village who might put you up for a few days. But what if he doesn't? Oh, he will if I ask him, don't worry.'

'How far is the village?'

'Doolin. Oh, at least ten, or more likely, twelve, miles from here, I expect.'

'I'll never make it. They're watching the roads.'

'We'll make it. We won't use roads most of the way. And they'll never see us. I'll leave my bike here for Dan to pick up when he's passing this way. Finished? Don't throw the paper away. This is the Burren, a precious place that we must keep well. Here, I'll put it in my pouch. Come on, we've got four hours walk in front of us.'

She took a long sloping track invisible to Ywain that first went up more than down, but eventually took them to the friendly barrier of a long wall behind which they were hidden from the road. After a while she added: 'Of course, you'll have to overthrow them.'

'Who?'

'Your pursuers, whoever they are. It's you or them, isn't it? But don't worry about it now. You'll have time. We need to find out more about them first. Right now you look a little lost, but that's only because you do not know your rôle yet. When the time is ripe that knowledge will come to you. In the meantime you must prepare yourself. At present you don't look like much of a hero, but perhaps I can help you grow into one.'

'What do you know about it?'

'Nothing, yet. I read only what is in your eyes, Ywain. Tell me more about this Ilona.'

'Oh, she was a girl I met at Ballinspittle. I helped her home. In return she ran off with my bicycle and stole some money from me.'

'I knew she was a bad lot. You shouldn't take up with strange women.'

He laughed joyously, for he felt free for the first time in days. 'What about you?'

'What about me, indeed! You should show a little more respect. I'm not one of your pick-me-ups! Don't you see that I'm above that? You do not look into me as I look into you. I came to help you.'

'But how did you know?'

'Of course I didn't *know*. I had just been given an idea. It's no good asking me to explain. I can't explain it to myself except to say that I am one of the high ones. Perhaps you too are one of the high ones but do not know it yet. I think you may be, for I was sent to you.' She glanced at him seriously.

'You mean, sort of upper class?'

'Not in that sense at all. I have few friends, but everyone wants to be my friend. I am looked up to, but not because of my family or my father's position, or his wealth, which he hasn't got, but for something in myself. That is why I am able to help you now. People usually do what I ask them.'

Ywain did not know what to make of this. She didn't seem to be putting on side or to be deluded about herself. She appeared to be trying to tell him something difficult to get used to.

'Well, in that case, I am certainly not one of the 'high ones', as you put it. I believe I know what you mean, though. I don't feel that I'm anything much.'

'That's a silly thing to say. Of course you are. I can see that right enough. You just haven't found out who you really are yet. What's your family?'

'My mother lives in Toronto. My father died ages ago, not long after I was born. I don't remember him at all. And I have a very clever and resourceful sister called Mira who is so much better at everything than I am.'

'You don't know your family really, do you? And don't do yourself down. Like it or not, I'm now part of your destiny, Ywain, perhaps only a little part, perhaps not, which means that yours is the destiny of no ordinary man. You're to be a hero and overthrow your enemies. Your father is involved in this somewhere. So cheer up and let's put on some more pace. You can keep up with a filly, can't you?'

Chapter 13

THE IMAGE, not clear even when computer-enhanced, showed Ywain opening the gate to his studio dwelling in Toronto. There was a better picture of him as he walked along Bloor Street with Debra. She also came in for some scrutiny, The ones taken in Ireland, jerky and indistinct, were evidently shot from a pursuing car. These were the last of a series featuring various people, including a hospital patient whom Ywain would have recognized. Earlier shots had shown him disappearing down area steps in a city probably in the British Isles.

The man Haynes said, 'That's not much, is it?'

Kerstow replied, 'We don't know exactly what we're looking for yet beyond the possibility that O'Keefe may be involved in or at least know something about Owen's people. It's pretty indefinite. Owen, of course, eluded us and we felt it was best to take the safest course, but then – he's gone! I find that inexplicable. I mean, we had him – restrained in a hospital bed one moment, gone the next – of course there's a cover-up – the likely liars have been dealt with, no fear, but we're no nearer the truth. O'Keefe may know nothing about anything – that'd be my guess – but we'll bring him in and put him through the complete wringer. We've got to find out. If he continues to make that inconvenient, we'll simply remove him. At present he seems to me to be just scared and on the run, but he definitely must be interrogated thoroughly now that Owen has vanished.

'Vandermeer was eliminated and we have no other leads on this one at present.'

There was a pause.

'I do need your agreement.'

'Yes. Let me know the outcome. Liquidating potentials is a high priority with the Council. Discretion is the key. No ripples, please, gentlemen. The Vatican Bank business nearly brought the house down about our ears. Don't let's rely on luck again. Security is a higher priority than ever before in an environment of electronic free-flow.'

A third man, rubicund, bespectacled and smiling like a latter-day Mr Pickwick, put in: 'I'm sorry, gentlemen, but I'm not happy with this situation. The lack of progress concerns me. I want much more leg-work, much more scouring for groups, much more and much more successful infiltration. My impression is that we're not getting to the springs. Cut off the heads before they get started.'

'I think we've found most of them, Sir. Owen and O'Keefe are probably the only survivors of their group –'

'"Probably" isn't good enough. I want action, not estimates and projections.'

'I should have thought, Kerstow,' Haynes put in, 'that letting O'Keefe run round on the loose so that he can lead us to his friends would have been better than scaring the daylights out of him. He certainly has valuable friends and an excellent organization, otherwise he couldn't possibly remain hidden from us.'

'Good point. He has a lot to tell us, and we'll get him. Everyone available is on the job and it's just a matter of time. He's a complete wimp, as terrified as a trapped rabbit. Whatever he has to tell he'll tell, don't worry. In fact he's the type we might have turned around, but now that's been ruled out, we'll squeeze him dry and dispose of him in the usual way, that is, if Mr Nickerson doesn't reconsider his policy.'

'If he doesn't lose himself in the Irish sub-culture, you mean.'

'Fine,' said Nickerson. 'I think we've settled that. I want him in custody this week. Have we finished with Potentials? Then let's get on with the next item.'

Chapter 14

A TINY BREEZE, hardly to be remarked, stirred the sands of Sligo Bay. In the twilight the coastal bens looked far distant in the deepening dusk. All day it had rained heavily; the miniature brown torrents had raced down the steep hills making some sections of the road impassable. But the evening was magic. Greater mountains of clouds reflected the rutilant brilliance of divine metals, molten, as the oblate sun sank silently beyond the oblique world. The sea, more peaceable, tore less relentlessly at the shelving rocks.

Harry Blake the farmer looked up at the ben whose kinder slopes were under his corn. A cave celebrated in legend looked out upon his fields, and once in a while a tourist would drop by asking how to get up to it. Harry would point out the way, run over the cave's hazards and hand the explorer a pamphlet published by the local tourist association. Sometimes he would go along if he had the time, especially if the trip was made worth his while, but he liked to have notice and he could not take the time at those seasons when the farmer is busiest.

He was a somewhat irascible but kindly man who could stand anyone for limited periods, except those tourists – particularly American tourists – who wanted him to be a character.

He was a good farmer. He had never had a bad crop, and he was regarded as the luckiest man for miles around. Perhaps his land had a virtue other farmers' lands did not have.

He had just received notice of a visitor, someone who would arrive in the late evening during the next week or two. And he was a little annoyed because he was very busy but now had to make special preparations which took time but had to be kept secret, even from the girl who came in to help in the house, to whom Harry blabbed just as if she were his wife. The instructions were very specific.

So every evening after dusk he was at work on an old hidey hole dug on the other side of a fold of land, invisible from the road, a chamber dug out, lined and revetted, equipped with several breathing tubes that could be pulled down flush with the ground. When he had finished the entrance was not distinguishable even if one knew where to look and looked closely. He carefully left out several markers unrecognizable as such except to himself.

Harry, like his father before him, was used to putting up reticent strangers from time to time.

Several other people from Kenmare to Letterkenny also received instructions to hold themselves in readiness for the same visitor.

In the meantime Dan was going out of his wits, saddled with several errands and told to look after a stranger who was not to be seen by anyone 'until arrangements can be made'. He cursed occasionally and resolved to tell Siobhan to find someone else to take the unwelcome guest off his hands, but he could not do this, for he could never say no to Siobhan. He knew he would get nothing, certainly not her company to himself, but she was the boss. And her requirements were rigid: Ywain was never to go outside until she herself came to give directions; he was not even to show his face at a window, let alone join the pub crowd downstairs or enter any public room. This worked well for the first few days. After that, even Ywain, now well-fed and feeling more secure, began to go out of his mind with impatience.

However, with all their reputation for easy conversation, the Irish have learned when to button up. Dan asked no questions.

At this time the nervous system of the small community became aware of intruders in their midst: several more off-key single visitors than usual roosted in the B&Bs. Although they strove to be seen as independent, the Doolin folks thought they all came out of the same mould, an American one. They tried to create the impression that they were on holiday, but it was obvious to the practised eyes of people who dealt with tourists year and year out and knew their clientele that they were a flock of blackbirds. Every one of these singular visitors had a passion for exploring the countryside. Some were out all day; the others were out all night.

At length Dan permitted himself a word. 'You're awful important,' he said with respect.

It was a slightly grotesque atmosphere. Something was held suspended over the village, and the rumours were gleeful. But what it was all about no one, including Ywain, knew.

The Guarda were puzzled too. They had not been let in on the secret and they were not inclined to be of any particular assistance to the strangers.

'What about to Aran, and from Aran to Galway?' asked Ywain when Siobhan appeared, as she did occasionally.

She shook her head. 'The boat's watched all the time and my father has a very poor opinion of McCory, who owns it. Don't worry. Your place is here right now. We'll have good help and we'll get you away from here some time after all the crooks are gone. After that we'll persuade them that you're still here. That shouldn't be too difficult.'

'Siobhan, what's this all about? I don't understand anything.'

She laughed. 'I don't either – yet. You haven't told me everything you know, and there will come a time when we have to talk about that.'

'Well, I don't want to be a hero. You ran on about that while we were out on the Burren. I'm scared stiff of these guys. I just want to get out.'

'You won't be doing what you want, or what at this moment you think you want. Nor will I. When life has a rôle for us it's impossible to refuse. We can succeed or fail. We cannot decline. When the time comes, your rôle will be made clear to you. That is what destiny means. These men think that they are going to find you and have an easy time of it wringing you out and then killing you, but it is not going to work out like that. They don't know what they're up against.'

'I think you're all mad.'

'All? How many is "all"?'

'I don't know.'

'Well, up until now it's been just Dan, me and Brian Collins whose van was destroyed in your behalf. Show a little appreciation you unfeeling block. Without us you'd be a corpse. What's more, they will make a corpse of you if I withdraw my protection. So far, in our collective madness, we've gone out of our way to help you. So, what have you to say?'

Ywain was silent.

'Ah well,' she went on, softening her tone, 'I'll get you all the help you need. That's my rôle, fortunately for you.'

'How?'

'I always have help when I need it, Ywain. I've a – say, a knack of having luck. Do you believe in luck? Did you know that luck is catching, bad as well as good? I'm very lucky. I can make you lucky too if you go all the way with me.'

Her voice fascinated Ywain, soft, firm, singing in the heart and exuding a royal confidence and security. He didn't know what she meant, but he was quite convinced.

'That's good,' he said lamely.

'Yes, isn't it? Now I have to leave you. No peeking, no company, not a step outside nor a peep through that window, or you may be dead. These boyos are not playing a game. Don't get yourself killed because I may need you. When I get a chance after we have these chimpanzees taped I may take you out somewhere and we'll have a yarn about everything then.'

Positioned well back in the room, Ywain watched her as she walked away. Her carriage was perfectly erect, her gait at once purposive and delicate, the step of a princess. She did not glance back. He heard a car door open and slam. Someone in a hurry gunned the engine.

Dan had to get Siobhan back to school before the beginning of the first afternoon period.

Chapter 15

By six in the evening Siobhan's parents had a full house: the dour American who had been there for two days was joined by three delightful ladies in their late twenties and early thirties travelling together, a couple from Canada who were delighted with everything except each other and a young German woman travelling alone, on leave from her job as junior secretary at the German Embassy in Capetown. Monika had chosen the rainiest summer in living memory to cycle round Ireland and she complained mightily about the single supplement she had to pay. She was fed up with the weather. Siobhan had to shift out of her own room, for her father was not one to turn away business.

Late in the afternoon they all gathered and chatted in the living-room, even the American, who said little but stayed long enough to satisfy himself that the visitors did not include anyone in whom he ought to be interested. As he got up to leave he bumped into Siobhan, who was bringing in some slides of the Burren that her father had offered to show. In trying to step aside he stumbled and grazed his left shoulder quite painfully against the door-jamb.

Mr Ward was not sorry to see him leave the company, for he had already identified he American as one of the blackbirds who had descended on the area. The latest rumour was that they were all working for a huge corporation considering developing this beautiful landscape into an industrial site. Mr Ward regarded that as too absurd to be believed.

The three youngish ladies who were travelling together were delightful: they had the qualities one associates with an earlier time. Even Monika recovered her good humour. The Canadians were enchanted. This what they expected in the old country. They had forgotten the wonderful spell of human harmony in a casual encounter. The three spoke to each other and the rest of the company inclusively as if they had known them all their lives, yet keeping from the near edge of intimacy.

Siobhan forgot her jobs and stayed to become part of the octet.

The Canadian man thought: how these people remind me of the folks I used to know when I was a child. But I don't remember anyone as fetchingly amiable in their strict courtesy as these girls who seem to spring from some previous century, so that is nonsense! Can something that one wants very much to be a part of one's past become a memory? Of course not. Then why did I instinctively associate this delightful encounter with a memory?

This occurred to him because once or twice when travelling around, some spot or another had brought a spontaneous feeling of association, although this was the first visit to Ireland for both of them.

The visitors' three cars – one each for the dour American, the three Irishwomen and the Canadian couple, together with the Wards' very old one, barely fitted into the postage-stamp parking yard, leaving one car blocking the others.

Siobhan, of course, could not stay in the living-room with the guests forever as she had to help her mother. The Canadians and the Irish had now asked for high tea, which was going to be late.

Finally, when that was in progress, Siobhan went back into the lounge. As soon as they had finished tea the two Canadians went off to make the most of the lovely late evening. The three Irishwomen, who had earlier professed weariness, came back in and sat chatting as good-humouredly and animatedly as ever, while Siobhan listened. As before, they talked to each other, but with all the expressions and gestures, with all the silent language of fellowship to include the younger woman. Their names of the visitors were Donna, Berenice and Maire. Soon Maire said, 'Let's go for a walk. We've done nothing but sit in the house since we arrived. How far is it to the beach, Siobhan?'

'Oh, there's nothing of a beach here. You'll want at least half-an-hour to the jetty. But if you turn to the left going out and walk up towards Liscannor, you'll see a narrow road – it's really only a track – cutting through the high fields down the slope. The village is at the end as you reach the little street at the bottom. A few hundred yards to your left takes you to the sea. You walk past the pub.'

'Ah,' said Donna, 'but we might get lost in the dark on the way back.'

'Here's a card in case you forget the address,' replied Siobhan, wise in the ways of helping strangers.

'That's a help, but, no, I think we'll wait until morning light.'

'No, let's go,' put in Berenice. 'I'd like to get out. And we can ask anyone. They'll be people in the village, won't there?'

'Oh yes,' replied Siobhan, 'the pubs are packed until they close. I often go down there. Once you find the road you came down all you've got to do is walk up it until you reach this road – it doesn't go any farther – turn right and walk the few hundred yards to the house.'

'I know it's easy,' said Donna, 'but I'll get lost in the dark. I always do. I lose my sense of direction. You're not going down this evening by any chance, are you?'

'I'd love to come down with you if I can help.'

'Well, then. Shall we get started?'

They put on pullovers and jackets and went out, Siobhan having got leave from her mother since she was helping the guests. Less than half-an-hour later they were in the pub, where three musicians played silently under the overwhelming spring tide of Irish conversation. The place was so packed that they migrated to one of the rear rooms where they could actually hear each other if they put their lips close to the ear and shouted only a little.

'Is it always like this?'

'Always in summer.'

'Pubs like this are the best places for private talk. Shall I tell you all my secrets?'

'I'll get them,' yelled Maire. 'What's yours, Siobhan?'

'Oh nothing. I don't drink. Really.'

'What about a ginger beer?'

'No thanks. If anything I'd rather have a bitter lemon.'

Berenice and Donna talked about the village and about the news reports taking up more space by the day of the number of statues of the Virgin said to have moved miraculously.

'I wonder, now, how that kind of thing gets started,' said Donna.

'Mass hysteria,' suggested Berenice, 'you know, first in one place someone imagines that the image has moved miraculously, then other people persuade themselves that they see the same kind of thing, so there are copy cat occurrences in neighbouring districts, then whole scads of people are gripped by the frenzy and it starts spreading. Not always in small places, in Cork, if what I've read is true. Is there anything like that around here, Siobhan?'

'Oh no.'

'Anything like what?' asked Maire, who had arrived with the drinks.

'You've heard. Statues that move – move their lips, speak, perhaps.'

'Oh that. What I wonder is how that kind of thing gets started. I mean, who is the first to see it?' pursued Maire.

'That's what you'll never know,' rejoined Donna, 'because it's mass hysteria.'

'But doesn't someone have to be first?' put in Siobhan. 'Someone has to be the first to say, "Look, it's moving!" or "Look! It must have moved during the night!"'

'That's what I was saying,' said Maire. 'Ah well, we're all terrible skeptics. Or are we?' She laughed at herself.

They all looked at Siobhan as if anxious not to offend her in any way, however inadvertently.

Siobhan regarded them steadily. 'Why couldn't the Blessed Virgin, the Heavenly Mother herself, move her own statue if she wanted to – or make people believe she had done so. Considering what people really do believe when they see it on the telly, or think they've seen it, it doesn't seem much,' she said ungrammatically and ambiguously.

'Well, there you are,' rejoined Maire, 'just what I should have said myself.'

Everyone knew Siobhan and she introduced her parents' guests to the nearest talkers. After half-an-hour or so they pushed their way through the crowd and walked down to the jetty. There was a small slipway alongside. The air had cleared. They stood looking out to sea for a few minutes trying to descry Aran in the darkness on the waters.

'Rocky it is, this part of the coast. Farther south there's lots of sand. They have races on the beach at Kilkee, horse races, I'm telling you, and nearly always you see a few riders at least on the sand down there. This is too harsh. You can't imagine any Aphrodite stepping out of the waves at Doolin,' observed Berenice.

Donna and Maire laughed.

'Sometimes I think the map of Ireland looks like a woman about to give birth. It's no Venus from the perfumed south but a child to shock the world into life that'll come out of Ireland,' added Maire. 'Tell me, Siobhan, this Burren your father was telling me about, is it within walking distance?'

'No, not really. I go there on my bike usually.'

'You know it well. Might you have the time to show it to us tomorrow, perhaps? We can all go up in the car.'

'In the early morning only, the very early morning. I sometimes go off there before the break of day to see the new dawn rising.'

'Do you now? That will suit us fine. We'll be ready when you are.'

'But,' said Siobhan, 'I'd like to bring a visitor, someone from overseas who is new to us.'

'Your choice shall be our choice. We'll look after him. And I am sure that Monika will want to come. We spoke to her earlier on.'

Chapter 16

His spirits restored, Ywain was now dying to get out of his little room, driven by competing urges to breathe in the freedom of the open air: to walk along the same village street through which his persecutors had chased him, now untrammelled by the fear of discovery; to know the joy of being with Siobhan; to revel in the sheer fascination she held for him; to know where she lived; who her people were. He was dying to know every little thing about her.

However, he was not exactly overjoyed when Dan told him he would be going on a promised picnic the following morning, the party to leave at 3 a.m.

'Why so early? Will Siobhan be coming?'

'I just do what I'm told, Ywain, my old son. And as to whether she's along for the ride, we'll find that out when we get there. Don't worry – it may even turn out fine.'

'And what about the creeps?'

'Oh, a few of those are still around, right enough, but we know where they are now. Mind you, I told Siobhan it was too soon and too dangerous to let you out, but she overruled me. "Never mind," she said, "just keep an eye on them. He'll be back soon enough." So I got several other fellows together, and we should be able to look after you if you don't do anything rash, like screaming for your mother or something.'

'And she was so cautious before!'

'Siobhan usually knows what she's doing. She's got a knack of being right about things. So you'll be O.K. And don't worry in the least about security. Secrecy is second nature with us. In spite of appearances, we're a pretty tight-lipped bunch here. Knowing Siobhan makes you one of us, you damned nuisance.'

'I know I am. I can't think why you're doing all this for me. I'm not worth it.'

'You're right there. But we Irish are always making poor decisions – it's our national character, like the North American habit of taking everything literally.'

The morning was chill but clear as Dan had said. He lay down on the back seat of a small car driven by a tall and muscular newcomer, Michael, with Dan in front beside him.

'There he is,' said Michael quietly as he took the left-hand fork in the lower road, 'thumbing a lift, the bastard. I've a mind to give him one he won't forget. If he's around on the way back, maybe I will.'

'No you won't,' said Dan.

Once well out of Doolin, Michael, an enthusiastic rally driver, poured the gravy. They went through Ballyvaghan cutting the acute turn past the pub and racing up the hill roads like the spark of a powder train heading for the keg. Once on the climbing roads, Michael drove like the devil, twisting around the curves and vaulting over the crests. He was definitely taking the long way around and precious few drivers could stay with him on these roads. Ywain was more than a little nervous but didn't say anything. Michael kept on talking the whole while about a deal involving some horses belonging to a friend of his.

When they finally stopped, Dan and Ywain got out and Michael drove off immediately leaving a backwash of gravel, dust and particles of rubber. Dan led Ywain off the road into a track that soon petered out or became invisible in the shelving stone of the Burren itself. It was still dark, but he knew his way around; Ywain frequently stumbled. They walked for perhaps twenty minutes, eventually reaching the overhanging miniature cliffs with copses of bramble, hawthorn and hazel at the base. Dan left him in one of these garden-sized forests, telling him to watch out for the other picnickers.

'I'll be around somewhere with a friend or two if you get yourself into trouble, but everything's quiet at the moment.'

The sky promised the magic first light before the dawn. Ywain was alive to every moment and did not care that he hadn't had so much as a sip of tea before leaving. The loveliness of the time raised his spirits. In the first long rosy light before the gorgeous sunrise he wanted so much to be worthy of Siobhan.

After waiting for some minutes he saw them as they made their way up towards the fringe of trees, but he stayed where he was concealed until they were almost upon him. Stepping out, he waved a hand in greeting, but did not know what to say. They weren't in the least startled, the five of them, all women. Face-to-face once more with the girl he had encountered so miraculously, he suddenly felt shaken and nervous in her presence, his dawn-engendered exaltation faltering.

'Ywain, I've brought some beautiful women to see you,' lilted Siobhan, and she named each of them. We are very close friends, as you may be if you really wish for that.'

'Indeed,' said Donna.

'Pretty early for a picnic, isn't it?' asked Ywain.

'Not at all. This is the best time, particularly for you,' replied Siobhan. 'Let's begin.'

Ywain was surprised to see that no one was carrying anything except Maire, who produced a stoneware bottle and some little schnapps vessels shaped like tiny beer steins about one-and-a-half inches high. These she set on the stony ground and carefully poured a small measure of liquor into each. Everyone stood in a circle around the offering, joined hands and raised arms over heads while Donna intoned an invocation in a language Ywain did not recognize. She then poured one of the vessels out on to the earth. Siobhan gave Ywain his portion.

'Drink this slowly – no! – sip by sip. This is good stuff.'

The liquor had that quality of the finest wines which leave no presence but their fragrance in the mouth, but it was not wine, nor any drink he had ever known. It did not have the instant fire of schnapps or brandy, but instead left the lasting redolence of some undiscovered spice. As they lingered gratefully over the final drops, the first beams of the emerging sun pervaded the sky. No one spoke a word.

Ywain was not warmed as a dram of cognac would have left him, nor was he aware of any other immediate effect. As the minutes went by, however, he thought he could see his surroundings with greater clarity than before; he felt an empathy with the landscape as if he and all things came together in a common harmony, not an insight but a merging.

In the meantime the others went off a little distance on the shelf where there was plenty of open flat space while he remained watching them from the brush. There they joined hands again and forming a rough circle, began a curious dance or mime. As he watched the dancers became a flowing shape, changing rapidly in a series of figures which at first held no meaning for him. After a few minutes, perhaps under the influence of the liquor, he thought that at any given time one of them was imitating something, perhaps an animal, possibly a tree or a feature of the landscape, while the others followed her lead. This rôle passed successively to each in turn, and the routine was repeated several times, but with different gestures. The dance lasted for half-an-hour perhaps. Ywain concentrated on every moment of it even though he did not understand anything of what was going on. The last to fill the leading rôle was Siobhan.

When, as he thought, the dance was over, they stood for a moment. Siobhan beckoned to Ywain, and they took him into the circle, gently pushing him around for one more circuit. Nothing was explained to him. They pushed him into place as they went through the motions without anyone in the leading part. This done, they walked over to the doll-house wood. Again, no one spoke.

Ywain now burst out of his preoccupation with himself and Siobhan. He was in some fantastic dream having the rigorous sharpness of surrealism. His mind was concentrated in itself, but on nothing external. The women, on the other hand, were concentrating on something outside themselves, and whatever it was, it was the same for all of them. They included him as well as they could.

They did not speak, had, in fact, some way of communicating silently with one another. Without saying a word, Monika, Maire, Berenice and Donna left together. He was alone with Siobhan. And still they were silent. A spell was on him and he did not wish to break it. He imagined how harsh and out of place his voice would sound in this divine morning after the rapture of the miming dance. Siobhan did not help him. She rested on a grassy tuffet between two roots and waited too. They both watched the transforming sky.

'Siobhan, what was that all about?'

'That was a dance of the stations of the year. Hardly anyone is ever allowed to watch that.'

'Yet you included me in it. Why?'

'Because I wish to make you one of us. I believe it is your destiny. It is on my word that you are here.'

'Why me?'

'We have a little time to talk now, perhaps very little. What I want to hear first is what brought you to Ireland – never mind all that stuff about your family. What made you give up your job and all your other chances in life? Depression does not normally impel people to action.'

'Depression –'

'Look, Ywain, I'm a woman, a very young one, I know, but still, a woman. I have a third eye. All women have it if they know how to use it, even little girls of eleven. You suffer from depression, whether you know it or not. What will you give me if I take it away from you?'

'Anything you can ask.'

'See? You knew perfectly well. So, why Ireland?'

Ywain told her about his encounters with Victor.

'You never found out his real name?'

'No.'

'That might be awkward, but he certainly gave you all the clues anyone could wish for. I'm apprehensive about him and I wonder what his motives are. Why should he of all beings wish you to encounter us first? Have you still got that bible?'

'Yes, it's in my pack.'

'Oh, good. I'll get it from you when we're back. Perhaps there's still something you missed. I wonder where your father comes into all this.'

'My father!'

'Yes, your father. He's in there somewhere.'

'But I know nothing about my father.'

'We'll see. You may encounter, shall I say, his likeness, his matrix, if you like. Expect to find what you never imagined if you stay with us.'

'What is your – group?'

'You'll find out more in time. For now, it's something very special, something old that's coming to light again. I have committed you to it, but I cannot answer all your questions yet. The easy name for it, which you must never mention outside of the group, is the Bridestone Circle. Each of us bears a sign that is recognized by the initiated.'

'Then how long have you and the others been together?'

'The villagers? Many of us grew up in it together; but if you mean Maire, Berenice, Donna and Monika, I never saw them till yesterday.'

'Then how –'

'Sounds difficult, but simple really. All of us in the Circle can reveal themselves to the others by using a secret language unperceived by any outsider. It's a very ancient art. The scholars who study these ancient languages never suspect that at least one of them is still in use today.'

'What is it? Explain.'

'All in good time, Ywain. To be one of us you will have to learn at least the elements of it, but that will be no problem for you. After all, Victor revealed a tiny bit of it to you. Up on the Burren that day I found you, I saw you make the sign of the Circle to me. I replied, discreetly, but you were not looking for any response and it was obvious that you couldn't really use the language. For a moment the thought crossed my mind that you had been sent to infiltrate us, but I soon saw that this was not so. Yesterday when Donna, Maire, Berenice, and, later, Monika came, we made ourselves known to each other immediately. No outsider watching us could have been aware of this. Later we walked down to the village and had drinks in the pub amid almost unbearable noise. We shouted some talk at each other, but what we were really saying was quite different from what we said aloud. Do you understand?'

'I think I understand now. I thought Victor was raving, but he was actually telling me something without my knowing it. He mentioned other letters too, but I don't remember what he said – something about *B* being a tree, I think. There was more to it than that.'

'Yes. Now you understand that we need such security, for we are in constant danger as you are, probably for similar reasons. No matter how secret the code, some goon brainier than his underlings can always commission a study and break it. In this case, he would also have to divine the language of communication. There's always the danger. For you there is another, more disconcerting danger. Victor. He has obtained some power over you, Ywain, and we cannot fight him if my suspicion is right.'

'Who, for God's sake, is he?'

'Wait, Ywain, wait. You will be better prepared when next you run into him, I hope. First, you must travel with us, and that will protect you a little. For the moment, remember: you cannot mention or even hint at the secret alphabet in even the remotest way except to one of us. And Ywain, what is expressed by word of mouth is never regarded as seriously between us as what is conveyed by the old alphabet, for that is the language of truth. It is the sacred language, never to be misused. If and until you are formally initiated into the Circle after a period of preparation, you depend on me and on no one else except the other four women you have seen this morning for anything to do with the Circle, or to some specific person to whom the Circle sends you. Otherwise you don't talk about it, you don't even think about it. You do not name the Circle: that and everything to do with it is to be expunged from your soul except as a love between us, a love. Do you understand that? It is a love.

'I think so, vaguely.'

'There can be nothing vague about it. The Bridestone Circle is a bond of love first, love in the widest and the deepest. There are no qualifications to love. Some people are on to you, so you're in danger, and it will seem to you that what I'm doing is very rash, revealing all this at a time when you could be snapped up and have it all squeezed out of you. But it isn't. That's the rational way of thinking. I think from the heart and something you would call intuition. We'll keep you safe and something will emerge from you, something you never believed you had in you. You have a great capacity for love, dear Ywain, the love of your lost father gone beyond recovery, the love of the natural land that drove you out of the grim soulless city, the thwarted love for your cold mother and distant sister and your love for me. Do you want me?'

Ywain quivered. His heart turned to water.

'That's bad, but it will get better. I love you too, Ywain, believe me, but I can't love you in that way. You see, one of us in the Circle will – well, soon, perhaps – become something very special. Until I know that it will not be me I can't promise to love you in the way your heart screams for, yes, you cannot hide it from me. That will sound like nonsense to you, but that's the way truth often comes, in the form of apparent nonsense. Some vision or turn of events bears it to you. It drifts into you and later on suddenly becomes a little epiphany, as a famous man once called it. A man always has one foot in the grave and one in heaven. A woman always has both feet in the same place. That is why only a woman can be truly divine.'

'This I don't understand.'

'It's not something you have to understand. It's something you know.'

Ywain did not speak. Clarity of mind did not help him. The morning rose before them painting shadows on the rocks.

'Well, aren't you bursting with questions?'

'I don't even understand what I'm supposed to have learned. I need to have the first lesson again.'

'Is that your need? This is all of it.' She embraced and kissed him and stroked his hand.

Her touch electrified him, and sent him quivering again. The intensity of his love carried him towards a blue and raging sun. He was terrified of his own ardent rage.

'How can I love you? You're not a girl of seventeen. You're a –'

'Do not say that word!' She placed her hand over his mouth.

'I can only worship you. And desperately want you. There is nothing else in me but you. You know that. And you can't help that. I'm weak at the thought of you, helpless at your touch.'

'Yes, I do know that, Ywain. That's the lovely beginning. But of course I can help you. And I will. I tell you from my heart that I will never let you down, but you cannot have me, not yet, perhaps not ever. I promise you that I will always receive your love and I will always love you in all the ways that count, so long as you are constant to me and my purposes. Remember this: no matter what happens, you can never do anything against me, and I can never, in my own person, do anything against you. You are overborne by love, Ywain. That is your supreme quality. We live in a age that does not want to admit that the greatest thing of all is love, absolute and pure love like yours. It often attracts scorn. It offends the puritanical humbug of the politically correct. But it's there, in you and in me. And as it is in us, I am no girl of seventeen. I'm a woman, eternal woman, as you are the eternal suffering man. All of us, men and women, are possessed by love, and to ignore this or to attempt to destroy it is to destroy humanity and divinity. Love is suffering. It always is. It is part of death. But it is also divine. And that is why there is a Bridestone Circle.'

'I love you, but I can't learn this lesson either.'

She laughed. 'You're learning very well – and that was the last demonstration this morning. Now we'd better be getting back. It will soon be broad daylight. I want to collect Victor's bible from you, don't let me forget. He had cunning enough for the two of you. And do be on your guard. You're going to see him again. Oh, and by the way, I'm eighteen, not seventeen, perhaps just a little older in love, a vessel of the ages, just as the youthful Mozart was in music.'

'It's an amazing coincidence that four other members should just happen to show up at the same time as I did.'

'In the Circle there's no such thing as coincidence.'

'What would you call it, then?'

'An interstice in the net of fate.'

'Do you often talk like a dictionary?'

'The precise word always comes to me when I need it.'

'Is this more of the help you always get when you need it?'

'Yes.'

This time Ywain went back in a bread delivery van, in the back, behind the shelves stacked with newly-baked bread. Siobhan rode in front with the driver.

To him, Ywain's presence was the most natural thing in the world.

Chapter 17

BLAKE'S VISITOR ARRIVED ON MONDAY NIGHT. The van that brought him didn't even come to a complete stop. A man jumped out and a small kit bag was thrown after him. The rear doors were immediately pulled to from within.

The newcomer had evidently been well-briefed, for he ran the length of the driveway against the slope. He didn't knock at any door but went round to the back and waited. Harry went out to invite him in.

'Put out the light, man.'

Harry switched off his torch.

'Quick! They may not be far off!'

In silence Harry led him up the path to the tiny bunker. The other slipped in.

'Do you need anything to eat?'

Yes, but go straight back to the house now. Bring me something in the early morning, before first light, only if you're quite sure no one – no one at all – can possibly see you.'

The revetted top went down and Blake walked back. His instincts derived from a long line of oppressed ancestors. He wasn't surprised when less than half-an-hour later a car raced up the driveway and someone knocked furiously at the door.

He took his time opening it.

Two young men in heavy sweaters stood there. They pushed past him into the hallway, went through every room and searched the house from top to bottom. They said nothing, not even to each other, and ignored Harry's pleas and questions. He made as if to obstruct them, but they simply turned on him, so Harry stepped back. The thought that crossed his mind was: so that's what a killer looks like.

When they had finished inside, they went out and got a halogen lantern from the car. After looking around, they traced the path up the hill.

'Are ye tourists?' asked Harry ingenuously when they came back.

They got back into the car and reversed down the track Harry called his driveway with never a glance at him. Evidently they and their friends were searching all the isolated houses along the route of the pursued van.

'The bastards,' Harry said to himself without any particular emotion, 'the bastards.'

Their complete silence puzzled him for a few minutes until he realized that they were not Irish. They had attempted to dress like the Irish, but their trousers were thinner and lighter, the knit of their sweaters not local. They weren't Irish.

He went to the image of the Virgin Mary and prayed for the safety of those pursued.

It occurred to him that the hide-out might not be safe for long. There was too great a risk of being observed from the road or higher up.

Before the light of dawn he took his guest a flask of coffee, a can of water, bread, cheese, cereal and fruit. He also threw in a few raw carrots, a knife and what was left of the leg of mutton.

The fugitive didn't need to be told to stay in there. Harry told him briefly of the unpleasant strangers and left.

Before he did, the man within replied, 'Don't worry. I think we're going to deal with them.'

Back inside the house, Harry began to wonder anew. The man in the bunker had an American accent; his persecutors were probably American. What could the Americans have to do with the fabulous Circle?

Something was up. This would not be the last time that intruders with guns would oppress him. There would have to be another hide-out, one less precarious. Perhaps there would be more than one harried man, although he had been told to prepare only for this one. If he were given enough time, he could stock certain caverns in the hill above with provisions. Some parts of the great cave were known only to a few, and a man well-supplied could hold out there indefinitely, provided he could stomach the bitter waters of the pool in that hidden recess.

Harry wasn't exactly surprised to hear that a van had gone off the road on the way to Sligo. Its occupant or occupants had vanished.

Out in the fields he was uncomfortably aware that there were always walkers or climbers. He descried two moving like lice along the brow of the ben, and once a helicopter flew close beside it, pausing at the cavern of Queen Maeve.

Early next morning three men came up his path, knocked on his door and requested permission to cross his fields. Harry pointed out the tracks and one took a tourist pamphlet which provided a sketch map of the shallow caverns. They were back in record time.

It was obvious that the whole area was under surveillance twenty-four hours a day. The hide-out was fine for a while, but it would not stand scrutiny forever. Sooner or later his ministrations would be spotted. He decided to supply his man once every two days. While examining his tractor he contrived to drop a note explaining this down a breathing tube.

On the second night at about 11 p.m. he took the next two days' supplies and change of clothing. No one answered his whisperings.

The man had gone, taking his sleeping sack and bottled water with him.

As soon as he got within the house, Harry disposed the man's leavings among his own, burned the note and pulverized the ashes.

Chapter 18

SIOBHAN'S SUBTLE MAGIC had drawn the sting of fear, but Ywain was as vulnerable as ever. If he were to take the last steep zig-zagging path up to the ben while the half-moon was still in the sky he would be visible to anyone watching from road, field or house. If he waited until moonset he would probably not reach the cave before dawn.

More by luck than judgement he was inside the great cavern before the summit was tipped by the first gold of the day. Perhaps the vestigial aura of the potent queen discouraged his attackers during the hours of night. Once there, he felt his way into the deepest recess, tripped into the pool and went right under. Coming as it did at the end of a nerve-wracking three days, the awful fall in the dark flooded him with panic. Yet here in the protecting cave the craziness of his headlong tumble was absorbed by the ageless silence. His sleeping sack, at least, was still bone-dry. He retrieved it, stripped, wrung out his clothing which wouldn't dry out in a week in the cool dewy cave and laid it out as well as he could in the dark. He got into his sack gratefully, careless of eyes.

After a short dreamless slumber he awoke. It was broad daylight at the entrance and he could feel death on the way. He noted that the pool receded into invisibility where the roof sloped down to meet it like a throat farther back in the shadows. He was in the mouth. He tested the depth gingerly with one leg. He could not move until he could see where he was going. He decided to take a chance and wait. He moved as far as he could to the side of the pool where it was darkest and waited, seemingly for hours, until his eyes accustomed themselves to the dimness, and he saw, or thought he could see, under the roof narrowing almost to the surface of the water, a yet darker space beyond. As he was nerving himself for the attempt, he heard distant voices.

The shock of cold water punched his breath out. Immediately he was out of depth as the floor fell off sharply within a foot or two, and he had to tread water, fearful of the descending roof. He inched his way forward until the water rose over his shoulders under the roof. He was wretchedly unwilling to go on, but with certain capture behind him, he had no option. The water was above his chin when, treading and staring, he could just make out the shimmering shapes of dark places apparently in a rising chamber. Thus heartened, he pressed on in a sudden flush of resolution, submerged, and came out on the other side into a clear space under a rising floor. He had seen enough. He dived back under, retrieved his belongings, taking the greatest care to leave no trace of his presence by sweeping out any prints, and returned into the farther chamber getting his sack soaking wet for his trouble.

He could not discern what kind of space he was in, but, fumbling his way around, found that this chamber was smaller than the first. Again he sat for ages, but hardly any light penetrated from the outside, and he could make out nothing of his wall-space. He trod painfully on several small hard objects, cutting his big toe. Turning them towards the soft ambient luminance of the pool, he found he had flint-hard fragments of bones in his hands, of what animal he could not say.

Returning to the darkness of his vigil, naked, he knelt and couched his thoughts into the form of a prayer Siobhan had taught him. When he had done, he sat on his wet sleeping sack, cross-legged. He felt fully alert. After a time in this place of night he could hear the thumping of his heart. In the huge silence he could distinguish a faint hissing in his ears.

Later there would be times when this faint sound would overpower him.

He did not think he would be disturbed here. Further than that he did not think.

He peered into the darkness, seeing vague changing shapes anchored uncertainly and always fluctuating. At times he thought he could see something of another dark entrance, but this too appeared as just another undefined emergent shape ballooning unguessedly in the deep waters of the dark. Yet the mind gave it a shape. At some time he must have dozed off, but when he came to full consciousness again, he gazed again, scrying the darkness with unknown focus. Intermittently but ever more frequently the inchoate shade bodied out into a figure, the form of a man wearing a prominent helmet marching with slow deliberation back and forth across the exit as if to bar both entrance and escape, perhaps to guard, perhaps to harrow his soul. At times he appeared to pause facing Ywain, with a weapon in his grasp. His bearing suggested the soldier.

When Ywain closed his eyes he did not have the impression of any such thing before him. The apparition disturbed no air, had no footfall. Yet as soon as he opened his eyes, it again took shape, nor could he will those floating degrees of blackness to take any shape but that.

Hunkering back, he felt a dry burning in his mouth; a heaviness oppressed him. He leaned back against the cool dank wall. A cataclysmic rushing as if of a rock slide breached his ears and filled his brain. It waxed inexorably in a long crescendo until the sound beyond sound passed what was bearable or unbearable and simply crushed him. He opened his eyes. The universe, all of it, in its infinity of suns and galaxies ever more violent in their wild spirals, cascaded towards him as water cascades out of a tilted jug, gradual for a blind instant, and then overturned as the universe leapt at him, infinite and colossal, ceaseless oncoming spheres, some bright but others not, streaming at him flattened against the rock. There would be nothing left. Every star in creation would hear his screams as it passed through. Horror had vanished. This was the speech of the streaming stars.

Thought left him. In the infinity of terror he perceived no time.

When he came to, the intense headache and griping nausea had left him. He was alert, but felt a great calmness in himself even though he was, isolated in the pitchy-dark, as vulnerable as ever. He was conscious of being high up and he now saw that the night had a red quality about it which he did not see, but felt, as if outside every liquid thing was blood. His vigil was dreamless but he did not know whether or not he was asleep. He was in a state neither conscious nor unconscious in which his whole force was intent on something within himself.

The sound was long in coming, but at last it broke in upon the threshold of hearing, a terribly rapid rushing. Water. The whole ocean was racing to the coast where it would briefly pause to gather its energy before flooding across the littoral to surge into the hills. Without seeing, he was vividly aware of monstrous mountains of water rising and subsiding in some astronomical coincidence of sun, moon and passing star. It would not take long for this tidal wall of white water to drive over the hills drowning to the deepest depths every burrow and cave, extinguishing life once and for all. The rock walls shook and the crescendo of unceasing thunder passed hearing. In blind anguish he saw clearly the white of the sea locks rush in to strangle him in his retreat. In ghastly panic he felt himself borne into the rock and knew the agonizing disgust of salt water cramming into his nasal passages and invading his lungs. He drowned trying to retch.

He was as white and helpless as a maggot stuck on the knife's edge.

After a while, he cast about for the wall, but could not find it. Nor could he feel any bone fragments on the floor. He had been carried some distance by the flood, perhaps, but whence? At the cave's end, up against the wall? He had no place to go, in space, at any rate, unless turbulence had swirled him into the main chamber again. Was he in the same time as before? Such catastrophes could not be in the age he knew.

Again the idea of blood, red and pulsating, came to him as if the tactile quality brought vision to the blind. It was only then that he became aware of slow breathing not far off. He froze. There was something – something big – sharing the cave with him. It was not just the breathing. He could feel its spirit pervading this place where it had been for so long. Soon that spirit would sense his smaller spirit trespassing in its sanctuary, and the thing would rise up, crush him and eat him. Then his spirit would become part of its spirit, never to be separated, never to be independent, never to be released. He had no choice but to possess it. He would have to take as his own its white and grinning skull. He had the faintest hope of doing this only if he had a weapon. But he was naked. He remembered the restless sentinel at the entrance, and saw him there, dimly before him, on the other side of the Beast. The sentinel was proffering his sword, hilt turned outwards. But the presence of the Beast made the naked man mortally afraid: he did not even remember his own name. He dared not move because the whole cave was possessed by the spirit of the Beast before which his own small and weak one quailed, and begged him to do nothing. Meanwhile, the sentinel was growing impatient of the man's hesitation in accepting his help. A man who hesitated was not worthy of any weapon. Some words spoken by a woman of great power entered his mind.

He stood up, and as he stumbled towards the sentinel he brushed against the coarse matted pelt of the Beast. Grasping the sword, he turned. He could feel the terrible rage of the creature as it stirred itself and cast about. Then he knew that it saw him, but it saw his weapon too, and instead of lunging at him immediately, it too hesitated. The man stared unseeingly and courage left him until he forced himself to remember a prayer the woman of power he had once known had given him. His grip firmed and his fright receded, but did not disappear.

It was the suddenness. The Beast rushed him. He jumped aside, bringing down his blade as soon as he could. But the unbalanced blow glanced away harmlessly from the flying hide. An intolerant warrior told him not to be a fool. He would not win that way. Plunge it in all the way, using your foot when you can. He could smell its blood and dimly saw its outline as it haunted a curve in the wall, head down, tushes to the ready, a great boar whose shoulders stood almost as high as his own. The small eyes hated him. How could he resist the impact of such weight in a charge? The odds were simply too monstrously against him.

Space had been enormously extended; he did not now know the limits of the great chamber.

Curiously he stepped closer. Don't make a mistake, the warrior within told him. Wait until the last possible moment until he is all but upon you before you turn just out of his track and drive your sword into his eye. As he swings back he will be hampered, a little slower. Go for his neck at the shoulder. Go right in. Don't let your blade glance through and out. If it does, don't lose it.

Clever and dauntless, the Beast watched him while he moved. A moment before he stopped it charged again. Only a warrior's cutting command kept him where he was. He saw that an attempt to thrust his adversary frontally would be his own death, and following looked impossible, for the Beast went on fast and far, much farther than the extent of the cavern. He was not confined within it as was the man. These thoughts raced through his mind as he realized that he had darted aside without striking and that the Beast had turned in an instant and was coming upon him again. As it arrived he outstepped fast and aimed his stroke at the eye. His swipe was ill-judged, he thought, but by sheer good luck or a warrior's touch it had taken the eye, and the monstrous boar hesitated a little in its furious swing back, a trifle confused in direction, giving the man a chance to move closer to its blinded side. His attempt to stick it in the neck was poor, for the head swung round knocking the weapon out of his hands. Had it gone for him then, he would have lost his sword. As it was, he managed to recover his weapon, but now flustered, feeling the warrior's scorn, the man forgot his strategy and underwent a desperate period dodging the Beast's rushes, closing ever more narrowly as its judgement improved. A single misstep, let alone a fall, would end his life. Keeping his feet on the floor and the sword in his hands was now his exclusive task. It was bleeding. He wasn't. He had to survive long enough to take advantage of that, but the venomous fury of its charges took the heart from him and made the chance of a decisive thrust an uncertain thing. Both man and Beast were slowing a little, but the Beast waxed desperate as the man retreated. This state of affairs favoured the Beast, for it knew that the slightest brush would have its enemy on the floor where he could be gored to death in a flash. Otherwise, blood meant death and its hour had come. The man, however, was still quicker, and at last he adroitly got in a good slash which produced a noticeable squeal to mingle with the martial snort. He now kept back, the warrior telling him to wait a little. Now a deliberate killer, he realized that killing is purely a matter of calculation, a changing counterplay of minds as the game moves. The enormous boar was heavier, fleeter and immeasurably stronger than he was in its elastic space, and it had a deadlier weapon. One touch of that would end the contest. But its calculations were not quite so good as his even on its own ground. Man is the finest of killers. And unbidden the thought sang through his mind: I have died twice and live again. This Creature knows that its life is lost for I shall take away its spirit and then it will be nothing but bones on the floor of this cave. And his spirit rose and flourished even as the Beast's quailed and sank.

It is exceedingly difficult to stab a large and tough animal in deep unless you have been used to doing that kind of thing for a long time. As the sentinel had said, it is better to use your foot once you have purchase. Spade it in where it counts and leave it. It still moves menacingly for a few minutes, but it's finished and now you can leave your sword to dance around for a while and stay out of the way. You also need your foot to get it out again, and then it's safest to cut the throat, saw a wedge out of it, not a neat butcher's job, but a horribly bloody ragged mess, extremely tough when you are dealing with an immense boar weighing over two tons.

But he *could* move it! He noted this fact dispassionately, putting it down as astonishing.

Hacking off the head gave him little trouble for the same reason: he had mysteriously acquired strength. The sinew and gristle were a nuisance, but the bone was a simple hacking job which the sword performed perfectly. He placed the head on a high shelf. Then he wept for the hero who had given him life and thanked him in many words of praise for its strength, its courage, its kindness and the gifts it bestowed.

The darkness of the extended cavern now lifted a little, although it was still dim to his eyes. Strangely, he could see tall trees.

Grasping both sword and head and ignoring his bleeding feet, his cuts and contusions, for he was conscious of some pain, he began walking towards them, finding himself amid a thick forest. When he stumbled upon an almost circular glade, he halted in the ring of trees on the verge. A mystical awe came upon him. He knew that he was in the presence of the supernatural.

Many people were gathered about a grassy knoll on which stood a woman with gold skin clad in a short tunic and a long tiered dress. Her breasts and navel were exposed. She was a sorceress bringing back to life a dead heiress in order to decide a question of inheritance. She was holding a pair of scales in her right hand the pans of which were dusty. At this point it was only her figure that was now clear to him. The other shapes were dim as if in shadow.

Yet all present, seen or unseen, were horrified at the thought of the dead rising. He was not. Suddenly this scene was replaced by one in which the background was just as vague, perhaps that of an old tropical town in Mexico, and the golden sorceress was replaced by her sister clad in silver and completely draped.

Again, although everyone else present was terrified, he, though in awe, was minded to go forward and present the Beast's head to the sorceress. As he proffered it with bent head, the figure she was leading on a cord stretched forth a long hand and took it from him. Beneath in the flowings of her robe he noticed for an instant the bared fangs of a black dog.

The silver-clad one said: 'For this offering take a virtue given as long as you shall do service, until She Who Is Chosen dismisses you.'

She and the gathering vanished.

He was part way up a gentle rise which grew steeper to his right. The sky had darkened and a storm was blowing up. On the left came a huntsman riding whose face was completely hidden in his hood. Running alongside was a forester leading a great stag which frothed at the lips, obviously near exhaustion. It was pursued by a most evil-looking small creature somewhat resembling a stoat with a long narrow sharply-pointed snout, brindled yellowish pelt and a barred tail, also pointed. Without changing his stance, the man could see the four move past behind him to the top of the rise on his left, where they halted. The mounted one nodded without looking round, whereupon the forester cut the stag's throat right out, and, to make sure, brought down his heavy blade on the creature's neck just where the spine joins the skull.

The evil stoat-like creature glanced once at the man who killed the boar. In that moment it was called to order by a single word from the huntsman and dropped its gaze again.

The three with their victim went on their way.

The man who had no name went on his way, coming to the edge of a great deciduous forest in the bright golden-green of early Spring. As he walked animals in their hundreds emerged from the thickets, every kind, from black jaguars to goats, a streaming host from every grove and copse, all going into the depths of the great forest. He followed.

Again he saw a figure in a glade with a lion between her knees, surrounded by eager animals. She was looking down at her meinie, but when she raised her head, she gave the man a glance and smiled. It was Siobhan, transfigured. She rose and turned away, the beasts following, while in his head he heard her singing as she went out of earshot:

> *After her came fawning wolves,*
> *Bright-eyed lions and bears,*
> *Fleet leopards ravenous for deer . . .*

He stood gazing while the creatures of the forest still streamed around him, all seeking the Goddess until at length the scene grew still again.

Again he was on the bare floor of the cave, but not the same man as he had been when first he entered it. He could not remember his surname. In any case, he must now take the name of the Beast when he could find it out. Before him he discerned a dim figure, hardly to be made out, black on black. He rose and offered back the sword, presenting the hilt. As it slipped gently from his grasp, he bowed, but the other had gone, whispering a single word in parting, 'Coll'.

After a while he went under the pool back to the main cavern without the slightest difficulty or hesitation.

The cavern entrance exploded on his vision like nuclear fire, and he withdrew with burning after-images of the cave's mouth searing his brain. Two or three days of almost complete darkness sensitize the eyes wonderfully, he thought.

He had to accustom himself to the light again as the deep-sea diver comes up in slow stages to avoid the bends. When the time came for him to walk to the entrance and look out upon the scene, he saw nothing but a flood of liquid light. Later he saw that it was not only the incandescent sun that whited out the colour; there were also vestiges of snow or frost in the dark winter furrows. Lean and desolate was the landscape that he had left in the tints of summer.

He felt bodiless and full-spirited as he took the slope in record time and strode towards the house oblivious of feet wounded by the thrusts of stubble and sharp stones, the frigid winter air invading his skin and exposure in broad daylight.

Blake, cup of tea in hand, was on the phone when the naked apparition walked in. He dropped everything and crossed himself.

'Don't worry about anything,' said Coll. 'If anyone bothers us I'll break his neck. I see you've got a cup of tea ready. That'll do to start with.'

Chapter 19

'Cults – the Hidden Valley – what was it you said? – the something Circle? There are no hidden valleys left in this land, I'm afraid.'

'It was the information I had –'

'Quite. You were quoting or citing –'

'Citing?'

'– some passage or another. My dear man, what in this land is there that has not at some time been rased, ploughed over, apparently obliterated? Who among us has not been beaten down or killed? That is our history. You do not know us.'

'Naturally. That is why I am here. My foundation is a friend of Ireland, which has contributed so richly to our own country.'

The Bishop stirred through the papers in his tray and finally produced a letter which he carefully read through again.

'Oh, I know what confused me. You don't speak like an American, if I may say so.'

His visitor had a pleasant smile ready. 'I was born in East Prussia, but my family managed to escape, with the infant in arms – that's me – to the west before sea transport was cut off, in April 1945, I believe. Fortunately my father was a local government official, so he was able to get ahead of the thousands of refugees camped out at the dockside.'

The Bishop nodded. 'And something else I find unusual: this Maxima Foundation you represent. I have never heard of it. My secretary couldn't get any information about it from your Embassy.'

His visitor's smile broadened as though nothing could have given him greater pleasure than to expound upon the Maxima Foundation.

'The Maxima Foundation is an old one and a well-known one in the United States. Although it does not have the international fame of – of the Ford Foundation, or, let's say, the Smithsonian, it resembles the latter in that it was founded upon a bequest, the gift of John Calvin Frost, a successful small arms manufacturer who became very wealthy in the course of the Civil War. Frost, a noted philanthropist, wished to devote his wealth to advance the interests of mankind. As a matter of fact, we have a great many corporate sponsors, some of the biggest names in the United States. I am proud to be the representative, however minor, of this wonderful organization. You, Sir, know only too well the immense satisfaction of working for all mankind. I am privileged to be able to contribute my part to the understanding of all peoples.'

'Indeed. You interest me. What are the purposes of the Foundation? Theology and small arms seem strange bedfellows.'

'Well, anthropology as well as theology.'

'All right. *Anthros*, not *theos*.'

The visitor, a tall sallow man with lean shoulders like a wooden coat hanger, caught the thrust uncertainly.

'The purpose of the Foundation is to promote awareness of human values through a knowledge of their origin and development based on comparative anthropology and religion, in order to promote the moulding of present and future human generations in the positive ethics of understanding one another in a framework of essential human and divine values. I am on a field work assignment.'

The Bishop sat back in his chair and laughed a little. 'What do you mean by "moulding"?'

'By giving guidance – based on research carried out in many parts of the world, Ireland included, by dedicated individuals supported by the Foundation. Although an old and very well-established body, we tend to avoid the limelight. It is better, sometimes, to do good by stealth, as I'm sure you're aware, Sir.'

'Well! That certainly covers everything! Now if you, Mr –,' the Bishop glanced at the letter again, '– Mr Luger should be so fortunate as to accumulate a large personal fortune and wish to use your wealth to establish a philanthropic foundation, what would be the terms of your project?'

Mr Luger looked puzzled. 'Aren't we a little off the track?'

'Are we? Still, indulge a man who is older than yourself and out of touch with what is happening in the bright young minds of today.'

The American thought. He had supposed the whole interview to be a mere formality. The old man had stopped being so charmingly archaic. He was no fool.

'What I would do. Well –' He hesitated.

'Here you are, someone who has done work, presumably distinguished, perhaps outstanding, in his own field in order for him to obtain the assistance of a – "long-established", I think you said – foundation, someone, therefore, who must have fairly definite ideas of where good research money should be spent.'

'What better object than to advance our understanding of human values?'

'Oh, none at all.' The Bishop paused and weighed the man's answers. 'However, that is a little vague, isn't it? How would you interpret that if it was your decision as to which of the many applications for assistance the Foundation must receive to entertain? You see my point? Your trustees must have a rudder to find some direction in this ocean of good intentions embraced by the phrase "human values". How are the terms limited? What is the scope? How is this big blob word actually to be applied?'

'Naturally the Maxima Foundation . . .'

'"Values" is one of the cant words of the day.'

'Cant –?'

'Ah, you didn't major in English. Let us say, the harping phrases of professional piety, jargon, perhaps.'

'Yes, well, there's a jargon for every line of work.'

The Bishop sighed. You have read Frazer? Author of *The Golden Bough*, one of my favourite works when I was young. I believe I got through the condensed version while I was still in the fifth form.'

'I don't think I've read that one.'

'Frazer is out of business now, I see. Not even heard of. Never mind. Dr Margaret Meade died not so very long ago. You must be acquainted with her – no? Well, there you are. I'm just hopelessly out-of-date. What are the up and coming minds in anthropology today? I'll have to catch up on my reading.'

Mr Luger thought furiously. 'Well, there's – I can see it, a big blue book, just can't think – Benton is the name, I think.'

'And what has he published?'

Mr Luger was out of his spiel.

'Still can't remember the exact name – it's out in paperback – something about – *Everything You Need to Know in Micro-Management*, I think.'

'So? And he's an *anthropologist*? Come, come, Mr Luger, you are jesting with me.'

'Wait, I know! There's Philip Samson, the man that's done such great work on the genetic differences between racial types. He's a Canadian, lives in Toronto, got some help from the Foundation. I believe I ran into him once. If I could just remember the exact name . . .'

'Interesting. And some of the others?'

Mr Luger thought. Nothing came to mind. There was a dreadfully long pause.

'By the way, what help is it that I can give you?'

Mr Luger's relief was palpable.

'Great! Well, I wanted to do some first-hand reporting on local beliefs and current values and I thought I would approach the different priests in your diocese. It would be a big hand up if you could give me some kind of authority, on paper, approving my work and asking them to cooperate. Not that they wouldn't, I'm sure'

'From me? But why should you need my recommendation?'

'It would help us interface.'

'I haven't heard that word before.'

'Well, you know, a letter from you would oil the wheels -'

'Oh, you mean that my formal endorsement of your activities would produce results for you.'

'Yes, of course. It's always a great morale booster if people know that their supervisors support their efforts.'

'But it's quite unnecessary. As far as I know, the fathers' morale doesn't need any boosting by me just now. You can talk to anybody you like. Doesn't concern me. Just tell them who you are and I'm sure you'll be very well received. They'll be glad to help you. Well, I fear that I have other people to see.'

Mr Luger remained seated. 'Sir, I'd take it as a favour if you'd give me something approving of the Foundation's work to help me along, and I'm sure the Foundation would take it as a favour. I know they would. They wouldn't forget about it. Might do you a good turn one day. It's a good idea to have them on your side, Sir.'

'Indeed. I'm sorry, Mr Luger, but my priests must have a free conscience in this matter. By the way, what's your university. I see you have an M.A. and an M.Sc.'

'The University of Niagara Falls, New York.'

'Ah, yes, I'm sure I ought to have heard of it.'

He picked up a crystal bell and shook it. His secretary appeared almost in the same moment.

'Would you show Mr Luger out? He's a very busy man, as I am, sometimes. And before you ask the sisters in could you take down something for me?'

After these matters had been taken care of, the Bishop studied the letter before him. He was amazed at the sheer ineptitude of the device.

What were the motives of his employers? He was not an investigative reporter interested in the current localized hysteria reported from several sites in Ireland. Why the big lie? Why such a silly subterfuge? Had he expected his path to have been prepared and his anointing to be a polite matter of form? What was he – or they – really after?'

When next his secretary came in he was no longer preoccupied.

Round Ireland, especially towards the west, the church was disconcerted by a renewal of the summer's hysteria. It was not only that statues moved, even came down from the pedestal, but, in one case, the Blessed Virgin Mary appeared in Her own Person to some children near Letterkenny. Publicly the church welcomed, non-committally, this renewal of faith. Privately the hierarchy hoped that the winter would put an end to these manifestations of religious mania beyond the church's control, and by the beginning of November they had died down, much to the relief of an ecclesiastical commission investigating them.

The respite was brief. A cottage on Aran suddenly became a popular shrine because, it was said, the Blessed Virgin Herself had entered it with Her Divine Child on Christmas Eve. Her image was rendered by a competent sculptor who could make little of what those who had seen the Holy Mother could tell him. At the darkest time of the year a rout of pilgrims rushed to the island. When the local boatman refused to risk lives in bad weather, a helicopter service was instituted for those who could afford it.

After that the Blessed Virgin did not reappear until high summer.

Long before that, within a week of the unwelcome visit of the American, the Bishop had received a letter passed on down the long chain of pastoral command, reaching all the way back to Rome, relying on those who beheld it to provide all possible help to properly accredited research scholars of the Maxima Foundation.

Chapter 20

Since Coll had no idea of where he was going, every evening's halt was a novelty to him. This one was Athlone. Like many Irish cities, Athlone was dull and grey, sunk in a landscape with no scenic character to compensate for its own lack of positive qualities. It is an inland nonentity which neither hopes nor despairs, as if its function is to be forever the neutral centre of a slowly-turning Ireland.

A small dull-green car in need of a paint job stopped at one of the uniform slate houses and two men got out. There was an undertone of last reminders. Then the driver got back in while his passenger unlatched the gate. The front door opened and a hand from within waved the driver off. He lost no time in speeding away.

Susan McGuire embraced the stranger.

'I'm so glad to see you. Did Michael tell you? I can only put you up for one night, for my sister comes back tomorrow. She's not one of us.'

'It's fine. Don't go to any trouble. No need to disturb anything. I can sleep on the floor.'

'No, dear. You'll never do that in my house. Your room's up these stairs.'

She preceded him, opening the door of a good-sized airy bedroom looking out over the front garden. He had an excellent view of the street below.

'Do you want to rest now, or will you eat?'

'Wash, I think. A bath would be great. I feel filthy.'

'Here, along the hall. I'll show you how to work the ascot. Then when you're ready I'll get some ham and eggs to your tea. Where are you headed tomorrow?'

'Don't know yet. Do you, by any chance, know what is said between two serpents?'

'What a question! Is it a riddle?'

'It's a puzzle, a clue, let us say.'

'I'll ask my neighbour. She's a dab hand at crosswords, you know, the hard ones.'

'No, better not.'

In spite of his hostess' obvious interest in him and her attempts to keep him downstairs talking, Coll went straight up to his room after tea. He examined every part of it before turning in very early.

With a sigh Susan went back into her kitchen. The anticipated magic of the afternoon which had so briefly flowered passed, she thought wryly. What had the poet Blake said? To possess something is to destroy it. Something like that. She had attempted to possess him and he had withdrawn himself.

Coll was up early, just before five. He tended to make a lot of noise in the bath. Wise in the ways of guests, Susan got up, paid particular attention to her hair, and made herself attractive. She was barely past thirty. She opened the bathroom door unnecessarily, hoping to catch him just out of the bath, but he was in the dressing-gown he had found in the wardrobe and seemed so lost in thought that he did not notice the rush of air at first, until he saw her standing there. She kissed him.

'What will you take to your breakfast? Coffee, lean bacon and eggs, and toast? Or would you like something else first?'

He met her eyes. 'Michael will be here soon.'

'He can wait.'

Less than thirty minutes later he came into the dining room and drank strong dark tea while he waited for his food. When it came, he devoured it and asked for more. His appetite had grown mightily since his sojourn on Blake's property.

'I've been thinking about your riddle,' said Susan, 'and all I can come up with is that there *are* no snakes in Ireland.'

Coll grunted.

At eight Michael came. Pulling his few possessions together, Coll left with a hurried word of thanks to Susan. 'Better luck next time.' She had expected something more, but disappointment was in her creed.

'Where to now?' demanded Coll.

'We're going to lose you in Dublin for a while. I'll just drive a bit out of town and we'll have a peep at the map. Pleasant woman, Mrs McGuire.'

'Oh, very pleasant. She wanted me to stay longer I think.'

'Did she, now? You made friends with her, did you?'

'We're all friends – more than friends, I thought.'

'And was she more than a friend?'

'She was most accommodating, loving and generous, in whatever order you like.'

'I'll bet. Well, she knows the ropes right enough, but her sister's liable to turn up at any time. It's best to tell her as little as possible. Rule one in security is never to tell anyone more than they need to know. You Americans are very careless.'

'Oh, Susan's all right. Besides, what do I know?'

'You know far more than is good for us. I don't agree with Siobhan on this. I know Susan is all right, but she's in danger just like the rest of us, and whatever a body knows can be screwed out of him by experts in inflicting physical and psychological hell. That's the other kind of world we live in, and it's just across the road.'

'Yes, I expect she is in danger. By the way. I'm not an American.'

'No? What are you then?'

'I was born and brought up in Canada, but I no longer know what, or even *who* I am.'

'Ah well, it's close.'

Long before twelve they went down a narrow side road and pulled off on a track going into a field. Here, hidden from view behind trees, Michael produced sandwiches and a flask of coffee.

'May as well take a nap. We'll be here for hours.'

'Why?'

'No use in getting there too early. Better to mingle with the rush hour traffic and arrive in the evening.'

'How far away are we?'

'You're still used to Canada. Ireland's just a tiny place. Belfast to Dublin is an easy three hour drive. We're about half-an-hour from the outskirts.'

Coll was inclined to be taciturn and Michael dozed off.

When they moved again under a darkening sky of late winter, traffic had picked up and they merged into the anonymous rush.

Michael dropped Coll off at a pleasant suburban house with a large garden.

'How long will you be here?'

'Don't know.'

'Better not stay more than two or three nights. Keep out of sight in the daytime. Mrs Anstell will be looking after you while you're here. If you attract trouble make sure it doesn't feed back to her.'

'I know that.'

'Just making sure. You'll like Mrs Anstell – she resembles you a little:

tough, prickly, mysterious and strange at times. You'll understand each other. But you won't find her as friendly – or should I say accommodating? – as Susan.'

It was nearly eight o'clock when Coll crossed the narrow parking space set between the imposing garden of the large house and a row of rented garages. The front door was old, wide and painted a shiny black. He rapped smartly with the brass knocker. After a while a pale girl of eighteen or nineteen answered the door.

'We're full up,' she said.

'That's all right. Just let me in. I have to see Mrs Anstell. She's expecting me.'

'She's upstairs resting.'

'I'll wait.'

'Well, I don't know. You've got your luggage with you. When Mrs Anstell says she's full up she means it.'

'Look, she's expecting me. Can you give her a message from me?'

'Sure, if she's up. What is it?'

He thought. He couldn't entrust anything to this girl. She saw his hesitation and made as if to close the door.

'No, don't. Tell her that I bring a message from Athlone and further west, a message from friends.'

She looked at him doubtfully.

'Look, do I have to stand out here. Couldn't I wait inside?'

'Very well, then, but please stay in the hall. Mrs Anstell is very particular.'

After about ten minutes Coll began to get impatient. Entrance to the living room on the left was blocked by a closed door with bevelled glass panes; green curtains were tied back allowing him to see that the room was full of heavy furniture; the walls were covered with many small drawings or photographs. There was a short hallway leading to another room on the right. Its solid oak door was shut. Ahead the stairs right-angled away from the front door just before they reached the landing, itself protected by a box-like case. 'Like a small fort,' he thought. Evidently the house had been enlarged and remodelled.

Then as he yawned and turned to face the living room again, there she was, behind the panes observing him. The door opened and she emerged. She could have been in her late thirties, but he would not have been surprised to learn that she was fifty. She was slender and a little below medium height. Her thin face was hard to read. Her eyes were the palest blue, exactly right for her pallor. 'So that is what they mean by grey eyes,' he thought. Oddly, they were too widely spaced for her narrow face.

She waited for him to begin.

'Hello –' he ventured.

'Well?' she demanded.

'Michael dropped me off. I –'

'Tell me something important.'

'Important?' he groped. Then he caught on. 'What is said between two serpents?'

She gestured impatiently. 'Is that all you have to say?'

He thought. She gazed into his eyes. He closed them.

'I offered up the boar's head and its spirit entered into me. It will abide until I have completed my task. I saw the dark huntsman and the Lady of the Beasts. She glanced at me and I recognized her.'

'That's better. Now I know you, and long have I waited for the moment of your coming. Come with me.'

She insisted that he precede her upstairs. From the upper landing they turned right along the hallway to the back of the house, to a small room on the left. Coll was surprised by the large expanse of garden whose rear boundary was defined by tall Lombardy poplars tinted Martian in the ambience of the street sodium lights and Dublin's vapour-laden atmosphere.

'Do sit down. You are to stay here for a time.'

'Michael advised only two or three days.'

'He's not sure they've lost you. I think they have. So you'll be here for some little time.'

'What makes you think they're off my track?'

'I *know*. Michael is merely following his instructions.'

'Your young lady knows I'm here.'

'Cybele? Don't worry about that. She knows better than to breathe a word of who comes and goes. You can trust her in all ordinary matters. She is one of us.'

'I think I understand some of my experiences, but not the death of the stag.'

'Describe, please.'

As he related the course of his ordeal in the cave she nodded from time to time as if each successive episode fitted an ancient story of her own.

'The divination given to you to fit you for your task was proleptical. The real battles are to come. The death of the stag means that not only will the spirit of the boar be translated out of you, but also that some other expiatory sacrifice will be demanded of you. It is better not to ponder these things. What they portend will come and in that time you will not take such great notice of what is happening in the course of your struggles. It is part of the *me* of the Goddess.'

'The *me*?'

'An old word for an old thing. For now you must excel in cunning and lies, be wary of anyone not in the Circle and ruthless in using your brute strength. When you come upon the enemy, strike so that he shall not rise again. Those are the powers you have been given.'

'My dream – vision – was a warning then?'

'Of course. All visions are warnings, whatever else they may be. What was yours?'

'When I saw all the animals streaming together, unheeding of each other, to follow the Goddess I was aware that I was not to go with them. I felt that if I did I should be as one of them, treated as one of them.'

'Like Adonis, eh?'

'Perhaps.'

'It was not for you to merge with them. You must now assume the guise that suits your purpose, when that is made clear to you. You have been reborn, given the power and fury of a boar, in addition to any other gifts. Do you know your own strength?'

'Funny you mention it. A doorknob came off in my hand a few days ago, just before I left Blake.'

She got up and rummaged about in the window-seat, coming back with a solid hard plastic bouncing ball about three inches in diameter. 'Here,' she said, throwing it to him, 'see what you can do with that. Can you tear it into two?'

He caught it. The material was sadly flawed; before he had begun to exert much effort the thing practically came apart in his hands.

'Very good. Even better than I thought.'

'There's something wrong with this stuff. It's deteriorated.'

She took one of the pieces from him and tried to tear it. She managed to peel a single minute fragment from the rough edge where it had been torn apart. She shook her head and looked at him. 'Have you noticed any change in your appearance within the last week or so?' She placed a hand on his shoulder over the coarse woollen pullover he was wearing. 'Were you always this big? Your shoulders are what the ad man would call massive. You have a remarkably heavy bone structure.'

'Well, all my clothes are new as I lost my old ones at Blake's, but I think I've put on some weight.'

'And you probably thought it was fat – after your long lean ordeal in the Cavern of Queen Maeve? With those thick legs and long trunk you'll never win a race, but that muscle is on an unusually solid frame of bone. I'd say you've put on a lot of bone. A *lot*. And, if you'll excuse me, if you start exercising now you can add some more of the muscle it was designed for. You'll soon be able to punch out a heavy door, like Chaucer's Miller – and you'll smash your hands. Let me see.'

She left the room and came back with a set of brass knuckles. 'Isn't it amazing what some people leave behind them? These will have to do for now until we can let you out. But take care of your hands. We can't afford to have you smash your fingers or break your wrist. I think I'll call Pat Clune. He'll give you some training. He's one of us, but don't tell him too much. Ah, he's up in Galway. I'll make sure he's here tomorrow. However, we mustn't forget the important things. Tomorrow you start learning your Beth-Luis-Nion, for you must know how to talk to us and understand us. And that will take more than three days, poor Michael, bless him.'

It did. He was to be in Mrs Anstell's house much longer than the two or three days Michael had anticipated. For nearly a fortnight he trained in the cellar, mainly on the weights Pat obtained. Even Clune was shocked by the results. On his back Coll could pump 2700 lbs with ease.

'They used to build 'em solid in the old days,' observed the pupil.

'The old days? What do you mean?'

'Just a rhyme. I can't remember the rest.'

'One thing you won't have to worry about is getting into a fight, you great clueless lump of brawn.'

Coll grinned. He liked Pat and the two traded good-humoured insults for hours at a time.

'I probably won't even catch on to the fact that it's started.'

At the end of the fortnight Mrs Anstell thanked Pat.

'You can't stop us now,' he boiled.

'Sorry. We may have less time than we thought. Just leave him a note of what he's supposed to do.'

'We were only just beginning,' pleaded Coll later on.

'I know. Pat's an enthusiast. It will be hard enough for him to keep his mouth shut as it is. You carry on training by yourself – now that you know what to do, keep doing it. You'll be needed soon enough. What do you make of this?' She handed Coll a sheet of notepaper that exuded a faint perfume of sweet pine. On it were four straight lines carrying sloping or vertical strokes in groups. Sometimes the strokes crossed the line, sometimes not.

'Where did this come from?'

'Surely you can guess.'

'Siobhan.'

She nodded. 'Indeed, I gather that you know something about this.'

He shook his head but clung to the paper.

'Didn't you give her something that contained this message?'

'Of course. The bible. But I went through it. I don't see how I could possibly have missed this stuff.'

'She and her friends went through it page by page, sorted these little marks out and grouped them according to the versicle numbers they were at. They were, I believe, made in invisible ink.'

'Invisible ink! Come on, how could the man conceal invisible ink?'

'All you need is a lemon. If you have an ordinary pin, slightly modified, you need not even cut into it or leave any obviously visible marks on it. It's a child's trick. Do you want to know what it means? I think Siobhan is hinting that we should get on with our studies. These marks are a way of writing the Beth-Luis-Nion. Let us work them out together.'

They sat down. Coll spread the page.

'Ah, we begin with a group of four vertical strokes above the line. That is *Coll*, followed by a single vertical stroke crossing the line, *Ailm*, but surely the man knew that you could not possibly read this?'

'No, he left an outside message, I guess you would call it, in clear English. It was this message that brought me to Ireland. Without my being aware of it, he gave me the one Ogham letter, *Onn*, which would help me get into touch with the Circle.'

'A clever man, indeed! Well, here is the first line – *Caer Sidi*. I'm sure you know *Caer* by now.'

'Castle, isn't it? *Sidi*?'

'Originally *Aes Sidhe*, I fancy. *The Castle of the Magicians* – does that mean anything to you? Did he ever mention a castle?'

'No, he talked about trees – a forest under looming clouds with the moon breaking through, and the figure of a man hanging from a single tree.'

Mrs Anstell drew back. For the first time Coll saw that she was not above fear. Her face went a little whiter.

'But a moon riding in the sky. That is something at least. May the Great Goddess protect you, Coll. But why Ireland, why the Circle? Oh Coll, there are many other things that you do not know, nor I either. He sends you to us in all your ignorance. This a deep matter for the Circle, too. I hope that it may not be a dark one. But who can guess at his purposes. Describe him.'

Coll did so.

Mrs Anstell put her face in her hands. 'Yes, indeed, but there was no doubt before.'

'Well, who is he?'

'Someone who intends that you and he shall meet again. Be wary. Always take Siobhan's advice, for she knows the exalted ones. That is all I can tell you. But I am deeply troubled. Let us look at the other three lines. *The Castle of Children* – that help?'

Coll shook his head. 'No. Wait a moment, though. Yes, he left a slip of paper in my pocket saying that I should find something opposite a castle where the children could enter.'

'All right. Now the next is *Godless Belvedere*.'

'What's the meaning of "belvedere"?'

'A belvedere was a kind of lookout tower, often set into the wall of a house or a garden wall whence the occupants could see what was happening in the street below without themselves being observed. Later on they came to be known as gazebos.'

'Then why "godless"?'

'Perhaps this last line makes it all clear. Ah, and it does. *AIN knows*. Who is AIN?'

'I haven't the faintest idea.'

'Well, it's someone we are bound to know. It would have been silly to put anything else, wouldn't it? And the – man – who sent this message was not silly. When you were still in Toronto you didn't know anyone in Ireland, did you?'

'No, of course not.'

'Then who is AIN? Your man – what was his name?'

'Victor.'

'Victor referred to someone certain to be known to whoever deciphered this inside message. And that leaves only one possibility, doesn't it?'

'I can't think.'

'Of course you can. It will hit you soon enough. You weren't Coll the Boar then, were you? What were you before?'

'My name was Ywain.'

'Why do you want to avoid the answer, Ywain? Is my fear catching? You knew that AIN was none other than yourself as soon as I mentioned those letters.'

'Because I don't know anything. How can I?'

'Well, but perhaps this is another case of you knowing something without knowing it, so to speak. What was your message?"

'What is said between serpents in the emerald isle – that's why I'm here.'

'What have you thought that might mean?'

'I can't make head or tail of it.'

'Well, here is a map of Ireland. Go away, look at the map and think. Victor gave you something you could dig out on your own, if, indeed he has not already arranged some apparently serendipitous discovery at the fated point in your life, your life in Ireland. I'll put on my thinking cap too. Let's talk about it again in the morning. And, incidentally, you are AIN because, as you should know by now, there is no *Y* or *W* in the Beth-luis-Nion. You know that much yourself. Now do start figuring out what it is you do know.'

But try as he might, his brain simply refused to function that night. It could not get hold of anything to start on, and he now wished more than ever that he could see Siobhan again. She would have been able to work it out, he thought, if anybody could. An impulse to throw off the yoke of Mrs Anstell passed over him like a wave, but the urge soon vanished.

Chapter 21

He got up early after a dreamless sleep, tired behind the eyes, desperate for a cup of tea or coffee. Not even Cybele was stirring. He didn't feel like staring at the map and no revelatory serpents uncoiled their delitescent enigma. There were no books on Ireland in his room that might provide a clue but it occurred to him that he could do worse than skim through a few guides looking for a pointer. With this in mind, he went downstairs as quietly as he could, to the living room where he remembered seeing several shelves of books. He was going through these when he heard Cybele come in.

'What are you doing down so early? It's not six yet.'

'Looking for something I can't find.'

'I'll help you if I can.'

He turned to look at her. She didn't look so milky pale as he remembered her in the late evening. She was one of them and wanted to help him.

'I was just trying to find some kind of guide book – looking for a place I don't know the name of.'

'Hm. Sounds as if you have a long search ahead of you. I have to get on with my work now, but when I've got time I'll come and help you, if I may. There's nothing much here. I'll look around for you. I know where most things are. In a few minutes I'll have some coffee ready if you want it.'

'I'd love it.'

He went back upstairs, bathed, shaved and dressed and went down again. He wasn't at all sure about confiding in Cybele. She was to be trusted, Mrs Anstell had said, but only in all ordinary things. Hell, it was only a guide book.

She brought a cup of coffee to him in the living room as he was scanning the map, north to south, east to west, trying to read out of it anything vaguely relevant.

'Here you are. Not having much luck? Shall I give you some? I'm not much good at research, but I'm not at all bad at passing on luck.' She had a delightful little giggle.

He told her he was going to wander out and clear his head, as he thought a short walk wouldn't really matter, but Cybele shook her head. So he went back upstairs, picked one of Mrs Anstell's ancient paperbacks off the shelf above his head, hardly glancing at the title, and threw himself down. 'Orders of Chivalry and Vows' was the chapter he happened to come upon as he opened the book. The title drew him; he scanned the pages, apparently at random. One passage in particular held his eye: *There was not a prince or great noble who did not desire to have his own order . . . The chain of Pierre de Lusignan's sword order was made of gold S's, which meant 'silence'*. It was something about the repeated letter *S* and the sibilant sound which reminded him of snakes, and even though while he had often run across the harmless garter snakes at home in Canada, he had never heard one hiss, yet it was this hissing that brought the image of snakes to him. The thing burst upon him. He suddenly saw it. Two snakes speaking to each other: he saw the printed page. He saw what was being said between two serpents. He was marvelling at his own lack of comprehension, but no, it was not something to be understood, was it? It was something to be seen, just as Siobhan had said. It was at that moment that Cybele tapped at the door.

'I haven't started yet because you haven't really told me what you're looking for. Give me a hint at least and I'll do my best to think of something.'

'Is there any place in Ireland called "Swords"?'

'Swords? I should think so, indeed. It's not far from here, and you've been there. That's where you landed – at Dublin's international airport.'

'The snakes,' he blurted out involuntarily.

She smiled and undulated her body. 'Like this?'

He looked at her, envisaging a great gold chain of intertwined snakes encircling her bare neck and dipping for warmth into the gentle shelter between her breasts as shallow as two little rocks, sunning themselves on a clear Fall day in the Shield country amid the Muskoka lakes. She became part of the memorable vision. He drew her to him. 'Like that,' he said.

'Ah,' she said, disengaging herself, 'and what have snakes got to do with Swords?'

'Perhaps they say interesting things to each other there.'

'Security's still tight, eh? Well, perhaps Esmirone will tell me.'

'Mrs Anstell?'

'Yes. At least I'm on first-name terms with her.'

'Meet Coll, Alpha and Omega, first and last and everything in between. What's your job then?'

'Looking out for blabbermouths.'

He grinned. 'You win, Molly.'

'Ah! Don't you call me Molly, you trog, or you'll need more than mollying when I've done with you. Why do you call yourself Coll? You sound like a high street butcher.'

'Doesn't it. But it was not my choice.'

'Whose, then?'

'Coll gave it to me when I killed him.'

She took a step towards him and looked into his eyes. 'On the level?'

'Oh yes.'

'Perhaps I'll have to take you more seriously then. But no, you're never a killer. I've met killers. They're all quite different from you – no sense of humour at all.'

'We don't choose our rôles, though, do we? What's yours I wonder.'

'Well, wonder on. You don't tell and I don't tell.'

'Would you be able to kill if you had to?'

'I knew you would ask that, and I'll bet you know the answer. If I had to, yes. Yet I'm everything of a woman, I believe. Coll, there's no woman, not even if she's an angel of grace, who wouldn't kill to protect her nest, and do it with less havering than any man. And what you and I have to protect is just that. So why do you bother to ask the question? Just to see what kind of a rise you can get out of me. You're not a killer. You're just as much of a softy as I am, but your job is essentially the same as mine, to protect. If the moment comes we'll neither of us have any time to reflect on the deep casuistry of human nature.'

'Pity I'm confined to quarters, otherwise I'd ask you out for the evening.'

'The time may come, Coll – oh, I have to find another name for you – and we'll see then. But if you're just hoping for a fling between the sheets, forget it. I need more from a man than that, so think on it. And now I'd better get back on the job, or I'll need protecting myself, from Esmirone.'

Left to himself, Coll considered what to do. He had to get to Swords and see if he could puzzle out the other clues. He went down into the kitchen to find Cybele.

'Are you any good at crosswords, Cybele?'

'I'm not good at them, but I sometimes try the one in the *Independent*. Have you got one for me to work out?'

'What does the clue "godless belvedere" come out as?'

'Sounds pretty simple. "Bel" was an ancient god. That leaves us with "vedere", which doesn't make sense on its own. It might be an anagram, "revered" for example. But, no, there's only one "r". I can't think of anything more just now, but I'll try it with a pencil and paper a bit later. Got any others?'

'I have a reference to a Castle of Magicians and a Castle of Children.'

'They might be literary allusions, but they don't ring a bell for me. I'll think about them though.'

'Can you think fast? I'm off to Swords.'

'Oh, that doesn't sound like a good idea. What does Esmirone say?'

'I haven't seen her this morning yet.'

'Well, she's the one who decides, so you'd better ask her.'

'When does she get up?'

'Stays in her room all morning sometimes.'

'To hell with that!'

'Coll, you're not going without her leave.'

'You're telling me?'

'I'm sorry, Coll, to put it so bluntly, but you are so impetuous. Yes, I'm in charge when Esmirone's not available, and so I'm telling you.'

'That's news to me. I'll go up and see Mrs Anstell.'

She walked over to him. 'When Esmirone is in her room, she's not available, Coll. You'll have to take no for an answer.'

'O.K., tell her where I've gone when she comes down.'

'Don't go through that door, Coll.'

He turned. She had a machine pistol. She was very serious.

'You wouldn't use that.'

'Coll, please believe me, I would, and I will if you attempt to go through that door, even so much as to leave the kitchen. A short time ago you asked me what my rôle was, and I told you: my rôle is to protect. You mayn't have taken my words seriously. I am the protector of this house, this tiny flower patch of the Circle. And, sadly, I have to protect it from you, from your heroic impulses, these pointless little fits of mad recklessness that men need to assume. These things have their place, but not here, not now. I could love you, Coll. You're a man, not one of the imitations I see everywhere. But I would kill my own child to protect this house, gladly kill, so think on it. No, don't move towards me. I'll have to disable you, and how are we to get in medical help for you? Before you act in any way think of the consequences, man. We'll tell you when it's safe to leave. You've been sent here by the Circle and you're under Esmirone's orders, mine in her absence.'

'Call her down.'

'No, Coll. This is not an emergency. Now sit down there away from the door where I can keep an eye on you. I don't want to lock you in the cellar. So stop being so – uncivilized. What is it about you men? Don't you see how difficult it is for me? How do you think I'll feel if I shoot you? Don't you have any regard for the feelings of your friends? Upstairs you want to make love to me. Downstairs you want to make me your murderess. It's not fair and very wrong of you.'

'I'm sorry, Cybele. I thought I was doing the right thing. I thought I would do the best I could . . .'

'No you didn't. You never think. What's wrong with you? You act like some one-dimensional character, a cowboy in a rotten little low-budget Hollywood film trying to bully your way through me. Were you never among sensitive, feeling people?'

'I suppose I met many of them when I was at varsity, but I never knew them, really. I don't think I even knew my own mother and sister well.'

'What a strange family yours must be. Coll, we are your family now. We love one another, and that means knowing one another. Promise me you won't leave this room until Esmirone comes down.'

'But how long is that going to take?'

'Does it occur to you that Esmirone might possibly be doing something important? You're not the only frog in the pool, you know. Get with it, Coll. Some of us are busy and right now you're more a burden than a help.'

'All right, I promise. I never meant to upset you, but how was I to know you'd react this way?'

'Something in that – but not much. Love me, Coll – no, not in that way just now, thanks – as I love you. I love you because you're as a brother to me, strong and protective. How would you feel if you had been made to shoot your own sister?'

'I'm wondering about that, wondering whether I'd feel anything like the pang if I shot you by mistake.'

'It's the same.' She laid the pistol down and gave him a kiss. 'Give me a kiss, too – just one is enough – to seal the little pact of love we have made. Now, don't forget: you're to stay here. I'm pulling rank on you, Coll, and those are my orders. Oh, I have to find another name for you. I simply can't face that one. You put me in mind of some fabulous heroics – I'll call you Byron.'

'Why Byron?'

'I don't know – the melting euphony, faintly French. He was the lovely lonely melancholy lord, a hard hitter and, like you, a bit of a pig sometimes. He was hard to handle.'

Chapter 22

'So I'M OFF TO HAVE A LOOK, FINALLY,' said Coll.

'Well, we have to balance your impatience to do something with the safety of the house. You should be all right. Michael will drive you in in the late afternoon. He'll drop you near the castle and tell you how and where you're to meet again. He's responsible for getting you there and back. You're responsible for coming back – and don't bring anything with you, understand? Get rid of any followers and get rid of them permanently. I don't think you'll be bothered, though. We've been through all this – the trick is to remain inconspicuous. Once again, do you know what you're looking for?'

'Not yet. But I think some things will add up if I find myself in the right spot. I'm glad Michael's along for the ride.'

'Yes, he's a good man, but remember that he's responsible only for the driving. It's not his job to play nursemaid, so stay out of trouble. And now there's just one other thing.'

Esmirone went over to the sideboard and unlocked one of the end doors. She reached in and chose from among several objects with deliberation and finally came back with a nice small automatic equipped with a squat unusually thick barrel housing. She checked the mechanism, looked into the breech to see if there was a perfectly uniform film of fresh oil, opened the butt, checked the cartridge clip and finally handed it to Coll.

'It's a lovely little Austrian job with the shortest silencer there is. Be careful with it. The ammunition is fresh.'

'I don't need that.'

'Oh yes you do. If you meet trouble we don't want any mess, thank you, and that means no marks of any sort on you. Get rid of the nuisance or nuisances without any sign of a struggle on your part. This is the safety catch. Keep it on, but don't forget to release it before you fire. When you've finished, reset and move off unobtrusively. I don't need to tell you again not to come back here or to implicate Michael if there's any chance that you're being followed. In that case you know what to do and where to go.'

Before shutting the front gate, Coll looked in all directions, then set off for the park where he was to meet Michael. Its grass was pale in the thin sunshine of March, its trees still brown skeletons. Outside for the first time in weeks, his heart lifted and his legs sang in their stride. He was intensely aware of an inner excitement at being set free in the open air, now certain in the promise of an enchanting future which included Siobhan. His exultant soul did not feed on the still-dormant natural beauty of the place. He would have been ecstatic in a January gale of driving sleet. He almost missed seeing Michael.

'Hello, beautiful dreamer,' Michael greeted him. 'As soon as you're fully awake we can get going.'

Spinning along the streets of close-packed houses, Coll felt a power in himself that he had never experienced in its fullness before. He had gathered together the strength of his ordeals and now knew instinctively that his new-found confidence in his natural abilities and brute physique would survive any further trials. He was now part of something, not, as in his earlier Canadian life, isolated from everything he was meant to be part of. And it wasn't long before they were in Swords, a community of top-hat brick-fronted houses interspersed with shops, very handy to the airport. The main street curved into a steep decline abruptly, so abruptly indeed that it seemed to end in a high wall which Michael was, apparently, determined to hit. And on that curve was the entrance to a pile of ruins long abandoned for any practical purpose, but nonetheless recognizably and undoubtedly a real castle. The sight riveted his gaze. Michael pulled over.

'Is this the main drag?' asked Coll.

'Shouldn't think so, but Esmirone thought that this was likely the spot that you were meant to explore, or whatever you're doing. A pub called The Gabriel is back along this street about half a mile, maybe. I'll be there from 2000 to 2300. Just walk in, get yourself a drink and sit down, ignoring me completely, of course. When I leave, you follow, not too obviously, O.K.? If there's anything I don't like, I won't leave. Then, after twenty minutes, you leave and stay away, understand? If you can, ambush and dispose of all the problems, but carry on with plan B – and that means you find your way to the safe house, staying completely away from Esmirone. Right, all the best.'

Coll got out and walked back up the steep slope. Wondering, he turned straight into the castle, avoiding numberless small boys chasing and fleeing in their games of mystery and concealment among the intricate passages, climbs and obstacles. Only when he was well inside among the youngsters did the conviction seize him that this was indeed a castle of the children. Was it also a castle of the magicians? The name 'Swords' was entirely fitting. As he glimpsed the word in block capitals on a newsagent's sign across the street almost exactly opposite the castle entrance, right on the curve, he experienced again an echo of revelation and laughed out loud in joy. How stupid he had been! It was so staringly obvious! Victor must have been inwardly grinning all over in spite of the terrible peril he was in. Or had he been in peril? That depended entirely on who he was: some in the Circle were in fear of him. More likely his keepers, ruthless and criminal as they were, had been more unwary than they knew. Did Victor revel in the gods' high mirth when they move the pawns on the board? St Patrick had not, after all, been able to chase all the snakes down to the last little twister out of Ireland.

And now what? He was here to look but not to linger. The children ignored him and the young mothers who came one by one calling out for their little boys gave him the merest glance. For all its backwardness in the eyes of other wealthier nations, Ireland had no need to street-proof its children against the pædophile predators so feared in any North American city. In spite of urgency and his own impatience, he stood there trying to enter into the character of the place: there was no incompatibility between the living archaic ruin teeming with young life, and the busy modern street, oh so much less alive, struggling in the sclerosis of its rush-hour traffic of dead mechanical vehicles. After a while it occurred to him, irrelevantly, that it was a long time since he had taken any interest in what was going on in the outside world, and thought he would go and get a paper. He went out of the castle, squeezed between the cars parked as close as books on a shelf and entered the newsagent's whose illuminated sign had again told him what was said between two serpents.

The shop was full and the morning papers were gone. He had no appetite for the tabloids and wandered out again, his curiosity aroused by the notice board pressed against the windowpane. Rooms to let, lessons given, articles and animals lost, found and for sale, services offered, sometimes ambiguous, help proffered, positions wanted, for housework, odd jobs and hauling, fortunes told (several of these) and a curious offer to provide traditional Irish music and poetry to the patrons of De Vere's Snuggery above the High Street. Visitors to Ireland who wished to experience the true atmosphere of her culture and history were particularly welcomed to hear in person one from the Castle of Bards and Magicians. Among all the notes and cards, this one, carefully handwritten like most of the others, stood out for its oddness and pretentiousness. It took him a minute or so to put his finger on the oddness, the mention of a Castle of Magicians. He noted the number. After all, why not? This is what he had come to do. At worst it would be a lighthearted entertainment. At best it might lead to something very much more. He felt like a lift. A drink wouldn't go down too badly either. His eyes flicked back to 'De Vere's' and he heard Cybele's voice saying that it was an anagram, but it couldn't be 'revered' because there was an extra *r*. Immediately he made his way back along the High Street in the direction of The Gabriel. There were many passers-by in a gentle controlled rush to get back to privacy, warmth and tea, a going and a coming out of shop doorways to pick up this and that delaying momentarily the culminating comfort of the day soft at home.

The number he was looking for was not to de found. Squeezed next to a small grocer's, a blank unnumbered door appeared to be the only possibility. This turned out to be the entrance to an elongated passage leading to the delivery lane. The patrons of De Vere's Snuggery had to know where they were going, for there was nothing in the way of a simple indication, let alone advertisement, to indicate its vicinity. It struck Coll as odd – or Irish – that this place of Hibernian culture etc. was publicized, apparently, only by means of a scrawl on a lost-and-found corkboard and in no other way. For himself alone? The casual visitor would have to be practically psychic to find the place, but, on the other hand, Coll reflected as he ascended the narrow staircase that twisted to the right, since the pub or whatever it was, was almost completely full, perhaps there was no need. De Vere's did not want for custom.

It was a single L-shaped chamber with a bar at one end. A cheerful glow from a dimly-lit chandelier relieved the companionable darkness, a comfortable gloom that is the right backdrop for whatever is to be said. Large tables were placed along three sides of the snuggery, with four small round ones in the centre. They were occupied for the most part by men. The hum of conversation was not overpowering, as if the subdued atmosphere did not permit loud talk, in contrast to the chaotic racket of the Doolin pubs, where musicians needed the voices and harps of gods to make themselves heard under the torrent of eager shouting. To the left of the bar was a daïs on which a single high-backed wooden chair was placed.

In Ireland you don't normally worry about finding an empty table before sitting down as you do in a North American bar or eatery. There were no empty tables. A man at ease with a dark-haired girl at one of the small round tables waved to the single remaining vacant chair at their table.

'Sit down. No reserved seats here. This place is usually packed out, so grab it before it goes.'

'Thanks. God helps those who help themselves.'

'In my experience, the ones who help themselves are not the ones who need divine assistance. By the way, I'm Thady. This is Anna.'

The girl smiled and raised her glass. She looked at him as if she had known him all his life. And you have a name?'

He smiled in his turn, feeling it easy to be his natural self in this homely place. 'Indeed. Coll. What are you drinking? May I get the next ones?'

'Sherry for me, please. Cream.'

'Another bitter pint for me, Colin,' chimed in Thady. 'I'm glad you came along.'

'Coll, not Colin.'

Coll went to get the drinks, not forgetting a tepid Guinness for himself, for he could not stop thinking of drinks served at room temperature as being warm. Its suave bitterness had something of the mock mystic quality of the pub. 'Thanks, stranger,' said the young man with only a mild guying of Coll's accent. 'What part of the world do you hail from?'

'Canada. Toronto, as a matter of fact.'

'That's a big place. Are you on your way back?'

'Not yet. I'm liking this land too much.'

'You like the land whose sons and daughters fled its shores, to a greater number than those who remained? This land whose quaint elfin humour attracts countless visitors from abroad, this land so charmingly fascinating, so disharmonious, which has the friendliest people in the world, outwardly, for that is the necessary mask for our inner misery of disruption and hatred. In all essential ways we remain the archipelago of tiny kingdoms that is our Celtic past. So we have invented this public medicine for the soul.' He waved a hand airily to embrace everyone in the snuggery.

'Oh, come on, wailing Thady,' the girl broke in, 'stop showerin' bitter drops. Coll wants heartsease, not sour flesh-tearing talk. Drink up your beer and relax. But God knows we could do without some of the drongos we do get. In Boston and New York there must be some kind of St Patrick's virus going around. Will you get a load of that, now?'

A man and a woman had just come in. They were obviously middle-aged Americans. She wore red slacks with multi-coloured sneakers and a polka dot top rather too revealing of ample breasts. Her hair was bright *bright* brand-new blonde with a dazzling fringe like the radiator grille of a concept car. It set off the copious lipstick, radiant scarlet. But it was her companion who was absolutely inescapable. Some souvenir shops in Ireland sell joke suits for men for £50 or £60. These are bright garish green of a revolting hue found nowhere else in the universe. They are cut from a thin crumply artificial fibre, probably made in Taiwan or Zanzibar, and are aimed at the same class of people who buy little plaster gnomes to put in the front garden. This man stood there wearing one of these suits with a self-conscious grin, obviously happy in the simple notion that by displaying himself in this sartorial atrocity, the colour of a badly overexposed photograph of pondweed, he was conveying a great compliment to any of these charming blarneying folks who encountered him to the peril of their eyesight. To complete the picture of frightfulness he was carrying in his hand a matching bowler, for the Grünewald of hellish taste who had perpetrated the suit was determined to leave nothing whatever to the imagination of the innocent. It was a strange mingling of uncertain climates, the gawping tourists in their gleeful vulgarity, the theatrical pessimism Thady assumed as being part of the stock Irish character the visitor expected and the cultivated Irish whose manners are normally faultless. It is well that they are compassionate as well as courteous. A *frisson* of pained shock briefly parted men and women from their talk, and in an instant the lovely conviviality flowed back as if good feeling had never been violated by the incubus of New York St Patrickism.

So far, apart from Anna, it was all beginning to feel a little phoney to Coll. What came next? Following ten minutes of desultory conversation after Anna had shut up Thady, the second layer was revealed

Coll was not paying any attention to what Anna and Thady were saying to each other in undertones, nor was he much interested in De Vere's other patrons once he had satisfied himself that there was no one there taking any unusual interest in him, nor were any particular thoughts occupying him. Yet he completely failed to notice the entrance of the harpist who was now seated on the daïs, got up in a red robe that (to Coll) looked almost as off-key as the extra-terrestrial green suit. A grey beard flowing out of the cavernous recesses of the hood completed the fancy dress. The face was invisible. Nevertheless, everyone except the two Americans shut up as if by command.

The Irish harp sounded a little out of tune to Coll until his ear caught its tonality and the ancient harmony which brought occasional jingles and clashes to him. It was a completely different, a music until now beyond his experience. Phoney or not, the harpist could play and play beautifully. Like the others, Coll was transfixed. Never had he believed that anyone could draw such sound from so simple an instrument, a primitive harp, as did this bard, for bard he must be. The red-robed one began with two berceuse-like pieces in a hush disturbed by the insensate whispers of the Americans who thought of music only as ambient wallpaper. Soon even they shut up. Coll began to realize what the music was about even though the language of many of the songs was unknown to him. Some, however, were in English. It was the music itself that spoke to him with an infallible voice, music that made the hair on the back of his neck rise and his spine tingle in the thrilling touch of the muse. The pieces were short, some of them illustrating dialogue on the great stage of comedy or tragedy; several of them were subdued marches, but swashing, as of confident men making their way to battle. These warlike pieces rose to no great climax; on the contrary, they faded away, as though the harpist marched with them into distant forests, or sometimes into lands of high romance. Then he returned to simple lyrics and rejoicing, the harpist bowing his head as if he were blind, or partly-blind, seeing within but not without. Then again battle supervened. Now the bard looked on, as it were, and sang words of encouragement, nothing clashing or heroic, but subdued and magic, gentle, almost, a quiet power drawn from another sphere giving prowess in the fight. Coll supposed the words were Irish. The singer ended with a curious mixture of song and declamation in classical style, always set off by chords, this time in English. Coll could make out some of the words:

> *The sons of Daire from Dun na n-Eicess*
> *Cast lots gleefully*
> *That each might know his share*
> *Of the enchanted fawn, without quarrel.*

Coll fell under the excitement of the magical song, knew that the fawn and the sons of Daire were as forever in the present as are Romeo and Juliet and felt their reality flow into him *and knew that he was one of the sons to whom a share of the wonderful fawn fell.* He listened now to a shadow of the singer's song that sent gentle, irresistible sea-waves into him: you and I shall meet again amidst those who unseeing stand. The blind shall see and the sighted shall be blind.

And there the spell ended. The hush remained but the bard was gone. Without seeing anyone else in the room, Coll left with the idea ringing in his head that those with nothing shall give while those with possessions shall be confined to what they have.

Out in the street it was completely dark. It was the darkness as much as the chill air which dashed into his face like water, dashing his dream, making him aware again of shapes walking with and towards him. Someone was leaning against the bus-stop signpost trying to read in the ill-lit gloom. As Coll passed, he folded up his paper and fell into step beside him. Immediately Coll grabbed him and turned him around, feeling as he did so a tremendous unmanageable resistance at once replaced by compliance.

'Gently, Ywain. Didn't you like my songs?'

It was Victor.

Chapter 23

As soon as he got in, he picked up the phone to call Siobhan, but Cybele's voice came on.

'Don't call out on this line, Byron. Who do you want?'

'Siobhan.'

'O.K. Come upstairs to my room.'

She had been in bed but did not seem to mind being disturbed. 'It's my job. Here.'

He took the handset from her.

'How lovely to hear from you – Byron, is that what I'm to call you?'

'That's only Cybele's little joke. My name is now Coll.'

'Ah, Coll, is it? Then I shall have to beware of you now, for you cleave even closer to me. I know something of your re-emergence and you can tell me all about it when we meet. Now what have you found out?'

'I haven't found out much in the way of information, but I have found someone, thanks to the clues you provided – Victor.' He told her about his encounter with the bard.

'So he did get away! I wonder how – but more, I wonder what he's up to. Is he a threat to us? What did he tell you?'

'When I grabbed him, he had amazing, almost irresistible strength, but it only lasted a second or two. He told me that he was glad to see me, glad that I had understood at least a fragment of what he was singing, glad that I would be bringing friends with me – that I didn't understand – that we should meet again in the forest and – oh, and that next time I should take care not to lay unfriendly hands on him. Does that make sense to you?'

There was a pause before Siobhan answered. 'Some of it, possibly. And I don't like it. When you and he were in hospital together, he refused to take anything from you or anyone else except this bible which has caught us all on its curve. Is it possible that he succeeded in giving you something, perhaps without your knowing it, something you may still carry around with you?'

'No, all I took from him were some slips of paper which I had filled out in advance –'

'– and on which he had written something, right?'

'Yes.'

'Where are those slips now?'

'I don't know. Probably left them behind in Toronto. In any case I've had several complete changes of clothing since being in Ireland, so everything I might have had is gone.'

'Well, look. And what did you tell him?'

'Nothing. He didn't ask anything. He just slipped off and gestured me not to follow him.'

'Well, that's that. Tell Esmirone about it in the morning and don't mind about Cybele. She finds out about everything in the end, so don't have any second thoughts about confiding in her. Her name is wisdom.'

'I'd love to see you again.'

'You will, dear Coll, I'm certain of that. You won't have to wait for long. But we shouldn't be talking on this link for so long. Cybele is probably getting impatient. Give her my love.'

'And what about me?'

'And what about you? I have accepted you completely. You will come very close to me, if that is what you wish. Didn't I tell you out on the Burren that I loved you, although possibly not in all the ways you wanted? I can give you my love; I cannot give you myself, at least, not at this juncture.'

'I still don't understand.'

'Goodbye until we meet again, Coll. Please say goodbye and ring off.'

'Goodbye, dear one.'

Cybele took the receiver from him. 'I can get into touch with Siobhan if you've something important to say to her, but this link is not to be used for casual conversation. Did she say anything to upset you? You look pale.'

'She told me just what you're telling me now – "Goodbye, dear Coll, until we meet again." In other words, don't call me.'

'What else do you expect? This is a security operation. But I'm sure she said much more than that. She does love you.'

'Only in the way she loves everyone, in the way she loves you. She asked me to give you her love.'

'Perhaps you don't know what you're asking.'

'I thought it was simple enough.'

'For you, yes. Perhaps not for her. In any case, whatever you ask you're going to have to work for.'

'I'm afraid I've made a fool of myself in front of you. Aren't you a bit jealous?'

She laughed, not too unkindly. 'Really, Byron, what do you think of me? You really are so old-fashioned, so *outré*. Do you really delude yourself with the picturesque notion so popular with the readers of historical romances, that I, the servant girl, am dying to win the favour of the young lord, yourself, so that one day in a grand fit of noble passion you can rip my dress off? Do you really think of me as a stock character in the weariest cliché of romantic comedy? I have a job to do and I like you very much so long as that doesn't interfere with it. Siobhan has a different problem with you, and it's plain that you don't keep in mind the distinction between her and me. I don't in the least object to being your substitute for her, up to a point, if it helps you to deal with your emotions, particularly with your sudden impulses to rush into action, but I think you're deluding yourself if you believe that Siobhan is an ordinary woman with an ordinary job to do, like me. She isn't. Now, have you finished, because I'd like to get some sleep in. Off you go. Write a poem about Siobhan tonight and make a full report to Esmirone in the morning. Poor Anne Isabella! No wonder she couldn't handle it. Goodnight, Byron.'

'Who's Anne Isabella?'

She gently pushed him out of her room and closed the door.

But once he found himself in his own room his thoughts turned to the fantastical duke of dark corners, man of fateful encounters. Was he part of the Circle or not? Siobhan had not given even a hint, but some were fearful of this gaunt figure, not much more than a skeleton, but a skeleton with unbelievable strength, far greater than his own. Now that he had revealed himself to his former friend, what was to be the next step? He had no answers to these questions.

During the night he did not sleep as long and dreamlessly as usual, but instead woke up several times feeling an unwonted thirst. Awaking for the third time at three, he thought he would never get back to sleep and had the wish to go for a long walk. While he was thinking about this he must have dropped off, for he went into a fantastic dream in which he felt supremely happy.

He heard himself talking to someone about the music he had heard played by the blind harpist. As he did, the scene shifted to a beautiful coast of tranquil sea, and cliffs completely covered with lush green sward. He was aware of Siobhan somewhere about, and was also aware that he now lived there, near her, miraculously transported by his father, whom he clearly recognized in his dream, now bearded and bearing a staff. The house belonging to Siobhan's parents, even the garden, had been translated to this paradisal spot. He walked in these lovely surroundings listening to the surging eloquence of the harp played by the absolute master who, though he had died on earth, was still making music.

Siobhan told him that his father was the author of this marvel, but that she had no idea of how he had accomplished it, and that she, Siobhan, gave the house to him, Coll, for his loyalty. He now realizes that his father is an angel.

Peering beyond, to the outside of this outside, he sees again the High Street of Swords, but all the shops are now decorated with works of art, some landscapes, some hideously grotesque heads. He knows that these are ancient works of art as fresh and vividly coloured as when they were first created.

Before the dream twisted and fled into the amnesia of the soul, his father told him that he could live in England if he wanted to. He thought he might want to if Siobhan did.

Chapter 24

ESMIRONE WAS NOT TO BE SEEN IN THE MORNING and Cybele either could not or would not tell him where she had gone.

'She must have been off early,' Coll remarked at breakfast.

'Indeed, I don't believe she went to bed at all. She was gone soon after midnight, for the car woke me up.'

Coll was more than usually grouchy. He didn't know where he was headed next, nor what he was expected to do, and it appeared that no one was about to tell him. He wanted above all to know when he would see Siobhan again, but Esmirone Anstell was useless as an oracle on that point. She shrugged her shoulders and opened her hands in a gesture not entirely sincere. He went upstairs, reviewed his few possessions and looked out of the window, dying to go for a long walk. He sauntered downstairs again to ask Cybele if it might be possible. She was not there. She was packing up electronic equipment in her room.

'What's going on?'

'I'm not sure yet, but I'm preparing to move if necessary. You had better do the same. It's not urgent, yet, just precautionary. Don't look so distraught, idiot! We're not deserting you. You'll be given adequate instructions if a shift of scene is desirable. Where is that revolver Esmirone gave you?'

'In my pedestal drawer.'

'Well, keep it on you. It's not going to be any good to you lying in a drawer if you have to use it.'

He went back, got his gear together, examined the revolver and put it in his back pocket. But in fact nothing at all happened that day and Esmirone was back in the evening. They had supper together. Coll described his visit to Swords.

'This Victor, do you think you could find him again?'

'No one was playing or singing last night. I'm not at all sure what I could do to find him again. I've a feeling that I can only encounter him when he desires it.'

'Don't let him go to De Vere's again,' said Cybele, 'at least not until we can find out what's going on. I'll go down in the morning to see if that notice is still in the window and find out anything else I can. I'm not very recognizable.'

'All right,' agreed Esmirone, 'arrange it with Michael, but hurry back. Don't stay away for more than two hours. I may need you here. The important contact is Coll. Victor doesn't know that he is a member of the Circle.'

'I believe he does,' put in Coll, 'after all, he directed my steps towards you in the first place. He knows what's going on, of that I'm sure. I don't know why I'm sure, but I am.'

'You told him nothing.' Esmirone was emphatic.

'Nothing. But I think that if he was sure that I had no connexion with the Circle, he'd have taken me off somewhere and I'd have found out much more. For all I know, when I met him in Toronto he may have been on some expedition – he's terribly brave as well as canny. I wonder if he's an Odysseus behind the lines.'

'You're improving, Coll. For that reason if for no other Cybele goes first. Then we'll come up with a plan for you. In the meantime, think about it. You may be moving on pretty soon.'

'Where to?'

'Oh, what a question, Coll!'

In the morning Coll went down to the cellar to do his exercises while Cybele and Michael went off to Swords. She was back within the two hours specified but could report only that the notices formerly in the newsagent's window were no longer there. Coll now went back with Michael with strict instructions not to get out of the car. They toured the area at intervals during the day but could not spot Victor. In the evening Coll was detailed to make a brief visit to De Vere's. He sat for half-an-hour. The crowd was as thick as before, but there was no performance and no sign of Victor.

Later that evening a man called Vernon came round and completed an Identikit drawing of Victor's features under Coll's direction. It was at that point that the latter began to wonder whether he was not, perhaps, being too helpful. He wanted to put his trust in Victor who, he felt, was a good, not a bad, angel. He thought of the sculptor called upon to render the features of the Blessed Virgin as she had manifested Herself in an Arran cottage. With a wry smile he wondered whether this was the first time a god had been proclaimed by means of a police identikit, but he kept his thoughts to himself. There was an air of uneasiness, if not fear. He was the only one who saw the Irishness of the affair.

After that they let him sit tight for two days. Esmirone was away again, but came down for breakfast on Friday.

'Well, you're off. After breakfast get your things together and give me back my Austrian beauty. We don't want them to find that on you.'

'Who?'

You have to go through airport security. You're off to London, moving up in the world.'

He now knew better than to express surprise.

'You want to lose me in London?'

'We want to use you in London – possibly – and before you ask, Siobhan wants me to tell you that she will keep in touch with you from time to time, but as you guess, doesn't want you to attempt to call her. Your people in London will pass up the line any messages you have and you'll have to fall in with their security arrangements. You must understand, Coll, that modern communications are terribly leaky. They're turning us into a police state. All forms of electronic transmission can be intercepted and recorded. We in the Circle have better methods, but they depend, as they ought to depend, on human encounters. Only in the Circle can we experience what nearly everyone else has forgotten, the lost harmony of simple honesty in talk between men and women. When you're ready, come down and I'll go over a few things with you.'

He didn't know whether he was glad or sorry to leave Dublin, for he had only his first rainy day impression and his glimpses of Swords, but he had grown to love Ireland in spite of the ghastly weather, for he felt that there were no lovelier people on the face of the earth.

There was no sign of Cybele when he came down. Esmirone gave him his air ticket, £200 in cash, checked over his new passport with him and received back the revolver from him. She then went over certain letters of the alphabet with him and gave him his recognition signals and responses.

'That's a marvellously authentic-looking passport.'

'What do you mean – "authentic-looking?" It is authentic, properly issued by the Home Office. We're not stupid, you know.'

'But how –'

'How little you've learned! My fault. Considering the time you've been with me I should have done much more with you. You've still got a long way to go in learning the basic Beth-Luis-Nion, but at least you've made some progress. You'll have more to do in England, I'm afraid. Michael will pick up your bag in a few minutes. You stroll off and meet him casually in the park in, say, a quarter of an hour. If you leave now you'll have nice time. Goodbye, Coll. It's been fine knowing you. We'll be seeing each other soon enough, I'm thinking, but keep that to yourself.'

They exchanged kisses.

'I'd better say goodbye to Cybele.'

'Go upstairs, then, and make it quick.'

Cybele was still packing up all the equipment in the room.

'So you're leaving too.'

'Looks like it, doesn't it? I don't know whether it's anything to do with you or not – probably not. I don't think you're that important yet. You're off too? Well, I'm sorry. You held some interest for me. Goodbye, Byron. Pity they didn't give you a bit more time. You fancied me, didn't you, wanted to have it off with me, you randy old boar, and you might have succeeded in the end. I think we would make a good couple. Too late now, and we may not have the chance again. But my love and good thoughts go with you.'

He kissed her, not really knowing how to feel about this reticent capable girl whose deep feelings were hidden from him.

'You're so ambiguous.'

She laughed. 'You think so only because I don't act in the way you think all girls do. In fact, I'm the exact opposite. I always say what I mean.'

'You really would have shot me down right in the kitchen that day when I wanted to go out?'

'Really, Byron. And I would have grieved for you, grieved right down to the bottom of my soul.'

'I don't understand.'

'I know. But perhaps you will before long. Now you're supposed to be on your way, so get off, and all the best to you.'

She gave him a most tender kiss.

Once in the open, the remote sunshine of the early spring day entered his soul. Again he practically tripped over Michael before seeing him.

'Hell, man, what on earth are they keeping you for? They need a resident philosopher?'

'Right. I'm the in-house bullshit bouncer.'

At the airport Michael produced his bag from the boot.

'We took all your stuff out and replaced it with heroin. Have a nice flight and don't worry about anything. See you if you're over here again – and awake.'

They hadn't left him much time to catch his 'plane. At Heathrow he had to wait for over three-quarters of an hour to pick up his bag and go through immigration and customs. He joined a queue five or six broad consisting of all the peoples of the world labelled on their baggage and T-shirts alike as though they were being processed through judgement day. He suddenly realized that he was never going to spot the subtle finger signals he had to watch for in this crowd, but he kept as sharp a lookout as he could. Not knowing where to make for, once he was through C&I he found a vacant seat in the arrivals and sat down. His fellow passengers were nearly all families, it seemed, including a silly over-sentimental young couple who drew attention to themselves by being oblivious to all but each other. He almost snarled in his impatience. It was unwise to sit around like this, but on the other hand he reflected, he really shouldn't mind it. London. Not much of an introduction: the modern airport has become a hostile place, thanks to the activities of terrorists and the contempt of the airlines for their passengers, but London all the same. The very name spoke of marvels. There was absolutely no one staying around to keep a lookout, and after more than half-an-hour he began to think someone's plans had gone awry when, gazing at the silly couple for the umpteenth time, he became suddenly aware that the woman's passionate hands made sense to him. Her crawling fingers were not as blind as they looked. To penetrate her target's imperceptive stupidity, she repeated the letters a little more slowly, *D, N, H*, oak, ash and thorn. He cautiously replied with *L, R, T*, rowan, elder and holly. After another moment or two, the two disengaged themselves, the man giving him an *O* as he bent down to attend to his shoe laces, and they went out without a glance at him. He followed at a distance. They were careful not to go too fast and led him to the tube. As he squeezed in behind them, the man handed him a ticket. When they all got out at a suburban station, he followed them to a car park. The man took his bag from him, threw it into the boot, all without speaking a word, and took off. Evidently he was a blood-brother of Michael with the same propensity to zoom through narrow choked streets and around blind corners at impossible speeds. They drove a roundabout course for about an hour. Finally they swept up a street of elegant brick buildings where the driver wedged the Volkswagen, God knows how, into a ridiculously small space between other small cars densely parked along the kerbside like a row of oddly-shaped books. He grabbed the bag before Coll could forestall him and led the way up the steps to a large apartment building with beautiful brick facing, five storeys high. They took an ancient lift to the top floor. The door to their flat was double-locked.

Inside the man took Coll's jacket and the woman introduced them. 'I'm Erin and this is Max.'

'Coll.'

'Come and sit down and we'll have some lunch. I expect you could do with something after your trip. The loo is along the passageway in an alcove to the right just before the dining room.'

Erin was petite, long-tressed, businesslike and precise in her speech and movements. Max was somewhat less than middle height, slim and impeccably casual in dress and manner. He went to a very good tailor and did something important in the City near Leadenhall Market.

Lunch consisted of romaine salad sprinkled with crumbled Danish Blue, smoked salmon and lettuce sandwiches, several cheeses including a nice one with a tantalizingly odorous sweat, a crumbly Lancashire and a ravishingly ripe Stilton on large thin round water biscuits, all accompanied by the nuttiest of brown ales. Coll still had lots of room for the fruit tart followed by thick Turkish coffee in small cups. At that moment London seemed bigger, older, more expansive and more comfortable than Dublin, an immensely rich sedate ancient city still replete with the good things of empire.

Coll's room overlooked the street. Directly across was a handkerchief park with burgeoning chestnuts lining the railings. The near kerb was, as previously, an unbroken line of cars parked so closely that a practical joker could have glued them together. A police tow truck brought up a mobile platform to the head of the street as it narrowed into Kensington High. They were removing someone's green Jaguar.

'Your job is security for now, if you want some kind of designation,' Erin told him. 'It doesn't really matter a lot. We don't expect too much trouble here, but you'll be going on the odd trip with Max and me, separately or together. You'll find some stuff in your armoire, the middle large outside drawer. Check it over and carry the gun all the time. You never know when you're going to need it. Apart from that we'll just wait for further instructions.'

'Can I go out?'

'Don't see why not, but check with whichever one of us is here before you do in case something has been scheduled for you. If you walk down the High Street to the right you'll come to Hyde Park and Oxford Street. Go across the park opposite and you'll come out on to Bayswater. Don't bring anyone back with you. If you find yourself with company you can't conveniently get rid of, go to Weimar Street, Putney, just off the High Street on the south side of the bridge. Ask for Peter in street number 11,

Flat 3. Here's the key if no one's in. If pursued, jump on any bus, jump off, get on another, jump on another and another until you're sure there's no one with you. Always lose yourself in the public transport system if you can. Yes, you ought to go out and get your bearings, but keep moving and keep an eye out. Memorize the main streets on this map before you go. Take a key from the basket on the hall stand and put it back when you return. If you need small amounts of cash, enough for bus or tube fares, take it from the fruit bowl. You have about £200, I believe. Otherwise I'll supply you according to your needs and the instructions I get. Ta-ta.'

For the first time in weeks Coll felt freedom as lush and irresponsible as on the first day of his life, as he walked airily across Kensington Park, past King William's palace. The trees were in the great green change of spring and even the ripples on the overstressed little pond were a live growing skin. He was not in the slightest tired. On the contrary, after a civilized tea with two civilized people, he felt wonderfully invigorated and alert, acutely conscious of his own life and the lives of all things around him, of his place in a new wonderful family. Some old exciting history arose from the earth beneath his feet which carried him along with it. In the park he felt that this part of the city was a natural outgrowth of the beautiful countryside, not something laid upon it, although he knew the opposite to be true. Here the city did not deny the earth. He walked for several miles down the Bayswater road, but the park pulled him back and he explored the gardens open to the public at the back of the palace before walking down the High Street, past the lovely brickwork of the Albert Hall and the bizarre Albert Memorial. After about three hours he remembered his instructions and kept a sharp lookout.

'Well, you weren't out that long,' Erin greeted him. 'Better exercise tomorrow. Max will be home in an hour. Dinner at eight.'

When Max came in just after five, they sat down to tea, which was rather like lunch, with cheeses and thin crackers, the cheeses tasting even richer, his palate increasingly alive to a spectrum of flavours; and the neutral crackers had a depth – is there depth in mere taste? – that said over and over to him, London, London, London. Max said nothing about his work and Erin asked him no questions.

'Trip into the country tomorrow,' said Max.

'Tomorrow's Saturday,' said Erin, 'that'll be nice. You'd like that, wouldn't you, Coll?'

Chapter 25

ON THE FOLLOWING MORNING, Saturday, the three of them got into the car and Max wrested his way through the clogged streets of London's Victorian suburbs on the way to the South Coast. He was one of those who can memorize maps and turn them around in their heads. It was obvious that he was highly familiar with the South East anyway, as he avoided the major roads in favour of those that still follow the ancient contours known to the old finders of paths, now overlaid with asphalt but not quite wrenched and straightened out of the natural influence of the simple ever-present hills and valleys known to centuries of travellers footing it before the teeming industrial ages. However, he was not driving these roads solely for pleasure, for once in a while he stopped, dashed into a house and dashed back again without a word.

He did not say where they were going, but once they got out of the blighted country of nineteenth century jerry-building Coll was entranced by the garden countryside and the rich little villages eccentrically fascinating. First they took him to Beachy Head, whose white chalk soaring above the waters sent shivers into his soul; thus it became a blessed day. His soul drifted in rapture over the green grass.

Then they got back into the car for hours as Max continued his brief house calls until well into the afternoon when, Erin protesting too much, they stopped at a pub for lunch. Max wanted to get on, but as soon as he looked at his watch Erin ordered a green Chartreuse.

Then they were off again, calling into several more houses on the way. Here there were introductions and Max left messages. In the high afternoon they found themselves in the ancient land of Wiltshire. At a little before five, Max stopped, opened a farmer's gate and pulled into a narrow trackway. They got out, stretched themselves and began walking up a path towards a flat-topped hill. The pasture beneath their feet was so liberally sown with sheep droppings that it was impossible to avoid treading into them and their shoes became thoroughly soiled. The path threaded itself around the hill, becoming much steeper as they approached the summit. When they were there they sauntered around to view the bare Wiltshire landscape. Soon they sat down together.

'I'm glad you have that spare jersey with you, Coll,' remarked Erin, 'for we might be here quite a while.'

'Are we meeting anyone?'

'Perhaps. Anything is possible in the month of May.'

'It's still April.'

'Possibilities are all in the future – and it's May eve. A feast normally begins just after sunset of the preceding night.'

They were waiting for well over an hour before two couples breasted the pathway at the summit. There was silence as they greeted one another in the hidden alphabet and with embraces. The sun was still well above the horizon when the greatest part of the group, about twenty people of all ages, were foregathered. Erin moved closer to Coll and asked him to help Max with the baskets in the car and to go with the other men to collect branches. By seven in the evening as the light waned a tall column of dead branches was ready for the match, while the men continued to pile up heaps more, enough to feed a fierce fire for hours.

It was a subdued group, for the language of truth flows slowly. Coll found he could not define the mood. Now that their preparations were complete there was nothing to do but draw in together. As the sun fell into darkness they pulled on jerseys and jackets. A few more joined them.

Yet as the twilight lengthened what little chatter there was flickered out and ceased; a stillness came upon them. They formed a circle which opened towards the track from below. For someone else was coming. Erin and Max had taken their places on either side of Coll as though to guide him through whatever developed. Not having the same facility in the Beth-Luis-Nion as the others, Coll was not fully aware of what was going on, although he fathomed an apprehension that it concerned him.

At last! A young woman in a loose-fitting soft wind-cheater drawn up almost to her face preceded a small group of others, all women. She took no particular notice of Erin, Max or Coll, but moved around the inside of the ring from right to left, carefully greeting everyone in the silent alphabet and embracing everyone there. She was received with marked respect, deference, even; she was someone special. When she had greeted everyone else in the circle and came to Coll, she gave him her warmest smile, but no other particular attention, resisting anything closer than a formal embrace. At last!

It was, of course, Siobhan.

In silence she moved over to the tall tent of branches. One of the women with her handed her a torch, a dry branch daubed with pitch. As it met her hand it burst into flame. First describing a circle of fire in the air, she thrust it into the tinder-dry kindling at the base. The whole mass blazed up in an instant like a minor explosion. Another of her assistants held out a large brass-bound box with a hinged lid. From this Siobhan took several handfuls of something finely shredded or powdered and cast these on the flames with oghamic gestures, whereupon the flames briefly raged with new potency in staccato fury. This did not send the men and women gathered there farther from the fire. Instead they drew closer to it so that their thick outer clothing now gave them protection from the fiery heat rather than the chill of descending night. For a space they grew graver.

Presently, however, they gathered even closer into each other, and a greater stillness possessed them in which some formed letters in their trance-like state; soon some began to mumble softly while others tripped the intricately figured steps of an inspired dance. Coll felt the same entranced delight as had seized him on the morning up in the Burren when the rising sun sang to him and the five women acted out their trope of the stations of the year. The fire now manifested itself to him as a wonderful renewal of something as old as the sun, now to be the whole principle of the rising year. He saw revealed to him a synthesized image of paths in the zodiac and the tracks in the fields already high with grasses and flowers. He saw the dense old forests in their sacred depths groaning under the yoke of a sterile winter god, waiting for the Great Goddess to bless them back into the world before it was reduced to a desert, and he wondered at the fantastic living organic architecture of the enormous trees shaped by every little pulse of life in their latent existence. He felt Her there, somewhere, not in the person of anyone, or in a hill or the sky or the nearer stream that wound a little out of its way near the hill and its adjacent spurs, but in the air itself, now softer in his breathing than a lulling breeze over a summer garden of magical poppies, billowing out from the little sun of the fire surrounded by faces, minor planets cast over with ochre.

As the fire waned, men threw branches on, but nothing more was done by Siobhan, and although did his best to look for her, he could not find her. Max and Erin never strayed from his side. He felt exalted and knew their all-delight, but there was no rite of any kind. At some time quite late, whether before or after midnight he could not tell – and what did it matter? – in the harmony that was the Circle he never thought to give his watch a glance – the baskets were brought forth, food and drink were produced, and everyone fell to, Coll discovering a hunger which had been completely repressed until that moment. He didn't note particularly what he ate, but someone, Max for sure, had brought a miraculous Riesling spiritually heady, a Mozart among wines, and the bread covered with poppy seed tasted heavenly.

Then someone brought out the cake, a very large one baked in one of those moulds with a central boss that produces a ring-shaped affair. This was distributed in a peculiar way. When the cake had been sliced up, all the pieces were put into an osier basket with a hinged lid. At this point Siobhan reappeared, from where Coll had no idea. She took the basket and offered it around in methodical order so that everyone got a single portion. Each one present reached under the closed lid so that selection was impossible, took his piece, but did not eat it right away. Eventually the basket came round to Coll who did as the others and took his portion blind. He, however, was luckier than most, for the cake had not been divided evenly and, as he could see right away, his piece was much larger than the others. It was also the only one dyed black. And this was not his only surprise. As soon as he knew what he had, Erin and Max seized an arm each and would have pushed him right into the fire if the others standing nearby had not intervened and saved him. Before Coll could realize what was going on, everyone broke up in laughter. He had been the butt of some joke or another, or perhaps he was being initiated.

'Don't worry,' laughed Erin, 'Max and I drew the task of sacrificing you to Baal. You were naturally a little reluctant to go into the fire – there is a somewhat similar show of reluctance when the Speaker of the House of Commons is elected. But you know that the idea of sacrifice to appease or propitiate a god is totally antithetical to our whole outlook. So the other kinder members of our Circle rescued you from our life-violating crime.'

'Baal?'

'The sun, in other words. Just a silly little charade. You have drawn the carle's portion and, well, you took it from the Queen, so she will have to explain it to you. I hope she does.'

Max broke in. 'All right? We always play this harmless little game on May Eve. It's just a variant of the bean in the old Twelfth-night cake, really, or the coin in the Christmas pudding, if you like. Just good clean fun – you hope, eh?'

'Changing the subject, are we going back to London this evening?'

'*We* are. You are staying. We'll send your things on to you. You'll have them in the morning, and really, you know, it's getting quite late, so I think we'll have to be on the way if we're to function at all in the morning. What do you say, Erin? Well, all the best, old man. It was nice getting to know you, and I'm sure we'll be seeing each other again. Take care of yourself. I've a pretty fair idea that you're going to move up in the world before the year is out. Ta-ta.'

'Toodle-oo,' added Erin. 'You're the honourary carline now. Make the most of it. It's going to be fun, I think. At any rate, it often works out quite well. I hope we'll be seeing each other again. You're the strongest man I've ever met.'

'Thanks. But what's the carle? I don't understand any of this stuff.'

'It's not a lot, don't worry. It was really lovely having you in London. I do hope we see each other again, but I don't know if we will. It's all in the lap of the gods, and they never tell.'

She kissed him and they left.

'Goodbye, and take it easy,' said Coll lamely.

As Coll watched Max and Erin disappear into the darkness of the track down, he realized that the last celebrants were just leaving and wondered whether he was expected to spend the small hours huddled up to the dying fire waiting to be collected by whomsoever might next have the task of looking after this particular piece of unopened baggage. In a few moments he was alone. They had all left without so much as a backward glance at him as though he had suddenly become infected by the plague. Even Erin and Max, in spite of their easy informal politeness, had, in their every gesture and inflexion, disentangled themselves from him. He was alone again. He stood and faced the languishing fire, then went to see if he could find a few more branches to fling on it, for the dog days were still far distant and it had become unusually cool even for England. There were only a few scrotty little twigs left. He gathered them and returned to the fire. He was about to add them to the dying flames when a cool voice spoke.

'No. Leave the fire alone. Instead, go down the hill on the other side, find a spade and return. Then cast earth on the fire to put it out.'

He went down, searched until he found the spade and returned to put the fire out.

When he had finished he followed Siobhan down the winding way. At the foot two other girls were waiting, showing the way with electric torches. An AWD drew up and they all got in.

They drove for about three hours.

As they alighted at the end of the final journey of the day, Siobhan remarked: 'You begin your service at the tide of day we call uht.'

No one greeted him or took any notice whatever of him when they went inside, and Siobhan showed him to his room in perfunctory silence.

After about two hours' sleep Coll got up early in the light of dawn to explore, walking down a hill pathway through a village overlooking the mothering fields scattered with trees partly shrouded in mist. Crossing the stream, he paused on the bridge. The boats might have been set in crystal. Few cars were visible, for most of them were penned in the walled ruin of an ancient stone gatehouse which served the village as its parking place. There was a hush on the morning as he walked back, fearing to disturb the living air around him. He did not resume his pace until he was well above the village.

It was a perfect first of May. The sun was now well above the horizon, but nothing stirred at Hazelridge, the huge and handsome house where he was now staying, with whom he did not know, apart from Siobhan, of course. Not knowing what to do with himself inside, he walked in the lovely gardens facing the South Downs, once more intensely aware of the mothering earth with life in all its folds. There was a pipe-fed pond with goldfish and three tall cedars of Lebanon, one encircled by a seat recently painted white. He sat here for a while. After half-an-hour or so he went back inside, nosing into the kitchen, where he found none other than Cybele.

'Cybele! How lovely to see you!'

'Didn't take long, did it? Well, you're really at the centre of things now. So am I. We have a last chance, you and I.'

'A last chance?'

'You can still choose. I am here, for you if you wish it.'

'The choice was made last night, wasn't it?'

'Was it? You can believe that if it suits you. If you think that something other than mere chance entered into your selection, then yes, a choice was made. What *do* you think?'

'Better, what do *you* think?'

'In answer, I'll throw out a further question: what were you chosen for? What is your rôle? Important to know.'

'So tell me then. I think it's obvious.'

'Are you overcome with excitement, then?'

'Yes, I suppose so.'

Cybele smiled. 'I don't see it. Anyway, Esmirone's here, together with some other people you haven't really met, although they were at the

Beltane fire last night. They left earlier than you because it's quite a long drive back. I had to stay here, looking after everything as usual. So you're among friends again, better friends than you know. You now need more looking after than anyone else. I will do that if you want me to.'

'I know,' replied Coll, deliberately misunderstanding her meaning. 'I've always been among friends, ever since I ran into Siobhan on the Burren. But can you tell me what's going on? Yesterday I drew a chunk of cake called the carle's portion and since that time I've noticed, well, a slight shift of attitude towards me, a certain coldness in the air.'

'Not on my part, never, never from me, dear Coll,' Cybele assured him, giving him her cheek to kiss, 'but you've been allotted your rôle and that means people know how they stand with you.'

'Yes, but what rôle? Apart from putting out the fire last night I haven't had anything to do and no one has told me anything.'

'A rôle is not necessarily doing something all the time. It may be just a part in our – let us say, play-acting. But whatever it is, don't worry. You'll find out what you have to do when the time comes. At present you are our protector. Doesn't that make you feel proud?'

'No, because I don't believe it's true. The important work is all being done by you. I went out for a walk this morning without your leave.'

'You're not in my charge now, Coll. You're independent of everyone except Siobhan. You take your directions from her and absolutely no one else. It is a critical time for us both, Coll. I need to be quite clear as to your intentions. For the last time, do you want me or Siobhan? She will release you if you ask and you will always be here, with me, in the Circle. I cannot even hint to you what your fate with the Queen – Siobhan – might be.'

'I have already chosen, not without a pang for you. You are the strongest woman I have ever met.'

'It's that kind of strength you need.'

'Is she in, by the way?'

'Siobhan? I expect so. She'll be in the first large room to the left off the top landing. The upper hallway brings you out at the back of the house, so the back rooms overlook the garden. Knock on her door if you dare. Everyone's meant to be down by eight anyway, so why don't you knock them all up?'

He did this, but left Siobhan until last and then gave her door only the gentlest tap.

He found Cybele outside. She took him to the potting shed where he saw a large oak sapling with its roots balled. It was heavy but well within his sheer animal strength. He carried it out on to the lawn where she told him and dug out its place, filling in a base of sphagnum mixed with earth and water. He left the tree leaning in towards but not touching the water and went back inside with her. Here he had to sit in the kitchen; as in Dublin, he was asked not to leave it.

'They're up to something, but it's meant to be a surprise,' Cybele told him.

Half-an-hour later all members of the household sat down to breakfast. He was looking forward to seeing Esmirone again, and he recognized another Irish girl he had seen briefly in Doolin whose name was Diane, but the other four women of the magic morning out on the Burren were absent. He was never to see any of them again. There was a couple in their mid-thirties, Maxine and Gerald, Esmirone and, last of all came Siobhan, radiant in a strange beauty that typified the May morning much more than herself, for she had none of the conventional good looks, the symmetrical framework for the painted mask that fashion magazines push at us as the ideal female face. Indeed, her face had something of the exalted complacency of the divine twins at Delphi, Artemis and Apollo. Her eyes were now much more important than the noble forehead. Some change there was, something important. The greetings were cordial enough, but Coll missed the sense of full participation in the Circle, particularly in greeting Esmirone again. Something was missing, he sensed, as though his earlier membership had been devalued. Cybele – was she a novice or an established member of this inner circle? – appeared still to be his handler, despite her previous disavowal, and if Siobhan had any special feeling for him she certainly did not show it. He did not worry or rebel at this, for Siobhan was everything to him, but he was surprised by it.

Later she walked with him in the grounds. The new tree stood straight. Under Siobhan's direction, Coll pulled it into place, filled in the cavity and tamped the earth well down all round. The May Queen was still wearing the short skirt she had on at breakfast. After an hour she changed into jeans and she and Coll went for a walk together. Weather and season were at their best for the feast in the year as young as she, and Coll now felt as deliriously happy as Romeo when the winged messenger of heaven bestrode the lazy-passing clouds.

Chapter 26

SIOBHAN WALKED BRISKLY. They did not retrace Coll's earlier route but instead took old rights of way partly overrun with bramble that brought them upland until they glimpsed the distant sea. Here they stood for a while letting the gentle air of springtime England refresh them within and without.

'Do you love me, Coll? Really, that is?' she asked, turning to him.

He put his arms around her, and this time she did not resist. 'As the sea loves and laps against the land,' he replied.

'Ah, you will have to, then.'

'Have to?'

'Have to love me, in spite of everything, to the end. Will you, can you, do that?'

'Yes, my dear one.'

'Perhaps you can. But who knows what love may run up against in its lifespan? You are not committing yourself to an ordinary girl, but to someone with an extraordinary fate, and if you agree to become my chosen lover you will be bound up in that fate, good or ill. Loving you with all my heart, as I shall love you, I tell you that you would be better off, much better off, with Cybele, who is dying to have you. She worships the ground you walk on. No, I'm not exaggerating very much. She is hard-headed and intensely loyal, two qualities you will go a long way to find. And she is free. I am constrained.'

'I knew you had it, had become someone very special, as you told me you might that morning out on the Burren.'

'I also warned you then that I might not be able to love you in all the ways you wished and that I would have many other things to do. Still, look at yourself, Coll, as you have now become. Do you remember what you were before, living with your loveless inert family doing its sterile duty by you, existing in a city devoid of roots or life? Man-made caverns inhabited by slaves with all the mental limbs inessential to their occupations lopped off? That city is a machine, its people mere functions, a city of the dead. Now look.' She indicated the green expanse to the horizon with a sweep of her arms. 'You have found another more vital family who offers you this. We give life to you who did not know what life was. In exchange for feebleness of spirit and limb you have arrogated to yourself the rash strength of the boar. On this heavenly morning you have in your arms the May Queen herself, who, far from spurning you, is willing to have you as her consort when the time comes. So I offer you myself. What do you offer in exchange, Coll?'

'Myself.'

She nodded. 'Yes. But what do you mean by that? Do you mean your body for my pleasure?'

'Body and soul.'

'Ah, soul too. How should I understand that? And there is much more. What if I am attacked?'

'I will defend you.'

'If I am injured?'

'I will restore you.'

'If I am killed?'

'I will revenge you.'

'If I need – whatever I need?'

'I will bring it to you.'

'If I point out to you those who seek my destruction?'

'I will destroy them.'

'If I require your life?'

In his rhapsody he paused. 'What do you mean?'

'What will your answer be if I ask you to lay down your life for me?'

'I will defend you with my life.'

'But suppose I require your life for no particular reason?'

'Siobhan, what a strange question. Is this a test?'

'No. That will be later. This is a love-parley. Look, if I needed an organ transplant and it so happened that you were compatible with me, would you give me a kidney?'

'Yes.'

'An eye?'

'Yes.'

'A lung?'

'Yes.'

'A heart?'

He hesitated for a moment. 'If it were the only way of saving your life, I think.'

'Think?'

'Yes, I would.'

'But what if it were only to revive my spirit?'

'I don't understand.'

'It's something that you can't understand. Will you give me your heart?'

He laughed joyfully. 'My heart? Is that all? Take it now.'

She placed her hand on his chest where his heart was and massaged it gently. 'I shall look after my heart, then, Coll. From this time, then, you are my servant, in the old sense of being a faithful lover. No one shall have any favour of love from me if you do not, as long as this compact lasts. This I give to you as the sea laps the land. But you have become nervous and shaky and do not embrace me properly.'

They turned back but took a different way, passing among some huge oaks, where again they stopped to gaze down the slope at sheep grazing, many of them still lambs. Even the odd swish of a car from a nearby road could not take away from the magic of this morning of mornings with its bliss of Siobhan. Hardly anyone was stirring as they passed through an unfamiliar village of red brick set over its green. The old houses had quite forgotten the day that once had budded from its people in past ages. Now at their jobs up in London they too were cut off from their own roots.

Siobhan cut up a street climbing the highest rise from where, standing below an unexpected windmill with immobile sails, they once more caught sight of the sea. Once clear of the village, she opened a farmer's gate and as previously took one of the old tracks which, for someone who had arrived from Ireland only a few days before, she seemed to know pretty well. They walked around little fields, plunged through copses and belts of trees, paused to take stock of the water as they lingered on a bridge over a stream and at length entered Hazelridge from the back. It was now quite warm and Coll was beginning to sweat a little from the effort of walking without rhythm below his usual pace,

The house was breathlessly still, as if waiting. No one was in the grounds, back or front. Everyone seemed to be out. He followed her round to the front where the oak was newly planted. They looked at it. Siobhan walked around it several times, touching it. She spoke words in an unknown tongue, calling out for someone, Coll didn't know who.

'We're both sweaty from our walk. Let's go up, take a shower and change,' she said, calmly removing every stitch of clothing until she stood before him quite naked. 'Come with me.'

He followed in a dream too startled to realize what was happening.

'Together, Coll, but no touching except as I say. I need you now.'

Showering with Siobhan was like standing in a rain of warm wine, in spite of his nervousness, for her attraction was tempered with a sense of awe. He tried to envelope her, but she kept him at bay, letting him have only one full embrace. When they came out, she touched him on both shoulders and the navel, making the sign of the cross, saining him. Without looking for towel or clothes, she scampered out of the bathroom down stairs and outside.

He found her standing at the new oak, a silver halter in her hand, a torque with an attached cord. Her divine nudity was irresistible. As he rushed at her, she said, 'First, put this on.' She made him kneel in front of her. Then, kneeling herself, she touched him in the most ravishing way, making the desire surge up in him, and took his seed from him in her hands. She then rose, spurned him with her foot away from the tree and anointed the earth and bole with his sperm carefully and ritualistically, speaking in a language unknown to him.

He lay on the ground wondering, for he did not know what was going on and he was suddenly in awe of her. She exuded power; her face had become otherworldly as though she was now possessed of a cosmic wisdom, some knowledge far beyond the mere human experience of ages.

When she was finished, she led him by the halter back inside and told him to go and get dressed.

At that moment she was a being completely different from the girl he had walked out with less than three-quarters of an hour before.

Chapter 27

AT LUNCH CYBELE GAVE OUT THE ORDERS, primarily to Gerald and Coll. They were to share security, taking it in turn to be up and constantly on patrol; around the house. In addition, Coll was put in charge of maintaining and driving both the AWD and the car with Cybele taking over his guard job when he had to be away on these duties. Diane and Maxine shared out the housework and cooking, but in practice the kitchen was Diane's domain. Nothing was said about Esmirone or Siobhan.

Whatever Cybele might say, she, in fact, was still in absolute charge of security. Back-up was provided by the nearest village where the Circle, apparently, was very strong. Coll gathered that, among other responsibilities, Esmirone was the liaison between this and other Circle foundations. It was obvious that Siobhan, now that she had been designated Queen, whether appointed or elected or whatever, had been set here in a kind of fastness where she was the central figure. He had no idea of how far or deeply the Circle reached, but he was sure she was highly protected. It followed, so he was convinced, that he and Gerald were there more for show than anything else, that his own function was going to be something quite different, and that the whole schedule had been put in place by Cybele just to keep everyone busy until their real duties were revealed. In this he was largely but not quite right, as events turned out.

As for Siobhan, he was aware of a surreal quality in his attachment to her, a delicate balance of extreme urges, of heaven, of awe, of sacrifice, of painful desire, all combining in a fantastic garden temple in the softest greenest part of the sacred earth.

It was something much more weighty than tricky surrealism that possessed the most direct and honest girl who had ever drawn him: this morning she had been more than human – some transcendental creature? He knew no word for it. She became something greater, something beyond his comprehension.

Diane was about the same age as Siobhan. Had she been a rival candidate in whatever choice had been made? If so, she did not show it in word, deed or gesture. Like the others in their casual ways, she treated the May Queen with a tiny touch of awe. More about her later.

Gerald was one of those people, apparently engagingly frank, who in fact are hard to get to know. Almost as big in build as Coll, but without the animal strength, he instructed the latter in pistol shooting and in handling a pretty good selection of other firearms. Initially they put in a lot of practice by arranging four with eight hour shifts week and week about until they could ease into the schedule and decide what was most comfortable for them. At first Cybele made no objection, but after a week she restored the original scheme. This brought an end to firing practice. Each of them had two-way radio communication with Cybele monitored by a security person in the village in case anything unusual should turn up. Coll soon became aware that other invisible people had done a thorough job of setting up a system in which Hazelridge was only one of several units. Gerald knew no more about this than he did. Others could be called in at short notice. The more he considered this, the more superfluous did he and Gerald seem.

It became clear, too, that initial training completed, under Cybele's scheme he and Gerald would see very little of each other.

Everyone gathered at meals, including afternoon tea, except the security man on duty, whose food and drink were taken out to him. Siobhan sat at the head of the table; Esmirone and Diane sat next to her on her left and right hands, followed by Cybele and Maxine opposite each other and either Gerald or Coll. No one sat further down the table. This order was for the first six or seven weeks invariable. If someone was away, the place was left vacant. Apart from this visible ranking there was little evidence of a pecking order in their chatter, except that when Siobhan spoke, everyone else was silent. She was never contradicted, even in jest. Very occasionally there were guests. These displaced those of lowest rank, namely Gerald or Coll down the very long table.

Much later on that afternoon when Coll was pottering about ostensibly doing his job, Siobhan came to him again. He waited for her to speak, but she said nothing, walking with him in silence along a track penetrating the thick yew hedge at the rear of the property while he called Cybele to let her know he was leaving with Siobhan. At first they walked in the sun through springtime fields pasturing sheep, pausing at a perfect scene of pastoral peace emphasized by a few scattered oaks, enormous rock-like trees; here they looked down a gradual shallow valley where a few peaceful sheep troubled only about their bellies clipped the shaven grass even closer. From here, in some completely mysterious way, they made a transit into some other completely different scene, passing under trees growing so closely together that their branches met in a common canopy. A fortnight would block out the sky. She took paths invisible to him until they came upon the great roots of dark pines creaking a little in the slight breeze. They were dark, dark trees, centuries old. Here she found a place where she could sit down and rest in a hollow formed by large roots below a grassy mound. He said nothing. It was as though they had reached another country.

'Still feeling hurt,' she asked.

He paused. 'Only for a moment or two. I can never hold anything against you. You never explain and you never justify yourself. You are the Queen – my Queen.'

'I know,' she said, 'and I'm sorry afterwards. But that's the way it has to happen. It's so hard for me to tell you about things I myself hardly understand. I'm still new at the job. If you could look at it from another point of view you would feel proud, not sorry for yourself that you were not at the centre of your – how do you see it? – manhood's rite? It wasn't. It was something even more important. Your time will come, Coll. That I promise you. When it does, you won't be disappointed.'

'I know. You became someone utterly different. Now you're just the same Siobhan again. Until next time. Just tell me: what about us? Yes, I know you warned me that something like this might happen, and I followed you with open eyes. I didn't expect that I would become just a low form of life around the place.'

'Low, you call it? Aren't you just a little proud that yours was the fructifying seed? Dear Coll, be proud and let it go at that.'

'Are you still going to be the Siobhan who saved me when I was waiting for death on the Burren? Sometimes?'

'Yes, of course I am, silly. Coll, have you any idea of how – exceptional – it is that you should be in the house at Hazelbridge in the very centre of the Circle, you who have been with us only a few months? You are here for one reason only: because I wanted you here, you jumped-up little general. What shall I do to restore your manly self-respect? Have you any idea what I could do? Produce spirits from the earth for a pageant as Prospero did? I might. Serve you precious wines here in the forest? I could. Dance naked in front of you to restore your lascivious desires that would do for Cybele or Diane as well as for me? I shan't. Isn't it enough for your ego that I'm here with you, talking with you, walking with you, even loving you in my way?'

She caressed him a little, stroking his shoulders and back until he felt wonderfully relaxed and confident in her company, but preventing his hands from wandering. He had the odd fancy that a continent of a forest from the past grew up enveloping them. He sensed life constantly on the move all around them.

'Do *you* still want to love me, Coll?'

'I love you.'

'If you have any doubt, tell me now. You must be quite sure and utterly steadfast.'

'You know I love you. Otherwise we should not be here together.'

'Cybele wants you and she would make you a good companion. In the Circle we try not to change our life's companions once chosen. She is freer than I am.'

'You are the Queen. I shall share your fate.'

'In myself I am much less than a queen; in my sacred rôle I am much more. It won't be share and share alike. Don't expect that.'

'I'll take my chance – for a kiss,' he replied, cheered again and laughing.

'Here's your kiss, then, and two and three. But no more. The way to my bed is more difficult.'

As they got up and walked on further into the forest he was so charged with happiness that he did not notice where he was going. They passed under unreachable boughs he did not remember seeing, and, since the Downs are under cultivation or in pasture, could not, as far as he knew, exist in the extent it did, for they spent several long hours amid giant trees whose silent presence was unbroken by any whisper or glimpse of a world outside. At length she rested again, seating herself between heaving roots, the gigantic ribs of an ancient earth.

'What do you see here, Coll?'

'These trees haven't been disturbed for centuries, God knows how many! I don't know how large it is – it looks enormous. There's not a sound except – it's almost frightening. I mean, I should have thought, this can't possibly exist in Southern England, can it?'

'Outside the forest there are many roads, the great scarring traffic ways that obliterate the land and the little tracks so hard to see that bring you back to it. In here there is another way, a way that you have chosen to take with me. So now I have to lay something else on you: that you shall never reveal to anyone that we have been here together, that you have been here with me, nor what you see or hear within this place. If we meet anyone, say nothing. I'll do the talking.'

She then plunged deeper into the thickest part of the wood, but by and by found a narrow path that gradually tended downwards. Here the giant pines were, if anything, even taller, darker, more spacious; They had entered a region where no ray of sunlight penetrated. After about half-an-hour he could make out the rushing of a stream. She paused and warned him again: 'Be quiet, say nothing, nothing at all. Don't even squeak.'

Breasting a scarcely perceptible rise concealing a hollow, they looked down upon a circular cleared space. He could see several figures on the opposite bank of the stream. A spontaneous feeling of thankfulness that the stream was between them arose in him. There was something familiar about the tall gaunt figure on the right even though his face was turned away from the newcomers. The central dwarfish figure was dressed in a faded green jacket that looked as though it had been displayed far too long in a museum case. The third figure, on the right, was that of a very pale slender lady clad in a dress that covered her completely from a high collar at the throat to the ankles. It was dark, dark red.

As Siobhan and Coll slowly made their way towards the three, those turned their gazes on the two who came. No one spoke or moved for minutes. At length, the dwarf sitting cross-legged on the turf spoke.

'Greetings, Siobhan the Queen. You come in good time. If you desire anything of us so early in your reign, speak. You will not find us unwilling to hear you. But first tell us the name of your companion, whom we do not recognize. Have you brought him here as a gift for the great ones?'

'No, honoured cousin, whose name I do not reveal. He is a servant dumb in my company whom I have sained for the sake of the season.'

'Yet let him speak for himself, Siobhan,' said the woman in a voice that reminded Coll of a serpent uncoiling. He must surely have the manners to greet us.'

'I have sealed his tongue, sister, and I ask you not to be offended. One who has a treasure naturally wishes to keep it as long as possible.'

'Prudence is one thing,' she replied, 'rudeness quite another. But I see he is a pig without manners. Yet surely his Queen should redeem him. Should we ignore her as he ignores us? Young man, tell me who you are and I will give you my name. Then we shall have power over each other and no one shall be the loser.' She looked at him with such bewitching supplication that he opened his mouth to stammer his apologies. Siobhan punched him hard in the back and he closed it again.

'A lovely man,' she went on, and she looked young and beautiful with all the urges of her blossoming girlhood turned towards him. 'Am I the first pretty woman who wants you – and you will not give me so much as a single word, not a look, even? Grunt me a single syllable and you shall lie with me to your heart's content. Believe me, I can give you heaven in my body. Your Queen gives you nothing but temporization and procrastination.'

This was true, but Siobhan had her hand upon him and he said nothing.

'A gross hog,' the slender lady said.

'I greet you,' said the man whom Coll recognized, both the Queen and this young man whose name I once knew well. That name he has lost. If he does not speak to me on this occasion, I shall, on this occasion only, choose to understand, for the sake of his Queen and because he was in his own way good to me in the past. I do not seek to alter his fate. His nemesis is with him at this moment, loving the one she has to destroy. Shall I change that?

'Since you are come to us, O Queen, what is your demand?'

'O Father of Insight, he and I have raised an oak sacred to you. He has given of himself in oblation to you. We have honoured you in our rites. In exchange I ask that you shall not demand him of me.'

'You have brought him here to our very earth,' replied the dwarf. 'What do you expect?'

'I ask that he shall wander here without harm.'

The three were silent.

The gaunt figure spoke: 'It is through my means that you have him. I therefore have some title. What do you offer me for my part?'

'Allfather, I took him by my own free choice. You did not give him that; and we have since made an offering and built an altar to you in recompense and reconciliation.'

'O Queen, I sent him to you. He is mine for one day of the year, the day on which you hazard his life. Acknowledge that and give me an earnest and we shall do whatever you demand beside.'

'But that is what I ask you to yield to me as you know only too well. Be kind in answer to the honour we do you: release him from his due on the day. Be kind, Allfather.'

'If I do you must pay it yourself.'

'Ask for anyone else; show the Queen some favour for my bowing down to you.'

The figure on the left could not be moved. 'Either you or he must answer, even if he did not stand here within our precinct on this day of all days in the year. Give me an earnest, or he shall not leave with you.'

In Siobhan's hand was a young oak leaf. This she laid on the ground. The gaunt one came towards them with great speed and picked it up. In his hand it grew suddenly into a strange shape, swaying and coiling. The woman walked over to Coll, hardly touching the water. Her face, now framed by coiffed hair, was as beautiful as a painting, the very image of perfection, with narrower lips than the current popular taste. It was lovely but had no depth. She studied him. Then she reached up and pulled her face off as if it had been a living mask. Beneath it was an old old face, depthless in its perception of the unending frightfulness of men and furious in its lust to revenge. The seated dwarf did not even move his head. Coll, overcome by this crescendo of horror, lost his legs and collapsed.

When he awoke he was among the few scattered oaks of his earlier walk with Siobhan. The sheep were still grazing undisturbed down the dell. He had awoken from a long vivid dream, but he could not remember falling asleep. The sun was shining, the day almost cloudless. Beyond the sheep to the left he noticed a curious latticework pattern. He later learned that it was the excavation site of a Romano-British villa. All this he could see without turning his head. When he did move he saw Siobhan some distance away behind him reclining on the pasture in the three biggest surviving oaks. She looked like an impressionist painting for she had taken off all her upper clothing. Her skin was angelically white. He thought of the first bursting forth of the naked bud on the tree.

He went over to her and crouched beside her. She took his hands to prevent his touch, not unkindly.

'I had a dream,' he began. He didn't know what to say. What was true, what false? Everything that happened had its own realm of conviction in the soul, an inescapable reality.

'I know. Well, at least we didn't meet the huntsman. I should have been hard put to it then. We've moved one tiny step forward, but there, I think, we hold. What did Victor give you in Toronto that obliged you to him?'

'Nothing. He gave and received nothing. That was his mania, that was why he was in there for treatment. Siobhan, you must tell me: do we share the same dreams, or did I walk with you into a forest that has no existence in this world? Did you speak with beings who have no business walking on earth? Tell me if you have any love at all for me, tell me for the sake of my sanity.'

'Coll, you are bound to me in ways that you do not understand. You have undertaken three times to love me and sealed that undertaking. I have accepted your love in the same way. You partake in a small part of me, but I possess you wholly. You are now mine, or nearly so. I told you it would not be share and share alike, remember? You were satisfied with that. I also told you from the beginning that you might never love me in the way you wanted most, so do not think of embracing me now. I offered you Cybele, but you preferred the higher road.

'At my side you are beginning to find divinity, for this time, the darker side. The shadow exists just as much as its primary does. In order to win through on your own terms you will have to meet, square off against and get on to equal terms with the shadow. And now I have to think what my next step should be. Please, Coll. I do not want your overtures now. Wait.'

'Ah, but perhaps your "no" really means "yes" here among these trees, the only lookers-on. Why do you undress before me, then? You treated me like a dog this morning, didn't you? I love you. Does that mean that I'm to have no feelings of my own? What did the lady in red say? "temporization and procrastination" – was she, by any chance, right?'

He did not attempt to touch her further, but anger gripped him.

'You are behaving like a fool, Coll,' replied Siobhan calmly. 'Every word you say makes it clear that you are succumbing to the blandishments of one who is nothing beside me. Have you any idea of what danger you are inviting upon yourself? Yes, I put you in danger's way today, but I thought you had enough discrimination to recognize my purpose. Did you not hear me venture myself in your place? I did my part for you, more than my part.

'You played the part you had to play, as I did. It was to have been for your own good. Don't you understand that you are in a bad spot, in need of rescue? As for sex, that too must be for me a matter of ritual, if it occurs. I am in great service. You have no rights over me, or any other woman, for that matter, but there are plenty of willing women who would be delighted with you. You have known at least one. Yet I'll help you, for Coll shall be satisfied, not angered – but not here. Don't, for your own sake, do what you are thinking of doing. Don't break the really big taboos, Coll, whatever you do.

'You're only my servant, my dog, my pig. That you chose at the Beltane fire. I feed and I water you: shall I also let you out among the sows? I take it you don't fancy the lady in the forest as much as she fancies you, in your "dream" as you think. Walk a little behind me on the way back. I don't choose to be disturbed by you.'

She slipped her clothing back on, got up and walked quickly away without another glance at him. His fury was almost ungovernable, but it was seasoned with a sense of her power, the fear left by the dream and a vestige of the awe that had overcome him in the morning. He trailed her back. There was no reality in his feelings or perceptions; he was unaware of his surroundings. He was in a transport of numb rage underlain by a sense that he had lost all grip on events.

When they arrived it was tea time. As he was still on duty he stayed out in the garden, but he paid no attention to what was going on around him. It was a long while before Diane brought him a vacuum bottle full of strong coffee, a large roll stuffed with lettuce and the blue cheese he loved and a large hunk of iced fruit cake. He liked Diane and wished to know her better.

'Here you are, stalwart and faithful man. You must have tired Siobhan out, for she went straight up to her room before we'd even got properly started. However, she told me to come out here and give you anything you wanted. I don't know what she meant. What do you think?'

'I want to tan her backside. Someone should have done it years ago.'

Diane began to laugh. 'That's very naughty, Coll, but you'd better abandon that scheme. She gave you a rough time, I gather. But you'd better be careful. She's as furious as you are.'

'This queen business – she takes it very seriously. It's gone to her head.'

'Not her head, Coll. Her heart. She has the vocation. You don't know her yet. We do. She's gold. You will find that out yourself. She is the pure gold.'

'And how long does it last? What's the term of her reign?'

'For a long time, perhaps a very long time. She will not always treat you like this. There will come a time when you will be more important to her than you are now. Right now, apparently, she doesn't care what you do.'

'But I'm responsible for her safety.'

'Yes, you are. And you'll have to weigh that against – what did you say? tanning her backside? – because she does have the power in our Circle. You know that much now. She's more than a priestess and she's sacrosanct. She has a rich sense of humour though, and I imagine she's laughing more than I am at your grotesque fancy that you're going to tuck her skirts up. Don't forget what power she wields when she wants to. You must have understood that. If you want to be her clown, go ahead, that is, provided you know how far you can go. Perhaps that's what she wants just now, although I wouldn't have thought that you had the talent or the inclination for the job.'

'Yes, well, she was up against it this afternoon.'

'Oh, Coll, don't be silly.'

'Not with me. I didn't mean that. There are things around that she's up against.'

He remembered the warning he had received and did not say what they were.

Gerald relieved him shortly after six and he was off until after midnight.

It had been a roller coaster of a day filled with new blends of emotion, from the lyric poem of the soft English dawn to the life of a tree strengthened by his blind act of nurture to the chilling reality of the dark forces arrayed against the people of Hazelridge, himself in particular, not to mention the ups and downs of Siobhan's treatment of him. He wondered if he should wander down to the village after supper while it was still a little light to look in at the pub, at least to have a glance at the neighbours who were such firm supporters of the household. It was another hour-and-three-quarters to supper and he was still hungry, so he sauntered off to the kitchen.

Siobhan was downstairs for supper as usual. Underneath the talk, he thought, there was some joke that he was being left out of, for the women glanced at him and smiled, not unkindly, no, that was not it, but knowingly. He realized that he would be stupid to go down to the pub and leave himself dead tired in the small hours. He went up to his room to rest, not bothering with the coffee, still feeling bruised.

Siobhan did not spare him a glance as he said goodnight.

Chapter 28

AT MIDNIGHT he went down to the conservatory and relieved Gerald. In spite of rest he was still tired and not inclined to move around much, so he took his time. Later, under a moon nearly full he made his first round, a circuit of the house itself followed by a search of the back garden with its ornate rectangular pond, fountain and summer house, then the sheds, walks and the outlying parts of the property. Here he walked along the tall hedges of yew and holly. In spite of his fatigue, he felt the ancient thrill of the bright moon riding in the sky. He spent some time sitting under the great cedar of Lebanon. There was nothing out of place or unusual. After an hour or so he went back to his spot in the conservatory. Strictly, neither he nor Gerald was supposed to be inside at all, but with all the lights out he had a pretty good view of the back.

On subsequent rounds he grew more alert, felt less at ease, and it was with a start that he thought he saw a figure moving among the trees beyond the boundary hedge. Unlatching the picket gate in the hedge, he searched the darkness with his torch, drawing a revolver as he did. A white face turned towards him in the dark, the face, he thought, of a woman. He stopped, for he did not in the least feel inclined to follow her beyond the property line. She remained as still as a statue until he hoped that his eyes might be deceiving him, but at length slowly turned away and walked with inviting motions into the wood as if encouraging pursuit. He felt as if he had been jolted by an electric shock and it was a minute or so before he gathered his wits sufficiently to call Cybele. She told him to stay within the grounds.

'I'll see if someone else can track her down,' she said.

This happened about three hours into his watch.

Normally he would have grabbed something to eat in the kitchen after Gerald came down and slept until lunchtime. On this occasion he was, however, curiously disturbed. The last thing he wanted to do was rest; he felt a wish to know more about the visitant, to find out the heart of the puzzle, the nettle of danger. The bed was a desert and the larder could not refresh him. He growled and pottered and waited for the others, who took their time.

At breakfast everything was back to normal. Siobhan was there. If she was still mad at him she gave no sign of it.

'Take your rest now, Coll,' she said. 'If you get three hours' sleep, will it be enough? I want you to drive me up to London. We'll have a late lunch there.'

It was just as well that Coll had studied the routes, for the main roads were clogged. In spite of his inexperience, he made no mistakes. Nothing was more important to him than keeping Siobhan safe and sound, and he had done his homework well. She did not like motorways, so Coll took secondary roads, and there was many a lovely village where he would have given much to pause before they came to the monstrous sprawl of London's brood of satellite towns and suburbs dated in degrees of degradation of a once breathtakingly beautiful landscape. Trying to keep the pastoral scenery as long as he could, he was on a relatively quiet stretch not far from Box Hill, a little off his route when, without any warning, a car pulled across the road directly in front of him. As he ground to a halt, another blocked him from behind.

He was out of the car in a flash as Siobhan locked up. The first man swung a baseball bat at him, but he seized it and punched the wielder's face, feeling the bones crack under his fist. The two others were on to him and he was rocked by their coshes, but one was already dead, his skull broken horribly by his second blow, while the third he kicked down with his last strength as he failed. With a final huge effort he pushed the blocking car to the verge, knowing he had lost his divine Siobhan to the thugs in the following car. Whatever hit him was as convincing as a naval broadside, for with a giant flash in his head he was out.

Later on he was aware that he was stretched out in the back of a car and tried to pull himself up, but someone gently pushed him back, someone who was holding his head. He heard Siobhan's voice and was confused. 'Keep still, dear Coll. There's a lot of bleeding. Everything is all right. I am fine and we are with friends. So just keep quiet and stay still. You must lie still, or the bleeding will start again.' From time to time he would come out of his daze, and once in a desperate fit he made a giant effort to get up, but she held him back, evidently with some help from another. After that he relapsed into unconsciousness, for the next thing he knew he was wide awake propped up on masses of pillows in a darkened room. Someone had done a professional job of bandaging his head. He put his hands up. There was no trace of blood.

After twenty minutes or so, as he thought, he opened his eyes again and decided to get up, now feeling perfectly well. The room no longer had to be darkened. It was night time. He could not find the switch on the lamp beside the bed, and when he made for the door he stumbled on to his knees. He still felt perfectly well, but his coordination was off. In the hallway the light was blinding. He was upstairs in a pretty large house, and he made his way down to the foot of the stairs facing the front door at the end of the passage. There were rooms to right and left. Set to the left of this elongated foyer was a short hallway with a picture window overlooking the garden and lawn fronting the main street. There was a very large room at the end. It was lit and voices were coming from it.

As he entered, they stopped.

'What on earth are you doing out of bed?' asked an Irish voice he had heard before somewhere.

He couldn't think whose it was although he knew the speaker.

'Look, man, your head has been stitched up, and if you move around the stitches will loosen and the bleeding will start all over again. When I first laid eyes on you, you looked like Agamemnon in the bath – or am I thinking of someone else? – anyway, it's back to bed with you. What time is it? After eleven. Siobhan? She nursed you the whole way in the car and she'll be along in the morning too. Come on, there's a good chap.'

He and another took him upstairs again, firmly but as gently as they knew how.

'Do be good, Coll. If you get lively, one of us has to sit by your bed all night. So don't get us in bad with Siobhan, O.K? You're not allowed any pills at all, so what are we to do?'

'Did you drive me around in Ireland?'

'Man, I'm always driving you around, there and here. And somehow you always seem sort of knocked out to me. although this is a real beauty. Perhaps I just happen along at the awkward moments. However, you're not supposed to talk, so sleep tight till morning's light.'

'I know you, you're Michael,' said Coll a long time after the other had left him in darkness.

He did not, however, sleep tight, for several times the other one came and woke him up on the accursed orders of the anonymous doctor.

When he finally woke up by himself, it was after ten. The day was fairly fine (for London). His windows looked out over a large back garden with a row of ugly Lombardy poplars marking the far boundary. Someone had thoughtfully supplied him with new clothes which felt good after a bath. Downstairs in the dining room he exchanged the sign of greeting with the housekeeper, Mrs Scott, but Barbara the kitchen maid did not recognize it. Both were from Scotland. They too had been enslaved by the tyrannical doctor, for he got a much reduced breakfast. They told him the papers were in the lounge, their name for the huge room he had wandered into during the night, and shunted him out of their business in the kitchen.

Michael and his friend were nowhere to be seen and there was no Siobhan, indeed there was no one else at all. He felt as if he were in a dream. He felt so comfortable: there was an atmosphere of self-satisfied peace in the house, in stark contrast to the bristling psychic energy of Hazelridge. He felt that nothing could possibly break through into the calm of this Victorian island in Putney. Several callers came and went at the door. He did not bother about them.

One wall of the lounge was completely lined with shelves filled with books. There were two large french windows opening out on to the back garden. About ten feet from these nearer the other wall was a Bechstein; near it the lovely marble mantelpiece survived, but the fireplace had long since been converted to gas, the only off-note in this calm of big leather sofas and wing chairs, newspaper racks and the dark-stained floor under opulent red rugs, all of it well-used and familiar. Much more a place for men than women it was. Nothing in Hazelridge, in spite of its ancient forest and lovely pastures, gave him such a feeling of permanence, a secure establishment for the comfort of men, as this place did.

The large back garden was more lawn than anything else, and nothing to compare with the one he had just left, but the brick-lined walks were pleasant enough even in the uncertain sun wavering above the crossing clouds. Attempts at flower beds waved their colours. The front garden was narrow, the driveway short, obviously truncated by road encroachments over the years. There was practically no room for parking, although spaces had been marked out for four cars accessible simultaneously by drivers of genius. There was a tiny red car, a nondescript Peugeot, but no sign of the car he had driven on the previous day. He wondered why he was not worrying particularly about the three men whose lives he had taken. While he was thinking of this, another car pulled in and Siobhan got out.

'Inside, Coll, quick. Didn't they tell you to stay inside? Michael's the very limit and Don's no better.'

Inside she gave him the old warm and loving embrace and a kiss that spoke eloquently of no reservations.

'You were wonderful, Coll. You went for the three of them, big fellows they were, too, and skittled them all without a thought for yourself. I still don't understand how you managed, even with your enormous strength, to shove the car aside before you went down. That was as important as anything else you did, for if we'd stayed blocked we'd have been delayed quite a while, more than enough time for something else to go wrong, such as the police arriving on the scene. The fellows behind took you while you were busy. Be sure you stand high for what you did yesterday. I shall never forget it.'

'What about the ones behind? Why didn't they kill me and you as well, or kidnap you, or whatever they wanted to do?'

'I always have back-up, as Cybele must have told you. Matt Hewer and a couple of his men from the village were following close enough to bring their weapons to bear. When the beauties, saw what was coming, they took care of their own, bundled the bodies in and drove off on their way covered by the village team. I never moved from the car until then. One of them wanted to make a grab at me, but he could see that he'd be shot dead if he did, so he sensibly decided not to. It was only then that I could attend to you. We got a doctor to you as soon as we could and she did a dandy job of stitching up your poor head.'

'So the police are not involved?'

'We don't think so – officially. In any case, we've got rid of the cars. Nothing like them will be found again.'

'Who are they?'

'Enough talk. You're supposed to rest.'

'Oh come on! Don't hold out on me.'

'All right, then. I don't know.'

'I'll bet you do!'

'At the moment I don't. There are simply too many possibilities – it could be a rogue section of the CIA with its own special agenda, a part-time secret police working for interests not uncongenial to the U.S. government. That's my suspicion. The whole right-wing slate of well-connected scoundrels, usually extreme evangelicals, sponsor this kind of murderous violence. They certainly don't have the cooperation of the British police, but favoured groups might operate with the tacit blessing of M.I.5. Another possibility is a rival group like ourselves, but much less enlightened. We know about these people, but so far, the rivalry has been muted. I think myself that there is a U.S. evangelical connexion here somewhere. We'll find out, don't worry.'

'Before they kill me, I hope!'

'You bled on me, you know. I did not flinch from your blood, but tried to keep it from flowing out of you. And there was so much! But that which touched me I cherish. What a nice room! Let's sit down, not too near the window. Doesn't it just smell of men!

'I'm off to Hazelridge today. You are going to stay here and simply take it easy until you're thoroughly well. Now don't argue. I know I need you, but while you're away I'll have others to look after me. I'll ask Michael to look in on you whenever he's up in London. I'll let you know when you're to come back, but you may be here for three or four weeks, in spring, you lucky dog. What more could a young man want? Here's something that will help you enjoy life.'

She handed him a fat envelope.

'London's prices are extortionate, but you won't need a great deal, because everything is found here. If you need anything, speak to Michael Wainwright, the House Director. I have quite a lot of business at Hazelridge. You can't help me there at present, and I'll have you back by Midsummer. But I've got to get away now, dear Coll.'

'Aren't you even going to stop for lunch?'

She looked at him curiously, smiling slightly. 'All right,' she said, a little reluctantly, 'may as well, but we'll have to make it a short one.'

Michael and Don showed up soon after and joined them at lunch in the dining room just off the kitchen. They ate rapidly while Siobhan confined herself to a single cup of coffee. In spite of her hurry, she embraced Coll most tenderly before taking off.

Coll was about to speak when Michael started the engine.

'Good God, you're not about to tell *me* to take care, are you, you joker? Have a good time you lucky bastard. She's mine on this trip, perhaps forever. Eat your heart out.'

Siobhan gave him another kiss before closing her window and Coll knew what the old poets meant when they spoke of losing their hearts. She had his in her hands.

Chapter 29

Left on his own without any instructions, Coll felt at a loose end, even in London. He was surprised that he was apparently the only resident in this large house, apart from Mrs Scott and Barbara. Barbara was lean and angular, rosy-cheeked and pleasant, but not at all attractive to him. Prowling the upper halls, he found that all the rooms, doors left open, were indeed occupied, but the whereabouts of their inhabitants was indeed a mystery. He asked Mrs Scott about it.

'Oh dear, yes. We're always full, with a waiting list. They've all gone off for the weekend. They'll be back for supper tonight, though, don't worry.'

He went out and took the bus into Piccadilly, but did not find much of real interest there, lively as the scene was. Walking around Putney was more interesting, especially when, striding up the hill well into his own pace, he found the heath at the top.

Back at Richmond House he prowled the lounge. The bookshelves yielded little, mainly unwanted books former residents had left behind – decaying paperbacks and old small-print pamphlets produced in accordance with the regulations of a wartime economy by authors now unread on topics archæologically outdated, for example, *The Citizen and the Beveridge Plan*. Someone had kept the piano in decent tune, though, and he wondered who the musician might be. When Mrs Scott heard that he had gone into London she was annoyed. He had, she said, been told to stay inside by Siobhan, and how could he think of not doing what she asked. He liked her. She was interested in music and told him about some of the concerts and recitals going on. He resolved to hear the Tallis Scholars on the following Wednesday.

By seven the tables in the dining room had been laid to capacity, but at eight there was still no sign of the residents. Mrs Scott grew restive.

'It's the traffic,' she said, 'worse now than it's ever been. There aren't the twenty mile-long queues there used to be before the motorways were built, but people were still polite in those days when I first came to London as a girl of fifteen. Now! It's so different. They're even killing each other. The tube is still the same, only more dilapidated, but the buses are worse, I don't know! And people simply walk right into you on the pavement – knock you off the kerb they do.'

It was at that moment that a coach pulled up to the gate.

At last! An hour-and-a-half late, not so bad after all. That's why we always have a cold supper on Sunday.'

She went to the door to greet them. 'Mr Wheelwright, back at last? How was it?'

He heard Michael Wheelwright's apologies for their slow progress until the men crowding in drowned out any particular voice. He sat in the kitchen near the open door to the dining room. The noise made him dizzy. He was still feeling the effects of his head injury.

Soon afterwards he joined them at supper, introduced by Michael Wheelwright, a trim slim man with an air of quiet command, about ten years older than the average resident. He had no hope of memorizing the string of twenty names or so. He sat next to Derek, opposite the tall Robbo and the small slim and lithe Eddy (these two in a continual ferment of comic dialogue with each other; both of them could extemporize in blank verse), and there were a John, a Tony, a Jack, two Peters, a Robert, two Alans, a Roger, a Vincent and a Gordon; the rest were too far away for him to try to memorize. One of them was called Trevor. Tony and Roger were brothers. As far as he could make out, they all had regular jobs of some kind, but chose to live in this glorified boarding house rather than independently. There was a lovely conviviality that embraced him, but demanded nothing of him. No one asked him questions; he was included immediately, especially by Robbo and Eddy who probed him only for a sense of humour.

The hour being late for these people who had to get up early in the morning to go to their jobs, supper was briefer than usual. Coll wandered into the lounge, but oddly enough only Derek was there, a young man of twenty-eight who was both tall and taciturn. He was one of those who find it difficult to mince their ideas into trivial conversation, and soon disappeared upstairs, leaving the directionless Coll to explore the interior, for he did not feel like turning in at ten in the evening.

The house had been extended several times, in order to expand the accommodation, so that there were enough single rooms for all, with one exception. The exception was the large upstairs room with easily the best view of the garden which he was to share with Robert. This did not please Coll at all, and he promptly went to Mrs Scott early on Monday to see whether there was any chance of getting a single room. She referred him to Michael, who would not return until evening. Michael was sympathetic, but could not help him. There was no more space. He was last in and could be moved only when there were vacancies further up in the pile. Michael told him that he and Robert had the best room. Coll, spoiled by the luxury of Hazelridge, mentioned that he would probably have to make his own arrangements, thank you very much, whereupon Michael looked at him sharply and gently shook his head.

'My understanding is that you are staying with us. Wasn't that made clear to you by your own people? I can't stop you from acting on your own responsibility, but I urge you to think it over in the morning. You might get yourself offside with your own gang.'

Coll thought it over and decided to stay for the present. As it turned out, Robert, the baby of the house, was a quiet young man; they didn't clash at all.

Coll noticed immediately that these people were ignorant of the Beth-Luis-Nion. He had given Michael the greeting, but the House Director had not shown any sign of recognition.

The following morning, Monday, Coll watched the residents depart to their jobs after a buffet breakfast. The house felt empty again. He noted that only two of them owned cars. The third one seemed to be a fixture in its parking space. Before looking at *What's On In London* he explored the house a little further. All he found was a locked door to the cellar, a hefty tom cat he hadn't met before comfortably asleep in the kitchen on a hard wooden chair and piles of old records, shellac discs, in cupboards under the bookcases in the lounge. All the bedroom doors were unlocked and he could easily have snooped around, but he did not want to put himself in a false position.

Siobhan hadn't said anything to him about staying indoors. On the contrary, she had implied that he was to have a good time until he was summoned back to Hazelridge. He went out to explore London riding high on the upper deck of a bus through its yellow brick streets, slightly tawdry, but still a place full of legendary romance for a young man.

By the fifth day, Wednesday, he was getting tired of it, and he wondered what on earth Siobhan was doing to him. But there was something different today. At eight all the residents gathered in the lounge. Here assorted chairs were arranged in a rough circle in the centre, while the sofas and larger furniture were pushed outside towards the walls. Twelve seated themselves in the inner ring, leaving one chair vacant, while all the others, including himself, were seated on the fringes outside the central group. He noticed that everyone had taken the trouble to dress up a little; jackets appeared to be *de rigeur*. The proceedings opened with one of the men in the circle, Trevor, standing and saying, 'We are almost at the height of the second quarter. I give you –' here Coll could not catch the word, for Trevor turned his face away. Three others, Michael, Derek and Gordon, marking the other three quadrants of the circle, stood up and apparently repeated the word Trevor had just uttered, but Coll still had trouble in picking it up. Trevor then turned to a paper he had in his hand and read a poem on spring and summer translated from the Attic Greek. Once this short ritual was accomplished, a visitor, Jack Corbin, produced some ancient records and gave a demonstration of great coloratura voices recorded acoustically in the early years of the twentieth century. This was followed by dark brown tea and Madeira cake so dry it might also have been a survivor of the acoustic era.

Outside in the garden there was the slight scent of stock in the night air under the diesel-laden fumes of London. Life within and without.

The next day, Thursday, Michael took him to where he worked in the City, very early, about five-thirty, long before there was any chance of a cup of coffee, let alone breakfast. At the top of a tall office tower Michael presided over a room full of manned computers, and while he reviewed the overnight markets coffee and sandwiches were brought to them by some factotum who did everything while no one else was there. They agreed to meet for lunch before Michael genially threw him out, telling him where to see a few sights. He wandered over to the Tower of London, but did not have time to go over it before he had to meet Michael again. In any case, Michael had told him that All Hallows was worth a visit, and had given him a card. By this means he got into the crypt, now only about five feet below ground since London has risen on its midden in the one thousand three hundred years the church had been standing. Cities rise on their dung. Although the nave had been largely destroyed by bombs during the Second World War, an awareness of the ancient sanctity of this place found its way into him. He knew with certainty that this site had been consecrated to divine power not for thirteen hundred years but for some immensity of time. The sacristan, a small intense man, noticed this.

'Wonderful to think who may have worshipped here since the seventh century. I hope they have in some sense left their presence here, at least some of them.'

'In this place they would feel safe, wouldn't they?'

'They would be safe. There are certain places that are under the special blessing of the Lord. I believe that here in All Hallows we are in one of them.'

'And before this church was built?'

'Sites for churches were chosen with great care, only after the most acute striving for divine guidance. They were not flung up as they often are now, as pieces of fancy bourgeoisie architecture, kitsch, if you like, at some point jointly dictated by the developer and the borough council, to become guitar-strumming social centres, rootless observance for those who know no roots. When this masonry was shaped and erected with devoted labour, the place of any church was chosen upon inspiration, or at a sign. The task was not first to build and then seek the Lord's blessing, but to find the place the Lord had himself chosen to bless, and build with reverence. The great cathedral at Chartres is such a labour, perhaps the greatest in the Christian world.'

'There might have been another building, another religious building, not Christian, already here.'

The sacristan looked at him. 'There might. There would have been some mark of the holiness of this ground, of that we may be sure. All the greatest Christian churches undoubtedly occupy sites that were known to be sacred ages before the new religion. To you I may be freer in my speech than to the normal altar-gazer who prowls the churches of London in tourist guise. Religions are like hyenas. They prey upon each other: the first-born tries to devour his brother as he emerges from his mother. The Christians have been no better in that respect than the others, and like hyenas they have often fed upon each other, in this land, with Catholic cannibalizing Celt. Oh yes, there are several sacred sites, divine foci, where we are only the latest comers.'

'For example?'

'There are more than you think. In this land the greatest of all is perhaps Glastonbury, where the story is not at all as the Church represents it. But, if I may be allowed to caution you, take care, young man. Know what holiness is before you go too far exploring. Do not lay your soul open until you know what the all-hallowed is. Trust none of us.'

Lunch with Michael was heedlessly rich but hurried in spite of the variety: wine (one glass only), smoked salmon, fresh asparagus flown in from Italy, cantaloupe dessert (the cantaloupes flown in from Israel) with real ice cream, not the muck commonly sold under the name in England, cheese, wonderful rich old cheeses in unlimited portions and coffee that tasted like coffee. They did not have much chance of sustained conversation because Michael had many interruptions *via* his cell phone. He was well-known in high financial circles. Coll wondered anew why such a man would choose to live at Richmond House when he could have had any luxury flat he wanted in, say, Kensington. Michael was glad that his guest had been to All Hallows and talked to Egg. 'We call him Egg because he's a good egg and because his parents saddled him with the name Egbert. Look, do you want to come back later to meet me at the office? We can return together. Or do you want to find your own way back? I'm afraid my late afternoon hours are a little uncertain, but I should be ready a bit before six and we'll grab a bite somewhere. Make a change from Dotheboy's Hall, hm? I'll let Mrs Scott know we'll be out for supper. Bit before six, then.'

Later, at another excellent and this time unhurried meal, Michael explained where he, Coll, stood.

'You see, the chaps at Richmond House belong to a society devoted to achieving harmony first in personal, then in intra-personal, then in social – and so on, all the way up to world affairs and beyond to the cosmic mind. I am deliberately vague about the upper reaches. We think of this endeavour as climbing a tower, and that's why we call ourselves the Tower of Cecilia, Cecilia being the grand matron saint of harmony, heavenly harmony. Doesn't sound like much, does it? A bit unrealistic and I suppose that any number of other groups or societies stand for much the same thing. To you I may confide a little more: it's really a seed-bed of male candidates to see which of them may be suitable to be initiated into the Circle, ultimately. At this stage they know nothing about this, and of course they have no inkling of the alphabet. I read the greetings you were displaying when we all came back last Sunday night, but had to ignore them, of course. Better avoid those up here in London, by the way. You entered the Circle by a very different route, from what I hear, and, being an initiate, have kept the secret quite admirably. At the moment, I'm not aware of any obvious leaks, but the possibility is always there, so while you're among us please keep your eyes and ears open. I'm sure we don't go unwatched in the modern police state.'

'Would you mind giving me some sign, since you seem to be one of the Circle. Michael gave him the greeting and some other words that he did not altogether follow – *castles and towers* were about all that he recognized.

'Good man,' said Michael. 'You are careful. I've already noted that have not said or hinted anything about your antecedents, notably your time in the Circle, and you've not dropped a single name. Our men will not ask about your past. It is made clear to all of them that a resident's past is quite irrelevant to his present standing. It's one of the first considerations in achieving harmony. If you encounter any queries, keep your ears open. Likewise, what I'm telling you now is to be kept under your hat.

'In short, it's my job to keep both my eyes on this group, which is already a pretty good pick, and cultivate the star candidates, if any. They're all idealists, some too much so, perhaps, and they all went on our weekend trip, which gives you some idea of how carefully we've selected.

'Now I don't know anything about your end. That's not my job. All I know is that you're here with us until your people recall you, and I take it as a privilege that our group should be chosen to help. I know that you got yourself into some kind of rough house, probably defending the Circle, or some particular members of it. Anyway, glad to have you. Long may Cecilia prosper in our hearts!'

They raised their glasses.

'I don't know how long I'm going to be here,' replied Coll, 'but I'll try not to be a nuisance. It's very comfortable here, but I've not got much to do, which makes it a bit boring.'

'I've been thinking of that. Actually, if you're willing, there are quite a few things you could do which would help me out. There's a lot of work in running the place, and while Mrs Scott does some of it, all the financial decisions are mine. If you don't mind, I could offload some of those on to you while you're here. Of course you'll have to work within a budget – one of the inescapable facts of life.'

And so it turned out. Coll found himself involved in contracting for maintenance, everything from cleaning windows to planning for a traditional annual fête at the end of May, which he mightn't even see.

Thinking of Siobhan, as he so often did, he remembered her scornful words, that she was going to let him out among the sows, and smiled. Of course neither of them had foreseen the attempted kidnapping which had altered the course of events. Well, attack was always to be expected, but all the same, she had a talent for irony never apparent in the freshness of her talk. It was, he had read in Homer, a god-like attribute. There were three oddly-assorted marks of a goddess by which she could be recognized: irony, slim ankles and a characteristic walk. Together they formed what would now be called in the self-important prolixity of this age of self-serving humbug the incomplete profile of the goddess. And the awe! She could turn it on at will, and when she did, he could not touch her. No anger of his could break it. And here he was wondering when it would be possible to caulk the door frames.

Another mark of the goddess, not out of Homer, the ability to appear, speak and disappear, in daylight or dreams. Could she do this? That would be utterly convincing.

As he sat over his daily ration of routine paper in the dining room he felt her daylight spell, something functioning as precisely as the latch on the front door.

Chapter 30

Frequently Coll's duties gave him the excuse to get out and walk, sometimes as far as Fulham in one direction or Wandsworth in the other. He loved going on these errands in spite of the toxic air loaded with aromatic hydrocarbons, chiefly the gift of London's diesel buses. Here he felt the past lying immediately behind the traffic-ridden present in a way he had never been aware of in Toronto: the two churches by the river, at either end of the bridge, even the one on the Putney side now sunken and squat, must once have been the greatest buildings in their little green parishes, must preserve the memory of that pastoral time when the town was still a mere interruption in the overwhelming landscape of magnified distance in the long ages of foot travel, a meeting of track-like roads from heath, pasture and forest drawing in to join the crowded high street, giant as it must have seemed, winding in to merge at the high lovely expensive bridge of new stone spanning the lucent Thames, today a belching bottleneck of cars, buses and lorries knotted over the turbid water.

It was in Fulham High Street that he ran across Roger, Tony's brother, who worked in an engineering firm nearby. Roger was one of those ever-cheerful people whose natural form of greeting is a joke. He had spent a year in New Zealand and was constantly parroting the style and accent of that country, something that amused most of the lads but tended to grate on Coll.

'Coll, me lad of all people, out looking for the long grass at this time of day, you randy old sucker. Why didn't you let me know?'

'Bound to trip over you.'

Roger added it together in a flash and grinned. 'I was about to grab a bite. Feel like lunch? There's only a Wimpey's.

His tone was frank and inviting, but Coll detected some reserve behind it.

'No, it's O.K., but I'll have a cup of tea with you. I'm pretty well on my way back.'

Roger told Coll about his job. 'I insist on getting out. Most of them send out for grub and eat it in fits and starts, greasing up their keyboards. There's no let-up. But I go crazy if I don't get out. If they don't like it they can find another programmer. But there's a shortage of us right now and so I couldn't give a tin of shit what they think. What are you up to?'

'Just trying to get some painting done before the fête. Just an excuse. I like to get out too.'

'Yeah. Is that all you do for a job, mate? Doesn't seem like much. No pay in that.'

'You're right there. There's f.a. Strictly a voluntary job to help Michael out.'

'What do you live on then?' Roger grinned. 'Your folks got piles?'

'Not really. I'm just taking a holiday between jobs.'

As soon as he spoke, Coll wanted to recall his words and wished that he had had more foresight. He braced himself for the inevitable question.

'What's your real job, then?'

'Not much, I'm afraid. My last one was as a bar bouncer in Toronto.'

'Yeah, but you've got university education. That's not going to be your real job, is it?'

'I'm afraid I haven't done very much – I worked in a bike store. Otherwise just casual jobs over here. I'm a stereotype of our time, an over-educated underachiever. Over-educated in subjects of no practical value in the job market, except perhaps teaching, which absolutely nauseates me.'

'Well, you might have trouble breaking into the job market here, that's true, unless you apply yourself to some skill in demand. Sorry, mate, but that's where the money is. So you're Michael's first assistant. Good, good.'

Coll heard the doubt in Roger's voice. He was not believed, either in the truth or the lie.

'Maybe you can help me to a job in your place.'

'What can you do with a computer?'

'Not much.'

'Well, better learn old chum. Look, got to go now. More than a few nanoseconds I don't have.'

Roger bagged the remainder of his hamburger and waved it at Coll as he went out, nodding to the man behind the counter as he went. Coll finished his tea thoughtfully. He now wished more than ever that Siobhan would either call him back to Hazelridge or let him get on with his life. The encounter with Roger had left him with a feeling of disquiet, the source of which he could not identify. He wondered as if in a daydream why he could not simply walk away from everything, now, in his new invigorated state, his new self, go back, and get on with the career that had been the chief concern of the little family who in this brief passage of melancholy showed up through the mist like an unexpected island in the passing ocean of his remembrance. He saw the old pit again, the pit that he himself had painstakingly gouged out, not as an open menace before him but merely as another unsummoned object in his reverie, as near and as unapproachable as his family. Nearer, much nearer, were Siobhan, the Circle, his new family and the deep forest in its ancient power. Yet he too had acquired power. Where was it? Nothing directed him. There was no application. And as for people like Roger: they were quicker on the uptake than he was. Roger grasped the simple realities of daily existence and succeeded; he, on the other hand, had dredged the deeps, but lacked the common skills that would give him a 'job with a future'. And as the cliché blotted his silliness away, he knew that none of this mattered. If he ought to think this way, he didn't. It was completely irrelevant to his rôle in the Circle. Yet ingrained habits of thought die hard.

Michael, however, was pleased with what he was doing and now left him in complete charge of day-to-day administration. Unfortunately, there being no change in the roster of residents, he was unable to deal himself a single room. His immediate task was to arrange the May party and dance, a dance being held on the last Saturday of each of the spring and summer months. The residents were unusual in that they, unlike other young people, had realized that decibels devastate eardrums, and had therefore gone back to an older, gentler style of dance. As Coll had the time to do the organizing, he assigned the various residents their parts. He asked Derek to arrange the music. Derek was a lover of the classics.

When the day came, everything was in place. He had done the job thoroughly and could sit back and enjoy himself. The several tasks had been delegated. At the lounge door John collected the entrance fee.

But there was one thing he had not been able to do. He had not been able to invite his own girl because he didn't know any women apart from Barbara and his friends at Hazelridge. In any case it would have been highly impolitic, since Siobhan or some other member of the Hazelridge set might have decided to turn up. However, it didn't much matter because everyone else had brought one and several more had strayed in, and although most of the dances were strange to him he managed to compass them. And here, all of a sudden, he felt marvellously free, as though he hadn't a care in the world – well, he hadn't. Somewhere in the great room he could feel a culture, a home calling that answered to his soul, something completely absent in rootless and dead Toronto, even though London was bigger, dirtier and ruder than his own city. It had not begun as a violation of the earth and the land beneath had not forgotten; and each delightful girl – how entrancing was the careful articulation of their casual voices – gave him the renewed desire to live here forever. Not a single tear in the web. He was beyond remembering their names. It didn't matter. He threw open the french windows to let the cool garden air play upon the fevers in the moving room. And during supper when the lounge slowly drained and partly filled again he sat almost in a trance until he wandered over to the black piano mysteriously potent. Then he noticed Roseanne. She was near the fireplace carefully looking through some old records left there by Derek.

'My father would simply love to get his hands on some of this stuff,' she said as he went over.

'Don't know much about it myself,' he replied. 'May I get you something before everything on the tables vanishes?'

'Mm, yes, let's go. I'm Roseanne, do you remember? And I don't have to ask your name twice. Who could forget Coll – or its referent? I liked dancing with you, but I'm no good at this old-fashioned stuff. You're an odd bunch here, aren't you? All men living together like monks, well, not quite monks obviously, but close to the contemporary equivalent, or is there one? When I came in here I seemed to be going back into my grandmother's past. And that's nice in a way, really it is. I shouldn't ask, but I will. What makes you stay here? Don't you make enough to move out on your own?'

She had given him the ideal opening for the obvious answer, but he blundered.

'Well, actually, I'm here only for a few weeks while I'm up in London. I've a job in the country.'

'Must be a gorgeous one if it lets you spend forever in London whenever you feel like it. You're from the States.'

'Canada.'

'Well, I'm going to have some more of this simply *marvellous* cheesecake. Who makes it like this?'

'Do you live around here?'

'Oh yes, I'm one of the few natives left in London. We've been overrun, haven't we? My family goes back a long way, but the old house is now a public school for girls and I live in a flat just off Putney Hill. It's slightly ironic that I work as a teacher in the former family house. We've all had to branch out. Shall we take our coffee and wander out into the garden since it seems to have turned out fine after a dull day? That's the silly thing about this summer so far – dull days, fine nights.'

The dance had died down. Many people had filtered back into the lounge and there was a half-hearted attempt to ignite the whirling fun again, but the talk was over-loud and insistent as though something other than coffee was in the veins. There was another couple in the garden, Trevor and Daphne; Roseanne waved to them. The weak pale radiance from the windows and the unearthly sodium lights behind the garden made it a yellow and black plot floating in space.

'Why are you here, really,' asked Roseanne suddenly.

'As I told you, I've a job with some very nice people in a place on the Downs –'

'What's the name of the place?'

'With some very nice people. They are away just now and so I'm free to explore London and meet fascinating girls like you.'

'What's the job?'

'Look, it's nothing grand. I'm an odd-job man helping out in the garden mainly, but anywhere else where I'm needed. The lady who owns the place is old, her family have mostly gone out west, the place is big, she can't afford full-time hired help –'

'You know, Coll, I'm sorry to say this to a man whom I would dearly love to have as a friend – I'll say that much – but I don't believe you. I don't know the difference between the Canadian and American accents, but your speech is that of an educated man; so is your behaviour. You're not some simple odd-job man. And all that about the old lady in the big house and the talk of going out west sounds so much more a Canadian than an English situation, *I* think, anyway. And if you do have these big gobs of time off and if you're over here on a trip, why would you sacrifice the whole of your young life cohabiting with these monks?'

'Well, they can't be completely monkish, or beautiful and intelligent girls like you would not be looking for action out here on a lovely summer's night.'

'Who said I was looking for action, Squire? Answer my questions – and then, perhaps, if I still like you, I'll consider answering some of yours.'

'If you're not looking for action, then what are you looking for?'

'Coll, that's unfair, almost offensive.'

'I know, and I apologize, but I felt myself under the gun.'

'Why? Are you ashamed of something?'

'Now who's unfair? I don't know. I guess I've never done anything much. I haven't achieved anything. Yes, I have the usual degree from York, that's York in Toronto, a place full of Yorks, but I haven't done a lot with my life. However, my present job, whatever it is, is important to me, and really I don't feel much like talking about it tonight. I'm just the way you see me. No more, no less.'

'Ah', she said softly, 'important because of the old lady – I think you said she was old. I sometimes feel quite old myself.'

He did not reply. She clasped his hand in hers and they strolled on to the lawn. After a while she said, 'Have you been up the river by boat?'

'No.'

'I'd love to go. Tomorrow's Sunday. Are you free? Then why don't we go down to Westminster Stairs and boat up to Hampton Court? Can you start early? I'll look up the times and pick you up here at, say, seven. Better be ready earlier in case the boat leaves before eight, but I don't think it does. You don't mind being driven by me, do you? Someone told me you do a lot of driving. I'm afraid I'm not very good at it yet.'

He was attracted to Roseanne but he had his misgivings about her. She was inquisitive, and a long river journey provided her with the ideal opportunity to drill him with questions, pretty sharp questions. But she was undeniably pretty and charming, not to say, clever, and liked him and he could certainly do with a change of company, perhaps more than that . . .

Siobhan had left him too much out of her eye here.

Roseanne then considered the time and wanted to go.

'I have to be up and alert in the morning,' she said. 'Goodnight, Coll. I'm looking forward to it.'

'How are you getting home?'

'Walking. It's not far and this isn't New York.'

'I'll come with you.'

'If you like, but Alan invited me here, so perhaps it would be better for you to walk down Richmond Road to the East station and wait there for me to come by. I'll need a few minutes to take my graceful leave.'

Evidently Roseanne was a stickler for appearances, or possibly she wanted to avoid causing tension.

It was fully fifteen minutes before she paused at the entrance of the tube station. He joined her. He'd been thinking of what she looked like while he was waiting and couldn't remember anything about her that stood out. She had brown hair of medium length, but he couldn't remember the colour of her dress, or her shoes or even of her eyes. She now wore an enormous shapeless windcheater over her dress that reached almost to her knees.

She was right. She didn't live far away. Up Putney Hill the madly-hued trees of early summer looked like aliens in a space museum under the hideous lights. They went around to the back among miniature streets of a monstrous complex of flats, until at a certain entrance she paused.

'Want to come in, Coll?'

'What do you want?'

'To be quite frank, not this evening, if I can avoid it. I've still got a few things to do tonight, and we'll be seeing each other tomorrow, but if you can tear your thoughts away from the old lady who can spare you from her garden just because she happens to be away for a few days, take this as a gentle reminder that love also goes on under the garishly-lit yellow bricks of London.'

She kissed him gently with the symbolic yielding which is the salute women give to men whom they consider good friends.

Chapter 31

Coll was blowing out his shaver when a volley was hammered on the front door with the heavy brass knocker. There she was, dressed from head to toe in shiny black leather-cum-plastic carrying a motorcycle helmet out of *Star Wars*.

'God, you're not ready yet? Get the sand out of your eyes, Coll.'

'Do you want a coffee or something before we leave?'

'Coffee! We're going to be late enough as it is, man. I want the special sailing at half eight. Stop pissing around and let's go!'

Outside he was made to don a very feminine helmet in the form of an enormous ant's head complete with two long trembling antennae. Not having expected a motor bike ride, he wasn't dressed for it, but as Roseanne roared off this became the least of his worries. She knew her London all right. Preferring side roads relatively free of traffic to the main roads, she took the corners at angles he felt the tyres could not possibly sustain. As a man he was interdicted from betraying the slightest misgiving. From time to time she yelled something at him which he had no hope of hearing, pointing out this or that as they hurtled on their way in spurts broken by the lights. Traffic circles were no obstacle. For these she hardly slowed down, but, like a Bisley marksman at his deflection shooting, aimed for a moving space between the monsters and shot off with a burst of acceleration. More than once his legs were inches from being brushed by the wheels of lorries, but manly pride made him oblivious to the fact. They stopped at a lock-up behind some office buildings and after securing the bike inside, took a bus for the rest of the way.

He hoped that his cultivated air of easy nonchalance made an impression on her. He ventured a daring œillade when they had quite settled themselves in facing seats as near as possible to the bow. It was met with the sweetest and blankest of smiles; nor was there any sign of emotion in her dark eyes.

It was a perfect day to pass under the elegant bridges of London, dawdling up the muddy Thames into a countryside where houses and whole towns sloped down to the very edges, human fantasies growing out of the land; one longed to live in storied places with magic names – Putney, Hammersmith, Barnes, Richmond, Mortlake, and Twickenham, the last renowned for Donne's garden and Pope's grotto. It took three hours longer than expected to reach Hampton Court because of unprecedentedly low water. It being only an hour to closing time when they finally arrived, they had to content themselves with looking over the grounds.

'Oh well, luckily I know people around here,' murmured Roseanne as they strolled in pleasant propinquity. 'It might be more interesting to drop in on them than put in time on carpets, ceilings, paintings and beds flush with the fleas of royalty and distinction. We can't, anyway. So shall we?'

'Fine. But what about something to eat first?'

'Follow me.'

Near a bus stop the *Mermaid Inn* offered meals. It seemed as good as any other pub, so they went in. Evidently Roseanne knew her way around, for she immediately took the stairs to the upper lounge. The man behind the bar nodded to her. They sat down with drinks to begin with. It was just as Coll was getting into his second pint of rough cider, a dangerously heady drink, that they were joined by an older woman, perhaps in her late thirties or early forties, whom Coll was quite sure he had seen before, but for the while he could not place her.

'Lovely of you to drop in, Rosie. Who's your handsome friend?'

'Coll, former denizen of Canada, now a convert to civilization.'

'Well, Coll, glad to know you.' She gave him her hand. ' You should have come straight upstairs, silly,' she went on, addressing Roseanne. 'No need to sit down here.'

'No, it's better this way. Less bother for you.'

'Bother! Who's talking about bother? You're part of the firm. Jack's tied up for a while, but he'll be along later.'

'Good, then we can talk. Coll, do you mind if we leave you by yourself for ever so short a while? Back in a quarter of an hour. Just order whatever you like. Don't worry about paying anything. It's all taken care of.'

'But –'

'We've the whole evening ahead of us. Just trust me. Back soon.'

Left to himself, Coll reflected on the strangeness of things, particularly the extent to which he so often found himself in the gentle compulsion of women who told him nothing but were confident in their power of beck and call. This thought rankled a little in him. 'Give you twenty minutes,' he said to himself. 'After that I'm off home on the bus and you can go home by yourself.' But the twenty minutes was extended to twenty-five, and the twenty-five to thirty, for the woman fascinated him and he still hoped that she might want him later on that evening. Siobhan's angry words still rang in his head. He was not above a morsel of private revenge, or, if not revenge, retaliation. He could not remember the name of Roseanne's friend and wondered where he had seen her before. The second pint of cider had foozled him, and the very large sandwich with its wedge of cheese had done little to clear his head. He decided to ask for coffee. He got this with some chips for he wanted to think straight.

He awoke with difficulty in pitch blackness. He was in bed, a strange bed in a strange room. He felt so knocked out that it occurred to him that he must have got into a fight and it was a while before he could prop himself upright against the head of the bed. He remembered clearly coming into the *Mermaid Inn* with Roseanne, he knew that they had sat down together to order lunch, he remembered drinking too much cider, and he had a vague idea that some other woman was involved, but he had no notion of anything after that. He didn't know the time or even the day.

Moving was difficult, and he soon found himself on the floor clinging to the bed. He felt ashamed to be in such a state, but after a while he grew a little cautious. Two pints of cider couldn't explain this. Perhaps he had been led into a trap. It was almost impossible to believe anything so bad of Roseanne. He therefore did not go near the door, but tried the window. It was a sash window nailed shut. An impossible pitch of roof overlooked the yard. He could probably break down the door, no matter what they had done to it, but this was what they would expect. Then he noticed the surveillance camera projecting from the lintel and wrenched it out. It was probable they didn't know his strength. All he had to do was stay on his feet and crush them one by one. There was nothing he could use as a weapon, so he took the bed apart. It had a heavy cast-iron frame. They would now try to rush him through the door. He held the mattress in front of him and wielded a short angular cast-iron leg of the bed. If he survived he would pay Roseanne a visit she wouldn't forget.

He didn't have to wait long for trouble. As the door flung open he thrust the mattress into the rush. It didn't have much effect but it confused them for a second during which he got in a lethal blow. He felt the iron leg sink in through the sickening crush of skull. His foes retreated. He followed. Outside was a short length of passage beyond the door, the last on this landing. Above in the ceiling was a trapdoor, a door he could not reach. The man on the floor lay in the peaceful contortion of death.

Keeping a wary eye on the landing, he tore the door to his room off its hinges and wedged it across the narrowest part of the passage. It gave him a rise of about four feet, enough if he were given the time. Hearing the racket, they came on him again, this time with long-handled tools no doubt from the shed in the yard, but he seized one of these, a spade, and while taking several severe knocks, got in another lethal blow, slicing into the big fellow's head. He charged, and they retreated, demoralized, giving him enough time to run up, punch open the trapdoor and pull himself up with a surge of godlike strength. They tried to get at and smash his legs, but again he managed to kick someone pretty well.

Once up and inside, he was again weaponless. He was in a large attic, well-furnished with a long table and chairs, obviously intended for meetings. The entrance door could be barred from the inside, and he would make short work of anyone so foolhardy as to put his head up through the open trap.

Now at leisure, he had time to look about him. There were cupboards and chests, and he rummaged around looking for something he could use to help him. Several long knives came into his hand. They were slender, of peculiar design, with Celtic leaf-like motifs on hilt and blade, both chased with silver. A heavy wooden mace-like object completed his armament as he explored for exits. No matter where he went they would be waiting for him. Was there a phone? There was. The idiots had not expected him here and so had not thought to cut the lines. He called 999 and hoped the operator would trace the call before he was cut off. Evidently his enemies had not expected the trouble he had given them, for after reporting his kidnapping to the police, he called Hazelridge, calmly told Michael where he was and what was happening. Michael consulted Siobhan.

'Leave *now*, man,' he said emphatically. 'Get going. Get yourself well out of the way. When you're safe, phone me. Got change or a card? I'll be near you, for I'm off to your general area right now. I'll pick up your call in the car. Get going.'

'I've got to get through the other mob.'

'They've gone, you idiot. Don't you understand? Don't *you* hang around. For the love of Mike stay out of the cops' clutches. They'll be there in two shakes of a raspberry jelly.'

He left. As he ran down towards the river he heard the cars. He met no one on the way and had no idea of whether the bodies had been removed or not.

It took Michael nearly an hour to find him. Coll, uncertain of any car, was wary of exposing himself and did not attempt to phone until he was quite sure he was not observed.

'Greetings, O Samson the Invulnerable,' said Michael. 'We'll just take a fast tour of these riparian environs to discourage any pests you may have picked up. You didn't notice any, did you?'

'No, but there's one I'm not going to leave behind. We're going to Putney. I've a little engagement to keep.'

'Wrong, Captain. We're going back to Hazelridge. Your Officer Commanding was very definite on that point. Someone called Michael Wheelwright is packing your things. I'll collect them tomorrow. You're back where the lady can keep an eye on you, and you're staying put, with your souvenirs. They look very nice. I wouldn't mind one of those knives. What on earth are you going to do with that barber's pole?'

Coll began to fulminate. 'Listen, Michael, this is important to me. The bitch tried to murder me –'

'I daresay. But Siobhan says not so. What can I do? Take a bus when you have time one day. But you'd better think it through very carefully first. You're the security man, you know. What about our security, eh? Don't forget about that. Like, what have these people found out about us already that they shouldn't know? Whoever she is, she isn't worth compromising Siobhan for.'

Coll shut up.

'And maybe it's better that you're not out in front always fighting battles on your own. So far you've wiped the decks. You mightn't be so lucky next time. At least back at Hazelridge you'll be among friends who can give you the help you need when something like this comes up.'

In the earliest light of day they pulled into the driveway. Coll suddenly realized that he was still groggy from the drugs and didn't care about the breakfast, hours away, that he had been looking forward to. He climbed into his bed with an unutterable sense of relief. As he relaxed his limbs and felt the pain of his bruises and contusions he realized where he had seen Roseanne's coarse friend before.

He had seen her in the forest, transfigured.

Chapter 32

ALTHOUGH ZONKED OUT BY DRUGS and tolerably well-exercised in the course of the night's adventure, Coll found sleep elusive, partly because the punishment he had taken declared itself in no uncertain fashion, particularly in his legs and arms. When he did manage to catseye, his fitful rest was troubled by dreams of Roseanne's companion and her sinister confreres who forever pursued him with menaces. They were not visions but shadows waiting in the hallway or next room.

When he awoke he was sweating and thought he must have picked up a fever under the bridge where he had hidden out for an hour. It was only just after ten, and as he didn't want to sleep again, he got up, bathed and went downstairs, noting that the house seemed to be empty. Outside he found Michael on the prowl.

'Oo, what a lovely sight! I didn't get a good look at your paint job in the darkness. It's absolutely splendid, no, spectacular. You should be waxed and put on display. What happened?'

'I ran into some Irishmen who disliked my tie. Where's everyone?'

'Esmirone and Siobhan have gone off somewhere, they didn't deign to tell me where. Maybe they're going to pay the visit you were so anxious to make a few hours ago. Diane and Cybele have gone shopping, or so they said. Don't worry. They took plenty of security, five cars between them.'

'That was my next question. We're up against it. Who knows how many we shall have to deal with.'

'Siobhan's party has Matt and Gerald in their car, with a car in front and one behind, from the village. Total of seven armed men. Maxine and anybody else left behind have been told to go to the village, the safest place to be. It's entirely Circle. From your altered but still roguishly handsome favour it's obvious that you've become our advanced striking force.'

'You've got it the wrong way round. They were the aggressors. That Putney punk misled the gullible yours truly into the clutches of the goons who passed an entertaining evening beating up the innocent and harmless me. And I'm just wondering . . .'

'What?'

'When does Siobhan get back?'

'Search me. Today, tomorrow, who knows? The two of them are up to something. They went out looking pretty determined, like a Maori war party out snooping for a little excitement and some native cuisine at the end of the expedition. As a matter of fact, I read a book recently which asserted that this was also an old Irish custom, so with Siobhan in charge an atavistic reversion is not out of the question. You must have done something pretty drastic along the line. I hope you gave as good as you got.'

'Quite as good. Two dead. Some more damaged. And their base has gone. We should go back and burn it down. Anything in the papers?'

'Nothing in the news this morning. They evidently looked after their own, as usual. By the way, you're not meant to be outside. I mean, we don't want you of all people spotted, do we?'

'Jesus, why not? I'm pretty well-known to the away team by now. Didn't you tell me that the place is crawling with back-up?'

'Siobhan said, "Tell him to stay inside and look after the stuff,' meaning, I guess, the shopping you brought back.'

'Shit.'

'Did you know that grammarians masturbate their minds in a rare old dispute as to whether that is rightly a weak or a strong verb. It depends on what you think the past participle should be . . .'

Coll went off to look at the loot he had brought back.

He had some trouble in finding the things. They had been laid in the bottom cupboard of the heavy oaken sideboard in the dining room. The key had been left in the lock, oddly. He drew out two knives or daggers, one shaped laboriously out of obsidian, its hilt wonderfully chased with silver, a heavy and dangerous weapon in the right hands, but obviously wrought with such loving care that it could never have been intended for the hazard of damage or loss in a fight; the other, a deadly-pointed flat shaft of hard bone or possibly ivory, but it smelt to him of bone, hafted with yew bound with silvered bands of hard steel, and, like the other, bearing carven devices and a monogram that looked if anything like an *A* married with a *K*. There was a strangeness to the touch of each of them not to be explained by mere unfamiliarity. He felt the presence of that palpable halo of awe that comes from great works of art or magic.

He took his hands from them and reached into the sideboard for the long mace-like object. It was a bare shaft of very heavy dark wood for most of its length. It supported a head crowned with silver, a head so realistic it might have been an ancient shrunken one. Underneath were letters or symbols he could not recognize. This was somewhat more than a metre long, quite handy as a weapon but intended for some other purpose. Compared with the other trophies of his adventure it was not particularly noteworthy. It did not exude power as did the two ritual knives.

He suddenly felt that he had had enough of them. His gloating vanished and he stowed them back into the sideboard with great care, aware that they were deadly and resolving not to have any accidents with them. He locked the door very deliberately.

Hearing cars, he went into the kitchen.

'Up already?' said Cybele, kissing him. Diane did the same. He was definitely back in favour.

'I'm starving,' he announced.

'There're a few mushrooms on the front lawn. Pick them and we'll whip up an omelette with those and some chives from the kitchen garden. When you come in coffee will be ready and we'll get breakfast for you. You have certainly deserved it.'

'That's right,' put in Diane. 'You look awfully pale under your bruises. What have you been up to this morning?'

'Nothing much.'

'I don't believe you.'

Over an excellent brunch of everything available in addition to the omelette, Coll told the two women about his day's outing up the river with Roseanne. 'So you see,' he ended with a wry smile in Cybele's direction, 'as you once intended to kill me, I have killed, I believe, two of our enemies. Have you done as much since then?'

'Don't be so sure I haven't, Byron,' she replied. 'And as for yours, well, they were out to kill you as soon as they had extracted whatever information you were able to give them. They did not realize what they were up against – a superman. Your blind boar's courage and strength served you well, even though you were a little obtuse in allowing yourself to be drawn in by this woman. But don't worry about Siobhan. She's impressed with your handling of the other lot. You know that she never says a word against you. She's always on your side, doing more for you than you can know. What you don't or can't realize is that your rôle in her life sometimes changes. But you still remember that I would have done anything to stop you from leaving the house in Dublin, don't you? Can't you see now that what I did then and what you did last night with an even deadlier determination are the same thing?'

'Yes I do. I never blamed you. I was just – surprised.'

'You were going to do something to him?' asked Diane.

'Yes, I was going to shoot him, not to kill if I could help it, but I might have, for in three steps he could have overpowered me. I had the gun on him. It was good luck that I was able to persuade him that I was going to use it, otherwise he would have been gone. I had very strict instructions. He had no idea of security.'

'That's a terrible strength for a woman to have,' observed Diane quietly.

'Every woman has to have it. Otherwise she's the victim.'

'I'd rather be the victim than a killer.'

'But Diane dear, your job is not security, is it? I notice that you didn't object to the instructions Siobhan gave you not so long ago.'

Diane reddened ever so slightly and said no more. Coll saw that the two women were miffed with each other. They ate in silence. After a while he said, 'Have you looked at those things I brought back.'

'They're locked up,' replied Cybele.

'The key was left in the lock, in the big sideboard. Very interesting indeed.'

Diane and Cybele looked at each other.

'Better not touch them, Coll,' said Diane quickly. 'Siobhan wasn't comfortable with them and even Esmirone wanted nothing more to do with them, although she, poor old dear, will be the one who has to deal with them. Leave them strictly alone. Don't go near them except in the presence of Siobhan, Esmirone, and us too. Please, Coll.'

She was anxious.

'I've already had a good look. Michael told me I was supposed to stay inside and look after the stuff, so naturally I went to see if they were O.K.'

This time it was Cybele who flushed.

'Where did he get that idea from? I'm going to have a word with him. You were in danger.'

'Those things could be worse for you than Cybele's gun,' put in Diane, 'at least that's what I think.'

'There's something disquieting about them, that's for sure.'

'I felt it too,' said Cybele. 'Take Diane's advice and don't touch them again. That bone ahamé is a very nasty piece of work.'

'Ahamé?'

'A sort of dagger. Ask Esmirone. She's the expert.'

'So what do I do now?'

'We'll clear up and you can do your job by protecting and amusing us at the same time. That's easy,' said Diane with a giggle. But in her little laugh there was the hint of a challenge.

For the first time, Coll regretted Cybele's presence.

It was dusk before Siobhan returned. She embraced Cybele and Diane, and then Coll with all the old warmth.

'Maxine is on the way back. Gerald is with her. But let's have tea now; supper can wait until later. Let's all go into the kitchen and you can tell me everything, Coll. Don't leave anything out.'

Siobhan listened with the most acute attention, betraying no sign of annoyance when Roseanne's name came up.

'There's one thing I regret.' remarked Coll as they went into the lounge for coffee, 'and that is I never got back to Roseanne. Michael wouldn't take me, but I'm going to settle accounts with her, don't you worry.'

'But that is exactly what I did worry about, and that is why I told Michael to deny your impetuous nature. What were you going to do when you got there anyway?'

Coll was stuck. 'I expect I'd have brought her back here to answer to you.'

'I think her pals knocked some of the limited common sense you once had out of your skull. You actually thought you should introduce this agent of that unregenerate cult into our headquarters? You just didn't know what to say, just as you had no idea of what you were going to do to her. She was prepared for you, you can be quite sure. If you'd been able to get in, which you wouldn't, she'd have phoned the police and you'd have been holding the bag. You didn't have anything like a credible story. Come on, Coll. You're not that stupid. Leave her out. She's not important. In any case, the attack against you was an attack against me, and I can handle her much better than you can. But you recognized her Queen and brought us several very valuable and well-chosen souvenirs. You don't know how well you did. In addition to destroying the headquarters of this cell you took from them the very things they can least afford to lose. In our hands they are valuable assets indeed. We'll be able to make peace with those. You did fantastically well or you had some real luck on you, which is equally likely, although I don't know why. Unfortunately they scored one telling point against you: the lady got your name. It's a pity your amazing luck didn't extend to getting hers. That was hardly possible.'

'Is that important?'

'Right now, yes. She's your Lamia and we'll have to be careful. After midsummer it will not matter so much, but you've now devolved from protector to protected.'

'Meaning?'

'I'll be looking after you now; you're under orders not to stray from this house or grounds without my knowing. You can carry on with your usual duties of watching and waking and fending off the burglars, but Michael will take your job.'

Coll was aggrieved.

'Cheer up, you chump,' put in Cybele. 'You don't know how lucky you are.'

'Yes,' agreed Diane. 'Don't push it, please, dear Coll. We all love you and couldn't bear it if anything happened to you. Siobhan knows best. That's why she's the Queen.'

'Fine. What is all that stuff in the sideboard?'

'Esmirone's the expert,' replied Siobhan. She's on the job of finding out about them right now, an unpleasant task. You have brought back two ritual knives, known in the trade as ahamés. They're highly personal and powerful things, as the wielder has to create them from scratch using only hitherto unworked materials, employing his own craft and magical skills at every stage. The mace-like object is ceremonial, not ritual and not imbued by the same magic potency as the ahamés. Leave them locked up, Coll. That's an order. They're not for your innocent and tender hands, believe me.'

'The key was in the lock, so I had them out to have a look. You told me to stay inside and guard them.'

'Guard them? That's news to me. What's come over Michael? Curb your curiosity until we show you over them. It's very easy to cut yourself on these things, very difficult to heal the wounds. I need you strong and healthy, Coll. Those things are going to attract attention, unwelcome attention. When you turn in tonight lock your door.'

'Lock my door? Why the hell should I lock my door?'

'Because I ask you to, my loving servant.'

'Are we all locking our doors?'

'For the moment, just you.'

'I thought I was the security man looking after you.'

'Well, you can still look after me, but as security man you can take a rest. We've enough people. Don't worry. You'll be my personal driver again, but later on. Michael's also very good, but he's a poet with a car and I don't like the anapæst. For now you stay here under wraps. So, once again your rôle changes.'

'When do we go to London next?'

'If you mean " When do you go to London next?" the answer is: when we've dealt with the London menace.'

'Who are these people?'

'They, as we, are the heirs of a very ancient cult seeking to flourish again. They are the direct-in-line appointed and initiated priests and priestesses of an ancient religion once so powerful as to rule the whole of humanity in these islands, now forgotten. In their decline they were at first persecuted and finally extirpated in fear and hatred by other religions that ruled in their turn. But although the holy places were vandalized, burned and ploughed over and the celebrants killed, the power remained, and remains now, well-disguised, waiting to grow again. And now is the time in this great vacuum, our age of fools' gold.

'They have a darker side. There is always a dark side, as you will see. Persecution changes the thing persecuted. In self-defence the survivors mutate into beings like their oppressors.'

'Do stop talking like a prof. It isn't like you a bit. I don't understand all this.'

'No, you don't. That's why I called you tender and innocent just now. We girls here are a lot tougher than you realize. We've been prepared.'

'Tell me why I have to lock my door.'

'You heard what I said about power. Isn't that enough? Stay away from the playthings in the sideboard and keep a watch on yourself. Keep your radio on you and call Cybele immediately if you even so much as sniff that things might not be quite right. She'll understand, and she'll move to counteract. Now the guard becomes the thing guarded. But you've got a powerful ally, fortunately.'

'Who?'

'Me. Try not to forget it.'

'What happens next?'

'Just enjoy yourself. We'll go off on a trip in June. Look forward to the sunshine and keep indoors at night. I don't have to tell you to stay out of the forest, particularly during the hours of darkness, do I? There are certain powers which are best left unsought, especially at times when your own spirit is at its weakest, the dangerous hours after midnight until the dawn, the tide of day we call uht.'

Chapter 33

LIFE WENT VERY EASILY AND PLEASANTLY for the household at Hazelridge for the fortnight leading up to Midsummer. Coll wanted to know more about the ahamés, but Esmirone, keeper of lore, put him off. His secure happiness in his new family would have been perfect had it not been for the one new development which caused him hours of disquiet: the amiable Michael now took his place not only as Siobhan's protector, but at the table inside. He had been moved down one. And in spite of her words to him, whenever Siobhan went anywhere she took Michael. Coll was never asked to drive her now. If he was given a job it was merely to give Diane or Cybele minor help in the household, or to drive them to the village or the nearest large town when they wanted to go shopping. They knew he worried and both of them tried to reassure him. Cybele told him not to let himself be troubled by Siobhan's preferences of the moment. Diane said, 'She will need you soon enough.'

Nevertheless, he resented being demoted to a Beaumains, even if it meant that he could now really get to know the other two young women. Cybele was always self-possessed. She had a fine restraining discipline, for her head governed her heart. Since she always kept things in perspective, she was always in complete control of her own sphere. She could still be a little unnerving to Coll, less demonstrative than, and totally free of, the selfishness of his sister, Mira, but equally masterful. He delighted in her small but perfectly articulated voice, yet whenever she spoke to him, delightful as she was, he felt that she was weighing him. She was slim, even a trifle bony, a little too pale, even for an Irishwoman, with hard small breasts and the hands of a pianist. She was surprisingly strong, wiry, not wilting. She was not a great thinker or scholar, and her spelling was erratic, but she was observant, canny and very clear in her perceptions. She was the model of sanity, one who had hardly ever made a choice without being able to define clearly her reasons for it. Her greatest quality was her transparent loyalty to her friends and the Circle and her quiet determination to protect those she loved.

He knew that if Siobhan relinquished him, she would claim him. This did not comfort him in his present state of mind, but he still loved her as much as at the first because, as he thought, she was such a strong decisive woman. In truth, all the ancient beckonings of the soul were there as they have always been. He knew that her loyalty to Siobhan – the Queen – overrode all her feelings for him, a vital point to bear in mind. She had a most graceful way of walking which he loved to watch. When he visualized her he saw her outside crossing the lawn or returning along the path, so graceful in the skirt she hardly ever wore. A neat well-tailored skirt is the sexiest garment a woman can wear, he thought to himself.

Diane was pure woman. With soft creamy skin, full mouth and enchanting blue eyes, she looked at you in glances. Cybele gazed at you; Diane glanced and turned her eyes to other things. A little plumper than Cybele, she had a full bosom and sensuous arms and hands, rounded arms and small very white hands. She was a honey pot. Her beautifully soft speech, as sexually potent as the lovely lips which shaped it, sent a riffling thrill through him. Her magic was as puissant as the others', for she had command of the kitchen. It was she who had baked the cake eaten at the Beltane feast. There is not much more to say about Dianes: they come out as mothers, but it is as crones that they rise to their full and awful power. This little woman who barely rose to Coll's nipple could eat him alive any time she wanted to. He was unaware of this, for he never stopped desiring her.

He had in truth been let loose as Siobhan had promised, but only the sows knew the rules of the game, and they were not letting on. In his idleness another question gnawed at him: the London business. Had the whole thing been an unforeseen series of events arising out of the attack near Box Hill, or had he been deliberately let loose as a decoy, perhaps to help Wheelwright spot any infiltrators, perhaps to induce the enemy to show himself, or herself, rather. He was going to put it to Siobhan when he had the chance, but of course he hardly ever saw her alone now. He rather missed Richmond House with its coterie of pure nuts living in a state of contumacious anachronism, and he hoped to see them again. He could recall their names and faces, but he was still uncertain of whether or not there were any plants among them. He thought of the brothers Tony and Roger. Michael Wheelwright was shrewd. He knew pretty well what was going on – which only raised the question in his own mind again.

The summer was behaving itself, and while England hardly ever gets the transparent heavenly days of the Ægean, there were times when the few clouds served only to soften the mutating tints of greens fading and chasing across the gentle rise and fall of pastureland in the still-virginal summer, the living temple of the motherland. He was now once more free of fear, except at night, when he was uncomfortably aware that he had interfered with something that greater prudence would have left alone, but no more than that. Once the three of them went for a walk, not far, but high enough for a glimpse of the sea. He would have preferred going with one of them, Diane, perhaps, but the game supervened. Each of the three covertly kept an eye on the other two. That, at least, is how Coll read it. It was on one of these occasions that Coll wondered aloud if he had been left in London as a sitting duck.

'But why should Siobhan or Esmirone want that?' asked Cybele.

'Or you,' added Coll, 'after all, you're part of it too. To flush out the opposition, of course, and give Michael Wheelwright a chance to identify any infiltrators. By the way, he asked me to keep an eye out for – anything unusual, I think he said. The thing doesn't bother me. It's part of my job, front line defence.'

Cybele paused. She wasn't at all pleased.

'What goes on at Richmond House is his job, not yours. But even if Siobhan and he were in cahoots – do you really believe this? – what on earth makes you think she wants to flush out the enemy, as you put it? That's very much a man's way of thinking. I'm sure she would rather avoid any sort of confrontation, avoid *making* enemies, if that's possible. She'd much rather cut a deal with them, especially now as, thanks to you, she has the means of doing so. You're thinking in terms of politics, where one power seeks to dominate the others. In fact each of these little groups is covert, reticent and hidden in all its essentials. Do you think that at this time, when the pot's hardly off the boil, she and Esmirone want you along when they're trying to negotiate peace? And do you think,' she went on, her voice rising, 'she would sacrifice you, I mean *deliberately*? What do you think of her, and of us, for that matter? I think you've forgotten the principles of the Circle. You're very much a beginner, you know, and your present position is quite accidental. You must know that Siobhan acts to protect everyone, notably you, or don't you realize that yet? She would sacrifice herself first if it came to that. How little you have understood! Of course people sacrifice themselves for the sake of the Circle, on rare and terrible occasions. We're at war. But sacrifice is deliberate and voluntary; one offers one's life in full knowledge. There must be, sometimes, an act of courage. You have not yet been asked to offer yourself. Perhaps you will have to make this choice some day.'

There was a uncomfortable pause full of tension. Then with a sudden fury she turned on him: 'Why did you go out of your way to sound me?' she exploded.

'That was unjust. I do apologize. But what about Siobhan? Does she really think me worth the effort? Right now she prefers Michael, haven't you noticed?'

Diane stepped in to forestall Cybele. 'Coll,' she said softly, 'Cybele has already told you why Siobhan doesn't want you on board just now when she's out on business. Your presence would be provocative. But that's not the important reason. Can't you guess why she prefers Michael over you just now?'

'She just prefers him, I guess.'

'"Prefer" is the word, all right,' put in Cybele. 'Just possess yourself in patience – and a good state of repair – you blockhead, and wait to see what happens. "Prefer" has various meanings.'

'Shush,' interrupted Diane, placing a finger over Cybele's lips. 'Be fair to the man. He doesn't know. We love you as you are, Coll,' she went on, taking his hand, 'and we couldn't carry on if we thought that anyone here could even think of using you like that. And Siobhan never would. Of course you know that. You're just having a little spasm of jealousy. Don't you remember her from when you first met? Didn't she save your life? She has never said anything to me, but I gather that you were in a tight spot when she ran across you, and got you out of it, I believe. I don't know what unusual circumstances caused her to bring you into the Circle, for it is a fundamental point with us never to seek actively for members. You know better than I do what set the whole chain of events in motion; was it anything divine? What do you think?'

She was right. He had forgotten in his rage, the silly and childish fit of jealousy. He hadn't been able to admit it to himself. But if he wasn't here as a decoy, what was he here for? To this question neither Cybele nor Diane had an answer.

In this game among the sows you were not allowed to turn over the next card until some other token landed on you.

And in his present position as the focus of some unfriendly force he might well be more of a liability than an asset.

As they reached the house again he asked jocularly, 'Well, who do I get to sleep with tonight?'

'With me, of course,' laughed Diane. 'Just get Siobhan's permission first.'

'Shall we go out tonight?'

'Where to? If you want entertainment you have to go to London.'
'What about the pub in the village?'
'There are several,' said Cybele, breaking her lengthy silence. 'It would be nice to try them all – what do you think Diane?'
'Oh, wouldn't it! And I'm bored with this place too. I'd love to go.'
'Right then,' rejoined Cybele, 'but not with Byron.'
Coll was hurt.
'Poor Byron. He's having a rough time today. Not because I wouldn't really like to go out with you this evening, you jolly old dog, you,' replied Cybele, 'I'd love to get out among some other people and have a few drinks, although I detest the smell of stale beer, but you heard what Siobhan said, my wonderful lordly Childe Harold, didn't you? Keep indoors at night. That's what she said.'
'There are three of us, and I'll bet you carry a gun.'
'So do you, Byron, but I doubt whether it's what we might need. And we need to keep you safe and sound, really and truly, whether you believe it or not. But we can ask Siobhan when she and Esmirone get back.'
They did, and much to Coll's surprise she not only agreed they should go but said she would come along with them bringing Michael. This was not quite what Coll had in mind, but he liked Michael well enough. So, leaving Gerald on duty with a direct line to village security, they set out.
They didn't get to try all the pubs, but settled into The White Hart, certified by Michael to be the non-pareil. Its façade of Victorian brick belied its thirteenth century provenance, but it looked as new as Ramsgate in a painting by Frith. It occupied the V conjunction of two roads combining into a tiny narrow high street, whose lovely buildings were pleasantly interrupted by a large village green running along the river. This widened out into a handkerchief park after the bridge took the main road into the forest opposite.
The pub was middling full, and of course no one was a stranger. Siobhan's party picked several tables gathered along a wall seat. Coll had taken a fancy to stout, Diane stuck to pales, Cybele touched nothing except Drambuie and Green Chartreuse which she sipped alternately, while Siobhan quaffed a single large goblet of Spanish red wine. Michael was either a teetotaller or had his instructions, for he confined himself to tonic water without anything.
The locals, being Circle anyway, treated the newcomers with great respect. No one seemed to be paying for anything, as Coll discovered when he tried to buy for the house, although the landlord was keeping score right enough. He got talking to several men whose shouted names

he didn't remember. They all wanted to shake his hand, which he thought was credit due for defending the Queen on the first trip to London, but as no one offered an explanation, he was never sure. This and the dark stuff made him feel pretty good and he was really beginning to enjoy himself when Siobhan gave the signal to decamp. He couldn't get near her in the pub, but he got out ahead of her as she was leaving and tried to persuade her to stay.

We've been here over two hours,' she replied. 'We can't leave Esmirone and Maxine alone any longer, can we? Sorry. But you certainly enjoyed being the lion, didn't you, you old roarer. So did I, just as much as you. We'll do it again if we get the chance.'

She linked arms with Michael as they all started to walk back over the hill, straggling along the footpath. Coll fell back with Cybele, Diane dropping behind.

'You're supposed to be taking us out, not Siobhan, you shyster,' said Diane jokingly.

'I know. I wanted to stay. Things were just getting wound up.'

'You were certainly getting wound up. I don't know if the ale or the applause went to your head first. You practically ignored us.'

'Oh.' He paused. Had he been inconsiderate?

'Never mind, you chump,' put in Cybele, 'don't let Diane operate on you. We had plenty of attention, as you evidently didn't notice. The men outnumbered the women for once, thank heavens. Diane fell in love with that wonderful slob with the blue eyes and the dirty blond knotted pony tail, so you've lost her.'

The walk back over the hill under a moonless sky was pleasant enough. Every now and then Siobhan would pause so that the rest could catch up. She did not want them to scatter. Under the banter every single one of them was only too keenly aware of a lurking threat.

When they opened the gate Gerald was not to be seen. Of course he might be round at the back.

Inside, there was no answer to Siobhan's call, 'We're back.' In a long pause, the three women looked at each other. There was no need to call out twice. Something was wrong.

While Siobhan, Cybele and Diane, walking in file, checked the rooms, Michael and Coll, weapons drawn, went outside to find the missing Gerald. There was no trace of him.

The two men thoroughly searched the grounds and sheds. Not a trace of Gerald could they find.

Both cars were in the garage.

Coll called Cybele only to be told tersely that help had already been sent for. In a matter of minutes cars were pulling in to the driveway.

Matt Hewer, the man in charge, who had been with them in the pub, listened and immediately contacted the village.

'We watch the roads as a matter of course,' he informed Coll. 'That doesn't mean that the pair can't get away – or be snatched away – without our spotting it. However, we've got all the traffic on the roads in and out in two-hour loops. We're scanning them now, but a proper combing of the whole area is going to have to wait until daylight. Better make doubly and trebly sure that neither is inside somewhere safe and secret. It's been done before. Don't worry about damage – tear the place apart if you have to. Compare the measurements inside with those outside. If you find any big discrepancies, rip the wall open. I'll leave you three men right now. Can't spare any more, but I'll send you extras later on tomorrow. The village is buzzing like a hornets' nest. The Queen – what a hell this is! – it doesn't bear thinking of.' Matt couldn't find words.

Coll knew what was passing through his mind. This might have been an attempt to abduct or kill Siobhan which failed only by the sheerest chance.

'How long were you all away?'

'Not more than two hours.'

Matt shook his head. 'You should've left more than one man on. Hell! Let's go. They're calling us inside.'

In the lounge Diane and Siobhan were on either side of an inert Esmirone stretched out just inside the door. She lay on her back as if she had been mown down. There was a good deal of blood evidently from lacerations to her head. Cybele had sent for the doctor.

Hewer started in to help, but Siobhan motioned him to stay put and shut up while she gave her own help, gently massaging the injured woman and whispering words into her ear. Cybele took everyone except the two priestesses out into the hall.

'There's nothing more we can do until the doctor arrives. Matt, will you leave at least three men here? Maxine's gone too, I'm pretty sure, but will all you men check the house again from top to bottom under Matt's direction. Everyone is to carry weapons and have them handy. Matt has notified the whole village that we're seeking both of them. So far, and it's early in the investigation, Village Security hasn't been able to come up with anything, and I'm not sure they have the resources for a full-scale search, even in daylight. If anyone sights either one, act with caution. We can assume that they're both carrying firearms. As a last resort, shoot to prevent escape.'

Matt shook his head. 'It looks as though there was someone else involved. Neither car has been moved. It will be difficult to find out who was responsible for what unless Esmirone can tell us. Are these two accomplices or victims? As far as I'm concerned, this is an inside job, something already planned awaiting the right time, which came tonight when you all decided to take a jaunt down to the pub.'

Coll had never felt more miserable.

'Maybe,' said Cybele, 'but we don't know that for certain yet. Maxine and Gerald were married within the Circle. That's what strikes me. If one of them was an infiltrator, then who recruited whom? They didn't strike me as being like that.'

'They never do,' replied Hewer, 'not the successful ones. And what did they do it for?'

'I can guess that,' put in Coll. 'Where is that stuff I brought back from London?'

'Never mind that now,' interrupted Cybele sharply, 'I'll check that later. Let's look after Esmirone first. That's why I have to have some men here. The doctor will need their help. I expect Siobhan will try to keep Esmirone here, but she'll probably need hospital treatment, and that's going to be awkward. She'll be in greater danger there than here.'

Coll was struck by the organization behind Cybele. There was no doubt as to who was in charge.

At long last, although it was in truth only fifteen minutes, the doctor showed up. She brushed in down the hallway and straight to Esmirone by an instinct that made directions superfluous.

She didn't take long.

'I've got to have an ambulance,' she said. 'She needs imminent life support. Got your story ready?'

'Not sure,' said Cybele, 'we're working on it. Can we have a little more time?'

'Not a chance. It doesn't look good. Siobhan should come along, but she can't stay at the hospital. And once they've got Esmirone, they'll keep her. They'll have to. It's a tough choice, but there's no alternative. It's my job to save her. What do you want to do?'

'The decision is Siobhan's.'

'Well, you've got to tell me now. It's not going to do you any good if I lose my licence.'

Siobhan came out.

'What are her chances?'

'If she gets hospital treatment now, perhaps fifty-fifty. And of course she'll be vulnerable at the hospital unless you can protect her. There's no saying what influence this lot would be able to bring to bear on her there. I'm sure you're taking that into account.'

'What can we do now?'

'I can't do much. It's a mess. But if against my medical conscience I leave her in your better care, you know – you men especially must know – that no hint of my presence must leak out. I was never called. And I need a complete alibi, Cybele. Get it arranged now, and in the meantime you men get a hard mattress down here. I'll need it when I'm finished, and you'll have to carry her up if she doesn't die, which, I'm afraid, is quite on the cards. Siobhan is here, and I believe that she can do much more than I once the pressure is relieved. She's still breathing on her own, but that could change at any time. Matt, make sure that your friends here and the whole bloody village knows that I was never here, didn't know about any injured woman, wasn't called and was in the *White Hart* with all of you tonight, if that's the story.'

She brushed back into the lounge.

This time she was there for the best part of two hours.

Coll thought of Diane.

If Esmirone wasn't dead when four men carried her up very slowly and gently, keeping her as still as possible, she certainly looked it.

The climax past, everyone became listless. There was no further news of the missing couple that night.

Siobhan was with the dying woman constantly. She told Diane to rest. But before Diane went to bed, she knocked on Coll's door.

'No, I'm not coming in. Too tired. I have to take over from Siobhan in the morning. But she sends you a message and wants you to know that it's important.'

'O.K. What is it?'

'Mm, you do have a nice room – bigger than mine,' she said, peeping round the door. The message is: lock your door and keep your room intercom open. I'm going to connect you with Cybele's room. There. Siobhan's still not sure who's around. We're under the gun, it seems, and there may be another attack tonight. Your windows are pretty solid, aren't they?'

'Are they? I just keep them shut.'

'Good – and goodnight, then. Everyone feels absolutely miserable. I can't face the morning.'

'What about those ahamés and the other thing?'

'The sideboard cupboard was locked as it usually is, but they were gone, unfortunately.'

'So the bastards got them back?'

'Looks like it.'

'So what now?'

'Right now, I have no idea. I doubt if anyone has.' She gave him a little kiss and went on her way.

He hadn't really looked at the windows before. They were half-inch thick armoured glass set in steel frames moulded and painted to look like wood.

Chapter 34

A WIND STILL TORE THROUGH HIS MIND as he started to wakefulness. The dream fled. There was a forest in which something deadly but fascinating lurked, something he desired very much to see. He sat up, thinking that it might be raining in or that branches stirred by the wind were gently tapping the window, but when he drew the curtains he could see nothing beyond the blackness: the night was calm. It was not until he was about to turn away that she slowly took shape like sense in the colours of a soap bubble, standing on the solid air as if in her own invisible crystal, at first trying to look like Siobhan, but soon reverting to the form in which he had first met the dark red lady of the deep woods, utterly terrifying and utterly alluring. He went weak, trembling at the knees, and would have drawn the curtains again except that he was overcome by an induction of such desire as no fear could master. With an effort more than human he covered her from his sight and sank back on the bed shivering. In the back of his mind he wondered what she would do next, and he jerked the intercom phone off its bracket in a desperate attempt to talk to Cybele, but a soft knock at the panes made him desist and the phone clattered to the floor. He now wanted to drag down the curtains so that they could not be drawn and it was well for him that he was too much of a wreck to get up, but the impulsion was there. He knew at the same time that he was committing the worst folly.

A seductive whisper hung in the air like a slow sweet and lovely litany about his ears.

'I have come for you. Let me in, O man I desire and shall reward.'

'I can't,' he blurted out, 'the windows are sealed and armoured.'

She sighed.

'Jealousy. What, does she grudge me a day, an hour, even a single minute with you? But even she cannot keep me from your arms if you ask me to come to you. Tell me to come to you, and I will give you everything you desire, not only the lovely riches of my body, but power as my consort, the walking with me in my domain and first place at the winter's fire, admirable and lordly man.' Her voice was a tongue curling lasciviously within him. At the same time in a daydream he heard Cybele's voice coming from the intercom speaker.

'What's the matter, Byron,' she called, still a little sleepy. He was aware that she had called several times already. Cybele! How tiny and narrow was she beside this preternatural creature who yet filled him with a terror he could never have admitted, even to Siobhan.

'One word, one little word to encourage me and I am at your side.'

He opened his mouth to reply as the subtle poetry of high sex thrilled him, pushing his lust to absolute folly.

'Say the words "come in" and your slave-drivers are powerless to keep us apart.'

They were slave-drivers. He wondered why he had been so dense, so lacking in a proper sense of his own worth to ignore the fact.

'Stay put, Byron. We're both on the way. Siobhan says not to do anything that would hurt you or her. Oh, and not to say anything either – anything at all to anyone, or you may be framed into an undertaking or pact. Someone with power is around.'

As he wavered in his reckless motion towards the window, he heard running feet, someone had his door unlocked and Cybele stood there, followed by Siobhan.

The spell was in him. He was gazing at the window, scrying it for the departed vision as he screamed with frustrated lust, not the lust for the great queen's body only, but also for the marvellous magic power, the ancient kingship deep in sacred woods, the whole lost landscape of the deepest love, the great secret of it all, the grand lottery prize that would never proffer itself again, and he wept.

Siobhan took him in her arms, the old Siobhan as simple as a schoolgirl. There was no greater comfort she could give him, but the dragging agony remained.

She took him back to her own room and sat with him as he lay on the bed and told her in staccato phrases what had happened. Cybele sat on the sofa while Diane was given the task of scouting for the dark one. There was no sign of her.

Later Siobhan decided to group everyone, including Esmirone, in the lounge, and summoned more men from the village to set the beds there and remove unnecessary furniture.

'We're under attack, Coll. You were the second objective. They're going for what they hope are weak spots in our defence. Thank goodness you held out long enough for us to get to you. If you hadn't . . . Well, never mind. We haven't lost Esmirone yet. We're still intact. What do I tell you now? You know that you were entrapped in glamour. She came on a little strong, fortunately, so you were not able to respond immediately. That kind of meretricious fraud should never be practised, but this bunch is completely unreformed. Don't worry about Diane. She has more power than you know. The dark queen probably knows that and will not be interested in trying conclusions with her now that her second attack has failed. Are you worked up very badly? Just sick and upset? Sleep here while we set up downstairs, and I'll sleep beside you, but no touching. If you want to touch, I'll have to leave you for the sofa. Here's Diane. Diane, you take the sofa and Cybele can stay up until it's time for first coffee.

But it was Siobhan who broke the rule on touching, for she gently massaged and hugged him into sleep. He had no desire left in his body. The fantastically glamorous one had taken it from him and he remembered it now as a disease. As for Siobhan, well, there was simply no connexion between the two. But it wasn't simply the old dichotomy of good and evil, the simple-minded dualism that permeates the current religions of the world. The dark crimson one was ill-intentioned, dangerous, potentially fatal, but not the embodiment of complete evil. She was no more than the emblem of a warring force. Once the old forgotten peoples had been governed by ancient ways of making power. It was now apparent that some of these survived. Conversely, nor was Siobhan completely 'good'; there was something dark in her intentions that she never revealed but which she could not quite conceal from him. She too was the embodiment of a force. All societies call on some sort of power to help them, successfully or unsuccessfully. That power is neither good nor bad in itself, but it reflects all the conscious and unconscious willing of the people who seek to employ it, harmful and beneficent together.

The simple faith in the efficacy of science characteristic of a modern technological culture is every bit as superstitious as the much earlier confidence in the protection of the Great Goddess: no one doubts for a moment that $2 + 2 = 4$, yet not a thousand people on the planet are capable of reading, much less understanding, *Principia Mathematica*.

At breakfast the whole episode had become a half-forgotten dream.

'Any news of Maxine or Gerald?' asked Coll.

'None,' replied Siobhan, who was pouring coffee from a tall Mason jug and spilling some of it.

'Which of them struck Esmirone?'

'What a question! She tried to go for her gun, of course, but the two of them were too much for her. She wasn't given time. We'll have to wait until she herself can tell us what happened. Maxine had arranged things very carefully, you may be sure, for Esmirone is a wise old bird and would not normally allow herself to be lulled into a false sense of security. I still don't know why none of us had the slightest suspicion of them. That is the worst thing about the whole business, something I've never dreamed of before. Everyone in the village is appalled. Must I now distrust everyone, even you, dear Coll, who has sworn to be faithful at the cost of your own life? That is how the poison could spread among us. We've suffered a very shrewd blow. We need to get the pair of them back, but they are well hidden and protected, Coll; only Esmirone can help us there, if anyone can. But I shouldn't think aloud. You're looking worried. You hit them harder than they expected, my champion.'

'They were out to get me,' protested Coll.

'I know. It must have been quite some time ago that our brace of beauties defected. That's why our rivals in London knew all about you. The loss of Esmirone, if that's what it comes to, is the worst blow they could have struck at us. You did your job even better than I gave you credit for, Coll, and you may have to undertake another commando operation if they become too much of a nuisance.'

'So Gerald and Maxine will now reveal your whole organization to this lot?'

'I'm sure they did that long ago. I wouldn't mind betting that there are plants in Richmond House.'

'Michael Wheelwright probably knows that, too,' said Coll. 'Why don't we go for their throats now before they have a chance to make the next move? Throw them off their stroke? But you tell me to stay out of trouble.'

Siobhan smiled. 'That's war, indeed, but it may be that everyone would prefer peace. We'll see. Let's put out some more feelers first.'

'But they've got the ahamés back. There's nothing to bargain with.'

'Yes, I need those in order to heal Esmirone. Well, we have Diane, who packs a heavy punch, and we'll succeed in spite of their attempts to strike us down. You'll see.'

'Shall I go back to Hampton Court?'

'What would you find there? They're gone.'

'I know where Roseanne teaches.'

'I can see the headlines. Come on, Coll, where's that brain of yours?'

'Michael can't handle this.'

'Right now he's taking your place. He'll do. There's something you don't know, my injured champion. Although at this time you are particularly vulnerable, to our common danger, this period will pass. After midsummer you will be in no danger from the red menace at all. Stay out of play until then. But take care: you still have to beware of the thin man with only one eye.'

'So what am I supposed to do now?'

'Amuse me.'

Chapter 35

ESMIRONE DID NOT DIE, but she did not live. In an unbroken coma, she existed in a region of the soul's cosmos out of time, like the dead. But where? Siobhan sustained her with miraculous strength of healing, aided by the priestly magic of Cybele and Diane. The doctor called every day, looked, but said nothing, for there was nothing more she could do.

Household life went on undisturbed by the group Coll had stirred into anger. When he asked Siobhan what was happening, she gave him no answer. He still had the idea that they should identify all the members of the hostile party and rub them out one by one in self-defence, for his acquired feral nature grew uppermost in him as midsummer approached. For once England was having an unusually hot and dry summer. Never had the swelling green fields, so strangely denuded of all their dark primal forest, looked so inviting. For all its menace the deep wood of mysterious existence was entrancing to him, not simply because of the glamorous allure projected upon him by its deadly denizen, but also because it manifested an invisible world stretched out over ages. Although she left the house less frequently now, Siobhan took several walks with him, yet neither of them brought up the subject of their previous undertakings to each other, the pact sealed in the shade of great oaks overlooking the ever so gentle drop of the vale where the new lambs bleated for their complacent mothers.

'The day after tomorrow is the longest day,' remarked Siobhan. 'Half-a-year to the shortest day.'

'What of it?'

'That is an important day for you, Coll. After it passes you will be able to ignore any danger posed by the enemies who have emerged so far, especially the one who comes guised in the face your soul fears. She has an awful strength, but it will not serve her then. Sometimes we are at our height, sometimes our depth and at all the degrees in between. You are now in great strength yourself; at midsummer you will be at your zenith. You will then come into your true place in the Circle. I chose you for that. But I'll admit that I didn't really know what I was doing at the time.'

'What is my true place?'

'Be patient, my restless carle, patient for a very short time, and hold out as you have done. You're a winner. I saw that at once. You believed that you were a loser, but no one can be a loser who finds his soul. Perhaps you will find out more about your father whose absence was so painful to you. You'll have something to do again. That's what you really want, isn't it, a rôle?'

'Tell me.'

'You will realize your dream. There! I'll leave you to the delight of guessing, because I can't tell you any more. For now remember the important things – that I have chosen you and that you ate your carle's portion at the Beltane. Soon you will be completely mine under the crowning aspect of the Goddess. Walk with me and the other one will be powerless to impugn your state. But still be cautious, faithless man: no more nocturnal chats through the window pane or flips with motorcycle minxes. Let's walk home under the high sun. For the rest of the day and the whole of tomorrow you stay inside and we'll be with you, all of us, together in the lounge. With Esmirone barely clinging to life, we've got to take great care that we don't suffer any more damage. You noticed the check-point set up on the road?'

He hadn't. 'What are you afraid of?'

'Personally, I'm not afraid of anything because I think we are a match for them. If you're not afraid, then perhaps you should be. You may not know it, but you are about to become our chessboard King, and we have to screen you. I am the most powerful piece, the Queen, so I have to be screened too. As the sun begins to decline in the darker half of the year, things will change about again, particularly for you. But on the whole we shall have less to worry about.'

'You're forgetting the other enemy,' said Coll. 'I am afraid of him. You know who he is. Even Esmirone was a bit scared when she heard about him – Victor, the one-eyed man.'

'No, I was not forgetting.'

She fell silent, but suddenly looked into Coll's eyes as if weighing him up: was he strong enough?

'I wish I could help you.' She was troubled.

'Thanks, dear one. Can't you, Diane and Cybele get together on this? Surely the three of you together can call him off.'

'Call him off? My dear man! Let's get back while the sun is high.'

Coll was not happy to be told to stay indoors in such glorious weather when the whole countryside was a theophany of summer beauty, but he had now learned just enough fear to curb his fancy: no more pub nights for a while. Although he would not admit it to himself, it was fear, not keeping faith, that made him determined to avoid any chance of meeting again the lady of the forest, apparently Siobhan's counterpart – or was she? She could, it seemed, change her guise and encounter him anywhere she chose when he was least expecting it. He now knew well enough that one of her purposes was access to the house through him. So they all played a lot of rummoli as quietly as they could. He slept on a sofa alongside Cybele. For that night he fell gently into a dreamless sleep and the hours until broad morning passed without incident.

The following day was one of busy preparation, with several women coming in to do things downstairs, and men moving about the grounds. Siobhan asked him to stay inside out of the way and forbade him work of any kind. He practised pistol shooting from the window of one of the back rooms until he got a request *via* Cybele to cease and desist immediately as Matt's men strongly objected to Coll's slugs parting their hair however friendly his intentions.

No rummoli that night, Midsummer's Eve. When he was emerging from the bath Diane came in and rubbed him down with a herbal unguent. In spite of this he found getting to sleep harder than usual because of unbidden excitement welling up in him: something was afoot all right, and he was at the centre of it. He knew in his heart what was about to take place, but he dared not express this, the most sacred and ardent of his dreams, even to himself for fear of being wrong. He could not live to be so mortified. Everyone slept in the lounge, of course, everyone, that is, except Siobhan. He did not see her at all, and, as usual, no one told him anything.

The three priestesses rose early to celebrate the sunrise after performing their lustra, Coll and Michael watching with them. Breakfast was also ceremonial. The centrepiece of the meal was a very large brown loaf intricately decorated with a central motif and a mysterious emblem at one end. The other dishes were laid out around it on the sideboard.

When Coll attempted to go into the kitchen at lunch time to eat with the others, he was shoved out again. He noticed two women he hadn't seen before. As the dining-room and the lounge were also peopled with strangers turning the whole place upside down, he went back to his old room. There Diane brought him lunch on a tray, whatever he wanted, notwithstanding her feverish haste to get things done and the presence of strangers in her sacred domain, the kitchen.

She wasn't the only one having to suffer strangers in her territory. The grounds were teeming with men, their voices mingled with the sounds of nails hammered home, the whirr of a two-stroke engine, the click of clippers, planks slapping into other planks and the resonant pizzicato of mallets meeting wood. A touch. She stood beside him.

'What they doing?' he asked.

'Can't you see?'

'Marking the lawn, putting up a very long table which is going to be inside that enormous marquee they've just finished laying out, in addition to scads of other tables. I don't think there's room for all that lot.'

The men were obviously well-practised in their jobs. With several more tents and some stands arriving, they worked to a rhythm. The exuberance of a fair was now taking over. It was a high jinks day in the making.

All the long tables were arranged at the side, so the merriment would include eating and drinking. Meanwhile inside the house the village band were depositing their cases in the front hall and getting their awkward instruments out.

However, security had not been relaxed. As always, all comers were scrutinized and accounted for.

Without thinking, Coll went to go downstairs and outside, but Siobhan pulled him back.

'Not yet. You are to stay with me inside all day. Did you forget?'

It was not long before the musicians struck up Holst's *St Paul's Suite* and a few couples were dancing around on the lawn even before the earliest drinker. The day was coming up like a brilliant birthday balloon. There was a bubbling joy in the coming and going between house and garden. Everyone was caught up in wild anticipation of the Midsummer's fair, everyone, that is, except Siobhan, who was lemonade cool, and Coll, who longed to join the fun. After all, he now knew many of these people. Yet while they were out in the sun, copious in dance, music, food and drink, he and Siobhan had a private little lunch upstairs in a study he had not noticed before.

'Why this seclusion?' asked Coll, whose appetite had been destroyed by nervous anticipation.

'Well, we're not part of the preparations: we're the subject of them. We have to stay out of sight until we make our anticipated appearance. And we must not hang around downstairs impeding the work. We're quite enough trouble as it is. By the way, you're not quite out of danger yet. We'll have to stay on our guard.'

'With all that crowd down there?'

She nodded. 'Take a rest now. Your turn comes later. For now you stay up here. You can rest in my room.'

'With you?'

'If you like. You remember what we said to each other on the edge of the forest?'

'How could I forget!'

'Today you must stay with me all the time.'

But rest was the last thing he wanted on this day of days. She sat at her dresser re-arranging her hair. He could not resist putting his hands on her shoulders and kissing her on the back of the neck. She stopped what she was doing and looked at him.

'So you insist on reigning over me?'

The reference to reigning was lost on him.

'Reigning? Is this the day . . .?'

'Today yours is the choice. You can do what you like – afterwards.'

She was the pearl of his dreams. Desire hit him like a blow in the stomach. Her words had released him. At last. He did not know what he was doing.

'Stop it, Coll. I said "rest" not "rape me" – you cannot be forgiven if you tear at me like that. I am not to be mishandled.'

He stopped, catching his breath. She turned away and resumed adjusting her hair. How she entranced him! Yet she herself was not in the least moved, at least not visibly. He went to the door thinking to go to his own room, or downstairs, away from her allure, but she stopped him.

'You stay here with me all day, remember? If you can't resist temptation go and throw some cold water over yourself. I'll come with you.'

He threw himself on the bed and tried not to watch her. Much to his amazement, she woke him up several hours later. He had no recollection of dozing off.

'We're going downstairs now, Coll. Try to wake up. Here are your things.'

Not fully aware of what was happening at first, he stumbled a little on the way. There were a lot of people about inside, and he found himself guided to the head of a little procession beside Siobhan. As they went, others surrounded them. After going this way and that hemmed in by the whole population of the village, someone shoved him on to a raised seat. Siobhan was beside him. A solemn stillness fell. In the hush Coll noticed that Diane and another woman he had not seen before were flanking the Queen as if they were her assistants. A man in a loose-fitting white gown approached. Someone handed him an ornamental staff. With this he touched Coll on both shoulders and below the navel and handed it back to his assistant. Another assistant handed him a wreath of wrought gold bearing a serpent motif. This the unknown priestess took from him and placed it on Siobhan's brow. The serpent shone in the sun, as if it lived. Then it was his turn. He was crowned not with everlasting gold but instead with a green wreath woven from living plants, notably myrtle. Except for Siobhan's two assistants and the one robed man at his own side, all the other celebrants withdrew a space. The entire congregation began to chant rhythmically. After a time as the chant became louder and more insistent, the assemblage began to move purposefully and Siobhan and Coll found themselves at the centre of a dance of many figures moving sunwise in which changing partners approached and withdrew from each other. Siobhan turned to him. The King and Queen rose in their places and, clasping their fingers, raised their arms over their subjects. Immediately the pace of the dance intensified. This happened three times, inducing in Coll a hypnotic adrenalin of June madness, for he was sure that he was god of the whole world, buoyed up in the gleeful certainty of the dancers. This went on perhaps for hours, but perhaps not, for on this day of days time ran strangely.

At any rate, the sun was still high over the horizon when the entire gathering, spontaneously and at the same moment, danced as a procession into the forest which he now saw grew quite thickly much closer to the property line than he remembered. Again he and Siobhan were constantly surrounded by the same joyful people of the Circle. At some point on this long dancing journey Siobhan handed him a tiny phial of something. After he tossed it off he felt marvellously clear, even more lightheaded and imbued with limitless energy and stamina: he wanted to dance into the forest like this forever. He could dance across the Atlantic. All the same, he was not too self-engrossed to notice that they were climbing the gentle rise again, the one he had once remembered with a measure of dread not completely absent on this insanely blissful occasion.

There was no one on the other side of the stream. She and he stood together on the bank. Once again she had a spray of oak leaves in her hand. The others halted behind in a hush, the spell of the dance broken as spontaneously as it had begun. Nothing moved in the dell. Siobhan called out in a strange tongue. The merrymakers waited nervously. No one emerged to answer her. Nothing stirred. She lay down the spray. Finally, she called, 'Remember that I the Queen have made the long-wished offering.'

As the royal pair turned away, Siobhan gave Coll the most luscious embrace he had ever received. He noticed that the people of the Circle standing well back from them were far from comfortable. Their holiday spirits had given way to fear.

'It's going to be you or the fawn,' said Siobhan, 'but don't let's think of that now.'

'What fawn?'

'You should remember.'

The way out of the forest was shorter than the way in. In spite of that, the last rays of the dying sun threw deep shadows over the garden. At the same time the moon was rising, the luckiest of all signs, the sun and the moon in the same sky. If the villagers had been having a good time before, they went wild now, and the real binge took over. A good deal of ale was foaming, both inside and out. Neither he nor Siobhan were allowed to leave their seats. If they wanted anything it was brought. Coll wanted to get down and renew acquaintance with the fellows he had met in the pub, but Siobhan would not let him.

'This is our day, Coll. They want to rejoice over us. Our sitting above them here with all our friends is very important to them. So don't be shy or embarrassed, but look like a king, at least like a rural one, for that's what you are.'

He suddenly remembered that he had seen nothing of Cybele since the morning and that Diane had also disappeared from view after her brief appearance. And he had expected Michael to be here, but he hadn't shown up at all.

'Diane and Cybele are busy inside. You'll see them in the morning.'

At the moment of nightfall the Queen and the Falling King were escorted inside under a pale moon. Coll felt it was the last straw when a large company of the revellers insisted on accompanying them right up to and inside Siobhan's bedroom, some of them making coarse tropal gestures indicating what was now expected of them. He and Siobhan had to stand, embrace and kiss, and even lie down on the bed together before the village's riper aleskins could be induced to leave. When Coll had pushed the last one out, he sat down beside her. They looked at each other. He was furious. She laughed.

'Aren't they priceless, these oafs! I was about to start undressing, but I wasn't sure that they would leave even then! It's part of the rites, really and truly, you old crosspatch. You have to accept all this as a very ancient custom, fortunately watered down quite a bit nowadays. After all, it's still the same in church. What do you think placing the ring on the groom's finger means? I know it disturbs your beautiful state of mind, but we can't shut them out. What we do tonight is very important to my people, so go to your room, dearest Coll, bathe, change and calm yourself if you can. I'll help you. Leave your door open a little. In a short time I'll send for you.'

He had lost his exultant mood in the coarsened atmosphere those clowns had brought upon the night with their barnyard rollicking, but it wasn't long before some of his former excitement returned. In and out of the shower in short order, he found a silken nightrobe laid out for him, threw it on, went to the door and peered down the hallway. There a veiled woman was waiting. She came in, made him remove his robe and applied little drops of oil with muttered words. He did not know the voice. When she finished, two other women also draped completely in black from head to toe were waiting for him. He could not recognize any of the three but thought that two at least must be Cybele and Diane. He could not tell who was whom. Each took an arm and led him to Siobhan's room. There she sat at the mirror as before, combing the hair that reached halfway down her back. Why had he never before noticed this voluptuous abundance? For some reason he could not see her face clearly, and he suddenly thought of the story of Psyche. When she put out the single light, he found that something had been done to make the room absolutely dark. He tried the old trick of bringing his hand close to his face, but he couldn't see it.

Her voice was clear enough. There could be no mistaking that it was indeed Siobhan's.

'I am in bed. Come and join me.'

She was naked, harsh word for the living touch of her virginal flesh, nymph and angel. To violate her softness seemed a sin, yet she guided him as he explored the divine countryside of her desires, loving to linger but always torn away to some other nimbused lake or dark grove transfigured in the moon of her unbelievable love. From her breasts he drew a milk that gave him greater bliss than the sublime act itself, O sensuous angel of paradise. When, much later, she drew him into her as gently as dying he was crucified in ecstasy and heaven was too much for him.

When he awoke after a deep and dreamless sleep, it was high morning and the room was lit by the eastern sun as usual.

Siobhan had gone.

Chapter 36

THE DIVINE NIGHT PAST, how pale and inadequate the light of day! The towering forest itself and the oblique summer landscape, the loveliest of nature's poetry, cradling his bright-eyed queen in her circle was mere bathos, fading ghosts of reality. Only the precious Queen, his Siobhan, inspired him now. She was his world.

He bathed and went downstairs.

In the kitchen Diane greeted him with a kiss. 'Now we can have breakfast,' she said.

'Come on, you weren't waiting for me.'

'Yes we were, everyone, including Siobhan.'

It was true. They were waiting in the dining-room, Cybele and Siobhan. The visiting priestesses who had assisted on the previous day had left. But this was a change! No one had waited for him before. He embraced Siobhan, but could find no hint in her body's touch of the rapture of the night of nights; she was now quite *different*, but of course that was bound to be so on the morning after a wedding night that had bathed his body and soul in heaven. There were no words for it. Cybele was even more restrained. He waited for them to sit down, but Siobhan led him to his place, first on the right of the Queen, who always sat at the head.

'This is your place now. Esmirone will sit on my left when she is better, as she will be. I'm sure you don't doubt my healing power now.'

'Not after last night – it wasn't a dream, was it? I didn't believe that such heavenly joy could be. I don't think I do now.'

'I also had joy of you. It is sad that all these things must be evened out in the soul, that joy must be paid for.'

'Meaning?'

'You will see soon enough. But now you are head of the house, of the Circle even, but you are a constitutional head.'

'How so?'

'All the decisions are made by others. Your job is to earn respect, receive honour and approve of whatever we do while your reign lasts.'

'That means you're still going to be the real boss while I'm just a figurehead. Well, at least the job doesn't sound as though it's going to be hard.'

'Doesn't it? I hope not. But now my king replete with carnal pleasure and heavenly joy, look outside. We're in for another incredibly beautiful day. What do you want to do?'

'Don't I get my jobs as usual?'

'Very funny. Your only job is to be king and lord of everyone. Whatever we can do for you, we will.'

'Shall we go to the village later?'

'If you like.'

'Or up to London, perhaps?'

'Whatever.'

'Why not a trip to Greece?'

'Why not?'

'I'd prefer China.'

'All right.'

'Are you having me on? Up until now I haven't been able to do anything in case I shattered like a porcelain doll or was stolen. What's new?'

'You are now a part of me and you will naturally want me with you wherever you go, I hope.'

'Can you possibly have any doubt of that, after . . .'

He paused because the other two were there.

'Besides, your new status confers a certain but not absolute immunity on you, at least for a time. But we're still left with the dilemma: you or the fawn.'

'What does that mean?'

'Trouble, unless we can think of something.'

Coll rose and went to the window, gazing out at the garden, the lawn still pristine-green even after the rack and ruin inflicted by hundreds of pairs of feet, and beyond, the dumose rise to the old forest, fresh and splendid temple of the earth itself that sent a thrill up his spine.

'It's so lovely to be here. I can't believe that all this is true, you, Cybele, Diane, and the wonder of garden and forest.'

'Make the most of it,' said Cybele matter-of-factly, 'while you still have it. Your star is still in the ascendant. I don't grudge Siobhan her good fortune, for I love her quite as much as any man. Take your joy and the carefree kingship while it lasts.'

'And how long will that be?'

There was a moment's silence as often happens when a lively conversation is unaccountably struck dead by a kind of collective shudder.

'Who knows?' said Diane gently after the chill. 'For so long as it lasts each of us three is here for you. So you may find yourself in another kind of dilemma, a dilemma for you but not for us, do you see? For example, if you want to bed any one of us, we will oblige you in perfect love, well – both love and duty – and you will not be doing wrong in anyone's eyes, except, perhaps your own, depending on how you think you stand with Siobhan. You'll have to think that one out.'

Coll was indignant. 'Look, I've just married Siobhan –'

'No you haven't,' put in Cybele. 'She has chosen you as her lord for this time, and for us that means you are king just as she is queen. And as we, Diane and I, are also priestesses, it is given to us to share you, if we wish, which we do. Think, Coll, of the course of events. We have been working up to this all along, ever since your election by Siobhan was clear, nearly a year ago. Now if you had chosen me instead of Siobhan, let us say, and I had accepted, we should have married and would have undertaken to be faithful to each other all the days of our lives, for pure friendship and love in marriage is the essence of the Circle. Did Siobhan ask you to marry her?'

'No, but we did give some undertakings to each other which were sealed with solemn promises.'

'What happened,' broke in Siobhan, 'is that you gave me some undertakings and I said that I would be faithful to you as long as your kingship lasted. I didn't ask the same of you.'

'Now I come to think of it, you didn't, but – this is all topsy-turvy!'

'Is it? You are the King, but your position is quite different from mine. I told you the way to my bed is difficult.'

Coll laughed in pure happiness, not stopping to consider the implications of what Siobhan had said.

'Well,' he replied, 'if that's what you call difficult, a couple of punch-ups ... but why freedom for me and restraint for you? That's not fair.'

'Perhaps not. You may change your view of that. What do we get out of it?'

'I can think of only one thing, children.'

'Of course. The kingly line must continue. The College must have infants.'

'Why was I chosen, a stranger, a man on the run?'

'Well, dear one, I must remind you that you asked to be chosen when you fell in love with me. You were given chances to back out, but, like the stout fellow you are, you wouldn't be deterred: you were going for the girl or for broke. Now you've got her, no matter what. There are other reasons, too, of course. You have no strong ties, you passed your initiation, underwent the strengthening of the candidate – yes, candidate is the right word and you showed on several notable occasions that you had the stomach for a fight, your strongest asset now. And I love you. Of course you know that my love has a different quality: it extends to everyone in the Circle. My love symbolizes the life of the earth. This is not the kind of love that arouses your feelings of possessiveness, my King. For the kind of love that brings more life into the College of this Circle, I am bound to you only as long as you are King and so far as I am permitted, and I do not monopolize you. From this day on, if other women initiated into the priesthood join us, you will have to approve them and they you before they can be admitted to this household. You understand what that means, I think.'

'I'm just a stud!'

'Oh, don't be foolish, Coll. Look at it from the women's point of view. Just as your reward for your devotion and perseverance is me, so their reward for their great qualities which they have acquired by undertaking long ordeals, is you, the man of great strength, the King for his season. Forget your upbringing, Coll. You are now at the heart of an inspired community, older than you can possibly guess.'

'There's a lot in this that I'm not grasping. Do you want me to lie with Cybele and Diane? After last night I can't believe it.'

'It doesn't have anything to do with what I want or don't want. We would like the Circle to have as many chances as possible, and you already know that Cybele and Diane accept you and want you. It's the same as an *agape*.'

'It sure is, a trifle more on the sisterly than the brotherly side.'

'Listen Coll, what are you? Think of that for once. Both they and you have been chosen. After all, there's nothing you have to do in the next ten minutes. You have time to reflect and absorb. Anyway, what shall we do today?'

'I don't know. I just want to stay as happy and light-hearted as I am now. What do you want?'

'Shall we walk over the Downs for a sight of the sea?' replied Siobhan.

'And go through the forest that only exists when I'm with you? This *must* be a dream!'

'Are you sure? You may find it quite otherwise. And dreams can be more gripping than waking life, far more dangerous than any other reality. The forest is of the past, a past we have forgotten. We in the Circle try to recapture it, even its dangerous aspects. We must find the Great Goddess again.'

'Shall I find Her?'

'If you seek long and hard enough. I can't say, but take care to seek Her in Her beneficent aspect.'

'Well,' said Coll, 'let's get going then. Are you two coming?'

'Do you want us to come?' asked Diane.

'Why not?'

'Hadn't someone better stay to look after Esmirone?' asked Cybele.

'Oh, my gosh, of course. I'll leave you two in charge then. Who else is here?'

'Everything's taken care of,' said Siobhan, 'but I think Diane wants to come. Are we all ready? Together we make a team that's hard to top, your brute strength, my power and Diane's magic, if we don't wander into the wrong territory. In the end the gods will have their due.'

If Coll had been hoping for some enlightenment as to his rôle, he wasn't getting it. The sows were playing a completely different game now, and he had an idea that they weren't going to let him see the fine print in the rule book. Was this a test, the one Siobhan had mentioned?'

There was something else: none of the three had the very long luxuriant hair Siobhan had been combing out on the fabulous night. Yet the voice he had heard in his voluptuous bliss had been undeniably Siobhan's. The drunken villagers had seen them getting into bed together on his and Siobhan's nuptial night. That was what they had wanted to see – Siobhan in bed with her King. On the other hand his recollection of empirical events might be confused, drowned in the emotional sweat of love. She had spoken to him at the beginning. He racked his memory, but could not remember her speaking at any time later. But this was absurd! No one had switched places! The thing was impossible – and why should she? The moment had been prepared for this and only this, his union with the Queen. Yet he had an abiding shred of doubt, one which he dared not express.

In whose basket was the pig, then?

Chapter 37

Now for the first time Coll began to see himself as a member of a greater entity than the immediate household. When he and Siobhan walked down to the village, everyone greeted him with the same dignified respect that they greeted her, in fact people went out of their way to shake his hand almost as though his presence and touch conferred some virtue. At the same time he was aware of being discreetly guarded by men who walked behind, something he did not relish, for it detracted from the sacred privacy of his moments with Siobhan.

'What if we go on holiday somewhere?' he asked. 'Are we going to find these chaps roaming through our bedroom?'

'Yes. And consider carefully before you decide one something like this, for the Circle's resources, although at your disposal, are limited. Our expenses come out of everyone's pocket.'

'I don't really want to be anywhere else but here with you, and these other wonderful people.'

'There's nothing in the world like summer in this countryside. You feel as if all the poetry and music of a thousand years are mingled in its colours. And this is where your friends are, as safe for you as possible.'

'All the same, I wouldn't mind dropping in on the lads at Richmond House one day. I got to know some of them fairly well when I was there.'

'All right, so long as your visit doesn't include Roseanne.'

'I thought I was the King.'

'You are. To receive honour, not to make decisions. Even going to Richmond House is a risk since there may be men there who are not to be trusted. You have to understand, as you found when you were pursued into our arms, so to speak, that this beauty, this little paradise established here, was not built without risk and failure, without the loss of innocence and the hard-hearted means of gain. It has its darker side. It is given to both of us to enjoy, but we shall have to pay our share.'

'Meaning?'

'I can't tell you, for I don't yet know the full meaning myself. But why spoil such a beautiful day? Can you feel it as intensely as I do?'

He looked at her. Her eyes were alight with passion for everything around, the old houses, the shop windows the runnel carrying water to the river, the old water mill and the tiny bridge house that now served as a museum of folk art, the roads forking, one rising over the brow of the hill, the other edging the green and crossing the bridge to ascend other hills. When they reached the highest point of the near stone bridge arching over the river, they embraced. Coll felt such an urge to take her that he was not sure he could control himself. She knew this and made him walk her back to Hazelridge.

He hardly felt he was walking for he knew himself to be in paradise. When they got back, however, Siobhan disappeared, and, although she couldn't have gone far, neither Diane nor Cybele could tell him where she was.

'What have you been up to?' asked Diane, who could see that he was more excited than usual.

'I've been out with Siobhan, as you know, have been in bliss with her, and now she goes off and leaves me.'

'Well, she'll be back for lunch at least. Is there anything I can do for you?'

As his eyes met hers he felt the dilemma he was in in all its acuteness, and he stood there swaying as faith and desire pulled him first one way and then the other. This might be a test. But had not already reached the height of his ambition and desires in Siobhan? That could not be taken from him.

'I don't know what to do,' he said feebly.

'Shall I help you?' She stood beside him. 'I am here for you.'

The dilemma stifled action. He was fast in ice. He could not take even this magical girl after Siobhan.

'I know. Thanks. Maybe later.'

He went up to his room downcast and with revolving energy seeking an outlet, which prompted him to do something wantonly stupid, such as to seek out the dell where the two of them had encountered the three grotesque figures and stick it to the weirdos. He put the revolver into his back pocket together with two extra clips of ammunition, and went downstairs through the french windows at the back. Cybele was waiting for him. She asked him where he was going.

'Just taking a little walk through the forest. Back for lunch.'

'That could be very dangerous if you find it, Byron.'

'I plan to make it less dangerous by taking out our friends on the other side, you know where.'

'What does Siobhan think about this?'

'Nothing. She disappeared as soon as we got back from our walk, so I have to find myself something else to do,'

'Byron, believe me, you'll meet whoever you're looking for soon enough, and perhaps sooner than you want to.'

'Fine. Well, you can tell Siobhan where I've gone *if* she comes back.'

'Look, wouldn't you rather lie down with me? You practically asked me to do that the first day you were in Dublin with us. Here I am – for your pleasure whenever you like. I give myself to you.'

'I don't understand. First Diane and now you. Is this a test?'

'No, it's an attempt to prevent you from committing folly, since I haven't any power to order you back. You know you're being a fool, don't you, but you don't know what you're doing or you wouldn't do it.'

'All right, since I'm King, why don't you come with me?'

'That's an unnecessary hazard, Byron. You cannot ask that.'

'Either you're coming or I'm not King. Well – ta-ta, then.'

'Since you demand it of me, I have to obey you, but this is sheer folly. You'd rather be a hero than a sensible man. At least give me time to change into something more suitable.

Ten minutes later she was back, in jeans, jacket and heavy-soled shoes and carrying a single-barrelled automatic 16 gauge shotgun which she threw to him. 'Here. A slug from this will stop most things.' She produced a box of cartridges. He put a handful into his pocket.

'What did you bring for yourself?'

'The usual. I should turn it on you now, you idiot.'

'Come on, then.'

'Look, Byron, are you sure you wouldn't prefer a nice quiet time at home? Diane and I could make it very lovely for you.'

He was already through the back gate, so she followed him, the first member of the Circle to do so.

The dwarfish conifers planted in rows with the wind wheezing through them were their companions as long as they remained in the man-made forest, and they walked for over an hour before these began to give place to the hushed giants out of the world's weather for whom a century was youth. Coll could not remember any directions or marks from his previous journey with Siobhan. One track looked much like another, and now, within the confines of what looked more and more like a giant prison, he had a sinking dread of meeting again its strange denizens. Yet he also kept in mind Siobhan's assurance that he was not in so much danger now as before, forgetting her exact words. But what about Cybele? He stopped and looked at her. He had no right to sacrifice her, and he realized how utterly thoughtless he'd been in his frustration. Hell! Why hadn't he considered her! He remembered her words about heroic gestures, gestures in which he had now involved her.

'What's the matter?' she asked.

'I've been stupid – and thoughtless,' he admitted.

'Glad you realize it,' she sighed in her relief. 'Let's try to get out, then.'

'I shouldn't have brought you.'

'Don't worry about that. You're the one at risk, the big cheese. I don't count for much.'

'To me you count for – a great deal. But now I'm bound to Siobhan.'

'No, she's bound to you. Remember? To you, to you alone. There is no other man in her life now but you, only you. Only for you, the King, are the rules inverted. Well, if we're not stopping for the night, let's get going.'

He looked at her.

'Good heavens, man, don't even dream of it *here*.'

In his dream of her she was maddeningly desirable. He had a vision of her in Dublin sinuously undulating in front of him to imitate a cobra. But she was on her way back. He followed her, caught between one impulse to tackle her and another to get her out of danger. He stopped in his tracks again, struck by a sudden realization.

'What now?'

'I'm beginning to get the idea, I think. When we were all here yesterday we were using the forest as a temple. It is a temple. I feel it.'

'That's very clever, Byron. Not everyone, even members of the Circle, thinks of that.'

'So it's a temple, not one built by men, the only kind most people think of, but one built by beings who have dedicated it to themselves. We are strangers, foreigners, here.'

'You've put your finger on the danger, although you didn't think of the corollary. Yes, this is a temple into which yesterday by virtue of your position you were admitted freely. But mankind, meaning people like us, have been busily destroying the temples of the earth for a very long time, blind to their sanctity. That ghastly process has been speeded up in our own time. Is it any wonder that the gods have come to hate men and now rule them for their destruction? In particular, we two are not wanted here. You yourself have now, thank the stars, at last understood that.'

She turned to retrace her footsteps, thinking that this truth had finally become self-evident even to the most stubborn male hero. But Coll still hung back, then turned and continued his way further into the forest. When she saw that, she followed him again.

'How far are we from the house?' asked Coll.

'Not too far. Probably less than an hour's walk.'

'That's what I guessed. Then you can get back by yourself.'

'What on earth are you thinking of?'

'I'm telling you – ordering you, if that's what it takes – to get back to Hazelridge. I have some things to straighten out.'

She was worried. 'I can't desert you. I think you're making poor decisions, but my job is security and I have to stand by you no matter what. I won't leave you.'

'I'm not chickening out now. What would you think of me?'

'I'd think you were a wise man instead of an adolescent numbskull.'

He kept on walking, oblivious both to his own revelation and her safety, as he had been from the beginning. Occasionally he turned and looked about as they walked. When they paused for rest, he fancied he saw movement in the depths, movement of something big, a bear, perhaps. He armed the shotgun.

Resuming their former path, this time more wary, intent now on the slightest noise, they went a considerable way into the forest, without, however, Coll's actually seeing anything he remembered. And the forest was endless. In the hush broken only by their footfalls and the slow movement of the leaves he found a peace that was more balming than his happiness at the house, but it also struck him that this was the peace of death rather than life. It was while he was in this mood that he became suddenly quite certain that something else was taking an interest in his movements. On his left were the sounds, now nearer and clearer, that suggested someone, someone big, was following with a heavy dragging gait. When they stopped, it stopped too. Gun at the ready, he worked his way towards it. But before he could raise his weapon to fire, the thing, moving rapidly, had him in its grip, an incredible giant of a bear a good two feet taller than himself, a terrifying bear left over from the ages when bears intimidated men, and he was fighting for his life as it squashed the breath out of him, try as he might to get a grip on it. One snap of the jaws and he would be very dead. But Cybele was as quick as the bear, and before this could happen she put a burst of fire into it so as to miss Coll. The bear released its hold just long enough for Coll to push it against a tree and punch its snout as hard as he could. This seemed to bother the creature more than the bullets in the right shoulder. Coll, battle-maddened, gripped the bear with all the purchase he could muster and tried to throw it down, but his opponent was far from finished. He got himself into the bear's grip for the second time, but had sufficient strength to throw it off, although only with a tremendous effort at the outer reaches of his enormous strength. Then, finding more sense, he took the shotgun which Cybele handed to him.

'Don't shoot unless you have to,' she whispered, as she moved to cover the bear from the side.

He levelled the shotgun at the bear's head while the great claws made as if to scrabble at him. It moved a pace closer, hesitated, then finally grunted and moved off into the forest on all fours.

'Are you going home, or am I to be murdered at your side?' asked Cybele.

'You saved my life then,' said Coll quietly, kissing her.

As they walked back, a sudden whisper in his left ear caused him to spin round. His nerves were not as good as before.

'A happy reign, O King of the Falling Year!' it said.

'What's the matter now?' asked Cybele.

'I thought I heard a voice speaking to me.'

'Thank goodness the new forest is not far ahead. What did it say?'

'It wished me happiness.'

'You can be sure that it was an ill-wish.'

Back at the house he found security all in a tizzy and Siobhan in a storm. She was almost speechless, the first time he had seen her really angry. She looked even more beautiful, for anger did not take possession of her; she possessed it.

'Why did you let him go?' she accused Cybele.

'I tried to stop him, but he ordered me to go with him. What could I do?'

'Coll, do you realize that by going in there without leave or protection you were in worse than mortal danger? And you are being very inconsiderate by leaving your friends up in the air. Your detail have been blaming themselves for your stubborn silliness. Come inside and tell me what happened.

Upstairs he told her.

'Hm, what kind of a whisper was it – well- or ill-intentioned?'

'Oh, ill. It was malignant in a sweet kind of way, like being wished a happy new year by your worst enemy.'

'Well, let me tell you what you have done: you have made the forest even more of an enemy than it was before by approaching it in the wrong way. I want to unite whatever forces I can. Understand? Only in that way can I do my part towards finding the world lost ages ago. That's my job.'

'I don't understand.'

'I know, and heaven knows when you will. We need your strength *here*. That's all you need to know for now.'

'There haven't been any bears wild in England for – what? Twenty thousand years? Or has this one escaped from a private park?'

'Not only are there no bears roaming around England on the loose – there's no habitat for them – but if there were at any time bears the size of yours, it must have been an enormously long time ago. Not even the Kodiak bear is that tall.'

'Don't you believe me, then?'

'Where were you Coll, with Cybele? Think about it.'

'I don't know.'

'You will not find that same path again, I think. Look, instead of giving everyone here heart failure, could you think of something sensible and enjoyable for us both to do?'

'All right. What about London tomorrow?'

'So that you can splash around up there with your propensity for stirring up trouble better left on its own. I'm coming with you and I'm not letting you out of my sight.'

'What if I decide to go by myself?'

'Try it, Coll. You are King now, but I am Queen, and my rôle is the executive one.'

'I didn't really mean that.'

'I know you didn't.'

'In the forest, all I wanted to do was to find Victor. I could have talked to him one on one.'

'You were in his ground and if he had chosen to meet you, you would have had your talk all right. Do you really think you would have had much to say? As it was you were close to being mauled to death by a bear and you deliberately chose to put Cybele, a dearly-loved friend of us both, in peril of her life.'

'She saved my life. I feel not only stupid, but brutal.'

'You're not brutal, Coll. I could never give my love to a man who was brutal or even highly insensitive, but you haven't learned to think in our way yet. We think that men are on a wrong course, and that someone has to start treating the earth not with respect, merely, but with reverence, with devotion, in adoration, even. Have you any idea of who Victor really is?'

'It is the greatest puzzle of my life.'

'Don't be in too much of a hurry to find out. He's not destructive, but he comes from the North and has designs on us, or hadn't you thought that through yet? No, you're not brutal. I know you love Cybele. You were simply as mad as hell, and that was my fault, Coll. I don't blame you. Anyway, it's tea time, you ass. Let's see who's here.'

Coll was in for a surprise. Esmirone, terribly pale and weak, still, but otherwise quite her old self was there in her place on Siobhan's left. Coll was delighted.

'Siobhan told me you would recover. It's wonderful to see you up again.'

'I am indeed here. Don't ask me where I've been. At any rate I believe I can throw some light on the puzzles you brought us, later, not today, please,' for she saw that Coll was about to ask her more questions.

Coll took his new place directly opposite her.

'And what have you been up to?' asked Esmirone, whose tone of voice indicated that she already knew about his misdeeds.

'This afternoon,' said Siobhan, 'he was taking a stroll in the old forest, hoping to take a pot shot at its denizens. It is fortunate that Cybele went with him, otherwise he would not be back here having tea with us.'

'Cybele is pure gold,' said Coll her courage saved me. Oh, she should be sitting here and I should be in the corner.

Cybele looked up at him, smiling.

'When are you going to learn sense?' asked Esmirone, 'Trust to the judgement of your consort, and mine, and of the high priestesses Cybele and Diane. They have something of the Circle's high wisdom. You need our help and protection; we also need yours. Since we're all here together, let me be specific as to what that help includes. It is part of your duty and privilege to make Diane and Cybele pregnant. Is that explicit enough for you? They certainly attract you.'

'He regards himself as solely tied to me,' observed Siobhan.

'Quite. That is only natural. But you are King. Siobhan as Queen decides her own course. Love prevails among us all here sitting at this table, and you must realize that Siobhan and you are – horrid word! – functionaries. Don't feel downcast at my words, Coll. Siobhan chose you in love, and her love is also wisdom, for she chose you not only for herself but for the Circle. At the very centre of our Circle she has engendered wisdom in her choices. You are very important, your motives are the motives of love, but you still owe love to others here. Not logic, eh, as a university man would understand it, but it is our way of thinking.'

Coll could not respond to this because his emotions were still confused, so he asked, 'Which one of them hit you?'.

'Both. They got nothing out of me. I sensed that trouble was coming, disarming as both of them were, and went for a gun, but Gerald had a softball bat, so I didn't stand much chance.'

'It's a miracle they didn't kill you. But they got the ahamés. They were our bargaining counter, I guess. But that's what they were after, wasn't it,' said Coll unhappily.

'Esmirone shot a glance at Siobhan. There was a pause.

'So you see,' put in Diane, to break the spell, 'we get our turn too.'

Siobhan smiled enigmatically.

Once again Coll was quite unable to digest the consequences of his position. He looked helpless. 'Trip away tomorrow,' he said lamely. 'Just Siobhan and me.

He had made up his mind to sleep with Siobhan every night. Her room was now his.

At last the sows had revealed the laws of the game to him, as it stood now. But he would play according to his own private rules from now on. He was Siobhan's consort, so she could not refuse him, especially after the previous night's ineffable joy.

Chapter 38

As before Siobhan wore nothing but perfect darkness on the second divine night of his possession of her. Again she sent him into a heaven both sensuous and visionary as he tried to do the same for her. This exalted lovemaking was nothing that the poets would have called 'heaven' or 'dying' such as young people at the height of their developed sexuality feel, but something extraordinary, miraculous, even. Again his involuntary cries and disordered talk were answered only by her passionate fingers. She was silent. Again when he awoke, in broad daylight, she was gone, her side of the bed cold. The minute he got his feet on to the floor, however, Diane appeared and told him that if he still thought of going to London that day, he'd better get a move on. He did, and, as on the previous morning, found everyone, including Esmirone, waiting for him. Matt was also there. He had taken over the security detail at the house himself and was going to drive the car. Coll thought wistfully of Michael with his mordant wit, but could get no information about him from anyone beyond the fact that he was in London.

It was close to ten before Siobhan and Coll were in the back seat of a black Daimler. They glided away in state and drove fairly fast for about fifteen minutes, when Matt suddenly pulled off the road and followed a forest track. Here, in a clearing, they got out of their stately car and into a much less regal model, while a couple from the village took their places in the Daimler. After it had gone, Matt waited about half-an-hour. When they emerged from the trees, Matt retraced their route through the village, driving on for a few miles until speeding off into a maze of minor roads.

It hadn't been decided where, exactly, they were going in the afternoon, but Coll wanted to drop in on Richmond House even though its inhabitants were away at work. Mrs Scott and Barbara would be there. Michael Wheelwright would see them at lunch in the City. Otherwise they were as free as the traffic permitted. Siobhan wasn't entirely happy with the visit to Richmond House and she wanted to keep it short.

Mrs Scott was glad enough to see them, especially Coll, whom she privately regarded as a bit naïve. They had to turn down her tea since they were expected in the City at one. However, Coll learned that Roseanne had not, so far as she and Barbara could recall, shown up again. Coll was also pleased to find that the brothers Tony and Roger were no longer in the House. They had, apparently, got into a dispute with the House Director, but she did not really know what it was about.

'I think it had something to do with parking space for their parents' new car, but I think, really, there was more to it than that. I never thought they fitted in here, but of course it's not my business and I shouldn't say that. I'm sure your friends, Coll, won't let it go beyond these four walls. I wouldn't like Mr Wheelwright to think I was poking my nose into affairs that don't concern me.'

They had left shortly after Coll. Was there a connexion between Roseanne and them? He tried to remember who had brought her to the dance, but couldn't.

After that it was off to Leadenhall by tube from East Putney while Matt and another man from the village, Don Winston, drove the car into the City where Michael had parking for them.

Michael was very happy to see them. The village, apparently, had a kind of metaphysical extension of its physical boundaries, for Michael shook Coll's hand as if he had met him on the bridge. 'Very glad to hear of your success. I had no idea, really! I simply pine for the day when I can afford to drop all this and move down to the village, Siobhan, but I know you need me here.'

'Indeed, Michael.'

'The House is under constant watch now,' he said, 'but Tony and Roger have left. They didn't fit in and I was never sure what they were really up to. Fortunately they didn't want to stay on anyway' he said simply. 'I won't bore you with the details. I had your message, Siobhan, and that was more than enough for me. I hope Matt didn't park in front of the House.'

'Of course not!' said Siobhan. 'He and Don are on their way to pick us up here.'

'Why don't you come down to our garden fête next weekend? You'll have plenty of time to get away in daylight.'

Coll was keen on this and accepted. They had to turn down with regret, at least on Coll's part, Michael's invitation to dinner as Siobhan particularly wanted to get back before dark. Matt in the company of Don picked them up as arranged and they were back in Hazelridge in less than two hours.

The golden age of Coll's life had begun; he was living in a dream, and perhaps for that reason never thought to ask himself why he had been chosen or what his future with these people was, or indeed how long it would last. He was lost in continual delight, fed, watered and let loose among the sows. The village, now more familiar and closer to him than ever his own family had been, was a joy, so much so that he began to look upon it almost as his possession. Men no longer went out of their way to shake his hand, but everyone was as familiar with him as if he were a long-lost son returning home. Similarly, they regarded him as a prized possession. When Siobhan was with him, eyes behind windows followed them. He had never in his life had such an awareness of being wanted, although there was a profound difference in the way in which he was wanted and the way in which Siobhan was wanted: he was a prize of some kind; she was revered as a potent figure, a source or spring without which the village could not live.

None of this mattered. He had never wanted much more than he got, and now that he had so much more than he wanted, he was simply content, in his strength and occasional rages. When he was out in the village with Siobhan even the thought of visiting the men at Richmond House on the day of their fête was a diversion from his plenitude of Olympian contentment. Paradoxically, although every minute of his life counted, time passed rapidly and the day of the fête came before he knew it. So on the last day of June Siobhan and he arrived just in time for lunch, accompanied by Matt, Don and Ross from the village. The brass on the front door was lustrous and the marble steps had been scrubbed white. Although there was some disorder inside with a coming and going through the lounge, they were greeted by Michael Wheelwright almost as if they were royalty.

At lunch they sat at the head of the tables arranged in a U to enjoy the only meal in the history of the austerely-run House in which wine was served, a small measure of feeble Blue Nun. The attendance of Siobhan and her consort was an Event, although none of the residents had any idea of what the Event was, beyond the cover story that certain important persons in the exalted regions of the Tower were visiting. However, because there is always a lot to do on these occasions, lunch was short and snappy, with most of Coll's friends excusing themselves early, and as Michael had to do the same, it was not long before the visitors were alone.

'I like this place,' said Coll. 'There are a lot of good men here. Have you recruited any, Siobhan?'

'Heavens no. I have nothing whatever to do with the Tower.'
'But –'
'Your position was completely different. You had no idea of where you were going when I found you, but you were seeking something beyond escape from your pursuers, weren't you, when I took the risk of bringing you into the Circle?'
'Victor sent me.'
'He did, and that is the most curious thing of all. Why you? And why to us? He's not really aiming at you, but at us through you.'
'Who is he?'
'The more important question is, what are his intentions towards you and us. If I only knew . . .'
'I can't fathom the man.'
'I can't either, but I'm afraid of him.'
'Everyone is, it seems.'
'Now that we're now together in love according to our vows, don't fail me, Coll, now or later. I'm in your hands, Coll, believe it. If you weaken I shall be in pawn to him. Do you know what that means? He will have gained a footing in the Circle. I love you, I need you, I depend on you.'
'Do you know how much I love you? I'd die for you.'
'I know. That is why I have trusted you. I would not place complete trust in any other man I know, not even the two Michaels or Matt, not as implicitly and utterly as I rely on you. Don't ask me why. I don't know. I told you it was a love.'
'Then how can Esmirone ask me to . . .' He did not finish.
'Oh Coll. I know how you feel. I accept the Circle utterly. You still have difficulty doing that. But you will understand in time. For now, it is the King's prerogative and duty.'
'To hell with that.'
'But you are King. That is why you have been given your great strength. The boar shall serve the lady. That you are my consort doesn't really have anything to do with it beyond denoting you as – shall I say? – the sacred fount. It is not solely my choice: I can only say that there is some other guiding power at work. I love Cybele and Diane. Why shouldn't I ask you to love them too? And you do, don't you? This seamless love is at the very heart of the Circle. It is our magic, Coll, our living expression of the uroboros.'
'I don't care about that. It debases my devotion to you, even if I don't do it.'
'But Coll, I understand it, allow it and welcome it, and it certainly

doesn't debase (as you put it) my love for you. You can't possess love, Coll. You can give it, you can receive it, but it is never yours to keep for yourself.'

'Siobhan, please! You take my breath away!'

'Come on! Let's get out of here and give Barbara a chance to clear up. The sky is clearing and we sit here inside like two lovebirds squabbling in their cage.'

'No! I can never quarrel with you.'

It was always the same. She answered his questions but he was no nearer to the truth of things. Something had passed right over his head.

Outside in the crowded grounds there was a chattering bustle as the darts tent, the biggest, was finally hauled up for the third time with reasonable tautness while the delicious smell of hot spiced meats competed with the irresistible odour of that recent import into England, drinkable coffee. Derek was selling raffle tickets and passes to the dance to follow that evening, hoping to raise more money for the Great Project, the construction of tennis courts, long-since proposed which, good fortune permitting, might be realized this side of Judgement Day. The airgun range had not yet opened because of some technical difficulty with the moving targets and John was doing something with cards. The fortune teller away back in the left outfield had long been set up. That well of Indian lore, one Shirami, was willing, for a trifling sum, to reveal the priceless hidden secrets of life to anyone (with cash) who applied. Coll had an idea that Shirami was Robbo, but Eddie would have been as good a choice, both born clowns.

In the meantime he was wandering the circuit with Siobhan mindful of her warning and keeping a sharp lookout. He was soon dismissed from the darts by Peter because all his went in up to the hilt, including those that missed the board altogether.

A coffee after lunch seemed a good idea, but it was not nearly as good as it smelled. Perhaps it never is. He stood there with her thinking, for no particular reason, of the sea that surrounds this great island Albion, of seeing it green from the deck of a ship, glimpsing the first definite image of England, the white lighthouse on Portland Bill rising out of the sea level mist in the early morning.

Why so vivid? His present vision was a reverie hardly briefer: here in the best of summer, having the most beautiful and inconceivably clever girl at his side who was so much more than that. The unsummoned images of ship and sea he could not understand. He had never been on an ocean-going ship. It occurred to him that this might have been a transmitted experience of the father he had never seen, a memory so powerfully charged, this first sight of England, that it touched even his son's soul. Absurdly he fumbled for pen and paper to scribble a note to remind himself to ask Siobhan about it when they finally escaped from the enveloping polite chatter, for she was moving on.

They chatted with John and bought tickets for the dance from Derek. At the airgun range, now functioning, Coll came into his own, and to the chagrin of the operator, a new resident unknown to Coll, won every prize in the stall. Coll gave a large black jaguar to Siobhan and returned all the other trophies.

The most impressive of the shooting games was the cross-bow range presided over by Michael Wheelright himself. This was not as well-patronized as the other games, partly because Michael had to explain the workings of the weapon, one which demanded some effort and skill, partly because the bow looked heavy and unwieldy. Coll watched as one girl had trouble winding in the spring. Michael set the bolt in the right position for her, but she was unwilling to let fly, so he handed it to Coll. Coll found it difficult to aim, but not at all difficult to use.

'These things are pretty well toys,' remarked Michael. 'A real hunting model is much heavier and nastier than this. The sport has revived in quite a big way. You might be surprised, not that I am a fanatic, by the way. These little plastic darts wouldn't do much harm to a kitten, but a top-flight hunter twice the size of this charged with a steel bolt is just as deadly as a good-sized slug from a shotgun. Pity I haven't got one here. I'd like to show you what it can do.'

At last only the fortune-teller remained for them. Siobhan did not particularly want to go in and suggested that Coll do the honours for both of them.

It certainly wasn't immediately clear who was disguised in the darkness, nor was the voice recognizable as that of Robbo or Eddie, but then Eddie was a good mimic. The spareness of the figure inclined Coll to postulate the little Scotsman.

'What do you seek?' asked whichever one of them it was.

'Are you Robbo or Eddie?'

'There was no answer to this, as Coll had expected. Either one of them would keep it up as long as possible until someone exploded in laughter.

'How many times have I seen you before?' asked the postulant.

'More often than you wanted.'

Coll was surprised that either one would tell a joke against himself; that wasn't their way. He had seen both of them horsing around on numerous occasions, but never tired of them as they were infallibly amusing.

'Will I get rich?'

'Never more than now.'

Coll was at a loss.

'What kind of a future will I have?'

'Your future is uncertain and what there is will be a burden to you; your fortune is less secure than your future.'

Coll laughed.

'Don't be a clot, Nosnibor. Didn't you see who I came in with – at lunchtime? Siobhan and our little entourage?'

'I also came with you.'

This was about the worst piece of fortune-telling Coll could imagine, and he began to laugh. Shirami's face was hidden inside a cowl, and although he was dressed completely in white, probably of bath towels purloined from Richmond House, his face was in darkness. Coll could not resist. He was determined to see who it was – the poker-straight voice betrayed Robbo. He reached across the table and made a grab for the other's headdress. As he did, fingers of ice gripped his arm with a strength the boar could not match and hurled him to the ground. Right beside his ear the fortune-teller spoke.

'You fool. If you had shown reverence and asked the right questions you could have escaped, lived and found yourself anew. But you are shallow and easily-led. Do not be eager to seek me out. When we next meet your life will totter on the knife's edge.'

When Coll came to he had been dragged out of the tent. Someone was talking of carrying him inside. He tried to sit up. All the inhabitants of earth spun around him as he sank into a vast maelstrom. His right arm was paralyzed; jagged ice ran into the shoulder. It wasn't that he couldn't speak. He had nothing to say. He saw Siobhan, whose arms were around his shoulders. Matt, Don and Ross hoisted him up and took him inside through the french windows into the lounge where they tried to make him comfortable on a sofa. To his horror he saw the fortune-teller approaching and started up in fear, making Matt and Don jump too. But when the cowl was off he saw Eddie.

'What happened to you?' asked Eddie.

'Who are you?'

'Don't you know me any more? Eddie, you oaf.'

Siobhan signalled Eddie to leave.

'What happened, Coll?'

He told her.

'Eddie says you came in, peered at him, mumbled something, put your arm up and keeled over.'

'That man belongs to the enemy. He's a Scot – comes from the North.'

Siobhan shook her head. 'I don't believe that.'

'He says I have no future, or not very much. That seems pretty definite. I was supposed to ask the right questions – of Eddie?'

'The gods do not allow for human weakness.'

'Was I speaking to a god?'

'Very likely. We shall look after you as well as we can. I think from now on it is better for you to be near the village where we can concentrate our powers, such as they are. But what shall we do right now?'

'That other lot are in the crowd here.'

'That wouldn't matter much. We are talking to them. This is quite different.'

'I can't make head or tail of it. This was to have been a last chance for me according to whatever voice I heard in the tent. But I'm still on cloud nine, even though my arm is useless. Siobhan, this *is* the enemy. That man had a strength I couldn't match. Don't you see –?'

'Yes, I do see. You cannot wrestle with a god.'

Coll looked at her. He now realized what she was saying. A horrible fear struck him.

'What can I do?'

'Not much. But you can still help us. He will not collect his due yet. Perhaps you can win back some small degree of favour from the one you treated so lightly in your ignorance. Did you recognize him?'

'I never got a chance to see his face.'

'Let's have a look at your arm. It doesn't show any bruise. Don't worry, I have virtue in this.'

She touched his arm lightly and murmured, giving him a gentle massage. The icy pain subsided.

'That's better.'

'Yes, I'm good for some things.'

'Well, we can stay on for the dance now.'

'You still want to, after all that's happened? I'm not so keen on that idea. However, if we do stay at least we'll be going back in morning light. There's no room for us here; only single men reside here, apart from the housekeeper, that is, and I will not be separated from you tonight. I'll find out what's possible. You stay where you are. Matt, keep men with you and don't let him out of your sight for a single moment. Get some more men here.'

'On the way now,' replied Matt.

She was away for some time.

'Look, do you absolutely insist on being present at this dance? It's going to be difficult because there are no rooms free. Mrs Scott has offered to share her room with me, but that's out of the question; it means that you and I would be separated, and that I will not allow. The only alternative is a small private hotel within easy walking distance from here. It can accommodate us both, but it's all rather a bother. I can get Barbara to go out and buy a few things for me – I don't know what you need.'

'Well, if that's all, let's stay.'

'If you insist, I shall not oppose you.'

So they stayed for the dance. As on the other evenings there was no ear-destroying amplification of industrial rock, but only the gentler if equally junky dance music of previous generations which at least allowed for conversation and courtesies. On this occasion the great lounge was fairly packed, and while he could not recognize more than five or six of the women guests from the previous dance, none seemed particularly interested in him, possibly because Siobhan was keeping a close watch on him and his encounterings. This was, he fondly imagined, the first sign of jealousy he had seen in her, and he smiled inwardly. 'Perhaps she's afraid for herself rather than for me.' Thus deluded, he danced with several other women, hoping he might evoke just the tiniest tangible sign of jealousy from his beloved. If he had success, she gave no sign of it.

It did not occur to him that he was barking up the wrong tree.

When, an hour after midnight, the time came to leave, he saw that security had been beefed up considerably. There were three new men who had brought Cybele with them.

Mrs Dixon, who ran the Carlton Hotel on the street of the same name, was well-apprised of their arrival. Although full up at this time of year she had, apparently by miraculous means, found two extra rooms on the ground floor, both large, one for Siobhan and Coll, the other, next to it, as a security headquarters where two shifts of guards relieved each other. Apart from that, one man was outside, another spent the night in the lounge and Cybele had a couch in the hallway outside their room. Apparently Mrs Dixon knew of Siobhan, but he saw no signs exchanged.

Coll suddenly realized that he was exhausted. Once he'd got himself ready he practically fell into bed and was asleep before Siobhan came to join him. At some time during the night he felt himself being fondled most tenderly. His strength returned and he stretched himself in voluptuous anticipation. He did not have to wait. This time she took him through the buttocks, her face buried in the pillow, while he nuzzled into the beautiful soft mane that clothed her back. For the second time he felt a slight obstruction as he eased in. Still half-asleep he spent himself in a selfish act, not giving her the slightest thought. When his reverberating bliss died away he stayed where he was, and felt her building desire and greed for him. After some period he repeated the act, and this time her agony of heaven was unmistakeable. Again he waited, dozing into and out of incongruous dream fragments. She turned and faced him, putting her arms around him. But it was not Siobhan. The breasts touched him differently, and she was firmer, much more lithe. He opened his eyes.

Cybele had him in her arms.

'Remember, Byron, I'm allowed to have you. I've waited for the optimal time between periods and I think I'm going to have your child. I know how you feel about Siobhan, but you are not responsible for what happened between us tonight. Siobhan and I are. I raped you, you didn't rape me – and you enjoyed it as much as I did, you wonderful boar. How does it feel to deflower two virgins in a fortnight?

Chapter 39

For the next five months Coll lived the life of the fabulous Riley; he was at the apogee of his idle and self-indulgent life as King of the Falling Year: he had hardly a care in the world, for he was not one to brood upon warnings and omens. The abiding neurotic anxiety that had been his despair in the old life was barely a memory, for he had become a different being, one who had some power and felt it. Alone of men (he thought) he was freed from any necessity of earning a living or wondering where the next few pounds were coming from, pounds he didn't even bother to keep in his own pocket. He needed little enough over and above the rapid gratification of his wishes, a circumstance he was all-too-easily taking for granted. Paradise itself became a little boring from time to time, but he went on trips with his detail within the great island itself, stood on Scottish bens or within several of the neolithic stone circles surviving in their hundreds, obviously an attracting force for the group which called itself the Bridestone Circle, walked the heady coastal paths of Devon and Cornwall, outswam his security detail at Sennen Cove, reverently walked in the ancient island of Glastonbury and climbed the tor, and then, starting with Arundel and the poorly-lighted paintings at Petworth House, oscillated in leisurely luxury from one coast to the other, ever northering, taking in the castles and cathedrals. The Cotswold villages of honeyed stone drew him like a mother, but if he had to pick the finest day among these autumnal lovelinesses, he would have chosen what a medieval king characterized as the finest view in all England, the one from Greater Rollright. These trips went without any unpleasant complication: none of his fears took shape. He always wanted Siobhan with him, but she was extremely busy, and although he was sometimes tempted to insist, he knew he could never overrule her. It was beyond his power. When she did come along, she was always accompanied by Cybele or Diane.

Lost as he was in these ambling pleasures, it did not occur to him that the King might in fact be nothing more than a glorified fatted calf, stroked and indulged.

He was still mortified at the trick Cybele had played upon him, but he had after all been told clearly enough what he had to do. Her hair was shoulder-length, as Siobhan's and Cybele's was, so it was clear enough that the luxuriant hair stretching to the waist, uncut virgin hair, the most seductive of all women's allurements, and the only possible disguise in nudity had been part of the tantalizing and delightful deception Siobhan and Cybele had practised. He wondered again about Diane, for she no longer went out of her way to encounter him. One day he asked her whether she had ever taken Siobhan's place beside him. She smiled. 'Do you really want to know, Coll?'

He was momentarily confused, and she began to laugh uncontrollably. Few men understand women's sense of humour, and Coll was not one of them.

'Oh my dear, don't be offended, please, but you're priceless. Although we shouldn't, Cybele and I have never laughed so much in our lives. No – not Siobhan. She has been as perplexed as you. Of course you've had my cherry and I'll bet you can't even tell me when. Oh don't be offended, my very dear one. Even mothers in a maternity ward don't really know the difference between their babies and all the others for the first few hours after they are born except by smell. And we all used the same scent. You didn't even remember that! That's men for you. So why should it be surprising that one girl feels much the same as another in the darkness to a blindly passionate man? You *thought* that you were lying with Siobhan, being faithful to her despite the temptation offered you, so morally it's the same as if you *had* been faithful to her in the deed, as you would say, for you intended to be and, as far as you knew, you were, true to your Queen and true to your betrothed, particularly as she herself was part and parcel of the bed plot. She did it to maintain the essential customs of the Circle and ensure the rights of the priestesses. And we played fair. I could have used magic to make myself irresistible to you, breaking through your principled resistance. But that would not have been fair. It would have weakened and demeaned you. It was far better that we should simply trick you.

'You're a brick, Coll. It was simple because you are such a fair, direct-dealing man, true to his beloved. We have all respected you, Coll. Siobhan does not choose a man whom we cannot respect. You've slept with us both. Does it sound so bad that you gave the priestess her right?

And you loved it. Your love was sincere as well as passionate, and your reward was the heaven on earth that comes only from the Great Mother. If I wielded a little magic when you were in my arms, it was in Her cause, and for you because you too deserve your rapture in the highest.

'Now you know, is it so bad?'

It could not have been clearer, but he was still strangely bereft of words. He did not know how to respond. He felt neither resentment nor anger; he didn't know what he felt. For devoting himself to Siobhan and steeling himself against the undeniable attractions of Cybele and Diane, his reward had been the effect of his temptation.

It was still a paradox, part of the Circle's topsy-turvy world. Yet even that was not really so, for marriage was much more of a sacred state in the Circle than outside it. It was the position of the Queen's consort, the King, that was topsy-turvy. He was a mere functionary with no more real power than a pawn. His position was purely ceremonial, except in this one unique function which he could not descend to calling by its most rustic name, for it had to do with one who was very much more than a girl, a woman or any monarch, one who was the Queen, and perhaps much more than a Queen, a Queen the extent of whose power he had not yet comprehended.

'It's not something to philosophize over, Coll,' observed Diane, watching him. She seemed to know exactly what he was thinking, and for the first time he was beginning to see just what a remarkable woman she was. 'It's something for you to glory in, for we all look up to you. Do you think I could give myself to a man I didn't respect? You've played your part in the Circle with a courage sometimes bordering on madness. You're important to us. You are the very centre of our family at this moment, a family that is about to grow. And there's something you should never forget about Siobhan. She loves you. It is hard for you to see it our way. It is because she loves us that she gives you up so willingly. She is bound to practise self-denial by the rule of her order, but this is one-tenth self-denial, nine-tenths pure love. For do understand this, Coll (we see it, even if you don't, at least at this moment): when she gives you, either to Cybele or me, she agonizes for you just as she rejoices for us. She loves you. She sacrifices herself for you, if you can see it that way. She has *never* laughed at you. She cherishes every part of you and worships the ground you walk on. I know you don't believe it, but it's true.

'She loves you, Coll, but she is also the Queen. She lives a dilemma.'

Again Coll had no answer. Everything that had happened since his arrival began to fall into place with her words. He was now indeed at his apogee.

'Do you want to see what I look like in daylight now that the secret has been exploded?'

He looked at her. All his fine resolves had fled in the overwhelming realization that Siobhan the Queen had been the contriver of all. However, his sense of being put upon did not entirely leave him.

'I recognized Cybele all right.'

'Of course. Having played her part, she wanted you to know, even though that was not Siobhan's wish. Siobhan and I resemble each other physically, but Cybele is different. You couldn't make that mistake. You're mine and hers and Siobhan's, Coll.'

'Nothing in my life compares with the first night with Siobhan. It was then that I knew there was a heaven.'

'That was your nuptial night. Be sure that the Great Mother will give you more such nights if you place Her first in your thoughts.'

'You are a priestess, all right.'

'Yes, but there is more to it than that. We have to practise humility and self-denial in the eyes of the Goddess, and more important, nature.'

'You have to practise nature in the eyes of the Goddess? That doesn't make sense.'

'It may sound odd, but the sense is perfect.'

Something vital eluded him, as it always did.

'Stop trying to think everything out as though it were a scientific problem, and take me now.'

Her voice had softened; her lips shaped her loveliness. Ravenous carnality surged in his loins and they took their joy of each other then and there. It was sex and something more. There was now a different kind of blessing on him. Where was divinity? It was here.

During these months, from the last week of September to the end of October, Siobhan was away quite often, travelling back and forth to Ireland. She did not confide to Coll the precise reason of these visits, saying merely that she wanted to see her people again and prepare for the next round of festivities. He wanted to go with her, but she was reluctant to take him, so he did not press her. He did not have her with him nearly as often as he wanted. Again, he felt a little resentment.

One inhibition having been surrendered, others followed. Coll's life lost its aim; others went on their high purposes, but he was given none, and there came a time when constantly living the life of Riley without any thought for the morrow began to gnaw at his physical and mental stamina. The omens he had encountered at mid-year were now vague in his memory. He lost touch with the reality of his position to the extent that he could seriously broach the idea to Siobhan that they could all go to some warmer place for the winter. Siobhan demurred, reminding him that his presence was critical at the mid-winter feasts so important for the Circle.

But this is to anticipate. Lammas was approaching, lasting from the evening of the first day of August until sunset on the eighth. Normally this was celebrated in Ireland, for there were many suitable sites there. Moreover many of the English members were on holiday at that time of year and thus could attend. At first Siobhan was all for going to Ireland, but something made her change her mind. In the end she decided to celebrate at a suitable site in England, and so the Feast was held on the hill that had served them at the Beltane.

Unlike the Beltane, Lammas began in great solemnity. Coll was no longer the appointed black sheep of May Eve or the undisputed King of the Midsummer revelry, but merely a silent witness to the most sacred rites of the Circle. Of these Siobhan was the absolute centre on this, by far the most hallowed feast of the ancient world. The moon, so favourable at Midsummer, was not in its best aspect for Lammas. The celebrants preferred a moon just passing full.

On an evening between dusk and darkness, he and Siobhan led the members of the Circle in a procession spiralling the hill, reaching the summit almost at the last light. In complete silence, everyone gathered in a circle, leaving a large space around the Queen. At some signal everyone together sat down in the bare grass, Coll, as first of the members rather than as the Queen's consort, a little further in than the innermost ring. He had the best view of the events he would never be able to explain.

After a few minutes it became clear that both Siobhan's rôles, as Queen and as Temple Priestess, were to be manifested. She was formally disrobed by three priestesses, including Esmirone, who surrounded and draped her at the same time to protect her sacred body from the gaze of devotees. These dressed her in a birthing gown cut so that the breasts were exposed and drawn up a little. This was done so quickly that it was scarcely possible to glimpse her in the growing darkness. That done she was ready to become the central figure in a trope akin to the stations of the year Coll had seen played out on the Burren in Ireland.

In the course of the celebration, one of the supporting priestesses poured a pitcher of water to run around the feet of the High One. From then on the movements were extremely slow as though they were very deliberate demonstrations to the ageless Goddess, and possibly in order to accord with the moon's progress in the sky, but there was no mistaking the birth pangs which went on for a long time during which Coll could see that his beloved Siobhan was in such great pain that she could not always forebear crying out. A birthing stool was brought and here Coll, close as he was, could not accept, let alone believe, what he saw. For this final act was no trope, no fabrication of props and words: it was an actuality. She gave birth to a crying child. As soon as the cord was cut and the tiny thing cleaned up, it was held aloft by the mother, who could stand only with the support of her assistants, and offered to the Great Mother as a first fruit.

Seated again, the mother clasped the newly-born infant to herself and spoke or whispered something into its ear, something inaudible to anyone else.

Coll was mentally stunned. He knew that Siobhan had not been pregnant, or at least not so far advanced that she could give birth to a full-term baby, even if she had been impregnated five or six weeks before. And his mind was telling him that all this was irrelevant. This event had no place in the calendar of the apparent world.

In his stupefaction he did not move, not noticing at first that his bewilderment was not shared by anyone else. Instead there was throughout a deepening and palpable joy thrilling the silent air, perfect silence being the greatest possible mark of respect among the Circle. One of the priestesses took the baby off somewhere, the Temple Priestess and Queen was ceremonially robed as she had been ceremonially disrobed before. At last, standing without assistance, she told them all something that rivetted the attention of the celebrants; but although she used the Beth-Luis-Nion (and Coll was no speed reader in that alphabet), the language was strange. He grasped nothing of what she said. It is possible that she wanted to convey something which would be unintelligible to any uninvited stranger.

He remained sitting where he was until the time came for the Queen and himself to lead the others back down the hillside. She was absolutely exhausted, leaning so heavily on his arm that he immediately picked her up and carried her in his arms as tenderly as she had been the babe. An S.U.V. had been brought right up to the base of the hill. He set her as comfortably as he could in the rear. Esmirone sat beside Siobhan. Everyone, including Siobhan, had been fasting since sunset, a fast not to be broken until the morning. She took nothing but a little water and fell asleep with her head in Esmirone's lap immediately. It was a long ride home. When they arrived, she was carried in by the women and put to bed by Janine and Sibyl. He stood there in the front entrance feeling useless. Cybele came and stood beside him.

'Better get some sleep in your old room tonight, Byron. She is still with the Great Goddess. You, being a man, do not have to suffer what she has been through.'

Esmirone, immediately behind Siobhan, had insisted on fulfilling her rôle at this, the holiest feast of the year, in spite of her weakness, for she had not fully recovered from the assault on her and was almost as exhausted as Siobhan.

Coll thought that by this time he would have ceased to wonder at marvels, but this transcended all the others. He had seen, close at hand, a woman who was not pregnant, giving birth to a baby. That could not be faked, not as he had seen it. He could not believe what he had seen but could not deny that he had in fact seen it.

The house was more populated that usual tonight, for the other two young priestesses he had seen at Midsummer, Janine and Sybil, were staying, and another man had now been given Coll's former job in security. As there was nothing to eat until morning there was no particular reason for Coll to go downstairs again.

He had no doubt that this was the most hallowed night of the year for the Circle.

Chapter 40

IN SPITE OF THE WONDER, Coll felt at a loose end. He knew he could not sleep, and changed his mind about going downstairs, resolving to go out and chat with the detail. One of them, Ross, had come up to London with them. He looked a little old to be doing this kind of thing, but like everyone else, with the exception of those at Hazelridge, his job was strictly part-time. Coll wanted to know how an entire village had been brought on side. Ross murmured something about this being a long story, and he didn't seem inclined to begin it. In daily life he was a master at the grammar school, about five miles away. However chatty he may have been about anything else, he was, like Siobhan, distinctly uncommunicative about matters pertaining to the Circle. Coll, rather imprudently, tried to find out more about what had happened on the hill. He knew it was a stupid question as soon as he had let it go: he had seen more clearly than most what there was to be seen. He wasn't surprised by Ross' gentle rebuke: being the Queen's consort, he, Coll, should know or could find out more than anyone present except the Queen herself. Coll was not taken in by this disingenuousness.

A ramble along the back boundary revealed nothing beyond the fact that Ross and his off-sider, Don, were following him closely, so he went back inside no wiser than when he came out. He was starving, but as there was nothing going until breakfast time, he chose a book from the library (there was no television at Hazelridge), and went back to bed with *Twenty-five Years in the Rifle Brigade*. After ten laboured pages he got up again to prowl, partly in the hope of finding something more interesting. He met Cybele in the library.

'What happened to that baby? No one brought it back here.'
'It is consecrated to the Great Mother, Byron,' she said, 'so don't fuss.'
'Is it with its mother? Is that mother Siobhan?'
'Ask her.'

'Is it a boy or a girl?'

'Guess.'

'How should I know?'

'Well, if you understood anything at all of this miraculous time you would know that only a girl-child has the potential for bringing forth.'

A thought struck him. 'Was Siobhan such a miraculous baby as this?'

'Every now and then you amaze me, Coll, with one of these flashes of brilliance. Believe me, if you have time, you will come to understand much more than I.'

'Are you pregnant?'

'I'm not quite sure yet. I hope so.'

'Want to try again?'

She smiled. 'Converted at last I see. But not on this holiest of nights when the Great Mother has manifested Herself to us. You have to fast and abstain like the rest of us, O King.'

'I can't sleep, and do you know why?'

'No. Should I?'

'Yes you should. For some reason I'm a figurehead, nice, but nothing more. And no one, *but no one*, tells me anything, not the men outside, not you, not Diane – or Esmirone, of course – not even Siobhan. No matter what I ask, I'm just shunted on to the side.'

'Steady on. I have told you what happened tonight. Look, Byron, you surely can't expect to find out in six months what these people born into the Circle have spent a lifetime acquiring. We're a very retiring lot, subject to threats from other groups and cults and the subject of government surveillance, even if it goes no further, stepped up pretty briskly during the reign of the now almost-forgotten Mrs Thatcher. You were chased from pillar to post by U.S. government thugs and right-wing radicals, both in Canada and in Ireland. Weren't you told not to blab? From my observation I'd say you haven't exactly got a talent for discretion. Now it's not quite so critical because you've learned to be a little more cautious, and, being King, we've got you on a leash. You can move only one square at a time, suitably guarded and escorted. Siobhan is perfectly discreet, and, being Queen, can move all over the board. She's the one with the power, the one piece we can't possibly lose.'

'What about me? Am I dispensable?'

'Depends. Right now you're just as vital to us as she is.'

'I still don't get it.'

'You haven't yet understood the problem. What you are asking is akin to wanting to learn Mandarin Chinese in a month.'

He sighed. 'O.K. At least you've done your best. I'll try to absorb all I can.'

'How did you feel when you were with us on the hill earlier this evening?'

'Everyone was in awe, even fearful, and I, to be frank, just a little too. The birth of the child was so unexpected – it hit me like a shock wave. But I was more concerned in thinking how this thing which could not be was in fact happening. Even if Siobhan had been pregnant she could only have been in her fifth week.'

'You have to realize that this kind of approach is irrelevant, and perhaps I'm telling you more than I should, but if you had been able to enter heart and soul into the transfiguration of the Virgin – this is something you apparently did not see – your spirit would have been, at least for one blessed moment, in the bliss of the Great Mother. I'll say no more. I love you, Byron, with all the love of a sister and the passion of the beloved, but, more than these, with love in the *agape* of the Blessed Virgin and Great Mother.'

'Then why choose an uninitiated person as King?'

'Of course you are initiated! The Queen herself initiated you and took you into her own band of friends. You are merely innocent of the ways of the Circle as yet.'

He looked at the book in his hand, *Twenty-five Years in the Rifle Brigade*.

'Haven't you got anything I can read up on?'

'No, Byron. You still miss the point. It's not that kind of thing. Read my heart and the hearts of all of us here, read hill, brook and forest, the oblique landscape of this ancient Albion.'

She kissed him and went on her way. The touch of her breasts gave him a comfort that had nothing of the sexual in it. They were the vessels of some essential human milk that he now knew of but could not apprehend.

In bed again, his thoughts were drawn to her words, but missed the point: his mind could grasp them, but not his soul. One phrase reverberated in the turbulence of his perplexity: the transfiguration of the Virgin. Cybele could only mean Siobhan, the central figure in the divine drama, but that was impossible because, as he knew, Siobhan was not a virgin. He had been granted the bliss of taking her maidenhead. But if not Siobhan, then who? And what had Siobhan told him much earlier? That she might never be able to love him in the way he wanted. It seemed so impossibly remote now, for he had grown physically and in every other way. She could not love him that way if she became something special. Well, she had become something special and she had loved him in that way.

Or had she?

He would have to find a way of testing her. He now had enough sense of her power to feel very uneasy about inventing some subtle scheme of verification; he had never been underhand with her before, and in the back of his mind he knew that the whole idea was stupid, but the silly possessiveness he could not altogether discard drove him on.

He got up much earlier than usual, bathed, dressed and walked around the grounds, not alone of course. Matt was there together with another older man he could not remember seeing before. After what Cybele had told him, he no longer felt the need to pump them. Matt didn't have anything to report and, when Coll asked him, did not seem much concerned about the prospect of another raid by the London Looters, as Coll had taken to calling Roseanne's friends. 'Have trouble getting through now, they would,' he observed. 'And it's hardly loot when the things belong to them, you know.'

'But they got them back when Maxine and Gerald defected.'

Matt looked puzzled. 'Oh, did they?'

Coll was left with the impression that someone was most distinctly not on the ball.

Shortly after more men arrived in vans and erected three very long lines of thick plywood tables crossed by a line of head tables running roughly parallel to the back boundary, like an E. These were supported by metal banquet legs, easily attached. This arrangement made it easy to serve everyone from the kitchen. Evidently even more people were expected than had turned up at Midsummer, which he had thought included practically the whole village.

The kitchen was a beehive gone mad, but the queen bee, Diane, was cool enough. Here too the odd strange woman was flitting about. Diane could hardly shove him out in the presence of these visiting helpers now that he was King, but no one had any time for him. In spite of the buzz no one seemed to be thinking of breakfast. He now went up to Siobhan's room to see if she was awake and find out how she was feeling after the dreadful strain of the night, the events of which he still failed to understand. As soon as he saw her, all his adoration came back. She was sitting up, an unfinished glass of orange juice on the pedestal. She looked like an alabaster image, paler than usual, but otherwise not too badly. The deep colour was still in her lips. He kissed her tenderly and took her hands. They were cold.

'How are you feeling, dearest?'

'Fine. I'll be up and ready by eight.'

'What's going on out there? Is the whole village coming?'

'Everyone who can be spared and quite a few visitors from the wider Circle. And it's a special day for the children.'

'What can I do for you?'

'Seeing you helps me. But you look so worried, my dear one! Everything has gone well, very well, and we have an important day before us. I shall need your help, but having you beside me does me more good than you know, you great boar.'

'What can I do downstairs?'

'Stay out of Diane's way. We have lots of women working in the kitchen, too many, probably, but it's an ancient privilege for certain village women, and there are many more slaving in their own kitchens at home. It's the greatest feast and best meal of the year, Coll, this breakfast. You and I will be together at the head table with the five priestesses we have now – Esmirone, Diane, Cybele, Janine and Sybil – and several men with ceremonial positions. This is a very special occasion.'

He sat on the bed. She hugged him.

'You seem to belong to everyone but me.'

She laughed. 'Yes, that is how it looks to you and me, and I warned you about it. And what about you? You're much in the same position just now. But dearest Coll, to everyone else I am untouchable. Only you can touch me. Doesn't that make you proud? Of course, the others belong to me and I to them. This sense of belonging is what counts in the Circle. You have to understand that both of us, King and Queen, are looked upon as givers. That is what is really important at this feast.'

He pressed her close, jealous that a mouse should share her.

'You gave all you had in you last night,' he said, 'but what have I given? So far I've been nothing but a drone.'

She looked into his eyes, musing.

'It won't look that way today. You'll see how vital you are in the eyes of our friends, you who have won such strength. Have you forgotten the ordeals you underwent to tear that strength from your enemy? You don't know what future trials of strength you will have to undergo. At that time you will have to give as much as I did during this night past. Don't ask me now, please, dear one. Be my strength today. And now I ought to be getting ready, if you will let me out of bed. Please close the door.'

But this dismissal was assuaged by her embrace and the tender stroking of his hair.

'No matter how much I give myself to others, I belong to you. Do you know that?'

He nodded. 'I think so.'

'Yet there's a trace of doubt in you, you obdurate heretic. Your eyes tell me. This evening I'll try to prove it to you all over again if I'm still at the height of your desire. But remember, Coll, I cannot always do what I want. You must accept that. We are both in the service of the Goddess.'

In the kitchen there was a delicious steam as Diane heaped the living bread, newly-baked, into osier baskets. She glanced at him, catching his thought as she so often did.

'The bread is alive,' she said.

'I think I'm beginning to realize for the first time what the Circle is all about. I feel life rushing on all about me, not only in all this haste and preparation, but – I don't know. Last night, most of all – life.'

The words did not come to him, but every plant, every tree in the forest, the old hills, were alive, bursting with life. He had the urge to rush outside and tumble headlong into the teeming life-force, but Diane stopped him.

'There are a lot of people out there now. Better make your appearance in the company of Siobhan, don't you think?'

Outside, some had brought lawn chairs; nearly every place at the tables was occupied, and this time there were many children chattering in anticipation. Even the much-abused lawn seemed on this delightful morning to have a lovelier, tenderer green than before. As on the previous night, he and Siobhan were greeted with a hush broken only by the cheerful piping of the birds. They took their places at the head of the tables where all the newly-baked bread had been set. It was Lammas bread, bread baked from the flour of the first harvest. He stood with the Queen as she offered the bread to the Great Mother as a first fruit. This was a short and simple thing, but it filled everyone with a palpable joy mingled with wonder. Coll then picked up a basket and walked behind Siobhan as she gave a roll to everyone there, even to the smallest infants, while uttering a blessing in the Beth-Luis-Nion. When one basket was empty she waited while her consort fetched another. This time he felt even more poignantly than at Midsummer the profound sense in the gathering that this was a hallowed time, and that even his own supernumerary function was important to them. When Siobhan had made sure that every person had been given bread, she and Coll returned to the head table where in the same way she gave bread to each of the priestesses. Last of all, she gave Coll his portion and blessed him. Finally, she took bread for herself. Only now did everyone eat.

The basket containing the remaining bread, only a dozen or so rolls, was covered and given to Coll, who did not know what to do with it and so left it in front of him until Siobhan whispered that it should be left out for any creature to eat. He took it to a side table and uncovered it. Two men came, picked up the table and set it in a shady nook out of everyone's way.

The hush lasted for a few minutes. Far-off rural noises of the day broke through, from distant barking of dogs to the barely-heard chatter of the spring-fed stream in the forest.

The fanfare of trumpets tearing the morning's calm made Coll jump. Through the french windows a procession of women came bearing burdens on trays and platters, while men brought yet more tables to set down at head and foot so that there would be room for the food and drink. This was what the children had been waiting for and they restrained themselves no longer as the women set out more varieties of bread than Coll could have imagined. This immense amount of bread occupied the tables now placed nearest the house, and was subsequently divided up and a portion taken home by every family. It was the central part of the feast.

But not the only part. Close at hand on each side was breakfast, the great meal of the great day now that the fast had been properly and ritually broken. For the children it was the greatest feast of the year in the bright full morning. Endless hot trays held pancakes and waffles, syrups, fruit toppings, butter, jams and marmalades, eggs in all conceivable guises – scrambled with onions, poached, turned, boiled, embellished with cheese in little glass dishes – kippers, various smoked fish, kedgeree, trays setting out cheeses of all kinds, pineapple, plums, peaches, pomegranates (mainly for decoration), apples, bananas and some other fruits Coll had never seen before, such as loquats, curious little pastries with aromatic fillings, all accompanied by the delicious aroma of coffee freshly-brewed. More dishes were added as enthusiastic appetites cleared the trays. There was only one thing missing: there was no meat in any form. Coll couldn't guess how many variations on breakfast were being played as over the tutti of delighted children shouting to each other all at once the trumpeters went on playing. But not quite all. Two small bands of children aged about ten or eleven brought wreaths to the King and Queen and arrayed them. The girls dressed Siobhan, the boys Coll.

As Coll got up starving for a bite, Siobhan pulled him back.

'We stay here. If we move among them they will have to stand back, and that will spoil their fun.'

'Siobhan, I'm absolutely famished.'

'So am I, so are all the priestesses. They cannot move until I do.'

'This isn't necessary,' grumbled Coll.

'They are priestesses and must practise humility and self-denial when that is called for. It is now. Our people look to us as an example.'

Coll cursed under his breath. He knew all these men. 'Well, Esmirone shouldn't have to wait. She's still not well.'

'This is what she wants.'

Siobhan was transparently joyful for she had given joy. Her face had the virginal innocence that one sees in some medieval paintings of the Madonna. And like the figures in a painting, they who sat could not move. It was their function to sit above, protecting the joy, especially the joy of the children.

Finally the trumpeters laid down their instruments. Still the King and Queen remained fixed in their places, not able to leave them until the last celebrant had eaten his fill and the leavings had been divided up very exactly to be borne away by the families. Once again the notion of a ship came to Coll, a black ship sailing across an endless expanse of blue ocean. The idea of a ship and fair shares sprang into his mind together. Anything that came by luck was divided equally among everyone, from the youngest to the oldest. He was convinced that his father had once embarked on a voyage that had altered his entire life, and that his son, Coll, was remembering bits of it. But what had happened to his father? He must have been a remarkable character.

When at length they rose, two young children came and removed their wreaths. 'The children keep these until next year,' explained Siobhan, 'for luck.'

In the kitchen the famished King, Queen and distinguished college of priestesses didn't get much. They had to make do with the scraps left over from breakfast, mainly bread and butter. Some of the bread was flavoured with herbs and seeds. Coll thought he had never in his life tasted anything so delectable. The trouble was there wasn't enough of it, and Diane wanted them out of the kitchen as soon as possible because she wanted to clear up and get lunch. The two new women, Janine and Sybil, were particularly attentive to Coll. He would have stayed to chat, but they resumed work immediately, helping Diane.

Siobhan was in her room, lying down. She was still tired from the previous night. He asked her if she thought that he could possibly be having memories inherited from his father. She thought it quite possible, even though the experience was unusual.

'But you are unusual, Coll, very unusual, especially since the ordeal that brought you face to face with your own Shadow. You never knew your father, yet he has always been very important to you. Have you ever asked yourself why that is?'

'I'm grateful to my mother, but I'm not sure that I can love her as I should.'

'Surely. That, after all, is why you are here. You did not have a mother who could really love, so you did not have a motherland. You came here to find one, although that was not your conscious motive. Now you are here you spontaneously encounter vivid snatches of memory not your own, perhaps something of your father who, in some distant past, left the remote country of his birth to come here. Yet he must also have gone to Canada, or that would not be the land where you and your sister were born.'

'How well you tease it out!'

'So you are unencumbered, free to be in our family, aren't you?'

'My sister doesn't think much of me, never did.'

'She doesn't know you as you are now. She might get a surprise.'

'Might is right. I'll probably never see them again, and really, you know, I don't care about it one way or the other. I guess it's not a good time to go down to the village just now.'

'You guess right. It would make everyone there uncomfortable on their holiday. After lunch when I've had a bit of a rest, I'll go with you somewhere private. Perhaps some of the others can come along.'

Lunch was not as plentiful as usual, consisting of the remaining Lammas leftovers with some ripe Stilton thrown in and a salad. All the bread of the first harvest had to be eaten. None might be wasted. Coll polished off a pint of very dark ale deceptively smooth which turned out to be much headier than it had any right to be, for he didn't at all feel like going for a walk for quite some time. It was not until well after two that they set out, Siobhan, Janine, Sibyl and himself, with Matt and Don in close attendance. Diane was still busy and Cybele was feeling a little sick.

This time they took a winding way to the rise before the village where the sea could be glimpsed. Here they rested, sitting down in the shade of several tall beeches at the edge of a field of wheat. Matt and Don withdrew out of earshot. Coll noticed they were both armed. The three women huddled in a tight group, exchanging messages in the Beth-Luis-Nion, ignoring Coll.

After a time Siobhan turned to him and said, 'Janine and Sybil recognize you as being of the Temple; they offer themselves to you as King of the Fall.'

'Is that important?'

'Vital. All the holy ones must scrutinize and accept you.'

'What if they didn't?'

'They would have to leave and others would take their place.'

'Why "King of the Fall"?'

'We shall enter the season of Autumn soon, the Fall, when all is harvested in its abundance. The first half of the year is the Rising Year; the second, the Falling Year. And now they have to know whether the King accepts them.'

'Why shouldn't I?'

'You might not. You have the choice. However, they are both very pretty, wouldn't you say?'

They were both looking at him. He did not know what to say. 'Indeed.'

'I ask again, Coll, because they have to be attractive to you.'

He saw what she was driving at and groaned. 'I want you, no one else.'

'I know, Coll, but this has all been thrashed out, in theory and practice several times. You must choose now whether they stay or go.'

He looked at them. Sybil flushed a little. Of course they were lovely, and single minded in their devotion with a power he could not match.

'If you accept them, make these signs after me.'

When he had done this, Janine and Sybil came and embraced him, making it very clear they wanted their desires fulfilled. In spite of himself, he was aroused by their touch in the presence of Siobhan. He suffered a spasm of humiliation, for they took from her.

'All right, let's go back. I haven't forgotten the promise I made this morning,' Siobhan went on, whispering to Coll. 'Don't forget the qualification, though.'

When they got back to Hazelridge, Cybele was in her room not to be disturbed and Diane, her magic completed, had gone off somewhere without leaving a note.

Coll had the feeling that from now on the two new priestesses would take the places of the new mothers.

Chapter 41

LAMMAS WAS CELEBRATED IN MANY WAYS, not simply in thanks for the blessings of the land and prayers for an abundant harvest, but also by the men of the village in other rites to which Coll was not invited. They had a ceremonial gathering in which women did not take part. The latter had their own separate celebrations independent of the College consisting in traditional dances in newly-harvested field by which they hoped to produce a bountiful great harvest in this blessed season of fulfilment. At this time particularly the Circle looked to its King and Queen for protection; Siobhan periodically went into the village on healing missions. Her touch was known to cure the sick. At the end of the seven day Lammas season, the holiday-making came to an end, the work went on as before, though with renewed vigour and the urbanites returned to their jobs in London.

There was another change at the house. A new man, Patrick, took the last place at table. He was designated as Gerald's successor in house security. Coll, who by now was completely spoiled, was miffed at the consideration Patrick received at the hands of the woman, his women, as he had mistakenly taken to regarding them. He now sat at the head of the table whenever Siobhan was absent and tried in other more subtle ways to demonstrate Patrick's lack of status. In fact, he feared him as a supplanter. When he revealed his fears to Siobhan she told him that nothing had changed and that nothing would change so long as Coll remained with them. He was still unsatisfied. He began to brood, wondering how long his Golden Age would last now that Patrick had arrived. He remembered having seen Patrick before. He had been one of the new men at Richmond House back in June when the departure of Tony and Roger had left places to fill. As August faded into September and the woods began to promise the golden time of Autumn, he noticed that occasionally Siobhan showed signs of a fondness for Patrick. On several occasions they went on long walks together, and this enraged him, even though, as Siobhan reassured him, she was bound to him, Coll, only. 'But,' she added, 'that does not make me yours.'

'I should think it does!'

'Does the indentured servant belong to his master?'

'I should remember this –'

'Early settlers in Virginia who could not afford to invest in the venture often indentured themselves to a plantation owner for a term of years, at the close of which they were entitled to the agreed-upon benefits. What I'm asking you is: did these indentured servants belong to their masters?'

'When you put it like that, no, or at most only for the term of their contract. So at some point I'm to be dismissed and Patrick is to take my place?'

'Going back to the analogy, the servant received his benefits in land or cash or both at the end of his contracted time. That is why he had bound himself in the first place; but you, Coll, have been receiving your benefits from the time when, out on the Burren, the Circle, in my person, extended its life-giving protection to you. So here the analogy is not complete, if you get my drift.'

'You talk like a philosophy professor!'

'When I do, you listen.'

'So what do I get?'

'Look at yourself in your position now, Coll. You have all you could possibly want in abundance. You have become a part of the Circle as a result of which you stopped being a wimp and became a man; you have achieved your love, and more, you enjoy the honour that other members of the Circle give you. You are afraid that all this will be taken away from you and you will be cast out into the world, naked to the menace of the forces thrown up against you by your encounter with Victor, or the theft of the ahamés at Richmond, not to mention the determined and efficient enemies employed by the state agents who persecuted you in Toronto and were about to destroy you when we first met. Here at the very centre of our Circle you are well-protected against your enemies. So what are you asking me, begging me, I should say? I have given you standing which is certainly not based on your own merits; that standing, not to mention all your other advantages, depends on my constant favour. But then you swore to me that day at the edge of the forest that you, for your part, would give me anything, including your life, when I required it, and this undertaking was unconditional. I gave you everything I could and you gave me everything you could, and that is the position now, King High-and-Mighty.'

Coll, whose mind had been fogged with the self-indulgence and loveliness of his life, saw in sharp focus the implication.

'When –'

'Don't ask any more questions. Take your blessings, the honour of men and the love of women when you can.'

'Are you going to ask me to give up my life?'

'That is in our agreement. We have to placate our greatest enemy.'

'How?'

'Leave it to Esmirone and me for now. I too am in danger if I walk beyond the Circle, but I have weapons you do not have.'

Like it or not, this was the only answer Coll got. The days now passed with only minor ripples in their placidity, and while Patrick received many small favours and attentions from the women, Coll was still the undisputed centre of their attention to the male of the species behind doors at Hazelridge. He was still being stroked, his ego was being fed, but underneath the cushion of his facile complacency lurked the sharp needle of a nagging expectation that all this had a term which he would be well-advised to prepare himself against. Shakespeare reminded him that summer's lease hath all too short a date. He ought, he told himself, to get into training again, but his nights with Siobhan and his sessions on day beds had made him lazy and he did not have the resolve.

September had hardly begun before it was over; in the mornings he and Siobhan with Janine and Sibyl went into the small pine forest to gather mushrooms. They took all the ones that were reasonably fresh, valuing in particular the ones with white flecks on their dark pink caps, which, Coll could remember having been told, were deadly poisonous. However, they left alone any other *amanitas* they saw. They filled several baskets with various kinds, one to each species, mainly *russulas* and the fly agaric. When they returned to the house Esmirone dried out the fly agaric caps to put away and the others they ate for supper deliciously prepared by Diane, whose culinary magic would have got her the head chef's job in any great restaurant or hotel.

In the richness of the year's harvest and the changing colours of the trees, Coll reflected on his good fortune, but still beneath the depth of his contentment lingered the ugly thought that one day all this would be pulled down about his ears. There was nothing to stop him from walking away from the Circle if he could ever find the will to do it, but he knew he couldn't. In any case, whenever he left the house he was unobtrusively escorted. There were disadvantages to being King.

What happened to kings? Did they simply fade away with age, or was some other method adopted for getting rid of them? Who had been the last King and where was he now? But of course Siobhan was newly-chosen Queen and he was her first and only consort. Some other questions for Siobhan, or perhaps for Sibyl and Janine. Sibyl might be a little more forthcoming than her sisters.

Chapter 42

With November came the first hint of bitter winds and the woods began to look grey in the morning mist. Winter was surveying the land. Strangely, at this time when animals prepare to sleep away the cold months, Coll felt a new access of strength. His body's powers gathered to him. It was now that he learned to ride, and while he never became skilled, he absorbed his lessons well enough to pace along the better tracks in the new forest. After the first misgivings he felt exhilarated with a sense of great courage when he did this, high above the ground with a noble partner under him, usually a mare, who soon got used to the momentary separations that marked their early relationship, for he had not yet achieved the canter and still had trouble manoeuvring.

He was not the only rider. Both the new girls rode much better than he, having been used to horses from early childhood. He avoided them whenever he could since he showed up badly beside them. In spite of his efforts, he often met them unexpectedly. He had no difficulty in keeping up with them, for they rode slowly. They too liked forest tracks.

Both Cybele and Diane were pregnant, and whereas they had lost some of their former interest in him, the priestesses Janine and Sybil made it clear in every hint and motion that they were available. In this they comported themselves in perfect taste with no element of self-consciousness, at least not after Sibyl's barely perceptible opening blush on the day of acceptance. Siobhan's state was still as much of an enigma as it had been on the summit of the harvest hill on Lammas Eve. His standing with her was ambiguous to him, for she could work illusions, if that is what they were. He could accept what everyone else present on that night accepted: that they had witnessed a miracle, and moreover that the miracle was an annual event at the centre of their mysteries. He did not doubt that she had given him the highest possible bliss that any man could attain on that enchanted Midsummer night; nor could he doubt that she had given birth to a baby girl less than six weeks later, an infant he had glimpsed but once, briefly. He had not lain with her more than twenty times since then, for she was often away or unavailable. When in the closest act of love at night in bed he never saw her. He had no idea of how many times Diane had substituted herself. She was another enigma. He believed devoutly everything Siobhan told him, but from the strictly epistemological point of view, he did not really *know* whether he had ever enjoyed her at all, and the thought of a test recurred to him pretty constantly. With the last November leaves shivering down from the denuded trees, the strong man Coll was now less a clear vessel of summer joy; he was now more often moody, sometimes even truculent, like the November gusts. He was looking for a fight with somebody, but he knew he had to choose his opponents with care, as there are enemies beyond human strength. He did not try to find the old forest again. He was surprised, therefore, when out of the blue one day Siobhan insisted on going there with him. It was late afternoon of the first day of December.

'Just ourselves.'

'Matt will be annoyed. I'd better bring that shotgun.'

'No, that won't be necessary. Our intentions are strictly peaceful, so there will be no opposition to our going in. If you go there looking for trouble you will certainly find it. You're a bit of a bear yourself, Coll, and that's why you found your atavistic self trailing you.'

'Have it your own way. There are animals in there, and atavar or not, it was Cybele's bullets which made him release me.'

'Yes. When you go into that place you have to know exactly what you're looking for. In the old forest you will find every creature that has ever lived under the boughs if you know how to search it out. Every living thing inheres in its slice of history like the peppercorns in a slice of salami. You need the right knife and you must know the right spot to cut into.'

'I guess that makes sense to someone if not to me. What are you looking for today?'

'A swineherd.'

'A –?'

'Swineherd. Someone who keeps pigs.'

'I still think we should take the gun.'

'No. Don't worry about it.'

They walked among the huge knotted oaks for an hour. Coll had not the foggiest idea of where they were and hoped Siobhan knew her way out again. After much uncertain wandering they came to a fork in the track. Siobhan hesitated as to which way to take.

'Let's sit down here under the trees and see if anyone else takes this path,' she suggested.

Coll must have dozed off. He was awakened by the sound of voices. She was talking to an old but vigorous man whose face was concealed by a heavy beard. There were pigs all around rooting for the mast. He tried to make out what they were saying but the animals made too much noise.

Siobhan motioned him over.

'This is the Master of boar and sow. He is in the service of the Great Goddess.'

Coll bowed, feeling that this was the right thing to do.

'Well met, O King,' the Master greeted him. offering his hand. 'I make you free of my part of the forest from now until your time runs out. You shall be my guest and I will be a good host to you, for I like you and know you better than you can imagine.'

'I thank you,' responded Coll, 'I am honoured to be given such friendship, even if not for my own sake. Such hospitality is one more bounty I owe to my Queen.

'Not entirely. I honour your Queen as much as you do, but I am a friend to you in your own person.'

'Thanks again, Sir. And when will my time run out?'

'You must ask that of the Queen. She is bound to answer if you put the question in the right way.'

He looked at Siobhan. She shook her head ambiguously, said her farewell and turned to leave. Coll was drawn to the Master. Something about him left the conviction that they had met at some much earlier time. He wanted to ask about this, but did not know how to frame the question. Meanwhile, Siobhan was anxious to be on her way, so he bowed again, took the Master's proffered hand and followed her.

As they made their way back he asked her about the Master but she said nothing about his origins. She was equally uninformative when he asked her, several times, to explain what the Master had meant when he said that the King's time was limited. She replied only that if he wished for an explanation he would have to approach the Master again.

'But he will be your friend. If you ever need him he will help. He is much more potent than he wishes to appear.'

As usual, he was told practically nothing.

They walked back without incident.

As the second week in December drew to a close, Coll was more and more bored with life at Hazelridge. He began to spend too much time in the pubs chatting with anyone who would listen, but he got nothing out of them, and they, while still very friendly, did not treat him with the same unquestioning respect as formerly. Perhaps too much familiarity had tarnished their perception of the King. He now went on long walks as far as the sea cliffs, still solidly white under grey skies and watched the miniature waves far below folding into each other on the narrow beach. Then he went back to the pub for a drink or two before returning to Hazelridge. What he now wanted to do was to go up to London in the evenings and take in a few shows. The women seldom accompanied him, for they did not have the same tastes. He and his security detail went to several plays, but the last of these trips did not work out well. On the way back out of London in heavy traffic they were plagued by impatient drivers – London has some of the rudest in the world – the ones who regularly ran red lights and took chances in the traffic circles. At some point their car was caught by the amber light. Matt was a cautious driver not given to taking risks, impervious to the tail-gaters at his heels. This was too much for the speedway burner just behind. Evidently he'd had a bad day, for his frustration got the better of him. He got out of his car, wrenched open the driver's door and started to drag Matt out. Coll got out of the back, gripped the man's shoulders and hauled him back.

The other twisted free and tried to land a blow on Coll, but he had no chance against the man of strength who felled him to the ground with a hastily-judged punch that broke his neck. The idiot's girl friend in the car behind started screaming. Coll got back in and Matt took off like lightning, skidding around intersections and traffic circles, darting into profitable side streets where he could find them and generally making life tough for any pursuit. Fortunately, being an old taxi driver, he knew London pretty well, and got everyone home in record time. Village security immediately took charge of the car and it disappeared. Coll had no idea of who it was registered to.

'Why on earth did you hit him so hard?' asked Siobhan. 'You're becoming a menace. You'll need all your strength soon enough, don't worry. I'm going to have to give you something to do which will absorb your energies. Go and have a bath. I'm sending Sybil up to you, understand? Try not to break her neck, if it's all the same to you.'

'Siobhan, I can't,' objected Coll, 'after what I've been through. Hell, I've just murdered someone. I'm a criminal.'

'Oh what nonsense, Coll! The other man brought this on himself. You always forget your own strength. I don't blame you – isn't that enough?'

'I like Sybil and I respect her for her – what's the word I want? – sacred status. That sounds silly, but I don't know how to put it. I don't think the priestess should be serviced by the appointed stud. I want you, no one else. You tell me you're bound to me, yet I can never have you to myself, not even for fifteen minutes.'

He wanted to test her, to see how she really stood to him. Was she still a virgin or not? Had he been deceived all along?

'Oh Coll, what a fib. Have you forgotten Midsummer? Have you forgotten that I brought you in when you were shivering out on the Burren waiting to be picked up by a bunch of government thugs? Have you forgotten my trust in you in bringing you into the Circle and choosing you as my King? Above all, have you forgotten that you love me and that I have given my love to you?

'No, for you never stop reminding me.'

'Stop, Coll.' She took him in her arms. 'I do love you. My goodness, you're still quivering from the fight you had. Coll, what is this all about?'

'Siobhan – I wish I could say "my wife" – you have given me bliss beyond my deserving, understanding or imagination. And I'm puzzled. First you throw me, blindfolded, to both Diane and Cybele, and now you want to put Janine and Sybil into my bed in exchange for you. Why? Am I not good enough for you? I love you to distraction, heaven knows. I know I'm a little stupid and sometimes selfish in lovemaking, but in your charity you never complain. I love you as a woman and I worship you as queen and high priestess. I know only too well that you are a being exalted above me, as far above as is the sky. You know that. But I can't understand why you don't come up instead of Sybil since you chose me, for whatever reason. When I do come to your bed, why is it that we make love only in pitch darkness? Is it because if I could see whom I'm with I'd get a shock, like Psyche?'

'For none of those reasons. Your love rides on a rhetoric of obsession: something gnaws at you. You worry far too much, but you must have faith as well as love. Am I not worth it? Dig out that canker of jealousy before it kills the most precious element in your life. Of course I love you in exchange for your love; jealousy is not a luxury I can afford. *I am not free.* You forget what trusts I have to fulfil. And yet you come closer to the truth than you think. Psyche suffered because she disobeyed her lover's injunction, and her lover was a god. You should weigh that well, Coll. On the other hand, she triumphed in the end by means of an incredible determination, stamina, willingness to endure ordeals for the sake of her loved one, sheer luck and some divine help, all generated by a single fleeting vision. Do you think you can put all that together now, Coll, you who have become so lazy and short-sighted since you were given everything you wanted at Midsummer?'

'Tell me what I have to do to win, to survive whatever ordeal you have planned for me?'

She was silent.

'I ask you to lie with me now, this night or the early morning, in the light where we can see each other.'

'Psyche accepted the consequences. Are you prepared to do that?'

'Yes, if you are indeed the Lammas Virgin, for if you were, you could not have been the Siobhan of our nuptial night.'

'So that's what's eating you. The Lammas Virgin *Mother*, by the way, Coll. Think about that carefully. I shall ask you again. Every woman's body is a sacred temple which can only be entered with the Goddess' leave. No one who violates this rule can escape nemesis. We see this all around us today. Those who are born into hell, your average urban dweller, deprived of his spiritual inheritance and the glories of the mind, who has never been anywhere, physically or mentally, thinks that the stunted growths of pleasure he picks up from the ground once in a while are happiness. Happiness is not possible in hell, only its illusion. You, Coll, have brought a scrapbook of your hell into this house with you. But what if my body is sacred even beyond the normal? Do you think you will be excused your impiety? You can be given heavenly bliss as you experienced it on Midsummer's Eve, or you can be cursed into pain and darkness. Which do you choose?'

'I am initiated. I have your leave. This is the only power I have. I choose you.'

'Think about this carefully, Coll. Think about what I told you on the Burren, what I told you on the edge of the forest. You nod and smile at me. Very well. I have warned you. I am not allowed to tell you more. Gods and goddesses have an awful propensity for requiring of humans the full consequences of their actions. You have offended one deity and now you wish to risk alienating another, the one whose favour you have at present, the only one who can help you. You must realize this before you demand my compliance.'

'I choose you. You are bound to come.'

'I shall come. It is now after midnight. You will see me at the first light of dawn wherever you are. As for Janine and Sybil, they have accepted you and you have accepted them. As priestesses they are entitled by virtue of their dedication in the temple to any man of their choice, and that choice is invariably the King who has accepted them. You must give them the power and tenderness of your love as you have given it to me. I ask it of you Coll, and you are bound to obey.'

'Temple? What temple?'

'The living temple of tree and hill, of meadow and dell and the secret places of this land which have drawn you away from the lifeless concrete of your own city.'

Coll did not go up to Siobhan's room. Instead he went into the conservatory where the radiators were still warm. He could have slept there very nicely, except that there was nothing to sleep on. He sat there in darkness for a long time wondering at what Siobhan had said to him, and even more, at the way she said it. Her whole tone of voice suggested someone other than the familiar Siobhan he knew, someone 'appointed' was the word that occurred to him. Someone who was being sent to do what – punish him? No, this was becoming absurd.

He felt no inclination to sleep and spent some time wandering the grounds aimlessly. There was no sign of Matt's men. It was getting on for two when he went up at last.

He took unusual care with his ablutions. He still had difficulty sleeping, but must have dozed off, because he was roused by someone coming into his room. It was quite dark.

'Siobhan, is that you?' he asked.

She sat on his bed.

'Who are you? You're not Siobhan.'

'I am here now.'

He reached for the lamp switch. It was Sybil.

'May I come into your bed, Coll?'

She had taken pains to look her best, but she was there at the wrong time.

'Dear old Sybil,' said Coll, 'you're beautiful, almost irresistible, but I've got other plans tonight. What about later on?'

'I wish you wouldn't dear old Sybil me. Perhaps I can save you from a disastrous error. Think about it. We can give each other joy without offending the Goddess. Aren't I pretty enough for you? You thought so when we accepted each other.'

He sat up. 'You're more than pretty, but we can wait a little, can't we?'

'I'm not sure. Why do you insist on creating a crisis?'

'There are things I want to find out.'

'Oh misled man! None of your strength and cleverness can help you if you don't honour the Queen as you should. You have no idea. Why won't you listen to what I'm telling you? I know what I'm talking about. You are in danger as long as you insist on having Siobhan tonight. Don't you believe me? Janine can come if I'm not good enough for you. Would you like that?'

'My god! How can I reply to that!'

'Very well. I'm not going to abase myself in front of you, but if you will give me your love now I'll do anything you want. Remember that as a priestess I have power to help you, to warn and guide you. I can save you if you will let me. Oh, do think, Coll, please think before you throw me out. I cannot beg like a pet monkey, but I love you if you can bring yourself to realize it. Can't you see that I'm trying to help you as well as myself?'

She looked at him, and there was compassion as well as love in her eyes. He felt a love for her but could not admit it in his eyes. He was now torn and tempted.

'Coll?'

'Later, I promise.'

She left.

He had the impression that he had not had any sleep at all, not even a catnap, but he was wrong.

Aroused by the electric charge of Siobhan's presence, he took his time opening his eyes. It was barely light, but light enough. As before, she sat at the looking-glass, her back to him, combing very slowly the jet hair that flowed down her white back as finely shaped and drawn as an Amati. Her face was turned from him. The flowing motion of her hand and arm was a sinuous diapason hypnotically bewitching. He was set on fire by a raging concupiscence. In one motion he rolled out and rose to his feet governed solely by the all-engrossing impulse to satiate his lust. In the same moment she turned to face him and slowly rose from her hair. But it was not Siobhan he saw.

In a literal sense the face atop the body that had been Siobhan's was hers, but it was not she who regarded him with an infinitely wise and all-knowing look devoid of any human feeling, a gaze which included the satisfaction of one who puts off eating a particularly succulent dish until later when it can be enjoyed to the full. The breasts were exposed. He now realized with a start that the breasts were more to be feared than the expression, for they were the centres of awful power, the power of giving or withholding life. And this was not all. The apparition wore the golden wreath of Midsummer, but the serpent surmounting had a life of its own though in the power of the Goddess, for he was now struck with awe and knew he was in the presence of a divinity realized in the person of Siobhan, a manifestation terrible and unfathomable. Over Her head the serpent swayed, coiled about the Goddess' slender waist. Its body trailed on the floor and had no ending. Swaying, its eyes transfixed him with their single-minded focus; he was incapable of moving a muscle, for the fascination the serpent exerted surpassed even the fathomless fear in the grip of this ancient irresistible power. Finally the golden cobra thrust its head down at him like a grotesque and horrible phallus. He rose again to his feet, drawn at Her summons. He knew what was going to happen, but he had no power to withdraw or even to hesitate. The snake struck at his right hand, drawing blood from the soft of the palm. The stinging venomous pain was agony as if bundles of barbs were being drawn backwards through every vein and capillary. Paralyzed he accepted the flow of molten pain gradually up his arm and into his chest where it threatened his heart, whereupon he was released from the spell and allowed to fall back on the bed, every nerve alive to unbearable pain.

Here he had no rest, but endured the most searching and menacing agony as if some high art of causing pain were being practised on him. In spite of this, as the dull ache with the burning flicker spread to all the regions that a man can feel, he noticed that his phallus had risen, stretched out as taut as a drum, consumed with an unattainable desire overwhelmed by a monsoon of agony. If he was screaming, he didn't notice it.

As he writhed in pain without remedy, a veiled woman approached. He could not say when the Goddess had taken Her leave. The woman had in her hand a long sharp knife. With an effort almost beyond endurance he flung himself on to the floor, prostrate in front of the Goddess' priestess and begged for his virility. Her naked foot came down in the small of his back, an immobilizing iceberg. He could not lose consciousness. He could not die until She had punished him to the fullest. Sweat made his body slippery and as cold as a mackerel. He now knew that he had taken too much for granted, that he had tried to possess Her chosen priestess without any prayer to Her or even acknowledgement of Her presence. It was now borne in upon him that the sacred Queen remained a virgin. He had not bothered to learn what Siobhan had tried to teach him.

The Great Goddess might let him live for now, but would require his life at Her own moment. She would not again send him help against his opponent, he realized with sickening clarity. As for his pain, that was his to keep. It pulled every tendon in his body tight under a cold sweat

He had found at last the *Mater Potnia*.

Chapter 43

At some time well into the day, Coll felt himself being hauled on to the bed by two strong men. After they went, a veiled woman entered, lifted her skirts and with languishing deliberation, in agonizing rallentando, excited herself on his phallus still taut and painfully sensitized. She stung him. She took, as it seemed to the helpless victim, an infinity of pains to make herself ready, and when she was the act of her impalement was worse than any pain he had known, as if an organ was being wrenched out of him. He had no control over his own body. He spent when she wanted him to, only after she had enjoyed several preliminary orgasms.

He counted for nothing, not so much as a stray mongrel.

Long after she had finished and the room was darkening, the other one came. She stroked his body with sadistic glee, tracing the currents of pain, crawled all over him, exciting her body at the expense of his cruciation. This was Janine. She didn't bother to conceal herself. When she was ready, she did as the other had done.

Night brought no diminution of his pain; sleep did not come to him, although he managed to doze off for brief spells which did not give him respite, for in fleeting dreams he saw himself as a captured boar awaiting his certain fate, the death and disposition suitable for boars.

No one else came. If Siobhan still existed in human shape she left him strictly alone. He was now relieved at that. He never wanted to see her again. His whole being revolted at the thought that he was her consort, or King, or whatever she and her circle of celebrants called it. He now badly wanted to escape, to go back to mending bicycles in Toronto. He was too mediocre to have anything in common with these exalted but savage cultists.

The paralysis and pain of his body was increasingly subordinated to a most deadly fear of who or what might appear to him, helpless and isolated as he was, for he had as yet no power to get up and leave. The venom had deprived him of all capacity to move or act. He now learned that agony can be endured hour after horrible hour if there is no other way. By an inhuman effort of will he managed to move his head just enough to see that by his watch twenty-four hours had elapsed since he had first been aware of Siobhan combing her hair – she had still been Siobhan at that moment. He must be convinced of that – and time flowed over him, his pain undiminished. No one came through the long night, nor did they during the day that followed, nor the next night, yet he took nothing, not even a drop of water. Under the pain was nausea. The thought of food made his gorge rise. He was on the point of vomiting several times, but did not. Nothing in him had relief. As the third day passed into the cavern of the fourth night, the King lay recovering slowly. He was now without any shred of pretence what he had always been, a mock King. The King had no power.

At the close of the fourth day he could move enough to drag himself to the toilet and back. The fire in him burned all night. In the morning it began almost imperceptibly to recede. Weakly the hero with the strength of a boar made his way downstairs. Voices came from the dining-room. He went in. Diane, Siobhan and Patrick were there. The two women looked surprised to see him but did not greet him, although Patrick nodded to him genially enough. Why not? The poor fool didn't know what he was in for. The reigning hero's strength and standing were gone as a result of his rash injunction to Siobhan – or would it have happened anyway? He would never know. That much was clear. He had encountered the *Mater Potnia*, and knew it.

The table had been cleared, so he went into the kitchen, more out of force of habit than the beckonings of hunger, for he did not have the slightest appetite. Janine was there. She gave him the smile of Merlin.

'Sit down, Coll. You look as though you have seen better days. You didn't enjoy your encounters with Sybil and me, did you? I thought not. Well, I did.'

Coll had made up his mind that he thoroughly disliked Janine. He said nothing, but boiled some water to make himself a mug of instant coffee. He now felt a little better. He didn't see why his strength shouldn't return to him in a day or two.

'Sybil's very happy with the result. Of course she's not sure yet. I might have to make use of you again, so eat up. I need a more virile kind of juice next time.'

He had just finished stirring his coffee. She looked at him.

'You'll have to wait for a day or two. I'm still a little weak from whatever poison someone gave me.'

'Well, but you managed the first time, Coll.'

'You'll just have to exercise some consideration for me.'

'Consideration? Aren't you the great hero who lorded it over us?'

He was right. She was the nasty one.

'I don't have Siobhan with me.'

'Then eat while you can. I'll send for you when I want you.'

He still had most of his mug of coffee left. He did something that most of us at one time or another have wanted to do all our lives.

'What's this, Janine?'

'What?' She came over to look.

He stood up and poured the coffee over her head. She wasn't the Queen. And unlike Siobhan, she screamed on the way out.

He made himself another cup of coffee and got the bread out. Misery and pain had prevented him from thinking clearly, but he now remembered the unsolved mystery of Gerald and Maxine. Had Gerald tried to escape? If so he had taken the obvious precaution of engaging Maxine's affection on his side before making the attempt. Coll's trophies might have been just what he needed to enable him to enlist the aid of an external group to help him get away and stay away. They got their prized possessions back. He got his freedom in exchange. Unlike Coll, he had seen what was coming and acted to forestall it, whereas he, Coll, had blundered blindly on. He had ignored all the warnings Siobhan had laid before him, had been enchanted in Cockaigne bereft of ordinary foresight. They wanted him wild and strong enough to enjoy but, like the swine in the forest, under control and penned in at night. When his duties were done and their interest in him had faded he would be disposed of in some kind of sport devised simultaneously to provide the ladies with amusement and make way for the next sacrificial victim, whose kingship would date from the Midwinter's Feast. He had at most two days left.

Here he was, without internal or external aid, in the very heart of the Circle's home country. He could not move five yards without their knowledge, and even if he could, there were other enemies a-plenty, enemies he could not recognize, waiting with open arms to welcome him. Yet with all this, the ancient land still exerted an unbreakable spell upon him. He did not long for Toronto, although now the broad land of Canada drew him again.

He got himself upstairs again after his bread-and-butter meal, and managed to get some blessed sleep. No one disturbed him. He half expected Janine. He felt stronger, and resolved to go downstairs as usual for breakfast in the morning just as he had done since Midsummer.

He awoke early feeling almost his old self, but not yet quite ready to take on anything big. He still needed a day or so, some good meals – and he must force himself to exercise hard.

He found Cybele, Janine and Diane at the table. Taking no notice of them, he seated himself next to the head of the table on the right and picked up the paper. He pretended to read until others arrived. When Sybil arrived he took no notice of her. It was Patrick who broke the silence.

'I say, don't you think you're sitting in the wrong place?'

'No,' replied Coll, without moving his eyes from the paper, 'I'm saving the head of the table for Siobhan.'

Patrick was nonplussed. He did not know what to say and none of the women gave him any help.

'Of course Siobhan sits at the head, but the other places have been rearranged.'

'Fine,' said Coll, 'why don't you come over here and we'll show each other to our places?'

Coll's recent illness and his apparent weakness may have tempted Patrick into punching above his weight. The women now formed an expectant audience presided over by Siobhan, who had just arrived. It was plain that they were not going to interfere, and equally clear that something important depended on this encounter. Coll now became aware that Patrick might not be the insignificant opponent that his manner had suggested, but the newcomer made the mistake of trying to pull Coll from his chair. It is difficult to dislodge someone securely seated in a wooden armchair at the best of times, and pulling is not the way to do it. If Patrick had thought about what was happening he would perhaps have paused long enough to form a plan of attack. He might then have begun by upsetting the chair. As he strove to pull Coll out, the latter resisted until, suddenly letting himself go, he came with him, kicked Patrick to the floor, and waited for him to get up. Patrick jumped up and flailed his arms. Coll stood back and waited for the main punch. Siobhan was on the point of calling a halt. Patrick delivered his blow, easily parried, and took Coll's punch. It wasn't one of his best, but, as Mercutio observed, it served. Patrick was out on the carpet. Fortunately the blood was still flowing. Coll resumed his seat. The women took their places except for Sybil who went off to get a stretcher party for the fallen hero. There was silence.

For the second time in five days, Coll began to enjoy himself and ate an enormous breakfast.

But the four women were hard to read. When they got up, all together, Siobhan said, 'Build up your strength, Coll. Tonight is Mother Night, when light is conceived in the womb of darkness. Be ready tomorrow, Yule, the twenty-first day of December. The games begin then.'

She had become a being apart. He could not fathom her.

Chapter 44

LEFT TO HIMSELF for the remainder of the morning, his first thought was escape. He thought he could come up with an effective plan, but he did not know where that would leave Siobhan. He did not know what was meant by 'the games' but he fancied that his discomforts and dying pains would provide entertainment for the priestesses from Diane down to Janine. What he needed was a plan, and allies, because the difficulties were daunting. Watch was kept on the house. He would be followed from the moment he stepped out of doors. Yet the forest was even more intimidating. He decided to sound out Cybele, who had always been for him.

Cybele was not that interested to see the father of her future child. He asked her what was meant by 'the games'. She went straight to the heart of the matter.

'You should have chosen me when you had the chance. I tried to warn you as well as I could, but you were enchanted by Siobhan. You owe her your life and a whole lot more. Now it's payback time for you. You concluded a pact with the Queen, and you will be held to it. Everyone in your position is. But it's not all black, Byron. You do have a chance of coming through if you can win Siobhan to your side again. You still have some time. And you have qualities of strength and endurance that will give you an edge over your enemies. And something more: stop counting us priestesses as your personal foes. You have more and better friends than you think, and some of them are going to go out of their way to help you. So don't give in to despair – you're above that. You've proved yourself already, otherwise you wouldn't be here, would you?'

'Was Gerald in my position?'

'A shrewd idea, Byron, but a moment's thought should tell you that the two situations are not parallel. Siobhan became Queen, for the first time this year, so he could not possibly have been in your position. You are her only consort up until now. Let's say that he felt himself to be in danger, got himself a useful ally in Maxine and decided, unwisely as it turns out, to make other arrangements. His new friends took him over quite easily – he had planned to remain quite independent, but he underestimated his opponents – so I don't think his outlook is fair weather ahead. He may well have to take his turn in some festivities which he will find very unpleasant indeed. You've already made the acquaintance of their Queen. You didn't like her, did you? She's been established for a very long time. If Maxine and Gerald had been loyal members of the Circle we certainly would have gone to great lengths to extricate them. But no one wanted them back. Sure, we still had the ahamés you captured, but –'

'Wait a moment. Gerald and Maxine stole them! That was the whole point of their defection, wasn't it?'

'If they had managed to grab them they'd have had something to bargain with and might have saved themselves, but they made the goofy mistake of promising the pelt before they'd caught the creature. You surely don't believe that Siobhan or Esmirone or anyone else would be stupid enough to leave them in such a vulnerable place as a sideboard cupboard? Once everyone inside and outside the house knew, or thought they knew, where they were, they were secreted elsewhere, separately and securely. The two of them beat Esmirone until she was unconscious trying to screw the whereabouts of the loot out of her, but she has a courage and devotion that would not even occur to that pair of beauties.'

'My oath! I was completely fished! I should have guessed – saved themselves – you don't mean their lives?'

'I don't really know, but I think so. You should remember; they're a rough bunch. Byron, get help from Siobhan now, while you can. I still have great affection for you – no, I love you still, you wonderful and unpredictable boar, but events are now standing between you and me. My task now is to be a mother in the service of the Great Goddess on Her hallowed altar. In that you have done your part, for we do not reckon descent through the father, but through the mother only, which, by the way, is biologically consistent. We do not record paternity. Fathers are not expected to take part in bringing up the children they have sired, even if they know who they are, which is unusual. It would have been much better for you at this late stage if you had not offended the Great Mother.'

'Cybele, please, help me. Is it possible for me to escape without doing any harm to Siobhan? I don't understand what's going on!'

There was something akin to pity in her eyes, She shook her head almost imperceptibly. 'I think you will escape from us, Byron. Have no fear. It will be soon.'

There was a knock on the door and Janine entered. 'Ah, I thought you were here, Coll. May I borrow him if you have finished, Cybele.'

'Oh, indeed. We'd done with everything we had to say.'

'What a nerve you have!' exclaimed Coll. 'May you borrow me, indeed. What do you think this is? A circulating library? Well, I think I'd rather leave you on the shelf, thanks.'

'Do argue outside,' demanded Cybele.

On the other side of the door, Janine's fury rose up in a storm.

'You ruined my hair, you beast! I could ask Siobhan to –'

'Janine, my love,' cut in Coll sweetly, 'I've taken a dislike to you, regrettably, for I realize that all should be light and harmony between us. Coffee in your hair might be the least of your problems if you insist on copulating with me. Ask Siobhan. She has told me many times that I don't know my own strength, and I don't want to break your neck, not deliberately, of course, but in the unrestrained rapture of sex with you I might not know what I was doing and accidents – irretrievable accidents, perhaps – do happen. Snap, and then where are you? And think: even damage to some of your less vital body parts would at least give me a chance of visiting you when you were ill and in pain and taking pleasure of you then, when you least want it. That would be a lot less painful than what you practised on me you bitch, and I'm not going to forget it. So if you really want it, that's the way you're going to get it. Don't bluff, as I see you're about to. I don't really have that much to lose. I may as well take you with me tomorrow, sugar dumpling.'

He made as if to seize her, but she retired in good order.

It was time to seek out Siobhan, but she was not in her room. Esmirone, however, evidently expected him, for he had hardly brushed the door panel with his knuckle when she stood before him.

'I know who you're looking for and what you want. We're both here. Why didn't you ask me for guidance, Coll? Neither of us wishes to lose you, but there is a problem. Siobhan, he's here. Can you come out?'

Siobhan emerged from the bedroom. His words dashed out like a geyser.

'Did I really deserve what you did to me when I foolishly wanted to have you to myself again, just once – and, I admit, try to solve the problem of virginity, which was foolish. I know I was stupid and wrong – more stupid than wrong – but you came in the guise of an irresistible and implacable being. It was your body, but not you. The Terrifying Goddess . . .'

Siobhan held up her hand to stop his flow of speech, for he was about to get himself worked up.

'You are right, Coll. I don't know what you saw or heard, but it certainly wasn't me. Tell us exactly what happened.'

Coll had trouble describing the being he had seen, for pain had pushed some of it from him.'

'So you remember me combing my hair as I usually do before I lie down.'

He nodded.

'Don't you remember that we drank a glass of spiced wine together?'

'We didn't. I couldn't have forgotten something like that.'

'But we did. I brought it to you on the brass tray with scrolled handles. You've seen it hundreds of times.'

'Siobhan, I know you'd never tell me a lie, but I'm not so far gone that I could forget *that*. I can recall every moment we've ever shared.'

'Very well. You had insisted, and I was going to lie beside you where you could see me as you made love to me. I wanted it too, because I do love you, Coll, and I'd love to live the life of a normal woman who loves her man, and the man I love is you, you, no one else. Why is that so difficult for you to believe?'

'Why is this person Patrick hanging around like a fœtid pong from the sewer?'

'Shut up and let's talk sense. Patrick has been dismissed in the run-offs, by you, you great fumbly cuddly unbeatable bear. You and I can't live together like two normal people because, for one thing, I am consecrated to the Great Goddess and you are my consort. To Her I sacrifice my virginity twice a year. Poor Coll, it has been one paradox after another: virginity that is renewed and the Virgin giving birth. But these are not new paradoxes. They are exhibited in every culture that preserves close association with their deities, gods and goddesses. You and I were born into a world which has been ruled by empirical science for so long that our sacred festal seasons and our deities with them have dissolved away in our daily lives. The Circle has inherited these riches of the soul, but you have absorbed very few of them. However, that will change. You have great potential. It's a pity that your first transcendent vision was so negative. The trouble is – and it's not your fault – that sex was forbidden to me on that occasion.

'Each of us drank half the glass of spiced Lafite laced with a small quantity of a secret substance. This is something you have to experience before the games, a transcendent insight that I hoped to manipulate to give you foreknowledge of your day of trial and to add strength and cunning to help you to victory. I also had to think of creating the right aurae in order to make you recoil from your awful stubbornness, stop you from insisting on violating my body on an unhallowed occasion and induce you to find succour in me and strength in the Goddess. Taken together, this is a taller order than I with the best will in the world can put together. And I was forestalled. Like the man you are, you wanted to make a test of me, and you were strong in your determination to insist on your 'right'. But, Coll, you have no right to violate the temple of the Goddess; and the temple looks after itself.

'Like you, I was possessed. I have no idea of what I was doing once Esmirone's draught was in my bloodstream. You will find no sign of any snake bite on your hand, but your lasting agony was real enough. Both Sybil and Janine were determined to exercise their right – and duty – when they could. I could not forbid them. As far as they knew, you might not survive either of your ordeals. They are enjoined to take the King's seed into themselves. You treated Janine badly yesterday, but then she treated you badly, and it is not for me to interfere, unless I have to command you to do your duty by them. I'm not even sure I could go that far.

The Siobhan you saw was certainly not me. I have no idea as to what extent, if any, your vision was objective. You saw a manifestation of the Goddess Herself, but of only one of Her aspects, a terrible one. Don't forget that among all Her other divine attributes She is also the Terrible Mother. She is Death, but also Renewal; Love, Nature and Wisdom and so many other essential divine aspects that can bring humanity into harmony with Her.

'She has punished you for your intention only, so thank Her that in her merciful treatment of you She prevented you from carrying out your unhallowed purpose. I love you, Coll, whether you know it or not, and I was going to submit to you for your satisfaction and pleasure on a night when it was forbidden to me, if that is what it was going to take to recover your trust in me again, and my transgression would have been the greater. I would not have been forgiven. I should have been guilty of allowing the temple to be violated in the full knowledge of what I was doing. That is why you are such a danger to me, Coll. You can command me, for you have my complete loyalty and love as we know it here. That is why I have to try to stay away from you sometimes. You're dangerous.

'As for you, I believe you have been forgiven. Go out, walk around and try to pray to the Goddess using the words Esmirone is giving you. Then you will know whether or not you still have Her favour. You cannot do without it.'

There was a long pause.

'Esmirone,' asked Coll, 'am I going to die tomorrow?'

'There is a very good chance of that happening, a slight chance that it won't. You still think of escaping, don't you?'

'It had crossed my mind. Things sound a little better now, though.'

'The Circle cannot let its King go, for so much depends upon him. In him all the community is focused, for he is their offering to the Goddess. However, as far as that goes, you may be able to make a substitution. Siobhan will explain that shortly. You bring us an additional complication, a serious one. No less a personage than the god Woden guided you into our Circle very cunningly. You owe him one day of the year, this year which is nearly at an end. He has agreed to take the Queen, Siobhan, instead of you if you, for example, should escape our games. You must know by now that when Siobhan took you into the forest, she voluntarily offered herself in place of you if you were spared. She hoped her sacrifice would earn you some indulgence, but it didn't. It was an act of the heart, but a most injudicious one, for it opened up an opportunity for the god to step into the Circle, and perhaps in the end, alienate us from the Great Goddess. That has happened in the past. You must not think of passing your burden to the woman who loves you, the Queen.'

'Coll,' broke in Siobhan, 'I am content to let you go. I will help you leave if you want –'

'Out of the question!' stormed Esmirone.

'You will help if I ask –'

'That settles it,' said Coll. 'Now I know what you were talking about in the forest that day. You are the fawn, the intended sacrifice, to be shared.'

'It's not me he's after,' said Siobhan, 'it's the whole Circle. He's not playing for a single card. He's playing for the pile. He wants it all. If you were as much a wimp as he thought you were when he met you in hospital – it becomes clear why he chose a psychiatric ward for his recruiting ground – he would have no difficulty in getting his foot into the Circle. You first regarded him as a friend, but subsequently you defied him, purposely or accidentally, in London. So tomorrow you will have two foes – at least – not one. And the god is more to be feared than any other creature set against you. Yet, don't despair. I believe that you will have help when you need it. You may find unexpected allies Apart from that, Esmirone and I have done some of your homework for you. As far as we can we will help you, but we cannot do anything for you once the games have started.'

'Your chances are skin thin,' put in Esmirone. 'A doctor would throw you out of hospital and you'd never get life insurance, but you do have a chance, because much more is at stake, on this occasion, that your own personal success. Therefore other powers – Siobhan is one – are strongly on your side. And if you win through you will be in a unique position, precious to us. Go out now and clear your thoughts. When you come back we'll discuss your game plan. We're acting against the rules, but this contest is a special case. We're up against a god who has had considerable success in England.'

Outside, the ruined beauty of the garden helped restore him. Spring was latent in this new beginning, the infant light in the dark womb quickening on the morrow. Forgetting his resolution to exercise, he went out for a walk, taking the precaution of filling his wallet with as much money as he could find. If anyone was watching him, he was being very discreet. Perhaps Siobhan had kept to her word. As far as she was concerned he could go. He walked over hill and dale to Windmill Road, stopping just below the crest before the road descended into the village. It occurred to him that if he struck off across the fields and angled back to take the main road out of the village, he could hide until dark, try his luck at getting through undetected and make his way to an arterial road where he could thumb a lift.

But who would pick up a hitch hiker in the dark?

Tramping an unmarked course across the uncouth December fields is not a good way to go even if you have a stout pair of boots, and he hadn't. There are too many obstructions – furrows, walls, fences, ditches, folds in the land – and it is difficult to avoid these and farm buildings while at the same time keeping a clear sense of direction in failing light. He was on the wrong side of Windmill Road which dropped more steeply to the village than he remembered. He cut back over the fields and crossed to the other side, seeing the road he wanted slicing through the green, continuing over the bridge and following the contour of the hill on the other side. The wood was out of sight a mile or two further on. He could not possibly cross the main road unseen. He could blindly strike off over the fields not knowing where he was headed, or he could wait until dark and try his luck in the village.

At the same time he scouted around to find a barn where he could hide for the rest of the day if he had to. He found one, hurried down the road and went to look at the old mill, inhabited now, like every building in the village. When he got near it, he climbed the fence. This enabled him to peer down to the end of the road where it debouched into the main street. On the near side two men stood casually, chatting. Another lounged on the corner diagonally opposite. Every approach to street and bridge was covered.

He withdrew and went back to Hazelridge as if returning from his customary walk. In his room he picked up a revolver and several clips of ammunition, and, stroke of genius for a dolt, took all the car keys off the hook in the kitchen. There was silence in the house. Had they all gone off somewhere? It was so easy!

The thought of Siobhan flooded his mind. He went to Esmirone's room. She looked worried, but her regard was tempered with derision.

'What have you decided?'

'Is Siobhan here?'

'Oh yes, she's making herself beautiful for you. I thought you might take your chance. She was sure you wouldn't.'

Siobhan emerged from the bedroom.

'Siobhan, let's walk outside a little.'

'Haven't you had enough of walking? Look at your trousers! You look as if you've been dragged through a hedge backwards.'

In the garden it all came out.

'Siobhan, my dearest, just listen and don't interrupt until I've finished. It won't take long. You were saying that all you wanted to do was to live a normal life with me. That's what we both want – don't interrupt yet, please. All right. What's to stop both of us leaving? I have all the keys to the cars. We can lose ourselves in London in a little over two hours. I've got cash in a bank in Dublin and we can be in Toronto in two days. All you need is your passport. Now don't explode. Just tell me if this is a possibility.'

'Coll, I don't know what to say. Everything we talked about earlier this afternoon has been lost on you. Now if you want to leave, you still have the chance. I've cleared the house for you, but they'll be back pretty soon for tea. Of course I can't go with you. I've been over all that. But even if your plan works out for yourself, don't you think you're being terribly shortsighted? You cannot defy a god. He will have his way, whether you're in Canada or anywhere else, not to mention all the other nasties waiting for you. At this moment you're on the tide of our events. The Games are come. You may pull off a victory and have honour. You have a good chance of losing, still with honour. I am dedicated to the Great Goddess and I cannot thwart Her will. If you haven't seen that by now, I don't know how to make it clear to you. Trust to Her, pray to Her, and do your best.

'You still have time to take off, Coll. I'll stay here for you. I don't mind walking into the forest for you tomorrow if I know that you are safe. But you will never be secure.

'Is it Janine who's bothering you?'

'Before her I had a family, a marvellous family. Now I've got a bad sister.'

'No, not bad. You haven't understood her yet. Well, time's getting on. If you're going, go now. They won't be late for tea. Come into my arms. That's better. You're not only my first but my only love. Even my love is virginal. A kiss. Ah, you're weeping just a little too. There, be off with you.'

He clasped her round the waist and they walked slowly back inside, ignoring the shouted greetings of the others who returned at that moment.

Chapter 45

IN THE LATE EVENING SHE CAME TO HIM. He was looking out at the dark forest through his sealed window. Not knowing what he had to face, he did not know what to prepare for.

They were in each other's arms for a long kiss and a hug she prolonged for minutes.

'I hope against hope for you,' she said, 'and have not ceased to pray for you. You must do the same. You have shown what a man you are, and you are all man. Your readiness to hurl yourself against brick walls has sometimes been painful to your friends, but that is what a man does, and it may be the one quality that pulls you through tomorrow.'

'Dear one, for pity's sake tell me what I have to do.'

'One of the Great Mother's aspects is Lady of the Beasts.'

'I have seen Her.'

'Have you? Then you start with some understanding of your task. The swine is sacred to Her above all other animals. That is why you have never seen any pork in this house.'

'Yet I killed a boar and took his name.'

'That was the event that led you to the Lady of the Beasts, wasn't it?'

'To you. The Lady of the Beasts, whom I could not follow, was you. I saw you and you saw me, remember?'

'If that is what you saw then it is quite certain that my choice of you was directly inspired by the Great Goddess. It is the best indication of Her favour that we could possibly have. Oh, invoke Her favour that your falling off in the matter of the honour you should have shown me, the appointed Queen, will be forgotten tomorrow. It also means something else equally important to you: as totem boar, you are sacred to the Great Goddess.'

'Then what have I got to worry about?'

'Several things. The first is that the taboo on the boar as a sacred animal is lifted on one day of the year, the day following Mother Night, or Yule. On that day the Queen and her priestesses eat of the flesh of the boar. Are you following me?'

'I'm not sure. I hope you're not practising cannibalism.'

'Save your wit, Coll. This is serious. Someone has to supply them with that boar flesh.'

'I do.'

She nodded. 'But that's not all. The protection of the Circle is withdrawn from you, its totem boar and King, on that day from dawn until sunset.'

'I see.'

'Do you? If you go down to the village now, your detail will be looking after you, taking care that no harm befalls you. Go down at the first light of day and you, the boar, are now the game. Any man belonging to the Circle can slaughter you with impunity until the last second of sunset. And not only with impunity. For great reward.'

Coll became very thoughtful. 'But –'

'Wait. There are a few rules that favour you. The men of the Circle cannot use firearms or any weapon which you are not allowed to carry, so you don't have to worry about bullets or arrows. I'll tell you more about that in a minute. Nor can they set out before sunrise in order to ambush you – this will not happen in any case, I have been promised – whereas you can; nor can anyone torment you. Any man can track you and kill you promptly like a game animal because that is what you are, a prize game animal. For this one day at the end of your reign, the day of Yule, you are seen purely in your rôle as totem animal. Your killer will identify himself with his victim. You did exactly the same thing when you slew Coll and took his name together with his endowment of strength. The inducement is irresistible for the younger, stronger and more able men: the man who kills you takes your place as totem boar, which means that he succeeds you as King. In this I have no choice. His reign will cease on Midsummer's Eve in an equally dangerous but different sacrificial game. Only a new Queen is able freely to choose her consort, and then only the first.'

'I don't have much of a chance, then.'

'If I thought that, I'd have got rid of you earlier today, gone into the forest and offered myself. Let's not go into that. There isn't time. Incidentally, we, the Queen and all the priestesses here, are officially your enemies for the day, from sunrise to sunset, but of course we take no active part in the chase. If we see you we can denounce you to the men out there, though. But don't worry about us. No one is going to go out of her way to impede you. On the contrary . . .

'Now this is what you have to do. Leave here well before daybreak and go into the forest. If you find the Old Forest you will be in danger, but you remember the Master made you free of his own domain. It's not impossible that men of the house or the village will be able to follow you in there, but the Master has given them no permission to cross his territory. If you leave the Master's domain the god you have stirred up against you may turn fortune against you. I cannot say what he might do.

'Don't, whatever you do, harm the swine feeding peacefully under the trees or you will enrage the Master. I'll repeat that: don't harm any smooth-skinned pig foraging as part of a herd. He will not mind in the least your killing the wild boar.

'You are looking for a savage boar covered with reddish-brown bristly hair, an aggressive and unpleasant beast, a past master of ambush, but not beyond you as you are now. Kill it.'

'With what?'

'With the spear I am going to give you. When you've killed it, cut off its head and bring it back here, preferably just after sunset. If you succeed thus far, we'll send a party in to pick up the carcase of the boar. You will no longer be King, but you will have saved your own life and probably mine also. Moreover you will have gone some way towards protecting the Circle, for our adversary attacks us through the Queen. However, it will be a near thing, for you have something else to worry about.'

'The great god Woden.'

'Precisely. Let's come back to that shortly. Esmirone and I have explored the forest, or at least I explored it on her advice, for she is still too weak to walk far. I have left some marks which will guide you to the Master of the Swine. The signs are hard to see unless you know exactly what you are looking for. You know what the *Amanita Muscaria*, the red-capped white-flecked mushrooms look like?'

'Yes, but they're all gone now.'

'Exactly, but we've had no snow, so there are still a few dried-out brown specimens there. What you are looking for is a rough ring of these about three feet across containing always the same number of mushrooms, six, with a seventh out of the ring. This seventh mushroom is the pointer. Be watchful, for some of these may be small and hard to see.'

Coll nodded.

'And don't have any mercy if you encounter your friends from the village. I know you like Matt and Ross, but they, like all who participate, are after one thing: the honour and easeful life of the kingship, the power and immense prestige of being the privileged consort of the Queen herself.

They won't have any mercy on you. So strike first and strike best. Make sure that your man is not going to get up again. For this one day in the year we give ourselves up to the darker aspects of the deity.

'I think that's all you need to know. The one troubling footnote is that Woden claims you on this day in rivalry to the Goddess. If you can argue successfully that his claim is not valid, he will forgo it. Can you do that?'

'I have no idea what this is all about. It started with my doing a man a kindness, as I thought, although I can see now that it probably wasn't. But my motives were good.'

'That sounds pretty fair. Put that to him. His help instead of his hostility could make all the difference in the world to you in the game tomorrow. And there's one other thing. Janine wants to be reconciled to you before the night is out. She does not want to be your enemy. It is a very bad thing to pour coffee into a woman's hair, Coll.'

'Ah, but you don't know what she and Sybil did to me.' He explained it all over again.

'Well, you don't have to deal with them much longer. Will you make it up for my sake, then?'

'Oh, if you ask me to I can't refuse.'

'That doesn't sound right. Is your heart so hard against her? Anyway, I'll send her along. But first come downstairs with me.'

In the shed outside near the place where they had planted the oak in the spring Siobhan showed him a tall spear, well-hafted with a long shaft of bright steel ending in a razor-sharp point. With this she gave him a long knife in a hard leather sheath, well-ground and pointed, also made of the finest steel.

'These are your weapons. Take this flask of water, but do not drink from it unless you have to, otherwise it will be empty long before the afternoon. We've made you this leather jerkin and sewn steel rings into it. You'll notice that it's pretty long, reaching almost to your knees. It will give you good protection from a glancing blow, but a really good thrust by a powerful man or an enraged boar will penetrate. So hit first and hardest. Do not take it off the livelong day. Otherwise, good luck and the blessing of the Great Goddess in Her nature and wisdom fall upon you.'

The last words she spoke as an invocation.

Sometime later, Janine knocked at his door. He did not feel like opening it wide. She stood there, looking not so much cast down as something cast up, he thought with a strange flash of mordant humour on the eve of his almost certain death. He did not invite her in.

'Well?' he asked discouragingly.

'I think each of us has something to apologize for. I treated you badly and you treated me very badly.'

'I think I would reverse the emphases,' he replied. You tormented me when I was helpless. Instead of breaking your neck I contented myself with two or three minor marks of my displeasure.'

'I thought you were a bit of a wimp, I'm afraid. I was wrong. I say, may I come in instead of standing out here in this freezing hallway?'

'Oh, all right. There's a chair.'

'Why do you hate me?'

'Because you're supposed to be a priestess serving the Great Goddess, embodying the best principles in life, but actually you're a bit of a bitch, aren't you, not to say a little prig.'

'You wouldn't say that if you knew how it hurts me, coming from you. Do you know why I hated you? Do you remember the day when we formally accepted each other? You scarcely glanced at me. As far as you were concerned, so long as I was young and the right shape I would do. I thought: here's a man I could adore, but what an ass he is. If he knew my feelings, he'd just wipe the floor with me. You didn't see any of that because you're very imperceptive. Tomorrow I have to hate you again, and I ask myself, is this what I should be doing, or should I be abject in front of you, for those are my real feelings. I have no shame when I see how besotted you are with Siobhan because she's the Queen. But you can have unrestrained pleasure with her just once in your whole lifetime, if that – or hasn't she told you that?'

'Oh, all right. Let's join hands and make up.'

'I'm a woman, Coll, not a man. I don't want a handshake. I want a sign that you like me just a little so that I can say to myself, his liking can at least grow. Give me a hug. That's better, oh, much better. This may be your last night, Coll. I should like to give you everything I can.'

'Maybe later. I have to keep my strength up.'

'Take this.'

She gave him a knife in a sheath, about half the length of Siobhan's.

'Thanks, but I have –'

'*Take it*. But be careful not to cut yourself with it. This a far more deadly weapon than any other you have. I made it myself and put much of myself into it. I made it specifically for you and you alone, so that if you do have an accident with it, I'm in hopes the wound may not be fatal. Before you go out to face the lot of them, I want you to know that I love you, Coll, and if you come safe home again, I'll show you what I can do for you. I don't care if you kick me in the face. I'll still come crawling back, for I desire you above any man in the world. I'll even help you tomorrow if I can. Just tell me what it is I have to do.'

He was moved by the gift, but did not know how to thank her.

'Dear Janine –'

'At last! That word "dear" sounds divine in your mouth! Don't thank me in words. There's a better way.'

'You're not allowed to take part, my loving Janine. In any case, what could you do? You'd just get hurt and lose your status. If you want to be my friend, stay here where you enjoy the greatest power. If I need help at the end of the day, if I'm still alive, then give what help you can once the sun sets.'

After a pause she said softly, 'Do you know how much I love you?'

Coll started at the quiet intensity of her voice. He gazed at her.

She came closer. 'Your body is my temple, your mind is my soul. At the altar of my devotion, my absolute love, I worship your phallus. It is the divine fount which makes a man half divine. You think we priestesses disvalue men as being lesser mortals than ourselves, but you are very wrong to think so. I took you because it was permitted to me and demanded of me, yes, but much more because I craved – that is such a weak word for what I felt! – to receive the greatest gift of the Goddess this side of divine transport. I don't expect you to understand.'

'I don't, really, not in the context.'

'What does the sovereign of my love offer me? Nothing. That is so hard for me to accept because you are the man chosen to seed my fertility. Yet accept it I must if I cannot move you. Are you not moved by true love, a love unqualified, a love unhidden by any mask, yet a Himalaya of love you do not see, and one, moreover, that shall never weaken you but instead give you profound power. I have power. I have given you some of it. Take me, O love, and take it all.'

He looked at her. She did not abase herself or pretend a tasteless submission. Whatever her words, she was intensely proud of the love she devoted to him, for all such human love partakes of the divine. Coll suddenly saw this in her.

She did not plead. She summoned him to a divine feast before his setting out. Gently they took of each other in reverence of the body as she guided him, and as she received his strength, she gave him greater. She was an adept in all her arts and rites.

After Janine had gone Coll thought long: self-denial? humility? Her love was frightening.

This was too much. He had enough on his plate.

Chapter 46

COLL LAY DOWN but it was long before sleep came to him, and then only in fits and starts. When he did manage to drift off, dreams of the boar that he had slain in his initiation ordeal came to him. Its great spirit sensed that it had a chance to escape: it was bursting to get out of its prison in the man, longing to be free in its dark forest again.

After he had been turning from one side to the other for about an hour, as he thought, someone shook him. Looking up to the well head of his dreams, he saw Siobhan for a moment before he closed his eyes again, too utterly tired to keep them open.

'It's getting on for five, Coll. I didn't want to wake you at all, but it's time for you to be gone if you don't want to fight your way out of the garden.'

She pulled him up. 'Get the sleep out of your eyes.'

But he was alive in a moment, new with some resource he had picked up from Janine. He washed hurriedly and shaved carefully. When he was finished she sprayed him all over.

'This will mask your scent for a few hours and might go all day in a pinch.'

She arranged the soft undergarments she had brought in several layers so that there was no direct contact of the jerkin with his body and buckled his knife belt on him. They went downstairs together. Janine was waiting. She took and fondled the other shorter knife she had given him. He did not particularly fancy it, for it seemed to him strangely alive and menacing, but Siobhan said, 'Don't refuse help, Coll. This is a potent weapon. Take it and use it.' And Janine girded him with that, speaking strange words to it.

There was also a pair of soft leather boots, light and comfortable, made exactly to his size.

'These will keep you nimble. I think that is all. You have your water bottle? Do you remember everything? You must kill without hesitation or mercy today if you want to live. On you depends so much: if you return to us safe and sound over the bodies of your enemies, you will help empower the Circle to defend itself against a potent threat. May the Great Goddess send you allies against your assailants, for you are in Her service today even though, paradoxically, She withdraws Her protection from you. All my thoughts go with you. You know my love; you know its quality.' She kissed and blessed him.

He took his spear and opened the back door.

'Don't forget Janine even if she counts for nothing,' said Janine. 'I have given you the best weapon I could wrench out of myself and I would help you if I could, even against the rule of my order. I have already given you my love in all its nakedness, even if you do not want it.'

She embraced and kissed him.

'That was not a wise thing to say, Janine,' observed Siobhan quietly, after they had watched Coll out of sight.

'Perhaps. But, with all respect, I wonder whether the Queen herself has not overstepped the mark just a little.'

'We shall be blameless so long as our aid ceases before sunrise.'

Janine looked away. A huntress herself, she knew exactly what her lover needed.

Once beyond the property, Coll took the ways he had explored in the new forest. He had a good hour's start. His problems wouldn't begin until he reached the Old Forest, if he was allowed to. The darkness slowed him down, but it was not men he feared. He thought he could safely handle any two if he saw them first. If three or more caught him he was done for, but he expected his foes to come upon him singly rather than in groups, for the prize could not be shared.

The boots were exactly what he needed for this day's work: light and easy on the feet, real running boots. They would help him keep his footing in a fight.

Once the sun came up his pursuers would be able to move fast to make up the ground he covered so slowly. But there was no point in trying to hurry. The first task was killing the boar, the second, concealment. At least his ears were becoming attuned to the sounds of the forest; he knew before the faintest grey of the new morning showed him that he was passing out of the new forest planted by men into the great forest of the ages. Here he was not so safe. He might well be betrayed to his hunters here. He paused until it was light enough to look for Siobhan's guiding marks, for he now realized that they must be almost impossible to see even in broad daylight.

Yet even as he hesitated, he saw the first. It stood out to him in some peculiar way, though it certainly shouldn't have. Following the first pointer, he lost no time, but had to keep one eye out on the ground ahead, the other in all directions for men or a more formidable foe. Instinctively he adopted the woodsman's practice of walking in the greatest possible silence so that he can hear the others before they hear him.

So far, so good. Someone, namely Siobhan, was on his side for he had no difficulty in spotting the markers. He was careful to count the mushrooms every time. By this means he made good progress, yet it must have taken him a good two hours before he reached the forking of the tracks where Siobhan had hesitated. Here was a puzzle. The pointer clearly indicated the right hand fork, but when he counted he found there were only five plus one mushrooms. While he was considering this, a sudden rustle in the leaves made him grasp his spear. An Alsatian, not much more than a pup, though as big as an adult, stood before him, its tail wagging vigorously. It caught his eye with a look that said, 'Hail and well met. Let's go off by ourselves today and have a good time. What do you say?' It gave Coll a single mischievous glance, and then it started springing here and there as if it could never be too early to get out and enjoy the morning. Coll got down on his haunches and gave it his hand to sniff. With that the pact was sealed with one great lick and his new companion bounded off into the trees out of sight.

After deliberation he took the left hand fork, and he hadn't gone far before he saw the true pointer indicating that he had the right heading. He began to worry about the dog. What if he harried the Master's swine? Coll couldn't afford to have that happen, but he had no way of controlling the creature. He needed a leash. He stopped and sat down. The dog simply went rushing off, racing back at intervals to see that his new friend was still in tow. At least he wasn't yelping as do so many young dogs without breeding. It struck him that this dog, no matter how lively, was a dog of no mean nature. This thought cheered him, but would it bring him nearer to the boar or merely frighten the creature away? He listened as carefully as he could to all the noises in the forest, but his ears had not been trained by experience, so he didn't know what was going on. No great bear was stalking him this time. The dog tore back to see what had happened to his companion and stood there wagging his tail crazily, but still taking care to leave a good six feet between them. When Coll got up, the dog shot heedlessly off again. He wanted to get going.

It was a waiting game. He had to wait until the boar appeared, kill it, and wait again until the day was advanced enough for him to attempt to make his way out again, avoiding as many of the ambushes as he could. The dog might come in very handy at that stage. It sounded simple.

Some time later during the high day, the dog barked. The barking was followed by a snorting. Hell, he'd found the Master's pigs, and yet it was possible that the dog himself was threatened. Grabbing his spear, he raced along. If the dog was worrying the sounder he would have to go. As he ran he became aware that the dog was in trouble somewhere off to the right. He ran off the path among the trees, but could see no sign of him. The noise was farther off now. He followed it with one thought: to save the dog.

The dog was not in good shape when he finally ran up against it. Saliva ran down from its muzzle and its springiness was gone, but at the sight of Coll it cheered up and led him on through the thickly-growing trees into a glade. It approached the far end, on the right, with caution, always keeping close alongside its ally. Coll could see nothing, but he remembered the warning snort from the previous encounter with his namesake. He raised his spear, but did not make the mistake of positioning himself well down in the clearing. He kept trees behind him. Meanwhile the dog went behind the brush to worry his well-camouflaged opponent hidden in the darkness of the dense forest growth. The boar charged out like a rusty torpedo aiming for the dog, who skipped away. But one error and he would be a very dead dog, ripped right open. Coll had no choice, even apart from his task. He had to protect his ally and collaborator. Keeping the trees on his right flank he went in to stop the boar, more with the thought of saving his friend than of gaining his first success of the day. The boar had retreated unseen, but, watching his enemy's every move now charged up with a terrifying speed that surprised Coll. He stepped back into the trees where his foot struck a root and he nearly fell over. One fall would be fatal. It was now that he thanked Siobhan for her foresight in giving him the right boots, the boots of a forester. He saved himself and came out as the boar made another attempt to topple and gore him, hefted his spear and ran out for room to use it. But the boar was quicker. Coll marvelled at the speed and agility of such a huge, short-legged and apparently clumsy animal. No such thing. It was a better athlete than he. But he wouldn't have any leisure for admiration until he could devise a paying strategy.

He was fighting an able adversary. The boar had the untamed cunning look of the wild creature. It had a well-pelted hide of reddish-brown and stood over a metre at the shoulder, an unpredictable mass of muscle and bone probably weighing in at 900 pounds or more and much lighter on its feet than it looked. This unconfined beast used to all the recesses of its territory in the forest had complete freedom of movement. Coll, on the other hand, in his ignorance of the ground, had to play out the worser scenario, that is, stand in the middle of the glade, exposed, for the boar could charge out at him from any direction; he had to give himself as much warning as possible and rob his opponent of the element of surprise. He thanked Siobhan for his boots and the Great Goddess for his ally. It was the dog who marked the enemy and thus he had some chance of guessing its next move.

The next attack was another fizzer: Coll tried to transfix it with his spear, but he and spear were swept aside and he was on the ground. He would have died then and there – for the boar halted and turned in a flash – if the dog had not hurled himself upon the boar and sunk its teeth into its haunch. Coll got himself up and took the opportunity to stick the longer of his two knives into the boar's left eye. He thrust in as hard as he could, and his enemy was terribly hurt. For the first time its snort ended in a pathetic squeal for its now certain fate. Picking up the spear, Coll tried to stick it from the blind side, but this was more difficult than it looked. The boar flung the dog to the sward and disappeared into the shades.

The beautiful Alsatian lay as if dead, knocked unconscious.

But the fight was not over. The creature still had him in view. It rushed and Coll's stroke went wide. It was the man's turn to skip about frantically as he tried to recover his spear. The fight could yet end in tragedy if he didn't sharpen up. He saw now that he had to use his weapons in the right order. The boar again disappeared, possibly with the intention of escaping, for it was losing blood and it too was tired. The dog, up again, though whimpering and limping with cracked ribs and a hind paw off the ground, gallantly joined in. He led Coll to the deep covert where the boar stood awaiting his fate. In spite of its pain the dog stood off barking as the boar lurched out at his lesser foe. It was time for Coll. First, the spear. As soon as he touched the moving body he obtained purchase and gave a good long thrust with all his strength. The spear took and moved back into the leaves of the covert like the mast of a strange ship. A sudden stab of white told the man that the show wasn't over, and he went in to meet his adversary, long knife in hand. But in that instant his legs crumpled under him and the boar found him and drove his tushes in with a strength greater than Coll's. A gigantic shock of dull pain racked his body with a horrible gripping at the throat, and it was several minutes after lapsing into and coming out of semi-consciousness before Coll realized that he was not alone.

A tall man was trying to turn the prize boar over now that he had cut its throat and severed the monstrous head. Further off he saw his faithful and brave ally lying in the stillness of death. Coll had found unexpected help, and with that help he had been able to overcome his enemy. But the playful and noble Alsatian who had jumped and run in his morning joy was now as dead as the object of his game, as Coll would be in short order. In spite of the almost overpowering pain he said a short prayer for his friend. The stranger had put Coll's spear and knife well out of reach, but had not noticed his third weapon. In spite of tides of pain becoming unbearable, he drew it and concealed it under his body.

Someone was looking down on him.

'You're bleeding a lot, old man No matter where I run across you, you're in a mess. I'm sorry it had to be you, but we all play by the rule of the season, and the prize I have coveted – I admit that, coveted – is now mine by right. She's a fabulous beauty and she pulls power, oh hell, far far above me, of course. I have fantasized about bedding such a potent honeypot even against her will. Even sexier that way. God, it's not the sex, it's the absolute power. You've had your turn. Now it's mine. This is the only possible way a man like me can achieve such a prize. The ship of ships comes in. But I was never envious of you, no, for our society doesn't work that way. That's the best of it. It's all legit. I know it's impossible for you to see it from my point of view, but, well, you've got to be killed, haven't you, old boy? You've had your turn and it was great while it lasted. So, better to be eased out gently by an old pal than slaughtered by some brute you've never seen before.'

It was difficult to breathe and talk, but even on the point of death Coll was fascinated by the other man.

'Are you sure you played by *all* the rules,' asked Coll painfully. 'How did you get here so early?'

'You were making quite a bit of noise you know – you were never careful enough of security, were you – and, well, yes, I did stretch things a bit by starting early. In fact I told Siobhan – well, to be quite honest, promised her even – that I would not be going out on the Game at all. As far as she knows, I'm still doing her messages up in London. That's why I was able to use the car – yeah, yeah, against the rules too, I know – and, yes, I did start early, much earlier than you, why not? I'm here to win. While she's had me based in London I've actually made quite a few trips down here doing my homework. But as she's not going to find out about any of this from you, well, it's all a bit academic, really. And let's face it – no one who's serious plays by the rules, I mean that's all tosh. The old

Circle is not really as different from normal life as we like to think, I mean, is it? Look, if you want something badly enough you're going to bend whatever rules there are – O.K., I agree, your own principles too – right? Let's be realistic about this. Don't tell me you just blarneyed your way in. I've heard the story, of course, but things don't work that way, do they?

'By the way, let me know when the pain becomes absolutely unbearable. No use going through hell when there's no need. I must remember to pack a few pain killers next year. You're helpless, old chap, and I'm not going to take advantage of you. I've got all the time in the world. But it's no use clinging to every last second when you're in agony, is it? I mean, you're not going anywhere. This is it.'

'Do you think Siobhan will accept, let alone, love, my murderer?'

His assailant laughed gleefully. 'She has no choice, Coll. Why the hell should she put me down as your murderer? Today you're up for grabs. She herself would betray you if she had the chance, not to mention some of the other harpies up there. I wouldn't put much past Janine. I really liked you, Coll. and I'll remember our brief friendship all my life. And I believe that Siobhan really does love you. She will be quite upset by your – ill-success. I know that I'd have no chance whatever of succeeding while you were alive, I mean, I'm realistic. But she is Queen. Her love goes out to us all. No one has a monopoly on it. I'd like to take her a last message from you, but that would compromise my own conduct.'

'You're forgetting a couple of minor points. She will know that your victory is a cheat. And you are forgetting something even more important.'

'What, then?'

'You are forgetting the Great Mother. Have you seen Her?'

The man who had tossed his spear between Coll's legs laughed. 'Have you?'

'Yes. And my offence was trivial compared with yours. You will encounter Her and She will make known Her displeasure. You are more foolish than you think in dirtying your hands today. But I too remember that passage of friendship in both our lives. I don't wish to part company with you in a spirit of resentment. Much can be excused in a man who acts helplessly in the fascination exerted by the High Queen. Since you were so very good a friend of mine during my short time amid the wonderful people of the Circle, you might at least kiss me before you kill me. Help me up a little.'

He could only gasp in wonder at the intensity of whatever element Janine had imparted to her gift, for even with the feeble strength he was still able to exert, the blade slipped in as lubriciously as an eel into ooze. Michael lay across him dead.

Irrationally, he thought of the dog. 'You deserve a hero's honour, much, much more than I. You brought to the battle a courage I didn't have. Now I see that the Great One is indeed Goddess of all nature, for you came to me a stranger and gave me the devotion of a brother, more than a brother.' Whatever happened, he must, if he could withstand the loss of blood long enough to get back, have the dog brought in for proper burial. The pain was intense and disabling. He wondered now why he had omitted to take pain killers with him. Dragging himself over to the severed head of his victim, he found it too difficult to move, but by exerting all his willpower, he succeeded in dragging it and himself, inches at a time, to the edge of the clearing where he could rest as comfortably as possible against the bole of a tree. He began to hope that the rest of the day might be relatively uneventful. He had been sent the perfect ally for his task. He hoped against hope that this favour might be continued. At any rate, there was now less blood welling up under his jerkin. He resisted the temptation to start crawling back to Hazelridge now. Anyone with a crochet needle could end his agonies without fear of resistance. In spite of the overwhelming pain he drifted into the solace of engrossing sleep, submerged in a flood-tide of his anguish.

He awoke much later with the disquieting conviction that company was present. He cautiously drew Janine's knife and tried to look about. The pain was still very much present. But even if he had been able to move freely he would have missed his man.

'All praise to you, man of no name, whom I recognize.'

He made ready to lunge at whoever had stumbled upon him, but he could see no one, and the voice he knew. It was no good drawing any weapon.

'You look too far away, you who have the favour if not the protection of the Great Goddess. I am here, almost beside you. I will not cause you further pain.'

He was, just over Coll's left shoulder, completely masked by the trunk of a tree. He came round. It was the one he dreaded to see, Victor, hardly to be recognized, for he wore the clothing of a gentleman of the sixth decade of the eighteenth century, with blue jacket and tricorne extensively trimmed with gold and an elegant black eye-patch. He was fussy about his linen at neck and sleeve and toyed with a handsome cane topped with an enormous sardonyx.

'For every entry there is an appointed dress. In this one I returned to my adherents when I walked abroad again. Yet Inanna was yet more daring than I when she went down into the nether world. You, of course, will not know her name. Nevertheless remember it, if you should survive this day. Even without your present injuries that is, of course, debatable.'

'O great one, why do you want my life?'

'Your life, already given to your Queen, you owe to me for the wisdom I gave you. Gods demand a price for all they give. Only the Great Mother asks nothing in return.'

Coll groaned. 'Will you take my life, then?'

'You have not treated me as a man should treat a god.'

'That was in my ignorance.'

'Ignorance is never a justification. It will not save your life if you in your ignorance touch a high tension cable. Why should it save you from the wrath of a god?'

'Will you accept a substitute as Zeus accepted the bones and umbles in place of the meat and rich stomach fat?'

'He was tricked by the greatest of all shysters. You are not a trickster. Otherwise you would not have so many friends, remarkably good friends. Two priestesses of the Goddess have offered me their lives in place of yours. It is their acceptance and service I want, not their lives, and this they cannot give. And you have other great pleaders in your behalf, one you know and one you do not at present know. You will meet him. The second has power. He watches over you. I cannot have the service of the sacred ones who also consecrate you, man, although you do not know it, so I recoil upon you. My demand is as it was from the beginning: on one day of the year your life is forfeit to me, on this day indeed. Today you have triumphed twice, but victory has left you almost without defence, even if you manage to crawl the distance back with a wound ever opening anew. Men are hunting for you, and an easy kill one of them will have if you encounter him. You have the head of the boar; he will have your head, yes, that is the trophy the new King must carry back with him in order to claim his bride-right. However, I shall relent a little since you once showed me kindness after your sort, and give you a task which is within the bounds of possibility. Bring a man as sacrifice, alive or dead, this or another, to the bank of the stream that runs by my altar before the sun sets and I shall accept it as my due for this year only. Otherwise I shall take your life at the last light of this day's sun.'

'How can I do this? I am in pain and move only with difficulty at the cost of losing more blood.'

'It is for you to find a way. If you want further wisdom you must pay for it. In the meantime I shall take the boar's head as a pledge, to be returned to you when you have brought me a life.'

'Is this wisdom in a god?'

'Ah, you can pose an intelligent question. I thought that day when we met in London that the senseless liberty of your kingship had turned you into an utter fool. Yes, it is wisdom. Shall I tell you about wisdom?'

'No, I cannot afford your teachings.'

'That is shortsighted pragmatism, the kind that struck that silly ass Protagoras as being smart when wrapped up in the current cliché and jargon of his set, the kind that men and women still imbibe in order to be successful, as they call it, good for winning cheap arguments against men even shallower than himself. They who practise it are mere balloons. How did I lose my eye?'

'You drank at Mimir's fountain.'

'You know that much. Paying with your life for the wisdom a god has sacrificed himself for is no bad bargain. Yet I demand nothing further from you than what I have specified. If ever in aftertimes you seek me out I shall be there for you. You know my price. I speak in the terms you now understand.

'One more question, O great god Woden. Will you help me win back my life from you today?'

Victor smiled.' Gods seldom laugh, but this is rich. I give you a finger and you want the whole hand. Are you not afraid of getting into debt again? What, shall I carry your victim to the place of tryst myself or lead you to another at the moment when his back is turned and twist the knife for you?'

'It is not easy for me to kill – my friends, at least.'

'Do not rouse my ire by asking foolish questions. I am here as I have been for long in this south eastern corner of England, for I first came ashore here. Further north I walk abroad. I have been seen and recognized. If you survive this day be wise enough to give me my due from time to time – and when you meet old men take care to treat them with due deference. I will be revenged upon the savages of this generation.'

He took out and opened the most beautiful pocket watch Coll had ever seen. The size and shape of a flattened orange, it looked like a little sun. He could not take his eyes off it.

'Shall we say, a little before sunset? Yes, this is the lost Harrison, the last masterpiece of that most ingenious man. Watchmakers like great gods use only one eye.'

The figure that had once been Victor the lunatic moved back into the trees in utter silence and vanished. Coll stared after him, but not even the serest leaf on the forest floor showed a trace of his passing.

He hadn't been asleep.

He now tried to crawl through the trees back to the forest path, but in the same moment knew that he would never have the strength to return home, let alone carry a sacrifice to the stern god. Determining never to lie down and give up, he managed to reach the track at the cost of more blood. He was blinded by pain and nearly defeated by weakness, far from help.

But the Master was there, riding an ass.

Hardly conscious, he yet managed to greet this servant of the Goddess, a sudden ray of hope in his heart.

'Greetings, Master. I offer you my respects.'

'Greetings, O King. Your unimpugned reign lasts until sunset and beyond if you can stay alive and out of the paths of your enemies. But you are badly hurt. I have some skill in tending wounds. While I work you shall tell me of your success.'

Lapsing again into a stupor, Coll could not reply, but as the Master attended to him, he revived remarkably and did his best to satisfy his benefactor. After some time, perhaps half-an-hour, perhaps much longer, most of the pain had gone, the flow of blood had ceased and he felt incredibly better, almost as if he had a chance. He told of the boar, of the dog's courage and devotion and the treachery of a friend that had led to his downfall.

'And where is the head, man of strength and courage?'

'That is more difficult to explain. I encountered a great god, who took it in earnest of a life in exchange for mine.'

The Master nodded. 'You have good friends, friends who have exerted all the power they have to help you. One of them sent the dog to you. You are not as bad a man as once you thought, are you? Don't be surprised. I have known you longer than you think. I too have helped you, for without my ministration you could not have gone much farther, and I will give you further help, but I cannot stand against a god or wander far beyond my bounds. I will look after your faithful friend for you. What else do you desire?'

'Help me in taking the body of the man I killed to the stream that runs by Woden's altar, and in returning to the Queen if I am successful with him.'

'As for the body, we can sling it over my faithful ass who will serve you well. But first you must rest and be refreshed. In another two hours you will be able to do something. I cannot take you much further, but I see in you marks of the Goddess' favour. If the Great One is determined that you shall come through this day, believe me, you will. In the meantime while you are recuperating from your severe wounds which are now healing well, let us eat and drink. Yes, I insist. Do not neglect any help that is offered you.'

The Master produced a loaf of bread and a flask of water, which they shared. After the pain Coll felt weak and nauseated, and his leg muscles complained; the thought of food made him recoil. He was reluctant to eat, but both bread and water were amazingly light in his mouth, tasted delicious, banished nausea and revived his hunger. He was hardly aware of eating, so rapidly was normality returning. He felt a stream of energy; all his confidence returned.

'I am honoured to break bread with –'

'One who is no more than the Great Goddess' swineherd.'

'– one who is so high in the Blessed Virgin's service. But what if I have to take another life? The Blessed Virgin will not condone it.'

'You will lose your own if you don't. This is the one day of the year when the Goddess allows the darker side to prevail.'

'I thought . . .'

'You thought?'

'Once I thought that I had seen the Great Mother in Her darker aspect, as a Nemesis, perhaps.'

The Master did not speak until they had finished eating.

'Where do you think your next assailant will be?'

'There'll be plenty of chaps playing it safe by waiting for me in the lesser forest as I come out. They have an advantage: they've picked their spots, they've camouflaged themselves and they probably think that they themselves are not in much danger. They're not really a problem. Once the sun has gone down they no longer have the right to kill me. The real menace will come from some man with an instinct for tracking, someone between here and the dell.'

'You are right. Fear the real woodsmen. They are trying to follow your trail at this very moment. You can be sure that I will take care that any traces of you will disappear at the edge of my territory. Yet even the best woodsman may at first mistake you. He sees someone with a lifeless body slung over an ass. His first thought must be that the body is yours. Take swift advantage of his hesitation. A friend has given you a most deadly weapon. Try to use it. But do not underestimate those who are concealed in the trees. Lust for power and your Queen drive some of them to the very depths of their soul's darkness. You have already seen what reckless coveting of the prize can do to men you thought good and honourable. A man who is ravished by lust for the kingship will do anything to get it. He won't worry about breaking the rules. Now let's see if you can get up and walk.'

To Coll's astonishment he could, but he still felt quite weak.

'Your wounds will not reopen, for I have dressed them with an ancient skill that will hold until you return to the Queen. Now go and recover your weapons and see if you can drag the body back here.'

Again, to his own surprise, he found he could, although the effort of dragging Michael to the track was almost beyond him when he had to get him through the brush. But he did not lose a single drop of blood.

'Good. You will not get your full strength back, but you will, I think, have enough. Let us wait some time longer before you truss the body over the ass. The bread of the Goddess will suffice for your tasks.'

As the afternoon wore on, Coll sensed renewed strength in himself. When the time came to leave the Master, he found he could, though with the difficulty of one with little more than ordinary strength, lift the body and tie it down under the Master's direction. He was aware of great pain subdued.

'If you leave now you will reach the dell in good time. I play no part in these foolish games and I cannot tell where your enemies might be lurking, beyond the fact that there is no one apart from you within my own borders. If I see any of my friends I shall ask them to help you if they can. More important, I send you with a mark of high success on you. Have no fear. And now, until our next meeting, harried man, I leave you. Yet one word more: once, long ago we met. I knew your father. But there is no time for questions. Be on your way with all the blessings I can lavish on a brave man's son.'

As Coll took his way leading the ass, he raised his hand in farewell, and thanked the Master. The final revelation would have kept him back if his immediate task had not demanded his full and unremitting concentration. But his friend was gone. If he saw Siobhan again he would have so much to ask her, and perhaps he would get some answers this time.

This was the hour of greatest danger. Wounded almost to death and exhausted before the morning was out, he was brimming with confidence again, a fatal state of mind in a cat-and-mouse game. He had the sense to remember that he was weaker than before, that he was being tracked by expert woodsmen with three good hours ahead of them even if the trail had been obliterated at the place of his meeting with the Master. The ass was complaisant. It didn't at all object when Coll went off the track to the right, trying to guess a course that would take him well out beyond house and village once he had reached the dell. However, in view of the proximity of darkness if and when he survived for the final dash, it probably was not worth trying.

Eventually the Old Forest showed signs of thinning out, and he edged back in, not being able to afford drifting too far from the dell. From this time on he left the ass from time to time and reconnoitred, moving cautiously and very quietly from tree to tree while the creature of burden waited patiently and silently where he left it. He did not doubt that his opponents had adopted protective colouring. On his side the long spear was the giveaway and he wondered whether he ought not to discard it, but he could not cast off so lightly Siobhan's gift. The absence of a single man, apart from Michael, puzzled him. He wished now that he had tried to find out how Michael had found him so easily, but that would have to wait. He crawled back to where he had left the ass, as silently as he could go. Near at hand the ass was troubled. Standing up cautiously, he saw a figure slip away. He edged carefully into position and waited in cover with the ass in view. Whoever it was now knew that the King was still alive and active.

He decided to wait in spite of the pressure of time. No wonder the village had looked after him. No prize on earth obtainable by men was more coveted than he. There was still ample time and he had patience in abundance. If the other was aware of Coll's approximate position, he would wait until his quarry moved and pounce. Coll thought he must have been heard if not seen. The other was surely aware that the crowning prize was in the vicinity, but if he were no woodsman, perhaps not. In that case, then, he probably did not know where his enemy was and lust for the kingship and impatience would ultimately overcome caution.

What happened next amazed him. Looking up, he saw a leg that he would have mistaken for a bough if it hadn't moved. The fellow was waiting for his foe to approach the ass, the triple idiot. And he had a bird's eye view of the field immediately below the tree. Coll would have given anything for a shotgun. If he moved an eyelid he would be spotted. After a while, however, his enemy, not realizing, apparently, that his position had been discovered, decided that he could see everything and that no one was around as yet. Coll could hear him climb down and jump to the ground on the far side of the tree, invisible to him about fifty yards away. Evidently he had driven in spikes . He then came around to Coll's side and, after first looking about him with great care, began to pee against the trunk.

Coll calculated quickly. With a flying bound he ran. The other turned and Coll had a further shock, for the man picked up a weapon quite against the rules of the game, a mighty hunting crossbow. It was the ideal weapon for one who watched for his quarry while safely ensconced in the foliage of a tree, and if the bolt had found its mark Coll's chances would have been settled there and then. As it was, the cheat wasn't quite sure of his attacker's position until a moment too late. Although he drew a knife and parried so that Coll's spear glanced aside, yet it pinned one arm very deep into the tree, for Siobhan's spear had some unusual power of penetration. With his long knife, Coll hacked the other arm almost off, then went for the head. Again it was Janine's short knife that took the man's life. It slid between the ribs as if it lived there and blood like warm tea spilled out over his hand. The man was dead. Coll dragged the body over to the ass and roped it on to drag behind. Now without a halter, he went ahead; the ass followed as meekly as a girl at first communion.

Coll had originally assumed automatically that the games would be played according to cricket rules. What a fool he had been to assume that men of the Circle would be any different from the rest of mankind when offered a chance to claw a path to the top. Even so-honest Michael had been corrupted by the dream of adulation and possession of the Queen! They did not understand that they could never possess her. They did not know, as he had not known, that the idea of possession was alien to the love-ethic of the temple.

His time was now short, but his adventures were not over. His next opponent was confused, wondering why a victorious candidate should be carrying his burden in the wrong direction. He was also nonplussed by the fact that the man he had been stalking made no attempt to conceal his movements. It took him time to creep close enough to see that it was the King who walked so hardily, and perhaps he was a little unnerved to see the kill being treated so barbarously. In the interval the ass had given a warning and the quarry had slowed, ears attuned to the attacker's own carelessness in making a noise in his surprise. When the man struck, he drove his spear straight and true at the King's heart, but just as quickly Coll interposed the ass between himself and his assailant, which thus became a shield, and the body of the first victim received another gash. It was then knife work, but Coll had two knives and could parry with one while he wielded the other. He was just as liable as the other to a shrewdly delivered stab, for he now had no superior strength. It was the smaller left-hand knife that held off the other at the expense of several nasty cuts. One of them would fall and the first one would be the loser. Picking a moment when his foe was visibly wilting a little from exhaustion, he went in and kicked the other man's groin. This didn't work as Coll intended it to, but his opponent buckled enabling Coll to get in a glancing blow at the head, which, whether serious or not, temporarily blinded the man with blood. A second penetrating stab left no doubt as to the result. Janine's dagger finished off the third challenger.

Yet even as he triumphed, darkness was closing about him and he realized that this third diversion might prevent him from reaching the dell in time. Without a glance at the dead man, he tried to run in his exhaustion. The ass had trouble keeping up, but he had no time to cut the second failed candidate loose.

On the rise above the incurving stream the oblique rays of the departing sun picked out an eighteenth century gentleman standing with his feet already invisible in the pool of darkness at the pit of the dell. As Coll approached he took out his watch.

'It wants nearly a minute to sunset hereabouts,' he observed. 'Only the greatest of mechanical masterpieces, this lost creation of Harrison's, gives true local time. What have you brought me besides the Irish coachman, not a prize of any great value? Oh dear, another interloper. I don't think your Queen knew of his interest in this day's work. A cunning, skilful and ambitious man, not the frank and open friend you remember, I fancy. What a pity he did not understand his limitations, for I assure you, his talents were truly remarkable.'

For the first time in his labours Coll looked upon the face of his vanquished enemy, the one who had sought long the lovely Queen. How on earth could a cosmopolitan, versatile, talented and above all, covert individual like Michael Wheelwright, who could so easily become any of his masks, think of going in for this rough stuff? His citified way of life, which included constant coffee drinking, had done for him. He felt no pity, for Wheelwright had been after his life as ruthlessly as anyone, and, like the other Michael, had no scruples about accomplishing his ambition surreptitiously with an illegitimate weapon. What a spell *his* Queen had cast on others! On this day she had been emblematically destructive: the boars followed at her bidding as he had seen in a vision in the mystical West of Ireland.

'The boar's head on which the Goddess' taboo is lifted for the season is beside you. I shall see you again, O man of no name, for I take no further power over you for this time. On the contrary, I ordain that you shall return to your Queen. I am abroad again. See that you greet me properly when next we encounter one another.'

Even as the voice faded the darkness closed in.

The sun was below the horizon. The games were over.

Coll lost no time in picking up the final burden for the final task of the day. He knew now that he was close to complete exhaustion and that his burden was both awkward and unbearably heavy.

It was not quite an hour after sunset when he crashed through the back fence, walked round to the front, and paused at the open door. Throngs of weary men and their expectant women, adults of the entire village, had gathered to see and greet their new King of the Rising Year. The King, not aware of his appearance, was stained, filthy, his face black, covered with blood and criss-crossed by cuts, his jerkin rent, his hair matted, himself beyond recognition. Holding his burden close to his chest, he pushed his way through, elbowed those standing near the threshold aside and went in, slamming the door shut behind him.

He was hardly aware of the priestesses who greeted him, but went on heedless like a railway train that has forgotten its station. He collapsed on the first landing.

At that moment he was close to fainting, for his fearful injuries were now telling on him again. He had lost a third of his blood and the pain was surging back in tidal waves.

Chapter 47

Pain. All-encompassing, all-engrossing like an unremitting electric shock. He was imprisoned in a hellish basket, trapped in the high tension wires of the nerves. Knocked silly by the flood of agony no longer dammed up by the Master's skill, he was hardly aware of the tablets they made him swallow, of the bed they placed him in, of the shock of his friends when they stripped off his clothes and saw the extent of his injuries, the deep gashes in the thigh and the ghastly ruin of the genital region, some of which the Master had been obliged to cut away.

The tablets made no difference, but Siobhan brewed a drink that caused him to slip into torpor again while the pain abated somewhat. Agony draws out time. Although voices told him the doctor was on the way, centuries of hell passed before the same woman who had tended Esmirone came and looked at him. With a precious wonderful hypodermic needle she took away the pain and gave him blessed sleep.

'Hospital, *now*. Someone has done a rough job rather well – did he do it himself, I wonder? – but everything's cold, so it's surgery from here on. Do you tell me that after receiving these injuries he walked miles back here carrying that thing in the kitchen? I can't believe that unless he had some more effective painkillers than you were able to give him.'

'More than that,' put in Janine in a voice breaking with distress and pride, 'he fought with several men and killed at least two of them.'

'Not after sustaining trauma like this. That I cannot believe.'

'I think Janine is right,' added Siobhan, 'but we'll find out. Is his life in danger?'

'Yes it is if he's not attended to in short order – like I said, now. I've called the ambulance. If we get him to hospital in an hour or so, he'll be fine. What's the story?'

'I'm his girlfriend, engaged,' said Janine. 'Here's his national health card. Born locally, but lived in Canada with adoptive parents after being orphaned at the age of four when both his parents were killed in a motor accident, so has right of abode and British nationality. How did he get these injuries? I don't know. You tell me.'

'Just tell as much of the truth as you can. It's easiest.'

'He was charged by a wild boar in the forest. I was with him. I'll write out and memorize the scene. I'll whisper it in his ear at the right time – don't worry: I know how to make it stick. Unfortunately I've heard only a few disjointed scraps of talk from him, but I'm pretty sure that's what happened. I'll try to find out more.'

'Right, then the nearest hospital's best. There I'm on staff and can authorize you to stay close to him for as long as they'll allow. Arrange for someone to relieve you. It's going to be a long wait, for they have to operate as soon as possible. I'll try to get Mackintosh. He's about as good as they get.'

'Can he hear what we're saying now?'

'I shouldn't think so, but funny things happen. Come out into the hallway.'

After the doctor had shut the door, Janine had some trouble in finding words. When she finally was able to form a sentence her voice was very near breaking in spite of her self-control.

'It looks – horrible. I've never seen – I was nearly sick. Tell me, is he —?'

'Yes. I'm so sorry for you both, but there's no use in beating around the bush. I'm afraid he is. We have to look after the waterworks pretty soon, or he may be in real trouble. You know, making it back home – defending himself, you say – is the best news. The man has incredible guts. That should pull him through. As far as the other functions go, the genital functions, well, there aren't any. You are going to have to face the fact that he is completely emasculated, and I wish I could tell you anything else. You've seen the extent of the trauma. I'll probably never know what hell you must be going through. You love him in the deepest sense, though, Janine, so this is not the end for you, no matter how terrible it seems now. It's possible that Mackintosh will be able to suggest some kind of prosthesis, in spite of the damage. Do think that over most carefully, as I know you will. Oh dear, forgive me, Janine. I wish I could tell you anything else. At least it doesn't get worse than this.'

Janine shook her head violently and could not forbear an outburst of tears, but when she recovered herself, she said, 'He was in the hands of the Great One. She still has something great for him to do. It must be so. My tears are just the tiniest part of the sacrifice She has exacted. I shall never cease to love him, never abandon him; his life will be my life. I will be his servant in his great purposes, even if he spurns me with his foot.'

'Whatever his condition, Janine, he's more than a man; he transcends all the old fables of heroes I've heard of. He's real, not a statue on a pedestal, his grand feats true. I've never heard anything like it – after such injuries to carry on for a large part of the day and actually succeed, against opposition, you say, in getting back here with his prize, even if he did get some first aid on the way, very skilled first aid – or did he do it himself, do you think? It doesn't seem possible, but I almost believe the man is more than mortal.'

'He encountered a god.'

'Sorry?'

'What can I do for him?'

'That bloody ambulance should here now! Go with him, be with him, believe in him, be a woman to him. He's going to need everything you can give him, especially as he now loses Siobhan, although not, of course, her love, I'm sure. It's going to be a very stressful time for you. You'll need the strength of two. I'll try to do a little homework on his situation in the next few days. He's coming back here, of course?'

'What on earth can you mean! Don't you think he has deserved at least that?'

'I'm not the Queen, Janine. I am trying to understand your feelings. I know you are going through hell with him, but he is down and you are not. He will be very depressed when he finally comes through after a major operation, and, worse than that, desperate when he understands his condition. At this moment he may have no notion of what has happened unless someone has told him, and that person would most likely be the person who tended his injuries so well. You will have to have enough courage for both of you, no matter what your own feelings are. If there's anyone who can do that, it's you, my dear friend. Of course there can be no better place on earth for him to come back to than this house. I don't envy you the part you have to play. I could not deal with this in the man I loved, Janine, though he were a hundred times a Hercules, but you are a priestess with inner power above the ordinary. You will manage. He will need you, not me or Mackintosh when we've finished patching him up. It's going to take several operations, I would guess.'

'Can't Siobhan do anything? Are there no miracles?'

'Not real physical ones like this. It's not something like an unaccountable remission from cancer. That is a physical process that we can understand even if we don't know why it's happening. Complete remission is a miracle to the patient, but this is not the same thing at all. You are asking for magic, not a miracle.'

'He might want death rather than this. He's a real man, not one of your imitations. I shall pray that I have his child. That's the one thing I can think of that might help both of us.'

'Yes, it would. But the College perhaps can do things that are at present beyond my ken: there are several kinds of miracle he needs – first to be saved from himself. Siobhan played the major rôle in saving Esmirone. I spoke too hastily before – who knows what she can do? What do I know of her powers? Perhaps she can transform his soul. Come on, here are the paramedics. Grab whatever you need. I'll get you aboard. I won't be able to spend time with you once we get there, but I'll be along to see both of you in the morning.'

'I'm sorry for my little tantrum, Melinda. You've got more than enough to put up with. I was thoughtless. You're doing your best and you don't need people like me upsetting you.'

'Tantrum? No such thing, silly! Don't hold it in – let it all come out, Janine. I have nothing like your self-control, but don't sacrifice yourself to it. I love you too, don't forget.'

'I know.'

As the doctor had said, neither Mackintosh nor anyone else was able to do anything about Coll's condition. After the initial work he was in for reconstructive plastic surgery in a series of operations spread out over months, but none of this surgical ingenuity made any difference to his loss of virility.

He came out of the immediate operation in a reasonably cheerful frame of mind, when his pain was at last clearing, but, as the doctor had predicted, once back at Hazelridge recuperating, he fell into a state of depression that put him in mind of his Toronto days. He locked light and the world, even Siobhan and Janine, out. He wanted nothing and could stand only darkness, silence and solitude; he regarded death as a desirable exit from the hours of gnawing desperation. It is hard to say whether or not he was clearly aware that he had permanently lost both strength and virility, or whether in his soul's blackness, the full realization of his loss of manhood would have made a scrap of difference: the bottomless chasm after the peak was the hell of the moment. The destruction of his manhood would abide as long as he did.

Few dreams and no voices came to him, and he was as incapable of prayer as he was of everything else. He didn't want to eat or drink; in any case, nothing had any taste. Both Janine and Siobhan sat with him for long stretches; Diane, Sybil and Cybele looked in on him every day, but whatever magic these great priestesses adept in their craft practised to bring him back from the black night of his soul was no more effective than the endless anti-depressive pills out of little brown canisters. These Janine gently forced into him, but their only effect was to dry up his mouth.

He had the best possible care. His nurses, the priestesses at Hazelridge, knew that it was no use trying to push him along faster than he would go, but he was going nowhere and every time the next reconstructive operation came along he was set back once more by the renewed assault on his body, one that he and everyone else knew was making not the slightest difference to his underlying condition. He saw very clearly what had happened and what was taking shape under the skilful hands of an internationally-celebrated plastic surgeon, for he was being given only the very best, and he understood more clearly and more soberly with every detail that he had no reason for living. He had completed his kingly function. His stays in hospital were simply that many more laboured steps in the treadmill of his desperation.

This conclusion appeared to him a matter of simple logic unrelated to his state of mind. He cast no blame on anyone, not even on his treacherous friend Michael, the rally driver. When he had recovered sufficiently to walk about he would find out from Siobhan how best he could serve the Circle by giving the life he no longer had any use for, perhaps as a sacrifice to Woden to extract some concession Siobhan could negotiate. He was no use to them; they were no use to him except in the sense that even a piece of waste material, garbage, can have some occasional use.

He did not reveal his thought to anyone for the simple reason that he did not speak to anyone about anything except in the monosyllables of bare necessity.

Siobhan, for her part, knew nothing in detail of his doings in the course of events on the sacred day; she would have known that the two Michaels had played foul even if the crossbow had not been recovered, and she could guess well enough that their lust for power and her person had led them to cheat. The Great Mother had exacted the penalty for their temerity, but She had also imposed a drastic penance on Coll in the midst of his labours in Her cause. Siobhan was mystified that he could have had such a debt to repay. But what could she do now?

It was terribly clear that her chosen consort could no longer serve the College; she must therefore find another to take his place. Consequently a new King stood beside her on the night after the Winter Solstice. Thus at a stroke the Queen simultaneously broke and set a tradition within her Circle, for since no man had earned the right to claim her, and her previous King was now disqualified, she reserved the right to choose for herself a second time. If any member of the Circle could think of any reason why this should not be so, he kept it to himself.

The great Goddess had made manifest her will.

Chapter 48

DECEMBER, JANUARY AND FEBRUARY WORE AWAY. The oppressed Ywain, no longer Coll, hardly left his room and would have starved rather than go downstairs to meet the household gathered at meals. He was in the vice of self-abasement, too mortified to lift up his head in the company of men or women. Although he shunned Janine, neither looking at her nor speaking with her when she sat with him, she betrayed not the slightest resentment, spending long hours with him day and night. Siobhan visited him now for shorter periods and less frequently, but it was she who brought him paper on a clipboard and insisted that he write out in full an account of his day's adventures, stressing that he should omit no details. This he accomplished in fits and starts with the help of his faithful uncomplaining amanuensis, but in perfect detail nonetheless, for every scene, every word, every face, every tree, even, was embroidered tightly into the tapestry of his memory of the great day's events. Yet he hated himself for his loss at the hands of Michael and blamed himself only for his tragedy. Janine never attempted to correct him or point out the valour of his deeds, for he could see none of that; he was empty of any shred of self-esteem.

Siobhan read it as soon as she had it in her hands. One pale sunlit day towards the end of Winter she and Janine went into the forest to visit the Master.

Much better secured in her new power, thanks to Ywain, she resolved to battle the menace he had brought with him. She needed help in devising a strategy and went to a doubtful Esmirone.

March was a particularly significant month for the Circle since in this year the Paschal moon was close to the Vernal equinox. By this time Ywain was walking about (on the upper floor only); one day he decided to visit Esmirone whom he had not seen since the night of his triumphant return from the games.

She was pleased to see him, greeting him affectionately, much more affectionately than he ever expected. She had changed towards him in some way, had become more human, even to the point of a tinge of motherliness. He remembered with a forced smile Cybele's attempt to get rid of him when he had first called on her in Dublin.

'I wondered when you would come. We at the head of the Circle are incomplete without you now, although you probably don't realize that. It was no use my attempting to speak to you before now, for you had isolated yourself. I knew you would come in your own time when you were ready. I don't suppose it's any use my reminding you that you performed unexampled feats in overcoming treachery and carrying on to win after sustaining potentially lethal injuries which would have disabled anyone but you.'

'The Master helped me. He patched me up so that I could carry on. I should have died there on the spot otherwise.'

'You went on to discover and kill another calculating cheat who should have been able to kill you before you knew what was happening, and not only that, you struck down a third assailant whose attack nearly made you late for your assignation with our enemy.'

'Hell, Esmirone, the man was unbelievably incompetent. And is he our enemy, or at least, my enemy? I'm not so sure that he is, at least, not completely.'

'Is that what you think? He still has a hold over you and I don't know that you can undo it. Still, you won't have to worry about that for a while. Perhaps we can forestall him – a long reach, I'm afraid. First you have to rejoin us, actively, that is, for the month of Fearn draws on.'

'I no longer have an active rôle to play; that is pretty obvious.'

'Are you sure? And is that what you really want? As I told you once before your rôle may change. You think that you are no longer important to us, that we tolerate you only enough that you may stay among us, no more, since you are no longer the virile principle in our little polity. You are wrong. In fact you yourself choose the part you have to play. You can be sure that there is one. Even at the house level you could take over as security chief now that Cybele is soon to become a mother and Matt Hewer, poor fellow, is gone from us.'

'What happened to Matt?'

'You did not recognize your third kill? Of course not. You were in a desperate hurry at that point, weren't you?'

'I killed Matt! – my god, what must the village think of me!'

'They have always thought very highly of you, the first consort of their new Queen, whom they love beyond measure. They think of you now almost with awe, as someone with a strength and courage almost supernatural. They have not lost their affection for you, as you will find out when you finally pick up the courage to go out among them once more. You have now become a legend, Ywain, but you do not see it that way at present. I give you the name you have recovered. You have understood that, I know. You understand more than many in the Circle now. You have grown among us.'

'The Lady of the Beasts has taken my name and its endowments back.'

'Surely. But we are losing the thread of our conversation. You did not kill Matt. Another trickster did that on his way to murder you. As with the two Michaels, his participation was illegitimate, and if he had succeeded his claim would not have been recognized. He never was a bright spark. In fact, he was a desperate man whose own Circle regarded him as dispensable but still capable (from their point of view) of a little constructive mischief-making in the shape of murdering you. As with the others – well, you certainly know all about this – his dreams of power and boundless sexual dominance over our Queen were well-fed. I have a modicum of sympathy for him even though I too was his victim: he had several good qualities, poor fellow, but he was such a pathetic failure.'

'You must mean Gerald.'

She nodded. 'You were entitled to defend your crown, for during the games you were still King, King in fact, as long as you were victorious. The men and women of the village cannot and will not hold the loss of any of their own to your account. These are the Games. As it happened, by coincidence, they lost no one at your hands, while in addition you paid out Matt's murderer. And you know as well as I that there is no such thing as coincidence. It is merely a sign-board pointing to the purposes of the Great Goddess. It seems that I was lucky to escape as lightly as I did from him and Maxine. Siobhan has been learning on the job and you can be sure that such people won't get into the inner circle again, close to the temple priestesses. So now how do you feel?'

'Better, much better now I am with you again hearing the comfort of your craggy wisdom. What are the other possible functions I might fulfil?'

'The seasons of Ostara and Summer Finding approach. After your ordeals it is possible that you might be able to undertake a priestly rôle, this time in the women's college. Now don't shy away! You don't know what you may be offered. You will have to undergo rigorous training and sacral rites prior to your assuming any ritual function, however minor, and I am not speaking for Siobhan who alone can decide in this. You could be again among women, but differently. Think it over and let me know tomorrow if this is the part you would like. I'm afraid you have no more time to make a choice. If I'm not mistaken I think that something like this is the path mapped out for you. After all, the greatest of heroes hid among women for a time, and in fact, wanted to become one of them. Do you remember?'

'No.'

'Herakles hid in Sardis at the navel-shrine of the Ionian hero Tmolus. The High Priestess Omphale dressed him as a woman and taught him womanly arts, notably spinning. I'm not suggesting that you should take a woman's rôle, not for a moment. There is, however, a third rôle you might take, but we'll speak of that tomorrow. I have great love for you, Ywain. You shall be in my tenderest thoughts when I take leave.'

'You are leaving Siobhan?'

'She does not need me now. She has acquired great wisdom of her own. I am called away.'

'You are going back to Dublin?'

'No, but let's discuss it another time. Now we are both a little tired.'

When he returned to his room, he felt tired as he always did these days and reclined on the bed listlessly trying to get into Witt's *Isis in the Ancient World*, but could not concentrate. Someone, however, had left a copy of *The Golden Ass* by his bedside. It looked more interesting. In fact so interesting that he spent the rest of the night reading it. The ordeals of Apuleius' protagonist seemed to bear some relation to his own. He had not, ultimately, been cast out, but having borne in patience the consequences of his folly in forming a liaison with Fotis, the lowly servant girl, and in dabbling in magic arts beyond his comprehension, he had at length been saved by the Great Goddess and given an honourable place in Her mysteries.

Chapter 49

It was the first time in months that Ywain had dared to sit down at table with the others. He was still pale and perilously thin; his overwhelming strength had gone and would never return, he knew; and he was careless about his dress and appearance. He entered, determined to ward off pity, whether spoken or tacit, fearing that the priestesses who had so recently demanded of him in his strength would disparage him for his impotence. Nothing of the sort. They were delighted to see him, anxious to do him honour. Esmirone led him to the head of the table and made him sit as the others greeted him, overjoyed that he was once more among them.

'This is Siobhan's place.'

'She yields it to you, first in the Circle on the night of your triumph; the Queen ordained it.'

'This is your doing, Esmirone.'

'It is Siobhan's doing. Why do you always doubt the one who has loved you body and soul all your days in the Circle? Don't you know that she offered her life in place of yours?'

'I am always forgetting! I'm afraid I've been very self-centred these past weeks. And someone else made the same offer to the god. That would be Janine. I have not even spared a word of thanks for my friends!'

Janine, who was behind him, gave him a delighted squeeze. 'Of course we did, Ursa Major. You went out to sacrifice yourself at our behest. Don't worry: we all know about Siobhan's little test of you. You were not seduced by love of your life – oh, we must have a new name for you. Not Sir Gawain. He scored well, but succumbed at the critical point.'

'Byron,' put in Cybele. 'Now that you are no longer King you will always remind me of the lovely romantic lord who did rash things to prove to himself that he could vie with the storied heroes. I don't know if Siobhan will give you a name. To me you will always be Byron. I like it, and do you know why, you silly self-doubter with no faith in our love? Because it reminds us that you haven't gone away. You're here, forever I hope. We're women, Byron. We love you because we love you and for no other reason, not even because you love us, or on account of what you have done, the giant deeds you have performed, not even because you fathered our children, nor for any other reason. These are factors, not reasons. Have you forgotten the Circle again? You are at the heart of it, silly. Everything between us here is love. It's a pity that the odd Maxine or Gerald penetrates, but I don't think that will happen again. Siobhan has begun to establish a pretty strict college of priestesses who monitor the young initiates, and believe me, she knows what she is doing. She has a wisdom and a power beyond anything she could have acquired in the normal way of things. As for your assailants: the dark side manifests itself on the day of the Games, yet even the shadow is accompanied by an aurae of good. Men who don't really belong are filtered out, usually at the expense of the King's life. But you have realized, haven't you, that the King is there to sacrifice himself, hence the fatted calf treatment in the palmy days.'

'She puts it very well,' said Esmirone.

'By the way, O King of old, if I might break in upon more important discussion, I want you to know that I too am to have your child.' It was Sybil who spoke. With a flush of shame Ywain realized that he had practically forgotten about her. What she said was said in love; she was not merely shoring up his self-esteem. In the relentless underworld of psychotic depression he had forgotten what Siobhan had explained to him, so long ago now, in the enchanted other-worldly dawning on the Burren.

Diane, who was as obviously pregnant as Cybele, looked if anything twice as lovely as before. Her lips, easily the sexiest Ywain had ever seen, framed words that sent a thrill through him, diminished as he was: 'Your flame has lit many candles, Ywain, but the Queen keeps her own counsel.'

He realized in passing that impotence made no difference whatever to the aesthetics of sex. He was as susceptible to the beauty and charm of women as ever.

'And where is she?'

'Byron! Really! No one asks such a question.'

But at that moment the Queen arrived accompanied by the King of the Rising Year. With them were two new young women. They came immediately to Ywain. Siobhan embraced him and the new King shook his hand. Ywain had seen him before, but recognition flickered for a moment.

'Brian!' he shouted. 'Where have you been all this time?'

Chapter 50

Siobhan took Ywain's hands in her own, cool and soft. He was again on the Burren early in the morning when her touch had turned him to jelly. She kissed him, and sitting at his left, kept her hand on his.

Taking his seat facing Siobhan, Brian began to answer his question.

'Well, the crooks didn't leave me alone once I'd taken a tyre-iron to them. They became quite a nuisance, I can tell you, so Siobhan decided to shelter me in the valley –'

'What valley?'

'That's what we call it in the Circle when someone has to go out of sight for a while. You were sheltered in the valley yourself, the hidden valley most of them call it. Ah, you didn't know I was in the Circle? Nearly all Siobhan's friends were – all except her school set when she was still trying to learn something –'

'Punch him for me, Ywain dear. Since he got the job he's become very uppity, as the Americans say. He'll learn.'

' – and keep out of trouble. Anyway, she had formed a network of the best kind of people. I don't know *how* she did it, for it's simply not within reason, let alone credibility, that a fourth form schoolgirl who spends most of her time doing her homework *and* helping a busy mother running a B&B *and* riding her bike all over the countryside can do this, and do it undetected.'

'The obvious answer is that I didn't,' rejoined Siobhan. 'Of course I had help. It was merely that the – helping agency – was focused on me.'

'And what was this "helping agency"? I'd like to know that.'

'I'm sure you would. It's something I can't divulge even to you or Ywain. It can look after itself – and "it" is definitely the wrong pronoun. After that clue you can't go very far wrong in your guesses. "It" is at the very core of this present widening of the Circle. There are those who are making a last attempt, now no longer hopeless, at defending our mother, the earth, from the horrid denial of nature advocated by anti-life religionists and what is curiously called positivism, the blindness of callous science, greatest menace of all.'

'I wish I could put together a sentence like that.' Brian wasn't sure whether he was being ironic or not.

'We shall receive help so long as we are single-mindedly serving the earth mother. Incidentally, Brian, the hidden valley means something quite different to you from what it does to Ywain.'

The others hardly ate. They listened without moving as if Siobhan was an oracle. There had been a change in atmosphere since last year. The easy comfortable air of chat had gone. Now instead of being for the most part empty, the table was three-quarters filled and Ywain no longer knew the names of everyone present. In addition to himself, Brian, the Queen and Esmirone, there were another six women present: Diane, Sybil, Cybele, Janine and two others who had not been introduced to him. But that was when he had been King. Now he would be introduced to the newcomers rather than they to him. What was his place to be? The third woman present on the morning of the Lammas feast whose name he had never discovered was absent and never reappeared. He turned his attention back to Siobhan.

'Unfortunately we have been penetrated by unfriendly powers. We can't afford that. But that is all in the past. Everyone is to be vigilant, always, especially over the initiates. Esmirone and I have already made plans which will help prevent any other Maxines.'

The light-hearted talk that had opened breakfast did not return. Ywain felt the menace of a world against them all. But somewhere there was a 'helping agency'.

After breakfast Siobhan drew him aside and, sitting down, they looked at each other as if nothing had happened since the terrified man on the Burren had heard a voice calling out of the rocks.

'Now once again you want to know where you stand. Esmirone spoke to you, didn't she? She and I talked about you.'

'Is she the "helping agency"?'

'I wish I hadn't used that expression. No. It is something you cannot know about, so forget it. Anyway, I wanted to offer you several choices, because I know that in spite of what has happened you don't want to leave us, and in any case there's not much chance you'll survive outside the Circle in your present stage of development. Powerful international corporations and government agencies know all they need to know about you and can identify you, so you have to stay here. You don't wish to visit your home again, do you?'

'No. This is my home, if I'm allowed to remain.'

'If you are allowed to remain. Oh Ywain, what nonsense you talk sometimes. Of course you have earned your place, and now that you have faced death you may be ready to go on to another stage. First you have to know something of your own cosmos. The Circle believes in a divine cosmos which gave birth to a human one. Finding the harmony between them is the greatest bliss one can have and I think probably your next stage.'

'How does one do this?'

'In several ways, either ritually or by seeking the right kind of death. In the former a long period of meditation alone in the utter darkness of a sealed hollow or cave is demanded, and a fast almost to death. Indeed, there is the risk of death. Every one of the priestesses has undergone this ordeal successfully, I myself in a more drastic form, guided by the "helping agency". If you want to choose this, there is a lengthy period of preparation before the immolation. If you survive, you are then a lower order priest.'

'This is the strangest definition of bliss I ever heard! And I have already been isolated in a cave and would rather not repeat the experience.'

'You had not been properly prepared, and the purpose of your transformation then was very different from this.'

'I don't think I have a vocation for this kind of thing.'

'Everyone has, deep down, the desire to return to paradise, the cosmic womb that we have forgotten about but nevertheless hark back to. In many ways it is easier for young people who are still close enough to their childhood to accept the rites and experiences they have to undergo than it is for someone older. That is why our priestesses begin so young and why they have such power, the kind of power that only those who have passed through the invisible subterranean world successfully can wield. You who have lost your physical power should think about your next stage carefully. Of course, if you want, you can stay with us here, remaining as you are, doing some job we can use you in. But you have been a King, not an odd-job man. I can only give you until tomorrow to think about it. Events are on the move again. One of the year's great feasts is nearly upon us. There is, by the way, a shorter way to paradise. Esmirone will not mind if you ask her about it.'

Left to himself, Ywain did not think as much about what Siobhan had said as he should have. He did not have enough to go on. He had often complained of being told nothing. Now he was being offered a way to some occult knowledge that brought power and something else. But he simply did not see himself as a priestly kind of person. After dawdling fruitlessly for several hours he went to see if he could find Esmirone.

'You have not set foot outside the door for so long, Ywain,' she remarked. 'I was thinking of visiting a certain place today. Would you like to come?'

'Who else will be there?'

'Just the two of us. You can do the driving.'

'All right.'

'Good. Can we leave in half-an-hour then? Oh, and don't forget to bring your revolver with you. One never knows. No place is sacred enough to ward off the senseless violence of those who are blind to their own souls in these rootless days.'

Armed with maps and prompted by Esmirone's directions, they set off for Wiltshire, aiming for the Bath road but avoiding the major routes for as long as possible. Taking a side road. Ywain parked the car and they clambered over a fence bearing a notice warning everyone to keep out. They moved towards an almost perfectly conical hill flattened at the summit approached by a spiral pathway ascending from the base. Instead of walking to the top, Esmirone took him around the circumference. She pointed out a sealed entrance to a tunnel made by several archæological expeditions who had discovered in detail precisely how the hill had been constructed to prevent it ever from subsiding and the dates of its beginning and completion; they had also speculated on the purposes of the builders in ways totally irrelevant to a hallowed site. The logic of science, so effective in adducing and elucidating the geography of physical knowledge, barred from consideration anything that might promote the insight possible only in an awareness of the invisible world that was equally a part of the divine cosmos, that other geography long ago familiar to the seers of the day but now almost totally ignored.

'This place manifests multiple realities, that is, it is more than one place,' observed Esmirone.

'I don't understand.'

'This is not the only entrance,' she went on, ignoring his remark. 'There is another, hidden even from the efficient eyes and instruments of archæology. It snakes into the interior; its entrance is the mouth of a serpent. But let us go up.'

At the summit a young man admired the view. His Walkman poured saccharin ooze into his ears to relieve him of the burden of silence and the absence of live company. He had destroyed all hope of feeling anything of the sanctity of the place. On the other side of the fence below stood his motor-cycle. Ywain kept an eye on him. He had the impression of a hidden menace near at hand.

'Is that what you feel?' asked Esmirone as they retraced their footsteps to the car. 'I'm not surprised. That is the first stage.'

'The first stage of what?'

'The first stage of a spiritual journey, one of regression first and progression subsequently that you must undertake if you want to remain one of the inner circle, or in other words, become a priest. Do you want that? It is perhaps the hardest path to take, a journey more arduous than the King's ordeal. I chose it when I was younger than you. Now I choose what for me is an easier path.'

'And what is that?'

'You will see soon enough. For you, if you want to find paradise and begin again – well, the way is hard, and perhaps fatal. You must come close to death in order to understand the divine part of you. And this is enjoined on no one, in fact, it is permitted to only a few, those whom the Queen considers prepared. Siobhan offers you this path. If you accept and are successful, you return to the Circle, the inner circle, with another kind of power. You will then be one with the priestesses who serve under the Queen.'

'Am I to be locked up in the hidden passage?'

'Yes. You occupy a certain chamber when you have passed the stations on the way. You have water, but no food. I can tell you no more, and in fact to divulge even so much is contrary to our rule. I speak with the Queen's leave. You emerge a different being, one having power against the enemies threatening you now. You have noticed, haven't you, that Siobhan wields enormous power over everyone? What she has undergone I do not know. That secret she keeps in her heart. So what is your choice? This, or to live among the men of the village, weaker than any of them?'

'How long does it take?'

'That will depend upon you. There is a period of preparation which, in the normal course of events, I would direct. Then you are sent on your journey. I can give you no other details. Have you made up your mind?'

'No. Well, yes. What else is there?'

'That is for you to decide, but I warn you that if you embark on this course there can be no turning back. Once you have begun the rites you must continue. Be perfectly clear about that.'

'What does Siobhan think?'

'Oh Ywain, what a question! What does she think? She has just offered this divine gift to you and you ask me what she thinks! I think you're a numbskull for even asking the question.'

They got into the car. As Ywain started the engine he nodded to her.

The unaccustomed country air and the day's exertions took their toll of Ywain: he was tired, dead tired after an exhausting return journey in heavy traffic. He sought out Siobhan and told her what he had decided, but was too worn out to express properly his gratitude for her favour. He wanted a nap. Janine came to him as she always did, brought him a soothing tisane, looking as beautiful as she always did for him. Her loyal friendship was the jewel of his life.

He was not allowed to sleep for long. Esmirone woke him and said: 'Tomorrow is Ostara. We'll all be up early. I wanted to say a few last words to you, my dear friend Ywain, before I go away, so please listen now. Don't ever doubt that Siobhan loves you. She has done more for you than you can possibly know. Through her you can now take the hard way, in which you will succeed: I see that quite clearly. You will gain enlightenment, wisdom and power, and more than any of these, bliss beyond anything you can conceive now. Don't repine that you have lost your manhood, as you think of it: in ancient days priestly initiates were supposed to deprive themselves of it publicly. And it would have been no earthly good your trying to hang on to the kingship year after year until someone younger, stronger, more active and luckier than you took it and your life simultaneously. This time you had the luck and the favour of the Goddess. Do you think that Siobhan wanted to see your severed head brought back here?

'Add to that the loyalty, devotion and help of the potent Janine to whom you owe much of your success in the games, whom you undervalue and neglect, and tell me who has such favour and fortune now and in prospect?

'We have work for you, Ywain, work more important than you can imagine now. Your only future is within the Circle. Shall I give you my advice?'

'Yes.'

'Follow the course you have chosen with determination and without deviation. Your friends await you here, and when you return you will be part of a ring of such power as will enable the Circle to advance to its destiny. I do not exaggerate.

'But my mind is elsewhere tonight. I came not to give advice, but to take leave of you my very dear friend, for you have never been divided from my heart.'

'You are going back to Dublin?'

I am going to where my soul has longed to be for many years. I cannot tell you more; paradise is ineffable. So I kiss one of my dearest friends, give you what blessing I can and wish all the latent riches of the soul to bring you to a sight of the divine. Remember me and find strength when the way is hardest. Farewell, dear friend.'

'I'm going to see you again, surely?'

'Yes, but there won't be time for goodbyes in the morning.'

Chapter 51

*And till seven years were past and gone
True Thomas on earth was never seen.*

NEARLY AN HOUR BEFORE SUNRISE on the first day of Ostara, Siobhan at the head of her priestesses led a long procession through a silent forest down to the dell. The entire Circle, every man and woman in the village, led by her consort, crowded densely before the altar as, gathered with her priestesses, she usurped the place of a rising god. Even as the sun began her ascent a Celtic harpist joined the group on the rise, standing well to the side. It was now their own Queen, not a forest god, who filled her followers with fear as for the second time Ywain witnessed the transfiguration of the queen in the incarnation of the Great Goddess come miraculously among them. The face was recognizably Siobhan's, but it was not Siobhan he saw. Neither young nor old, but timeless, as in a statue come to life. There was no human expression on that face, only the ineffable remoteness of one existing in exalted serenity. The sculptor of the Divine Twins at Delphi came closest to the face of divinity: he too had seen it.

Ywain recognized the priestesses flanking the Queen, but Esmirone was out of place, behind. She too looked completely different from the Esmirone he knew so well. She wore an expression of blissful expectation that he simply did not associate with her. Not only that, she was robed in a splendid ceremonial dress in which saffron competed with white, and, oddly, there were decorative cords arranged around her neck. She wore no headdress; instead her long hair hung freely.

Prompted by Diane, Esmirone moved round to face the Queen with Diane on one side and Cybele on the other. She was saying something, perhaps praying, for some time. Whatever it was, the Queen gave no reply, but drew her supplicant's head into Her divine bosom, stroked her hair and fondled the cords, accepting her in Her love and giving tenderness in human kind. Esmirone was Her infant in love.

At this point Ywain still thought he was witnessing a formal farewell to Esmirone before she took her leave.

As the first rays of the sun threw light and long shadows down into the dell, the Queen gave the briefest nod. Five men drew Esmirone gently away, surrounded her, seized the cords and on a signal, suddenly pulled with all their strength, not only strangling her but breaking her neck. The victim offered not the slightest resistance. The last glimpse of Esmirone's face that Ywain caught expressed the contentment of the well-fed child. The two priestesses Janine and Sibyl examined the body of Esmirone thoroughly and satisfied themselves that she was dead.

Leaving the cords in place but symmetrically arranged to indicate that the corpse was a sacrificial offering and therefore sacred, the two remaining priestesses laid her out, enshrouding her in new white linen. The Goddess had received her even before her journey and waited to welcome her after. Throughout Esmirone's remains were treated with the utmost reverence. She was left in her place as she fell while the harpist played chords in gratitude for the presence of the Goddess and the consecration of Esmirone, who had persisted in begging the Queen for bounty seldom granted.

The Great Goddess had reached out to save Her fawn even as Her rival took his mancipiary portion.

* * * *

As for Ywain, he followed the Rhymer. It was long before he was seen walking the earth again.

Acknowledgement

I should like to express my gratitude for the valuable help I received from Melinda Tate who first patiently reviewed my writing, offering many valuable suggestions for improvement and subsequently took over the business of publication. Without her generous contribution this book would never have seen the light of day.

A Note about Quotations

The lines on page 99 are adapted from Hesiod's *Hymn to Aphrodite*. The quotation on page 116 is from *The Waning of the Middle Ages*, by Johan Huizinga.